PRAISE FOR THE DOOR WITHIN TRILOGY

"In the tradition of C.S. Lewis' Narnia Series, *The Door Within Trilogy* beckons the reader to come along on an epic fantasy adventure to faraway lands and the more near places of the heart. Readers of all ages will find that *The Door Within* delivers heart-pounding thrills as well as themes and principles that will linger with you long after you put the book down. *The Door Within* reminds us that there is much more to life than what we see before our eyes."

Josh D. McDowell
Best-selling Author and Public Speaker

"Batson leads young readers to a fantasy realm where faith and sacrifice serve as essential tools in an epic battle between good and evil."

Publisher's Weekly

"Those who enjoy fantasy, from young teens through adults, should feel right at home with this."

Liz Duckworth
Aspiring Retail

"*The Door Within* has all the trappings of J.R.R. Tolkien's *The Hobbit*."

Joe Burris
The Baltimore Sun

THE DOOR WITHIN

BY
WAYNE THOMAS BATSON

Published by
THOMAS NELSON™
Since 1798
www.thomasnelson.com

© 2005 Wayne Thomas Batson
First in a series of three novels.

Published in Nashville, Tennessee, by Thomas Nelson. Thomas Nelson is a trademark of Thomas Nelson, Inc.

Thomas Nelson, Inc. books may be purchased in bulk for educational, business, fund-raising, or sales promotional use. For information, please e-mail SpecialMarkets@ThomasNelson.com.

Library of Congress Cataloging-in-Publication Data

Batson, Wayne Thomas.
      The door within / by Wayne Thomas Batson.
         p. cm.
      Summary: Three ancient scrolls beckon high school student Aidan Thomas to enter a realm of knights, kings, and unusual creatures, but he must rely on instinct and his latent athletic ability to deal with the terror, tempest, and treason offered by this new world.
      ISBN: 978-1-4003-9243-8 (premium)
      ISBN: 978-1-4003-1011-1 (tradepaper)
      ISBN: 978-1-4003-0659-6 (hardcover)
      [1. Space and time—Fiction. 2. Christian life—Fiction. 3. Fantasy.]
   I. Title.
      PZ7.B3238Doo 2005
      [Fic]—dc22

                                                                                    2005009216

Printed in the United States of America
07 08 09 10 11 RRD 9 8 7 6 5 4 3 2 1

To the one true King,
through whom all good things come:
I bend my knee and await your command.

CONTENTS

Principal Cast

AIDAN (AY-DEN) THOMAS

When Aidan's parents move the family to Colorado to take care of his
wheelchair-bound grandfather (Grampin), the teenager discovers the Scrolls,
which start him on an adventure of a lifetime.

MR. THOMAS

Aidan's father.

MRS. THOMAS

Aidan's mother.

GRAMPIN

Aidan's grandfather on his father's side.
He is confined to a wheelchair.

ROBBY PIERSON (PEER-SON)

Aidan's best friend in Maryland.

ACSRIOT (AX-REE-AHT)

Glimpse warrior, who often questions the judgment of others.

BOLT & NOCK

Twin Glimpse warriors, who are both very highly skilled archers.

CAPTAIN VALITHOR (VAL-EH-THOR)

The new Sentinel of Alleble, and the Captain of the Elder Guard.

ELEAZAR (EL-EE-AY-ZAR)

Glimpse warrior. He is an emissary for Alleble and
is well versed in the Kingdom's lore.

FALON

The elder of all mortiwraiths, who are enormous, venomous underground serpentine creatures.

FARIX (FAIR-IX)

Glimpse warrior, who does not wear armor.

GWENNE

Glimpse swordmaiden, who is Aidan's guide.

KALIAM (KAL-EE-UM)

Glimpse warrior, who is also known as Pathfinder.

KINDLE

Glimpse armory keeper.

KING ELIAM (EE-LEE-UM)

The noble and wise monarch of Alleble, who invited Aidan to his kingdom.

KING RAVELLE

Ruler of Mithegard.

LORD RUCIFEL (ROO-SI-FELL)

Paragor's Lieutenant, who wields two swords.

MALLIK (MAL-ICK)

Glimpse warrior, who wields a massive war hammer.

MATTHIAS (MA-THI-AS)

Glimpse warrior, who is very competitive.

NOCK

Glimpse warrior. See Bolt.

PARAGAL (PAIR-A-GALL) / PARAGOR (PAIR-AH-GORE)

The first Sentinel of Alleble, who now rules over Paragory.

TAL

Glimpse warrior, who likes to compete.

Principal Settings

THE REALM

The world of Glimpses, once united with our world,
was separated by The Schism.

ALLEBLE (AL-EH-BULL)

The first Kingdom of The Realm. After The Schism,
Alleble remained the center of The Realm.

PARAGORY (PAIR-AH-GOR-EE)

A kingdom built by Paragor and his army.

MITHEGARD (MYTH-GUARD)

A kingdom in the northwestern part of The Realm.

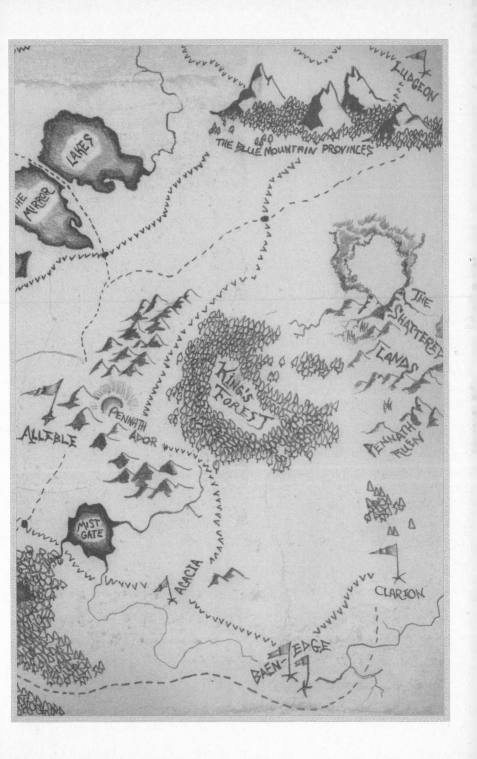

Adventures are
funny things.
They may creep out of holes,
appear down a seldom
trodden path,
fall out of a tree, or even
arrive in an envelope,
but they always start
the same way.
Adventures always
begin with
the unexpected . . .

FROM NIGHTMARE
TO NIGHTMARE

The first sword missed Aidan's head by an inch. It slammed into the massive catapult's wheel, stuck for a moment, and jerked free. In that breath of time, Aidan batted away the second sword and threw himself down the hill.

This foe was beyond Aidan's skill. His only chance was to get away, to escape with . . . Aidan looked down at the torn parchment in his hand. It was something important, this parchment, something of infinite value, the key to it all—only Aidan could not remember why it was so precious. He only knew that it was and that he must not let the enemy get it.

As he ran, Aidan glanced over his shoulder. The knight in dark armor crashed down the hill, gaining rapidly. His cloak trailed behind him like a gray wing, and he swung his two swords in wide arcs, carving the wind. The blades came closer . . . and closer.

Before Aidan could run another yard, the knight in dark armor fell upon him. Aidan turned, fended off a blow, then ran a few steps; turned again, sidestepped one blade, and barely blocked the other.

"Where will you go?" rasped a voice that seemed to reach for Aidan. "Your kingdom is in ruin. Even your King has fled. All is lost!"

The enemy's taunts threatened to strangle the small hope that lingered in Aidan's heart. But Aidan would not give in.

Aidan blocked another savage blow from the enemy and slashed away his second blade. Again, Aidan lunged away from his foe.

Suddenly, he saw his chance. Beyond the next hill a horse struggled, its reins tangled around its dead rider's arm. Drawing from his final reserve of strength, Aidan charged up the hill and dove for the horse. It shrieked and staggered under the sudden weight but did not fall. Aidan swept his sword up and cut the tangled reins. He thrust the parchment under his breastplate and slapped the horse hard on its hindquarters.

"Go!" Aidan screamed.

The beast reared briefly but then surged ahead with such force that Aidan nearly fell. He could not reach what was left of the reins with his free hand, so he clutched the horse's neck with all his might.

Aidan looked back. The knight in dark armor was now far behind and had given up pursuit. Just as Aidan allowed himself a grim smile, something hit him—hard—in the back, knocking him off the horse. He heard a sharp snap and felt the air forced out of his lungs.

He lay in a heap, his face to the ground. A dull pain throbbed in his right wrist. Dizzy, he spit dust and debris from his mouth, and looked up weakly from the ground. Out of the corner of his eye, he saw an enormous black wing in the gray sky.

Suddenly, Aidan was kneeling on a high stone platform. His sword was gone, and his hands were bound behind him. A pale warrior stood tall before him. His long gray hair was drawn back, and a thin black circlet—like a thin crown—rested above his strong brow and penetrating hazel eyes.

When he spoke, a shrill ringing came to Aidan's ears. The sound faded and he heard the warrior's words. He was saying, ". . . make you the same offer I made your companions." His voice sounded rich and kingly—above all else to be trusted. "In spite of my generosity, they chose the weaker path."

Aidan turned and saw two knights facedown beside him. They somehow seemed familiar, but they lay unnaturally still. And looming proudly over the bodies was the dark knight brandishing his twin blades.

Aidan looked questioningly back to the warrior before him.

"They have lost," he said, clasping his hands before his chest. "But their loss is your gain. You will have all that was to be theirs and so much more."

The warrior seemed to grow. His presence intensified. And when he spread apart his hands, Aidan saw visions of grand towers, high thrones, and vaults of gold. It was all there for the asking, Aidan knew.

"Look about you," the warrior continued. "All that you have defended is lost. There is nothing left."

Aidan turned and saw desolation. Everywhere were fallen towers, rent walls, charred debris, and broken bodies. The sky was black, roiling with dark clouds and smoke from a thousand fires.

"All you must do," said the warrior, "is deny the one who abandoned you."

A profound wave of peace washed over Aidan, and he looked

steadily into the eyes of the warrior. He spoke calmly. "I will never deny my King!"

The dark knight came forward with his two swords, but his master held up a hand. "I'll do it myself," the warrior said. The warrior's hazel eyes flickered red as he drew a long, dark sword and drove the blade through Aidan's breastplate.

"Uhnnn! Ah, ahhhhh!" Aidan screamed. He writhed on his bed and knocked his lamp off the table. It crashed to the ground and shattered, awakening Aidan. He shook violently, and his stomach churned. Something heaved inside him. Barely avoiding broken glass, he bolted to the hall bathroom and threw up. He collapsed and rested his head on the toilet seat.

"Aidan?" came Grampin's voice from the study downstairs. "Are you okay?"

"Yes!" Aidan lifted his head and managed a hoarse yell. "I'm fine!"

Aidan shook his head despondently and let it thud down on the seat. The dream had been horrible, but waking up to find that his family had actually moved across the country—to Aidan, that was the real nightmare.

THE UNEXPECTED

Grampin told me you had another one of those dreams," Aidan's dad said. He tentatively put his hand on his son's shoulder and gave a firm, reassuring squeeze. Aidan shrugged it off as if it were a wasp.

Mr. Thomas grimaced, exhaled, and ran a hand through his gray-streaked hair. Silence hung like a cloud between father and son.

Nearby, Aidan's mom stood with her head at a slight tilt and her hands on her hips as if to say, *I told you so.*

Mr. Thomas looked away and sighed. He started to leave the dining room, but spun around and quickly pulled up a chair next to his teenage son, who was sitting stiffly at the table.

"How long are you going to keep this up?" he asked.

"I don't want to talk about it," Aidan replied. He looked away.

"Look, it's been two weeks, son, and—"

"Yeah, two weeks and I still hate it here."

"I know it was kind of sudden—"

"Kind of?" Aidan interrupted. "One week into summer vacation and you say, 'Oh, uh . . . , by the way, Aidan, we're moving halfway across the country in two weeks.' That's more than a little sudden. You didn't even ask if I cared."

"We've been through this before," Aidan's dad said, his face reddening. "You know we didn't have a choice. Grampin needs our help. This is where he spent his whole life, and we can't just force him into an assisted living facility."

Aidan shrugged. He'd heard this song before.

"Besides," his father continued, "Riddick and Dunn has an office out here, and it was easy for Mom to get a teaching position, with her credentials."

"So it was convenient for everyone but me."

Mr. Thomas turned his head and frowned. "Listen, we left friends behind in Maryland too, you know."

That was it. Aidan sprang up and rushed from the dining room. He banged up the stairs in an angry fog, slammed the door to his room, and dove onto his bed.

Aidan faced his bedside table. The twelve medieval figurines—the pewter knights, dragons, and unicorns—were, as always, still, quiet, and ready to listen.

"Y'know what?" he said to them. "They don't have a clue what it's like leaving a friend behind. I bet they won't have any trouble at all finding people to play Bridge with."

None of the small medieval beings replied. They were good that way. They didn't offer advice. They didn't lecture. They simply listened.

"I mean, how am I supposed to survive high school when my only real friend is a thousand miles from here?" Aidan glowered at the fantasy figures and shook his head. There was no way he'd ever find a friend like Robby again.

Robby Pierson and his family had moved from Florida to a house in Maryland a block away from Aidan. The two boys had met in school, had homeroom together and lockers side by side, and everything changed for Aidan. Until that time, Aidan had been known to the kids in the neighborhood and at school as the overweight weirdo who sat around all day drawing castles and spacecraft. Then Robby showed up. He was tall and muscular and had huge green eyes, long blond hair, and an earring. And given his good looks and ability to play every sport better than everyone else, he was instantly crowned "so cool" by everyone—even the juniors and seniors!

For reasons Aidan still didn't understand, Robby had decided to become his best friend. They hung out between classes, after school, and sometimes had PlayStation sleepovers on the weekends.

It was as if *coolness* were a magical golden powder that could rub off on Aidan just by standing in Robby's shadow. Because of Robby, the most popular kids in the school paid attention to Aidan. They all seemed to think, *If Robby Pierson thinks he's cool, then he must be cool.* It was, after all, a large shadow, and Aidan liked it there. He didn't have to worry about being picked on, and better still, he never had to think about what to do in certain situations—Robby always knew what to do.

"Looks like it's back to being the oddball again!" Aidan's anger surged to the point that he was tempted to smack the little medieval figurines right off the table, but he'd already destroyed a lamp. So he hit his pillow as hard as he could and then threw it at his bedroom door.

Aidan suddenly sat very still on the edge of his bed. He had the most intense feeling that someone was outside his bedroom window watching him. He felt frozen in time, unable at first to summon the courage to turn around.

This is stupid, he thought. *I mean, who could be at my window? I'm on the second floor, and there's nothing out there to stand on . . . except, maybe one of the pines.*

Aidan spun around and looked out the window. The front yard was full of tall evergreens, but the biggest one was rocking severely back and forth.

. . . like something was in there! The thought leaped into Aidan's mind, and he pressed his face up against the glass.

Aidan looked left, right, up, down. At first he didn't see anything. But then, up the road that ran in front of his house, there was a shadow. It was wide, spanning the road at times, and it was moving fast. That's what caught Aidan's eye. And even through the glass, Aidan heard a peculiar swooshing sound. Aidan looked up in the sky. Nothing there.

The swooshes continued. And the shadow rocketed back toward Aidan's house. Aidan strained to see what could be casting such a shadow, but there was no passing cloud or low-flying plane. The shadow swooped over the house, and for a split second the sun was eclipsed by . . . something.

Aidan bounced off his bed, took the stairs two at a time, arriving with a horrendous thud at the bottom.

"Hey, watch the thumping!" Aidan's father bellowed from the kitchen.

"Sorry!" Aidan yelled over his shoulder as he ran out the front door to search the skies.

Treasures in Earthen Vessels

I'm serious, Mom, it was this huge shadow," Aidan mumbled earnestly, his mouth half full of pizza.

"I'm sure you saw something, Aidan," she replied. "Maybe it was an airplane?"

"Mom, airplanes don't sound like that. It was like, *swoosh, swoosh!*"

"I didn't see—or hear—anything," offered Aidan's dad.

"Maybe it was a helicopter?"

"Mommm!"

"Sorry," she said, holding up her hands. "But helicopters do go *swoosh, swoosh.*"

Aidan scowled.

"Besides, it couldn't have been anything like that because it was in the big pine tree out front . . ."

"It was in the pine tree?" his parents echoed. They both had raised eyebrows.

Grampin wheeled into the kitchen and parked at the table. Aidan got up immediately and said, "Oh, never mind!"

The next morning, Aidan sat at his computer, staring at the last email Robby had sent. In it, Robby had explained that he was going away for two weeks to a special soccer camp being held at Camp Ramblewood or Redwater or Rattleweed or something like that—Robby couldn't remember. Pro soccer players were coming to train promising junior players.

The bad part was that Robby said he wouldn't have access to the Internet. That meant no emails would come until Robby came home in August. "Great," Aidan moaned. "Some summer vacation."

In the three weeks since they'd arrived in Colorado, Aidan had run out of good books and had mastered every PS2 game he owned. Aidan's father was at the firm all day. His mom went to her new school two or three days a week to create lesson plans from the new math curriculum. And Grampin, well, he just wasn't an option as far as Aidan was concerned.

But the biggest problem was that there didn't seem to be any kids Aidan's age in his new neighborhood. He didn't even see any at the local shopping center. But at least he'd had Robby's emails to look forward to—and now he didn't even have that anymore.

With Robby, every day had been an adventure. Whether it was building forts in the woods, catching crayfish, or riding bikes on the winding trails behind the local high school—Robby found ways to make it exciting.

"That's what I need," Aidan said to himself, "an adventure!"

And there was one place in the house Aidan hadn't checked out yet: the basement. But he didn't like the thought of being underground, cold, and closed in. Still, he'd need to go in sometime, might as well be today.

Walking through the kitchen, Aidan passed by Grampin, who was asleep, snoring like a chorus of whoopee cushions, the coffee in his mug long since cold.

Then he spotted it—the basement door. It had a deadbolt, a chain latch, and a regular knob lock. Aidan had often wondered why Grampin needed three locks on the basement door. He'd wondered about it when he'd visited as a little boy, but not enough to ask . . . and certainly not enough to go down there. Aidan didn't like basements. They were uncomfortable, damp, and full of shadows. Robby's basement back in Maryland had always given Aidan the creeps.

Aidan had a feeling that Grampin's basement would be worse. Could this be the adventure he was searching for?

Quietly, Aidan slipped into the basement and shut the door behind him. He found himself smothered in darkness. He groped about, flicked the light switch—nothing.

After wrestling with second thoughts, he tried to tiptoe down the stairs. But each step Aidan took made a different creak or groan, like playing a wildly-out-of-tune piano. If there was something sinister lurking in the basement shadows, it surely knew Aidan was coming.

Aidan reached the bottom step and realized with great relief that the basement wasn't completely dark. There were three windows that, while painted a peculiar shade of green, at least let in enough light to make out shapes.

Eyes wide and straining, Aidan stepped down onto the basement floor. He half expected ghoulish, rotting hands to reach up from the ground to grab at his ankles, but none did. There were, however, other reasons for him to feel uncomfortable. It was cold—a kind of chill that seeped through clothing and made Aidan cringe. There was also a damp, mildewed smell. On top of that, it was unnaturally silent. No crickets, no rattling water heater . . . nothing. The only sound Aidan heard was his own heart pulsing away while he walked.

He saw a large cardboard box. It was overflowing with toys, but in the ghastly green shades cast from the windows, these toys were not a cheery sight. A wooden sailboat, a broken drum, and a doll that stared back with one eye—Aidan cringed as he passed them.

Aidan scuttled over to a workbench up against the far wall where, to his great relief, he found a small lamp that still worked. In the new light he made many discoveries: an old radio with large wooden knobs, a stack of newspapers from the 1950s, and half of an old baseball card of a player named Gil somebody. Thinking that there might be more old baseball cards, hopefully intact, Aidan began to search meticulously through other boxes nearby. No luck. The boxes were filled with musty smells, wads of tissue paper, or other smaller boxes. No '52 Mantle, no '81 Ripken.

Aidan sighed and furrowed his eyebrows. He marched over to the far corner of the basement but stopped abruptly when he heard something. It was faint and might ordinarily have gone unnoticed, but because of Aidan's nerves and the unearthly quiet of the basement, it was as bone jarring as an explosion.

Aidan stood still as a tombstone, but his eyes strained in wide arcs. The noise clearly came from the angular nook beneath the steps, but there was nothing there. No bike with a rotting, leaking tire. No box with a mouse family within. No tipped paper cup with a roach clicking about in search of food. There was just bare cement floor. The sound continued, a raspy, whispering sound like wind disturbing a pile of dead leaves. It was getting louder. Aidan thought suddenly of the thing watching him from the pine outside his window.

His heart now lodged somewhere in his throat, Aidan lunged toward the stairs—for there was no other way out of the basement. Just a few more steps, and he'd be . . . But on Aidan's very next step, the lamp on the workbench flickered, dimmed, and with an audible *pfffft*, died.

The darkness was almost total. Even the green light from the basement windows had been blotted out. Aidan stood frozen again, his eyes darting. He opened his mouth to scream, but his voice chose not to cooperate. He thought humorously that even if he had screamed, the only one in the house was Grampin. What could the old guy do?

The noises continued to get louder and sounded less like wind and more like deep breaths being exhaled. There was an especially loud breath and something sparkled on the floor beneath the stairs.

It was like blue electricity—flickering and powerful. There was a pause and the sparkles faded. Another breath, and the sparkles rekindled and began to swirl as if rapidly climbing a spiral staircase. Another pause-fade and then another breath-sparkle. This time two more electric spirals appeared directly behind the first. All three pulsed with energy and then dimmed. Suddenly, the electric sparkles glowed fiercely, bathing the basement in blue. Then, they waned and disappeared.

Just an electrical arc of some sort, Aidan thought, trying to calm himself.

Then the lamp on the workbench came back on just as suddenly as it had gone out, and there on the floor beneath the stairs were three tall clay pots.

Aidan shook his head. *Were they there before?*

Aidan took a few tentative steps closer. Each pot was dusty gray and at least two and a half feet tall. There was no writing or decoration of any kind on them. They had lids that made them look like huge, ancient cookie jars.

His mind whirled with ideas. His heartbeat raced off the charts. Only a moment ago he had been terrified, but now all he could think about was what could be inside! *Gold and silver coins? A treasure of emeralds, rubies, and diamonds?* Aidan smiled, his mind already imagining what he would buy with his newfound riches.

Then again, Aidan thought, *each jar could be filled with something less pleasant, like cobras or—yuck—somebody's ashes!*

Either way, Aidan had to find out, so he reached slowly toward the clay pots.

There was no blistering heat and no biting electric shock, but the moment Aidan's finger touched the first pot, all three of the pots shattered. Aidan flinched and pulled back, feeling very much in trouble for breaking something so valuable. He half expected his mother to run down the stairs immediately to lecture him about his carelessness. She didn't, of course; for she wasn't at home.

Then Aidan noticed that lying in the shards of each pot was a scroll. *TREASURE MAPS!* Aidan hoped as he reached down and picked up one of the scrolls. It was surprisingly heavy, and Aidan immediately saw why. For it was not one but many pieces of parchment rolled up and secured by a leather lace.

Aidan scooped up the other two scroll bundles. He carefully walked up the darkened, creaky basement stairs, but at the top he bounded through the door and rushed to his room—all the while wondering what was in the scrolls.

THE BETRAYAL

Carefully, Aidan untied the lace around the first scroll. As he unrolled it specks of parchment fell to the bed. He caught his breath, fearing the scrolls might be so ancient and brittle that they would crumble to dust if opened. Aidan's fears proved unfounded, for the pages were quite thick—more a stout cloth than paper.

A stone castle tower was emblazoned near the top of the first page and seemed to guard the beginning of the text—which, to Aidan's relief, was in English. Aidan read the first line aloud.

> **Outside of time and place,**
> **there is a realm of**
> **great nobility and renown.**

Aidan's mind buzzed with excitement. He read the words over and over, as if he was sampling some rich, delectable treat. Eagerly, he gently turned to the next page.

For the next three hours, Aidan lay in his bed reading the scrolls, his mind mesmerized by the fantasy world unfolding before him.

The first scroll told the story of another world, a region known only as The Realm. Early in the history of The Realm, a vast and glorious medieval kingdom known as Alleble became very powerful. The kingdom grew and gave birth to many neighboring cities. In time, castles and townships appeared in every corner of the known world. But Alleble was the Father Kingdom. And like a good father, Alleble protected all of its offspring, those who swore allegiance to Alleble, and even the many who did not. There was a great time of peace, for Alleble's power was absolute. Its King, sovereign. Its armies, unmatched.

There were, of course, occasional skirmishes between smaller armies, much as young siblings might bicker. And there too were natural threats, aggressive creatures that left their caves and other dark places of the world to assault the strongholds of nearby cities. But with each incident, the King of Alleble saw to it that all conflict was resolved and order restored. The Peace, as it was called, did not last. For in all its plans to protect its people from the dangers lurking outside it, Alleble never dreamed of a war within the kingdom.

Aidan had read lots of fantasy fiction before: *King Arthur and the Knights of the Round Table, Oswald's Quest, The Dark Mountain Chronicles*—all mysterious and exciting tales. But something about the story in the scrolls was different. Of course, none of those other tales were written on ancient scrolls Aidan had found, but it was more than that.

From the first word, Aidan found himself strangely connected with everything he read. Yet a suspicion grew at the edge of Aidan's consciousness. Sure the story was full of fantasy stuff—knights, castles, dragons, and other beasties—but it sure seemed real. *Of course, it could not be real,* Aidan thought. However, certain elements nagged Aidan to reconsider. The unbelievable detail, for instance. Things like the exact measurements of a castle gate or the precise number of knights killed in a specific battle—even their names! Some of these lists went on for almost an entire page.

Aidan wondered why the story's author—whoever it was—would interrupt the plot to include such precise details. At times, it almost seemed like a history book. And history was real.

Aidan could not help himself. He had to know more. As soon as he finished the first scroll, he picked up the second one and eagerly read on.

King Eliam, the noble and wise monarch of Alleble, decided to promote one knight from his Elder Guard to become the Sentinel of Alleble. This was a difficult decision, for the Elder Guard were the twelve most skilled and loyal warriors of the kingdom. But only one could be Sentinel. It was a new position—a position of great honor, great responsibility, and great power. For the Sentinel was in charge of guarding the King's throne room and protecting the King.

King Eliam favored a bold-hearted knight named Paragal, and chose him to become the kingdom's first Sentinel.

The King gave Paragal *Cer Muryn*, the Blue Blade. It was a mighty sword forged by the King himself from *murynstil*, the strongest and most rare metal in the land. On its hilt were three blue onyxes that blazed like stars when the sword was wielded by one of pure heart. In the beginning, Paragal was pure, and all the kingdom of Alleble, including the King, loved Paragal deeply.

So entrusted was Paragal that King Eliam endowed him with an unheard-of power. In the highest tower of the Castle of Alleble was a sacred place called *Sil Agal Lorinfal*, The Library of Light. It was where King Eliam would go to consult—and compose the history of Alleble.

Only the King had the ability to enter *Sil Agal Lorinfal*, for The Stones of White Fire surrounded the tower with an impenetrable barrier of unquenchable holy flames. Anyone else who dared an attempt to enter would be consumed in moments.

King Eliam gave Paragal power to endure the flames and pass into The Library to read the lore of Alleble. But still, only the King himself could write on the scrolls within.

Paragal spent much time in The Library, and soon his wisdom was unparalleled in Alleble, exceeded only by the King. So wise did Paragal become that ambassadors and emissaries from many of the smaller kingdoms came to Paragal seeking knowledge or counsel. This Paragal gladly gave to them. And in return for some portion of Paragal's sage advice, these dignitaries gave Paragal treasures from their realms. Over time, Paragal amassed a collection of extraordinary wealth. It became his undoing.

Greed for even greater gain began to gnaw at Paragal, for his fortune was but a trinket when compared to King Eliam's vaults. But greed was just the first fissure of evil to appear in Paragal's heart. For just as he grew rich on the gifts of the people of The Realm, he also grew prideful on their praise.

They called Paragal fair, and he was handsome like one descended from kings. They called him wise, and he was dauntingly wise. They called him powerful, and Paragal was powerful—a legend in arms and able to pass The Stones of White Fire without perishing. But in every facet of this praise there was for Paragal a biting insult.

For no matter what was said, it was always understood by all that King Eliam was greater still!

Jealousy festered in Paragal each time rulers of other lands came to King Eliam for counsel. When crowds bowed low as the King passed, Paragal watched and coveted for himself such love and homage. And when the King entered The Library of Light to pen the lore of Alleble, Paragal stood guard outside the throne room . . . and smoldered.

It was no longer enough to be the King's most honored. Paragal wanted to wear the crown himself.

In secret, Paragal gathered many to his side—some from distant lands—but most from inside Alleble's own borders. With riches, he bribed them. With wisdom, he beguiled them. With power, he coerced them. Then Paragal set in motion a plan to bring down the King and put himself on the throne.

Aidan was outraged. How could Paragal betray his King like that? King Eliam was good and kind and . . . generous. He treated Paragal like a son! It was treason. It wasn't fair.

Aidan flopped backward onto his pillows. He'd seen an awful lot of injustices lately, but nothing on the scale of what was taking place in Alleble. And though he kept reminding himself that it was just a story, Aidan found himself afraid for King Eliam. Aidan had to know what would happen next, so he sat up and read on.

Some time later, though he tried hard to stay awake, Aidan found himself blinking and nodding. Slowly, Aidan's eyelids drooped and shut.

It was a troubled slumber. He tossed and turned, grasping fistfuls of blankets, all the while muttering again and again, "No! No! No!" But the dreams did not stop. . . .

It was an hour before dawn would brighten the skies over Alleble, and Paragal was pleased. "So far, my plan is unfolding exactly as I had hoped. Well, almost," he corrected himself. "One of the Elder Guard's little runts has escaped and has not been found. No matter."

Paragal stood outside the throne room at his post. He was, after all, the Sentinel of Alleble, sworn and prepared to risk life and limb for the King. Paragal intended to honor that oath—just not as it was intended. He looked down at his sword, Cer Muryn. The three jewels on Cer Muryn's hilt were dull, absent of their former blue fire.

Paragal turned and, like a phantom, silently passed into the throne room. Darkened murals of heroes from Alleble's past hung high between tall, arched windows of stained glass. These knights and ladies of great honor witnessed Paragal's approach to the seat that should not be his. He did not look up at them, for they were but memories and powerless to hinder his plans. His eyes were riveted to the throne.

King Eliam's high seat was made of a precious white marble, and even in the dark it seemed to glow. Paragal ran his thin fingers over one armrest, closed his eyes and, intoxicated with the moment, let his head roll back. For now he allowed himself just a taste. Later, though, he would drink deeply of glory and would have his fill.

Paragal knew that King Eliam would be in The Library, as was his custom before sunup. It was his time to write, when The Realm was still and quiet, and all concerns could wait for the light of day.

By dawn, he would no doubt have penned several new scrolls to add to Alleble's illustrious history.

Torches flickered on the inside wall of the curving stairs as Paragal ascended. He ducked under a wooden arch and crossed the threshold of the King's sacred courtyard outside on a large gatehouse. There, in the center of the courtyard, Paragal paused a moment and beheld The Stones of White Fire and the great tower Library. Twelve stones, inlaid on the floor, formed a circular barrier surrounding the tower. Each stone was inscribed with a word from the sacred first scroll of Alleble. The first scroll was the only scroll in the entire Library that was kept sealed. Not even Paragal was permitted to read the first scroll. It was said in legends that the first scroll contained the past and the future, the entire history of every being in the realm of Alleble from beginning to end, the sum total of all the other scrolls that had been or ever would be written. But no one knew how that could be . . . if it was true.

The twelve words on the twelve stones seemed written in liquid fire, and white tongues spouted from them and rose into a great inferno. The Library was engulfed in a writhing wall of flame that would suffer no being to enter, except King Eliam and his Sentinel. And the Sentinel entered.

The flames licked all around Paragal, but no harm came to him. Once past the fire, he entered The Library and the writing sanctuary on the first level. There were nine levels in The Library, each above the other, joined by a central spiral stair and a network of ladders and trapdoors.

Hand on the hilt of his sword, Paragal entered and walked past shelves that reached from floor to ceiling. Each level held scrolls beyond number, and Paragal had read every one, word for word. All except for the first scroll kept in a locked chest on the ninth level—and, of course, the scroll on the desk in front of King Eliam.

The ink on that scroll was wet, and the pen was still in the hand of its author.

"You have come earlier than you are wont," said the King, his back turned to Paragal. "Come in, my Sentinel. Have you news?"

"Yes, m'lord," said Paragal. "There is a matter I would speak to you about."

The King dipped the pen into a dark bottle of ink and continued writing. "I will gladly attend to your wish, for this scroll is nearly complete."

"M'lord, if you please," said Paragal through gritted teeth. He despised having to beg like a mongrel at his master's table. "It is an urgent matter that will not wait."

"Very well, Paragal," said King Eliam. He turned and rose to look upon his Sentinel. Whether it was some trick of the candle's light, Paragal could not tell, but he thought there was an odd look in the King's eyes. *Surely he cannot suspect*, Paragal thought.

"Let us speak, then," said the King.

"There is some trouble among the Elder Guard. Will you come?" asked Paragal, gesturing out of The Library.

"Trouble?" echoed the King. "Lead me where you will."

Together they left The Library of Light and passed through the flames. Then the throne room—they walked by the marble seat of the King. The moonlight cast Paragal's large shadow over the throne as they passed.

No words were spoken as Paragal led the King down a long hall and then by the stair to Guard's Keep. They did not travel the stair. Instead Paragal guided King Eliam to a seldom-used door, the door to the great stone balcony above Guard's Keep. The King paused momentarily to allow Paragal to open the door and escort him out into the cool air of the fading night.

Beyond the waist-high parapets lay the still gray shadows of Alleble. Towers, cottages—even the fountains seemed to rest unaware.

Paragal walked out toward the center of the vast balcony and brushed his hand along a rectangular block of marble that stood about four feet in height and was about as long and wide as a tomb.

"What is this you have led me to see, Paragal?"

"It is an altar."

The King stared at the back of his Sentinel. "An altar for what purpose?"

"Come and see, my lord," said Paragal.

Paragal stepped to the brink of the balcony wall and waited for the King.

When King Eliam approached, Paragal pointed over the wall down into the courtyard. The King's gaze followed, and his eyes widened.

Men, women, and children, bound by their hands and gagged, trembled waist-deep in the vast fountain nearest the castle. Soldiers with torches ablaze surrounded them, and bowmen with flaming arrows fitted to their bowstrings stood at the ready.

"There is trouble with the Elder Guard, my lord," said Paragal.

"Paragal, what have you done?" said the King. His hand crept slowly to the hilt of his sword.

"It is simply what I have been prepared for my entire life. I am fair and wise and powerful, and yet, while you live, I am but a puppet—a servant never allowed to achieve the grandeur I deserve."

"Paragal, you have been as a son to me."

"A pet, you mean. A servant. Always I am second!" Paragal

raged. He drew Cer Muryn and slashed the air as he spoke. "But no longer. Your precious Elder Guard, their wives and children all wait to see what sort of King you truly are. The fountain is filled now with fuel oil and will kindle into a pool of fire with a kiss from a flaming arrow. I have but to signal and they perish."

The King's shoulders sagged and his head lolled to the side as if something he had long expected had finally occurred, but the weight of it was more devastating than he had imagined.

Paragal's voice lowered to a gravelly whisper. "Oft you have spoken of sacrifice. Will your deeds match your words? You must now choose, my lord: Your life or theirs?"

The King's eyes narrowed. "You are wise, indeed, Paragal. But your wisdom is tainted by this treachery. Do you believe that by murder, you will gain the love and respect of all the free folk of Alleble?"

Paragal's eyes narrowed. He stepped just a breath away from the King. "If they do not give me their love freely," Paragal said, "then I will take it at the edge of the sword or . . . by fire!"

"That is fear, not love," said the King.

"Nevertheless, it is what I will. And finally, my will be done— not yours."

Paragal gestured toward the altar with the tip of his blade.

"So, great King," he seethed. "Will you lay aside your crown for your people? Will you redeem their trust in you? Or would you watch them perish in such fire and allow their screams to haunt you forever?"

The King looked one last time into the eyes of his people, into the eyes of the children. They were frightened and shivered as much from fear as from the morning chill. But there was more in their eyes than fear. The King smiled at them kindly and removed his sword.

And then Eliam, the mighty King of Alleble, lay down upon the bed of stone.

Bloodlust gleaming in his eyes, Paragal approached the altar and gripped his sword, Cer Muryn, the sword forged by the King. The spark once kindled by Paragal's purity was gone. The onyxes in the sword's hilt were as lifeless and cold as ice.

Paragal held the blade aloft high above the King's neck. The captives in the fountain stirred restlessly.

"Have you any parting words, my lord?" the Sentinel asked, sneering.

"Your name," said the King. "Your name, Paragal, in the old tongue, means 'one of pure light,' and so you once were. But know this: When your stroke falls, so shall your own star fall. Your light will go out, and you will earn a new name. You shall be called *Paragor*—'one of pure darkness.' Darkness will be your dwelling place, and it will consume you. You will be ever hungry for what you can never have. No darkness in Alleble will be as you."

Paragal's eyes flickered and flashed red for a moment.

"You have no power to pronounce this," Paragal said through his teeth. His grip tightened on the sword, and he prepared to deliver a mighty stroke. But the blade did not fall. In fact, it could not fall, for King Eliam held it up by force of his own will. And then he spoke once more.

"What you are about to do, do it now, but know: You do not command this. I am allowing it. And nothing will ever rescue you from the doom you have chosen."

"No!" Paragal screamed, but it came out in a hiss like a venomous snake. And like the strike of a cobra, he brought the blade down swiftly on the King's neck.

REALMS THAT
LIE UNSEEN

"N oooooooo!" cried Aidan, sitting bolt upright in his bed. He raised his arms, trying desperately to ward off an attack. But the attack was not there in his room. It was back in his dream, his nightmare. Aidan's chest heaved. His bedclothes were drenched in cold sweat. Aidan shivered.

He looked down at the scrolls, the account of the Great Betrayal. He had seen it in his dreams, and it was horrible. Aidan tried to shake the vivid images from his mind, but they held on.

He'd done it. The, the—Aidan could not find a word severe enough to describe Paragor. He had taken the love of his King and kingdom, and their trust as well, and he had paid them back with treachery. Paragor's face, once noble and proud, had become twisted with rage and hate. That face . . .

Aidan realized with horror that it was not the first time he had seen that face. The warrior from the recurring dream. *It's him! It's Paragor!*

Aidan felt a sharp pain in his chest, and he doubled over.

Aidan staggered to the hall bathroom and splashed icy water on his face. His heart pounded. *But how did Paragor get into my dreams before I ever read the scrolls?*

Aidan dried his face with a towel, looked up into the mirror, and reeled backward. In the reflection he saw himself surrounded by the desperate, haunted faces of the children from the fountain. They were so . . . so sad.

Deep in a doubt-shrouded corner of Aidan's mind, an impossible thought stirred. But it was impossible, wasn't it? Aidan looked back at the mirror, and the faces were gone.

Aidan stood at his bedroom door and stared at the third scroll bundle. It lay, still secured with its leather lace, waiting.

No, as much as he wanted to find out what became of the Elder Guard and the Kingdom of Alleble, Aidan needed a break. Aidan went down to the kitchen. Grampin was there, still asleep in his chair.

All he does is sleep, Aidan thought disdainfully. Aidan slipped around him and opened the pantry door. *Mannnnn, the brownies are all gone!* Aidan cast an accusative eye on his grandfather. Sure enough, there were brownie crumbs in his lap. *Sleep—and eat,* Aidan corrected himself.

Settling for option number two, he poured a bowl of dry cereal, grabbed a spoon, and turned around. For a split second, Aidan thought that Grampin's eyes had been open. Aidan studied his grandfather suspiciously. His head was bent forward, chin resting on his chest. His hands were folded in his brownie-crumb lap, and his upper body inflated slowly with each sleepy breath. He sure looked like he was asleep. Aidan wondered.

Aidan set the empty bowl on his bedside table. Now he felt ready to open the third scroll. Aidan untied the lace, spread open the scroll, and stared.

He went back to the last few pages of the second scroll. He reread the horribly tragic balcony scene above Guard's Keep, and then looked back at the first page of the third scroll.

It didn't make sense. On the first page of the third scroll, there was what looked like a poem.

Aidan scowled. *But what happened to the Elder Guard and the children?* A cold feeling in the pit of Aidan's stomach suggested that whatever happened in Alleble after Paragal murdered King Eliam, it was not good.

He looked down at the poem. The words, written in black ink, shimmered blue as Aidan turned the page at angles in the light. Aidan ran his fingers over several verses and discovered that the text was slightly raised and had its own texture. *This text was meant to stand out,* Aidan thought. And he began to read.

There are passages and doors
And realms that lie unseen.
There are roads both wide and narrow
And no avenue between.
Doors remain closed for those
Who in sad vanity yet hide.
Yet when belief is chosen,
The key appears inside.
What is lived now will soon pass,

And what is not will come to be.
The Door Within must open,
For one to truly see.

Though he had no idea what the poem meant, Aidan read it
again and again. It was some sort of riddle—that much was clear.
And Aidan had an odd suspicion that the riddle was meant for him
to solve.

Eager for an explanation, Aidan moved aside the poem parchment. The next page, however, was blank.

Aidan scrunched up his eyebrows. The following page was blank
as well. He hurriedly turned over each of the last five pages of the
scroll, but they were all void of writing.

"AArrggh!" he growled, looking around his room for someone to explain this great injustice. It couldn't just end there—
with no mention of what became of the Elder Guard and no
explanation of the mysterious poem. But there they were: seven
blank pages.

Confused and more than a little annoyed, Aidan turned back to
the page with the poem. Perhaps there were answers there. He read
it through again, but froze on the last two lines.

The Door Within must open,
For one to truly see.
Do you see?

Aidan blinked. Gooseflesh rippled up his arms. There was a new
line at the end of the poem! He was absolutely sure it hadn't been
there before!

A car door slammed, followed by another, and Aidan looked

out his window. Both his parents were home. *Dad's early*, Aidan thought. He looked back at the poem and swallowed, for there was another line.

Believe and enter.

FAIRY TALES

W hat's goin' on?" Aidan asked. No one answered, but he heard the front door open downstairs. Adrenaline surging in his veins, Aidan bounded down the stairs and nearly steamrolled his parents.

"Mom, Dad, guess what I foun—"

"Please—Whoa, Aidan . . son," Mr. Thomas exclaimed, catching Aidan by the shoulders. "Ever heard of walking down the stairs?"

"Sorry, Dad," Aidan said, his heart still galloping. "But I just wanted to tell you something. See, I was exploring the basement this afternoon and—"

The shrill chirp of a cell phone cut Aidan off.

"That's mine," Mr. Thomas said. He reached into his suit pocket and pulled out a tiny silver phone. "Oh, hi, Doug. What's up?"

Aidan felt like he was about to burst.

Mr. Thomas frowned and turned slightly. "Are you serious?" he said into the phone. "Right now?" He glanced at his wife guiltily and at Aidan.

"Of course, I know this account is important," he continued. "Okay, let me go into my office." Aidan's dad put a hand over the phone. "It's Riddick and Dunn. I have to take a conference call. Sorry, Aidan, we'll have to talk at dinner."

"But," Aidan stammered. His father walked into his home office and closed the French doors. Aidan turned to his mom.

"So, Mom, I was in the basement—" Aidan began, but he was cut off a third time.

"Honey, tell us all about it at dinner," his mom said. "I've got to run a quick errand."

"But, Mom."

"You can tell us everything at dinner."

Dinner?! Wait until dinner?! The greatest discovery of my life and they tell me to wait until dinner?!!

But Aidan waited until dinner.

At dinner, Aidan's mother, father, and grandfather ate as Aidan told them the story about the basement, the sparkles, and the scrolls. He told them everything that he could remember from the scrolls, especially about the poem and the words that had "magically" appeared on the last page.

". . . and it said that if I believed, I could enter."

When Aidan had finished, he looked around the table. His parents wore raised eyebrows and crooked smiles. Mrs. Thomas put her hand on her husband's hand. They glanced at each other knowingly, then turned to Aidan.

"Isn't our son cute?" Aidan's mom gushed.

"What an imagination!" Aidan's dad agreed.

Grampin was silent.

"Cute! Imagination?!" Aidan exploded, widening eyes all around the kitchen table. "I'm NOT making this up!"

Aidan rushed out of the kitchen, nearly stepping on Marbles, his grandfather's cat, who had a terrible habit of walking leisurely in front of people. Grabbing the three bundles of scrolls off the bed, he ran back downstairs to show his family the proof.

As he unrolled for them the ancient pages of parchment, Aidan's mother and father gawked open-mouthed. But Grampin just nodded and smiled.

"Guess it wasn't jest the young feller's eemagination, huh?" he said.

"Yeah!" Aidan agreed, liking Grampin a small bit.

Mr. Thomas took a few of the pages and looked at them closely. "Hmmm," he said. "Show me where you found these, son."

Grampin, confined to his wheelchair, remained in the kitchen, but everyone else descended into the basement.

Aidan knew why they wanted to go check the basement. Proof. They wanted proof. That was it.

He wondered why his parents wouldn't trust him. Sure, he had an admittedly wild imagination—not to mention a voracious appetite for fantastic tales. But the strange nightmares, the thing lurking in the pine tree outside the bedroom window, and the scrolls . . . well, those things all really happened.

Or maybe they didn't.

Aidan felt doubt creep into his mind like an early fall frost, premature in its coming and dangerous to new growth. As Aidan thumped down the basement steps, he began to wonder.

Aidan bumped into the box with the one-eyed doll and awkwardly shuffled over to the workbench to flick on the light. Aidan
and his parents stared at the dark alcove beneath the stairs. Even in
the light of the small work lamp, there could be no mistake. There
was nothing there.

There wasn't even a trace of the three broken clay pots that had
contained the scrolls. Nothing. A numbing cold skittered over Aidan's
body.

"I can't believe I let you drag me all the way down here." Aidan's
dad shrugged. "Clay pots! That's a good one, Aidan."

"But, Dad! They were right here! I saw them . . . they just
appeared!" Aidan pleaded.

"The only thing that appeared, son, was your imagination."

"But what about the scrolls? I didn't make those up!" Aidan
argued, his own belief fading. "Would you at least look at the scrolls?"

"Aidan, I don't know. They're prob—"

"Please, Dad. Just look . . ."

"Son, look, I don't have time for this kind of . . ." Mr. Thomas
hesitated, shifted uneasily, and then changed course. "Okay, okay!
I'll look through them, a little—after we finish dinner. But listen, no
more of this stuff about clay pots. It was cute, but enough is
enough."

Later, Aidan's mom and dad took the scrolls and went upstairs.
Aidan vaulted after them, only to see their bedroom door shut.
Deciding that his parents would most likely need a good bit of time
to examine the scrolls, Aidan flopped down on his bed to draw.

He had just begun sketching the outline of a haunted house
when his parents came out of their bedroom. Aidan's father sat
down on the corner of Aidan's bed. He held two of the scrolls in his
arms. Aidan's mom stood behind him. She had the other scroll.

"Well, I looked at your scrolls, son, and—"

"But you've been gone for just ten minutes!"

"Aidan, please don't interrupt. The reason that I didn't keep reading is that I think I've read this story before."

"You . . . you have?!" Aidan gasped.

"When you described it to us at the table, it sounded familiar, but it's been fifteen, maybe twenty years since I've read it." Mr. Thomas glanced away. A look of irritation flickered on his face for a moment. "It's called *The Story*. It was very popular, for a time."

"But on scrolls?" Aidan blurted out.

"I've never seen it written on scrolls before. I'm wondering if these might be some of the original handwritten drafts."

"Who wrote it?"

"Uh, that I can't remember. But if these are originals, they could be worth a bundle—even more than your baseball cards! We should check on it. I heard that an original manuscript of *The Legend of Sleepy Hollow* went for a half-million dollars at an auction!"

"But, Dad, I don't think this is just a story," Aidan said. "It seemed so re—"

"What? Real? You've got to be kidding me!" Aidan's father snorted and looked at his wife, who had put her hand over her lips to stifle a laugh.

"It's not funny, Mom."

"I'm sorry, sweetie. But it just made me giggle."

Aidan's father handed the two scrolls to Aidan. His mom gave Aidan the last one. "Be very careful with these," she said. "If they are collector's items, you should keep them in a safe place."

Aidan looked down at the scrolls and shook his head. They didn't seem very magical anymore. "It could be real," he offered weakly.

"Son, this is a work of fiction, a fairy tale," his father explained.

"It's different," Aidan said.

"Oh, Aidan, Mom and I both think this is a wonderful story full of beautiful ideas, but it's just not true."

"How do you know?" Aidan said, a slight tremor in his voice.

"Awww, now look, son," he said sympathetically. "I know because . . . I know. That's all. When you grow up, you learn how to judge things—tell the difference between reality and fantasy. It's a story just like *Snow White* or *The Sword in the Stone,* or even *Star Wars.*"

"But it said . . . for those who will believe."

"Aidan," he said, stiffening, growing irritable. "Believing in something does not make it real. Life just doesn't work that way! This, this is nothing more than a fairy tale. Do you believe that *Little Red Riding Hood* is real? Could a big, bad wolf really knock on our door? Or what about *Jack and the Beanstalk?* What about geese that lay golden eggs?"

"Dear," whispered Aidan's mom.

"No, he's a teenager now. He needs to leave this imaginary stuff behind. Do you understand me, son?"

Aidan gritted his teeth and nodded.

His parents gone, Aidan sat alone with the scrolls. He felt betrayed both by his parents and by himself. *It wouldn't be the first time my imagination got the better of me. But just once, I wish they'd believe me.*

"Stupid!" Aidan yelled at himself as he recklessly knocked the scrolls onto the floor. He threw his face into his pillow and glanced one more time at the scrolls. They had unraveled, a page of the third scroll on top. It was the page with the poem.

Aidan drifted off into an uneasy sleep, with the words "Believe and enter" still dancing in his mind.

A New Ally

A car door slammed and woke Aidan earlier than he wanted to be up on a summer day. With some effort, he opened his eyes and uncoiled an arm from his favorite goose-down pillow, the one his mom had bought for him when he was five. For some reason, Aidan had immediately grown attached to it. And now, many years later, no matter where it was on the bed when he went to sleep, the pillow always ended up tucked snugly under his arm.

Aidan put his pillow aside, sat up, and blinked. Bands of light streamed in from the blinds and fell upon the scrolls, which were neatly bundled at the foot of his bed. The parchments looked golden in the sunlight.

Mom must have picked them up off the floor, he thought.

Aidan immediately felt the urge to read them again. *Why?* He did not know. They had, after all, gotten his hopes sky-high for nothing. Still, the urge was there.

Forget it! I won't give in! He shook his head and threw a corner of his blanket over the scrolls, leaving a peculiar oblong hump at the end of the bed. The sunlight lingered on the hump for a few moments more but faded as dark clouds rolled in from the Rockies and smothered the sun.

After a quick change, Aidan was online, checking email. Nothing but spam, as usual since Robby had been at camp. It didn't stop Aidan from jotting a quick note to Robby anyway. The message complete, his finger hovered over the mouse, ready to click SEND. But then he hesitated.

Aidan's stomach did a flip-flop and tightened uncomfortably— like he'd just broken something precious in a gift shop but couldn't afford to pay for it. Then, he glanced over at the hump on the bed and had a thought. Aidan clicked the mouse back in the email field and typed "P.S." underneath his original message. *After all*, he thought, *Robby would believe it.*

Then again, Robby might just say: "Ri-ight, Aidan. Magic scrolls?"

Aidan deleted the postscript and hit SEND. His stomach did another flip-flop.

Hoping to cure his churning belly, Aidan wandered downstairs in search of breakfast. As he poured a large bowl of cereal, his thoughts began to drift. There was a small part of him that wasn't convinced that the events of the previous day had been figments of his wild imagination. A timid but determined voice spoke up in his mind.

The clay pots were there, and I know it!

Well, where are they now, then? answered a blustery, skeptical second voice.

Maybe they dissolve after a few minutes.

Yeah, right! That's way out there, Aidan. So the pots just went "Poof!" and vanished without a clue? Good one.

But I saw them. I touched one even. It must've ju—

"Aidan, that you?" Grampin asked, snapping Aidan out of his dueling thoughts. He immediately realized that he had overflowed his bowl with cereal, spilling it all over the counter.

"Yeah, Grampin, what do you want? You need something to drink or something?"

"No, I need you to come here for a minute!" Grampin's voice snapped like a whip.

Aidan stomped into the living room, expecting Grampin to scold him for spilling the cereal. *If the old guy dares to lecture me,* Aidan thought, *he'll get an earful back, and then some.* Aidan didn't get what he expected.

Grampin was sitting in his chair, but his posture was different. He sat, shoulders back, chest out, chin up—far from his normal slouch-slump. Blue eyes, though faded with age, gleamed from under his wiry white brows, and his stubbly jaw was set firmly. All together, he looked like an aging but still-proud army general. The serious look on his face softened as Aidan drew near.

"I'm sorry that your daddy was so hard on ye last night," he said. "Didn't believe ye about the scrolls, did he?"

"No," Aidan whispered. He felt stunned. After festering all morning, he had tromped into the living room, walls up—poised for battle.

Grampin's question smashed down the walls, and disarmed Aidan's heart.

"Dad said I made it all up."

"So I heard, Aidan, and again, I'm sorry. He was wrong to say those things."

"No, Grampin, it's okay. He wasn't being that mean."

"You're missin' my point, boy. Now listen. What I mean is that your daddy, smart as he is, was wrong to doubt you."

Aidan stared.

Grampin smiled.

"I wanted to say something last night, but ye ran up to yer room 'fore I could make a peep. Then, I heard ye in the kitchen, so now here it is: Aidan, I believe you."

Aidan gasped. "You do?"

Was Grampin serious or . . . senile? Aidan wasn't sure, but having any adult agree with him felt pretty good.

"Heh, heh, heh . . . yes, sir, I do," Grampin replied. His volume climbed excitedly as he spoke. "The clay pots, the scrolls, the new words on the pages, and most important, the story in the scrolls—I believe it all!"

Aidan thumped down into an easy chair near Grampin. His thoughts and feelings were so conflicted it was like having a battle going on in his head. He had been dying for someone to believe him about the scrolls, but he never expected his ally to be Grampin. *This is the guy who ruined my life!* Aidan thought. *Why should I trust him?*

And maybe time had finally caught up with him. Grampin's face was so stretched and weathered, his arms and legs so thin and frail—maybe the years that had withered him physically had finally begun to diminish him mentally as well. Aidan stared hard at his grandfather for several silent moments.

"But, Grampin, Dad says it's not true," Aidan said finally. "And Mom doesn't believe it either."

"Yes, I know they didn't—or maybe *wouldn't* is a better word. For your parents, things just don't appear out of thin air. You, on the other hand, you were open. In fact, I bet you were just waitin' for something amazing to happen."

"I was, Grampin. Lots of weird things have been happening to me—I was kinda expecting it."

"See!"

"But, how come when we went back down there, the pots were gone?"

"I'm not sure, Aidan. Maybe your mom and dad talked you outta trusting yer heart. A little doubt can be poisonous to new faith."

Aidan nodded. His father had made a pretty convincing case against the scrolls' magically appearing. *He was right, wasn't he?* Aidan wondered. *Things really don't appear out of thin air, do they?*

"Look here, Aidan, I've been where your daddy's at. There was a time, years ago, when I was as stubborn as an alley cat on a diving board."

Aidan smiled. Then, Grampin leaned forward in his wheelchair and grew more serious. "I was a bitter young man then, Aidan. Mad at the world about my parents."

"What happened to your parents?" Aidan asked.

"When I was sixteen, my mother got sick. It was an awful thing to watch her go like that. Muscles seizing up. Always in pain. My father died a year later. They said it was his heart, but I knew better. That man died of grief."

"I'm sorry, Grampin."

"I was too, Aidan. But I didn't let it get me like it did my father. No, I threw myself into my job. I worked hard, but I guess people could always tell there was something wrong. Someone at the factory where I worked—guy named Kaleb Shipley, I remember—tried to tell me a story from the scrolls. Said it would help me understand

the world better, but I didn't want to hear a word. A whole lot a'
hooey, I told him. I just wasn't ready then. It took me fifty years to
get ready.

"But gettin' old makes you look at things differently—bein'
closer to the end, I reckon. Your heart either gets so hard that you
close up inside for good, or you start to wonderin' if there's more
to life than what meets the eye. Well, it seemed to me that there just
has to be more, so I started to wonder.

"Don't get me wrong, Aidan, aside from my parents dying when
I was young, I've really had a good life—met and married the finest
woman in the world, raised a good family, had decent jobs. I had
few complaints. Still, eighty-some-odd-years a' fun in the sun on
this giant spinning mud ball can't be all there is. I mean, what's the
point of it all? Is everybody jest goin' through the motions a' life
until, one day, life runs out? And what really worried me was, what
happens after?"

Grampin was speaking to Aidan eye-to-eye, man-to-man about
deep, meaningful things—it felt so good to be treated as valuable,
even as an equal. Aidan leaned forward; he wanted to hear more.
"What happened?"

"Well," Grampin continued, "it was about that time that some
scrolls showed up in my library. And there they were, the answers to
all of my questions. Best dang thing that ever happened to me!"

Grampin leaned back in his wheelchair and a joyful grin widened
on his stubbly face. He began to laugh, almost a cackle. "Heh, heh,
heh."

"What's so funny, Grampin?"

"Well, you probably don't remember, but when you were just a
little squirt and came to visit with yer Grandma and me, I used to tell
you bedtime stories. You sat on my bed in your blue footy pajamas

and munched gingerbread cookies, and I used to act out the stories with different accents and voices, heh, heh."

"Sure, Grampin, I remember. So what's so funny?"

"Those stories, Aidan, every one of them, came right out of the scrolls! Drove yer daddy nuts, that I was fillin' your head with such nonsense."

"Really?" Aidan laughed. Grampin's mood was contagious, but Aidan was still skeptical. "I didn't recognize the stories when I read my scrolls."

"That was ten or eleven years ago, Aidan. And I suspect that a person receives the scrolls they need. Besides, if the story is no more meaningful to you than bedtime entertainment, it fades from yer memory."

The clock's ticking grew loud. Aidan was silent. But his mind was like a beehive that had just been hit with a stone. Jubilant thoughts— *I was right! The scrolls are real! I knew it! Wait'll I tell Robby!*— careened around and crashed into demanding rebuttals and urgent questions. The latter were piling up and could not be ignored.

"Grampin, Dad said that lots of people have the story from the scrolls, that it's even in bookstores—is that true?"

"Yes, that much is true. There are dozens of different versions. Shame of it is, there are millions of folk all over who have *The Story* collectin' dust right on their shelves—and not the slightest guess that it's all real."

"But, Grampin, how can it be real? I mean, castles and drag—"

"Aidan, listen. Your father said that believing in something doesn't make it real. But what he don't understand is that there are things—incredible things!—that are real whether we want to believe in them or not. *The Story* is real, all right, but he won't see it until he's willing to believe."

Aidan squinted, wanting to understand but still questioning.

"Believing in something or someone is a very special thing, my boy. It can be risky 'cause if you believe in something, you stand up for it. You fight for it sometimes. If what you believe turns out to be a lie, you could end up humiliated or . . . worse. My own son thinks I'm a kook for believin' *The Story*, and he's not the only one, heh, heh."

"So, Grampin, you're serious—you believe it all, what the scrolls say?"

"I do, Aidan. The big question is, do you believe?"

"Well, I don't know . . . Dad said—"

"I know what yer father says, but ye need to decide for yerself. Now, you go to the scrolls, ye hear? The key is there. The Door Within is closer than you think."

"But—"

"Son, you best git! It's time for my nap!"

Aidan had never seen Grampin so stirred up before. He certainly didn't look ready for a nap. Aidan half expected the old guy to get up out of his wheelchair and boot him a good one in the rear if he didn't get moving. So Aidan flew up the stairs, threw the covers off the bed, and scooped up the scrolls.

A key? Aidan thought as he spread the first scroll. *I don't see a key in here.*

In turn, he examined every page of the scrolls, shook them, even waved them around like magic wands, but nothing fell out.

Outside Aidan's window, a catbird chirped angrily. The pines in the front yard were a playground for many wild creatures, but the birds took over around ten every morning. Squawking, twirping, and peeping, dozens of them hopped from branch to branch among the evergreens. Aidan liked to watch them at times, but today, he had other concerns.

The key. Grampin had said The Door Within was close, but how was he supposed to unlock it without a key? He was about to call down the stairs to ask when his eyes locked onto the poem.

There are passages and doors
And realms that lie unseen.
There are roads both wide and narrow
And no avenue between.
Doors remain closed for those
Who in sad vanity yet hide.
Yet when Belief is chosen,
The key appears inside.
What is lived now will soon pass,
And what is not will come to be.
The Door Within must open,
For one to truly see.
Do you see?
Believe and enter.

Like a connect-the-dots picture with a handful of lines drawn in, the meaning of the poem was slowly taking shape. It all seemed to hinge on believing, but believing what? *The Story?* Just believe it's true? Aidan needed more dots connected.

Maybe it's like making a wish, Aidan thought. Perhaps he could just hope really hard, and a key would come forth from the scrolls. Aidan reasoned that if three clay pots could appear out of thin air, certainly a key could. Aidan put down the scroll. He was ready to believe.

THE DOOR WITHIN

Aidan sat on the edge of his bed. His knees were together and his back was as straight and stiff as a post. He squinted his eyes shut, as if letting in a crack of light might somehow spoil the moment. Then thinking *I believe, I believe, I believe,* over and over again, Aidan started to hold out his hands. Then he opened his eyes. *What sort of key will I get? Should I cup my hands one under the other for a tiny key? Or hold out both hands shoulder's width apart for a large key?* Aidan wasn't sure. Then he had a disturbing thought. *What if the key is the size of a telephone pole?*

He risked it, cupped his hands, extended his arms, and again closed his eyes. "I believe, I believe, I believe, I believe," he chanted, rocking slowly and trying to will a key to appear. At last, he opened his eyes again. There in his hands . . . was nothing.

Aidan glanced sideways at the scrolls on his bed and then

trudged downstairs to the living room. Grampin seemed to be asleep, but he opened one eye as Aidan approached.

"Grampin," Aidan said meekly, "how do I believe?"

Grampin snickered. "Do you believe the sky is blue?"

"Yeah," said Aidan.

"Okay, do you believe birds fly?"

"Of course!" Feeling foolish now.

"Well, son, it's kinda like that!"

"Okay, I believe like that, but . . . I didn't get a key or find a door."

"There's more to it, Aidan. It starts in your head, but it's got to go beyond. Try this. Picture yerself standing on the edge of a cliff. It's a chasm, really, and there's an old narrow bridge you could cross to get to the other side. Now, you can look at the bridge and agree, it's fine—that it'll hold you—but believin' it's safe won't get you to the other side, now will it? You got to step out, walk right on out there."

Aidan swallowed and nodded. Grampin's fierce blue eyes held him there for a moment more.

"Now, Aidan," Grampin said. He coughed and cleared his throat. "It's up to you."

Aidan gritted his teeth and turned. He began to climb the stairs to his room, but glanced one last time at his grandfather. He was slouched again, spent from their conversation. Aidan noticed too that Grampin's right hand was lightly pressing into his chest as if he were kneading dough. Aidan took a tentative step back, but Grampin looked up and smiled. "Go on," he whispered.

Aidan grinned back and flung himself up the stairs.

The scroll with the poem was waiting on his bed. Aidan sat down and brushed his fingers across the script. They felt vibrant, textured with electricity. Aidan closed his eyes. No more chanting. No more wishing.

He cleared his mind. Then, rapidly, an image began to develop. There before Aidan was the cliff. And secured to the edge of it, just a few feet away, was the narrow bridge. It spanned a great gap, but Aidan could not see the other side, for it was whited out by distance and haze.

In his mind, Aidan stepped closer and peered over the edge. The depth of the ravine could not be guessed, but it had a peculiar, powerful gravity that entranced and pulled. Aidan shrank back. Were he to fall, he might never stop falling.

He heard the birds chirping, and he almost opened his eyes for the safety of his bedroom. But that would be giving up, surrendering. No, he could not surrender this time. And Robby wasn't there to bail him out. Aidan himself had to go forward.

First, however, he decided to inspect the bridge.

It was made of ropes and wooden planks. The ropes seemed tightly wound and knotted and were not frayed. The planks were cut from solid wood and were not cracked or rotted. The bridge looked sturdy. The bridge looked strong.

I can do this.

Aidan took a step toward the bridge, but at that moment a stiff wind came forth and caused the bridge to sway. The terror of death awoke and whispered icy thoughts into Aidan's mind. The bridge seemed at the mercy of the wind. Aidan began to shake. It was one thing to venture out upon such a bridge when it was still. That was enough. But to risk his life on rope and wood in motion?

The rope might not hold. A board could crack. I could slip.

Fear groped about for Aidan's throat, and again Aidan was

tempted to open his eyes. But then words from the poem sprang into his mind:

> Yet when Belief is chosen,
> The key appears inside.

In that moment, he had it—the key to the riddle: Belief must be chosen.

Aidan looked out at the swaying bridge and made his decision. Without looking back, he stepped forward onto the bridge and kept walking. He held on to the rope railings and watched to make sure each foot landed squarely on a plank. Aidan felt a gooseflesh chain reaction up his spine as he walked. They were not the bumps of creeping cold or of tingling fear—they were of pure joy and exhilaration.

Each step brought increased confidence. And though the wind picked up again, Aidan pushed forward. He swayed as the bridge swayed, and for once in his life he was not afraid.

He still could not see the other side, but he had come to the end of the bridge's down slope and began the slight incline that told him he was halfway.

Aidan was too intent on getting to the other side of the bridge to notice, but the cries and chirps of the birds in the pines outside grew faint as he walked. He pressed on, pulling himself by the rope railings and quickening his pace. At last, there was something visible. *It's only a darker patch of mist in a sea of clouds,* he told himself. But as Aidan moved forward, it took shape. It was a door.

Aidan reached the end of the bridge and stood before the door. It was as tall as a door from any home, but that is where the similarity ended. This door was gray stone. Designs were carved meticulously into its surface. And many were inlaid with silver. Knights on horseback carried shields and banners and followed a winding trail to two mountains. A sun rose between the mountains and seemed to light the way for the travelers on the road. And about halfway up from the bottom of the door, just waiting to be pulled, was a large, thick silver ring.

Aidan was certain that before him stood The Door Within, and it was time to open it. Hands slightly trembling, he grasped the silver ring and tugged it to open the door. It was difficult to budge, at first. But Aidan looked up at the graven image of the sun rising between the twin mountains. The image seemed to inject hope into Aidan heart. *It's all true!* he thought. And in that moment, the door came free and began to swing open. Brilliant golden light streamed out as if millions of stars were hiding behind it. Aidan released the ring, and the door opened the rest of the way on its own.

Aidan shielded his eyes with both arms from the fierce, pure light.

He had a strange feeling that Grampin was watching him. Aidan smiled as he walked through The Door Within.

PASSAGE

The light faded and flew away to a pinpoint miles in the distance. Aidan slowly became aware of his surroundings. The first images he saw were blurred and quivered as if viewed through water. He walked on a very narrow stone path. Darkness pressed in from both sides.

Suddenly, Aidan heard thousands of voices—all speaking at once. Yet, as Aidan listened, one voice stood out and the others diminished. It was a dreamy, peaceful voice, speaking in a language Aidan did not know but somehow understood. It called Aidan and guided him straight ahead.

This voice was ever before Aidan and drew him along the narrow path. He did not stumble and he was not afraid, at first, for the voice was comforting and strong like a father encouraging a young child. But as the journey continued, Aidan became aware of another voice.

It too spoke in a strange language, but it was not comforting. It made Aidan wonder, *Should I really be on this path? It seems so long.*

Aidan looked to his left and to his right, and the darkness looked less frightening and more like an enormous dark blanket in which to hide.

Aidan shook his head and continued forward, but as he did the darkness flickered, and unusual visions rose up all around him. There was a beautiful snow-covered countryside, but the snow faded into the pale face of a being whose eyes changed from brilliant blue to blood red. The face dissolved into swirling shadows that were soon pierced by a single flaming arrow.

Blazing across the sea of darkness, the arrow shed a weak flickering light on a cold stone maze. Vision followed vision until Aidan could not follow them any longer. He was somehow becoming aware of things—things, people, and places.

He felt overwhelmed, as if he had left an empty hallway and entered a stadium filled with eighty thousand people. And the second voice kept telling him, "Get off the path! Come to the darkness, and I will keep you safe. Get off the path, now!"

Terrified, Aidan ran off the edge of the path!

Like a stone Aidan fell shrieking and clawing at darkness, for it was a blanket—not for hiding but for smothering.

He fell, unable to see where he might land. Then there was an image beneath him. It was just a gray outline at first. But it grew and took the shape of a pale, almost ghostly form. It was a person! And as Aidan was falling, this being was rising to meet him. Aidan stared down at the being. The being stared up at Aidan. They were rushing toward a collision. And in the last moment before impact, before losing consciousness, Aidan recognized the being. It was a reflection of himself.

STRANGER IN A STRANGE LAND

Something tickled Aidan's nose.

He opened his eyes just a crack, blinked a few times to adjust to the sunlight, and saw a large scarlet-colored butterfly walking and flittering about, apparently in search of nectar.

Aidan thought, *Trust me, bug, there's nothing in my nose for you!*

As he swatted gently at the beautiful insect, his arm erupted in a chain reaction of tingles and pinpricks. It was a familiar feeling. It meant he had fallen asleep on his arm.

He sat up, rubbing the last of the pinpricks out of his arm, and watched the butterfly take to the air in front of him. A bit woozy, Aidan stood and watched the butterfly sail on the breeze up over some stony foothills and into a dense forest. Beyond the foothills and forest, a dark mountain range emerged, piercing all that was green. The mountains sprawled left and right. But in the center of the range were two jagged peaks that stabbed up from the cloud tops like black fangs.

Aidan turned in circles and searched for something, anything familiar. "Where am I?"

He was in a clearing surrounded by a variety of unusual trees. Some were short, no more than six feet in height, with dark, flaky bark. Their trunks were narrow, gnarled, and twisted. And their branches were bare except for massive paws of leaves at the ends. These strange twisty trees all leaned away from the dark mountains.

There were also huge, cone-shaped evergreens. But to call these *evergreen* wouldn't be quite right. They did have needles like the pines in his front yard, but they most certainly were not green. These maintained a dark purple and here and there a hint of navy blue.

But the most striking trees were the tall ones. Aidan didn't know what to call them. The trees' bark—if it could be called bark—was absolutely black. It looked smooth and polished, almost reflective, like an eightball. Their trunks rose in columns and were crowned by thickets of broad red leaves. The roots of these black trees rose out of the ground and spread in dozens of directions. Hundreds, maybe thousands of scarlet butterflies danced around the tree trunks, occasionally dropping to light on the tiny multicolored flowers that grew from the trees' roots.

Aidan shivered, taking in the scene. *It wasn't scary, really . . . just so different!*

Am I in Alleble? Aidan wondered. *Am I?*

Aidan turned again in a circle. There were no castles, no signs of civilization—nothing but nature. He was wondering what he should do next, when he noticed that he hadn't come into the world alone. By his feet on a patch of deep green moss was a scroll. Aidan smiled, picking up the bundle like a long-lost pet.

"I'm not sure how you got here," he said aloud to the scroll, "but I'm glad you did!"

Aidan plunked down on an enormous moss-covered rock and untied the leather lace. It was his third scroll, the one with the poem and the empty pages. He looked down at the bottom below the poem and hoped desperately for something new to be there.

There was, but it wasn't mysterious new text telling Aidan what to do or where to go. It was a handwritten note. It read, "Thought you might need these. Love, Grampin."

Grampin! How could he . . . ? Aidan smiled and shook his head. It seemed that Grampin was full of surprises. *Now, if only I had a map.*

Aidan felt a sharp tingle in his right hand. Instinctively he turned to the next page of parchment. And then his jaw dropped. As if invisible hands were busy sketching away, an incredibly detailed map gradually emerged from the parchment. Etched and shaded mountains formed on the page under a sun whose rays became directional arrows pointing north, south, east, and west. Forests surrounded and penetrated by roads and trails dotted the new map in a patchwork of gray splotches. Flags appeared in many places on the map.

The flags were puzzling. *Could they be foreign countries or cities? Are they borders of some kind?*

He decided that, whatever they were, he would set out toward one of them and see for himself. The only landmark he could identify from the map was the dark mountain range. There was a patch of forest just west of those mountains. One of the flags was on the other side of the range. It looked like the closest flag. Aidan guessed that if he could get over or around the mountain range, he could see what one of the flags was.

Feeling satisfied with his deductions, Aidan began his quest for the flag. He ducked under the boughs of a twisty tree and stepped over the black roots of the shiny eightball trees. He plowed through a row of everpurples, wondering what Robby would think of all this.

Their adventures in Maryland had mostly been exploring the woods behind the high school and crayfishing in Brae Brooke Creek. Aidan wished that Robby could be with him now to experience, well, to experience a real adventure.

Aidan gasped, dropped his bundle of scrolls, and froze in place. A unicorn stood just a few feet away. He couldn't believe his eyes.

A single ivory horn that spiraled out of the creature's forehead distinguished it from a horse. Its coat was not really any color by itself, but many colors mixed in with white—like an opal in the sunlight. *A real unicorn!*

Aidan's heart pounded in his chest as the noble steed approached him, bobbing its head in a friendly way. Timidly, Aidan reached out and patted the beautiful creature on its nose. It felt smooth like velvet. Aidan grinned and stared as if in a trance. The unicorn ducked its head toward Aidan's feet. Aidan looked down, saw his scroll bundle, and remembered his quest for the flag.

Reluctantly, Aidan picked up the scroll and walked away. To his surprise, the unicorn followed.

"I've been here less than a day, and I already have more friends than I did in Colorado!" Aidan said to the unicorn. Aidan jogged at first, and the unicorn trotted along with him. Then, as the trees thinned and the ground began to rise into foothills, they slowed to a walk. The beautiful trees and plants became less and less plentiful as Aidan's climb steepened. Brambles and bracken and scraggly thin shrubs replaced the trees, and a moldy form of gray moss covered everything underfoot. At that point, the unicorn stopped.

"C'mon, Girl," Aidan called. He wasn't sure, but it just seemed like a girl. "You can make it!" The unicorn blinked at Aidan and shook its head. Could it possibly understand?

"Please come with me," Aidan pleaded. "I'll be lonely without you." Again, the beautiful unicorn shook its head. Nothing Aidan said could coax it—the unicorn simply refused to go even a step farther up the mountain.

"Fine, then!" Aidan shouted indignantly. "I'll go by myself!" The unicorn shook its head again, whinnied twice, stamped one hoof on the ground, then galloped away. Frustrated and saddened at the loss of his companion, Aidan turned and continued toward the dark mountains.

After climbing for a stretch, Aidan began to think that maybe the unicorn was smarter than he was! The climb grew steep, and the footing became more uneven. The vile moss began to die out, giving way to crumbly stone.

How many times have I slipped? Aidan wondered. He looked at the collection of scrapes and scratches on his arms and felt bruises forming on his knees.

For the millionth time, Aidan wished he was thin and athletic like Robby. His all-sports-star friend would probably jog up the mountain, but not Aidan. No, his feet felt heavy, like cinder blocks, and his breath came out in pants. He felt hot and cold. Hot from the exertion. Cold because the air became brisk as he climbed. To top it off, Aidan's stomach grumbled. He was starving, and his head hurt. No, the adventure was not going as he had hoped.

The higher he climbed, the more he felt exposed. It felt as if there were millions of tiny eyes watching him clambering clumsily up the mountainside.

Even the mountain seemed to be against Aidan. Again and again, Aidan reached the edge of what he thought was a ridge he could get over and start climbing down, only to realize he still had to climb higher.

After what seemed like hours of back-and-forth climbing, Aidan made an all-out sprint toward a distant notch on the left peak. But it turned out to be just a plateau. And even worse, it looked like there was no way to continue up from there. The mountain rose up before him in a sheer face of stone—as if to say: "GO AWAY! IT'S NOT SAFE HERE!"

Aidan slumped down, his back to the mountain. The headache of hunger and fatigue continued its dull thudding while Aidan considered his options. He could either climb back down a bit to search for another way up, or he could edge along a narrow ridge looking for a spot more level to climb. Aidan opened the scroll once again—this time to the page after the map—but it was still blank. He rolled up the scroll, tied it, and let it roll off his hand to lie at his feet.

The moment he sat down, the sweat he had generated climbing turned icy, and Aidan shivered.

What'll I do? he thought, looking up as the sun sank behind the clouds in the distance. Here he was, high above the trees on the edge of a dreary mountain in a world no one knew existed.

He wondered what his parents would do when they came home and found him gone. What could Grampin say to them?

"Dad, have you seen Aidan?" Mr. Thomas would ask.

"Well, yes, actually," Grampin would reply. "Y'see, he believed in *The Story*, entered The Door Within, and ended up in The Realm."

Aidan laughed through chattering teeth. They wouldn't believe him if he told the truth. *Perhaps,* Aidan thought, *I could bring home some proof—to show them once and for all that it is all real!*

Aidan's eyes grew wide as it occurred to him that the scrolls had helped him get into this realm, but they never mentioned getting back out.

It wasn't at all like some of the stories Aidan had read. Stories where kids had run away without a care to strange new worlds. Stories where the characters never worried about food or where to go to the bathroom! Aidan trembled and hugged himself, for he was cold, afraid, achy, and hungry.

As the deep purple of night began to creep across the sky, Aidan succumbed to sleep. The temperature on the mountainside dropped even more during the night, so Aidan curled up, tucking the scroll under his arm like his old down pillow, and huddled close to the face of the mountain. Aidan's eyes raced beneath his eyelids while he dreamed. Visions of his basement back in Colorado Springs paraded through his mind. He was there again, staring at the alcove beneath the basement stairs, listening to the strange scraping sound he had heard before the clay pots appeared.

But something in the dream wasn't right. The scraping sound was too loud—out of place in the hazy quiet of his dream. Aidan's mind jolted to consciousness.

Opening only one eye, Aidan scanned the dark ledge lit only by the cloud-veiled light of the moon. There was movement in the corner of the ledge near his feet. A fuzzy basketball-sized black lump was scratching at the ground. Aidan sat there motionless, unsure of what to do, until the creature rose up on its hind legs and opened two pale yellow eyes.

"Aaah!" Aidan yelped, leaping to his feet and pressing his back against the wall behind him.

He looked again for the eyes, but they were gone. To be sure, Aidan waited a few minutes and then ventured toward the corner of the ledge. The creature was gone.

At that moment, the moon escaped the clouds briefly and rained pale light upon the ledge. Aidan looked more closely and saw . . .

"Fruit!" Aidan screamed aloud. Not caring where it had come from, he grabbed one of the four plump purple fruit and bit into it. Sweet juice trickled down his parched throat and all over his face and hands as well. It had a texture similar to watermelon, but the taste was different from any fruit he had ever eaten. Aidan's skin tingled warmly as he ate the delicious fruit. Its juice seemed to flow directly into his achy muscles, completely renewing their strength.

When Aidan lifted the last piece of fruit, he discovered an arrow that had been gouged into the ground. It glowed palely, as if it had been painted with moon dust. It pointed to the narrow ridge to the right of the plateau.

Go that way? Aidan wondered. *Why that way?*

"Well," Aidan said aloud, "I might as well go now while I have the energy."

Pressing his back to the sheer mountain, he moved cautiously on a ledge just wide enough for his feet. Gravel and stones toppled over the ledge and disappeared into the inky black distance. Aidan could hear them clacking and ricocheting off the clefts and crags far below.

Following that arrow was another bad idea, Aidan thought. But almost as soon as he'd thought it, the ledge path widened a little and there was yet another glowing arrow—this time scratched into a rock that jutted up from the ground. His confidence restored, Aidan continued along the ledge. As he crept along the ledge, more arrows appeared, until the path began to rise steeply up the mountain. He turned for a moment to see how far he had climbed and became dizzy with the sight of the dark world beneath him.

Don't look down, Aidan! he berated himself.

Aidan followed the arrows around a gradual corner. Then the path stopped, and Aidan was faced with another dead end. But it wasn't a dead end, not quite. For there in front of him, in the side of the mountain, was a three-foot circular hole about waist-high. Several arrows all around the opening seemed to indicate that he should enter.

"No way!" Aidan said, his complaint bouncing off the echoing cliffs. "I am not going in there!"

Spooky basements and nightmares were bad enough, but venturing into a pitch-black hole in the side of a mountain with who knew what living inside? That was just plain crazy.

What if one of those little glowing-eyed beasties is in there? Maybe this whole arrow thing was a trap meant to lure me in!

Aidan thought there might even be a whole nest of those things in there, just waiting to tear him to pieces like piranhas on some poor critter that fell into the river. Aidan sat down with a thud and sulked.

I guess I'll have to go all the way back, Aidan thought dejectedly. It was a LONG way back, with no guarantee that he would find another way over the mountain. Of course, there was no guarantee that this cave, or whatever it was, would lead to the other side of the mountain either. What to do? Neither choice appealed to Aidan, but going back seemed safer than a dark, mysterious hole!

Aidan knew what Robby would do.

That was the problem. Of course, Robby would go. Robby was brave. Robby was an explorer. And if Robby went in first, Aidan would follow. Aidan just didn't have it in him to be the leader. Or did he? Aidan thought for a moment, and a burning sensation began to smolder in his belly. He remembered exploring Grampin's basement. He had overcome that fear, and he was rewarded with the scrolls. Aidan looked again at the opening in the rockface. He felt he had to at least go into the cave a little. *Okay, I'll go in. If it seems to go nowhere, I'll simply turn back.*

Aidan jumped to his feet and walked over to the hole in the mountain. He peered in, straining to see anything that indicated its depth or whether it went straight in or curved.

Total darkness.

He couldn't even tell if it was indeed a cave or a tunnel. But gathering all his courage, he took a deep breath and put one foot up on the edge. Aidan grabbed the top of the entrance and swung his other foot to the edge. Balancing precariously, he stared for a moment into the darkness, questioning all the time if this was a mistake he would live to regret.

Aidan took a couple of tiny squat-steps into the tunnel when an alarming thought occurred to him: He had left his precious scroll way back on the ledge where he had slept!

I've got to get it!

He tried to turn around, but the cave floor sloped downward and was slippery like a newly waxed floor. In trying to clamber out, he lost his footing and began to slide.

Aidan yelled and clawed at the edge of the opening, trying to gain a hold, but he failed. With a final shriek, Aidan rolled onto his back and slid helplessly down the tunnel into the heart of the mountain.

Carrying Aidan's scroll like carpet installers delivering a huge rug, three of the dark, pale-eyed creatures came trotting along the path outside the opening to the tunnel.

The middle one hopped up on the first one's shoulders, and the last one scrambled up atop the other two. With a wobbly effort, they hoisted Aidan's scroll up to the edge of the tunnel's opening. The scroll lay balanced on the edge until the top critter lunged upward to knock it forward. The scroll launched over the edge, but so did the highest creature!

Together, they sailed down the tunnel, following Aidan into the unknown.

The Gate of Despair

Aidan's screams echoed as he flew down the smooth tunnel through the mountain. Nothing he tried could stop nor slow his descent, for the tunnel wound through the depths of the mountain at a steep angle. With every unexpected turn in the passage, with every jarring bump, Aidan expected to die. Smashed into a rock wall, skewered on a stalagmite, or wedged forever in some black crevice of the mountain.

How long can this go on? he wondered. And some distant part of Aidan thought, *This would be kind of fun, if I wasn't about to die.*

Aidan blinked as the thin air whooshed past him. His view was the same, eyes closed or eyes open. Black. And still he slid.

Aidan strained his neck trying valiantly to see where he might be headed. At first, there was nothing. Then, far in the distance, he saw a few points of pale yellow light. Then there were more than a few. Then there were many. Aidan swallowed hard.

Before he knew it, he was right in the midst of them—like swarms of stars on all sides. Aidan whooshed through them, fearfully trying to figure out what they were. Some kind of luminous stones, maybe? Sparks? Subterranean lightning bugs? Or maybe . . .

Eyes! They are eyes! Aidan could see only blurs and flashes, but he felt sure they were eyes. Hundreds, maybe thousands of them winked and blinked as Aidan slapped and scraped to keep them away.

Fed by this new terror, Aidan thought that perhaps the little glowing eyes belonged to the parasites of a gigantic beast that disguised itself as a mountain! The tunnel was actually its enormous esophagus, and Aidan would soon enter the great beast's stomach and be dissolved in its digestive juices.

Aidan yelled, shut his eyes, and launched out of the backside of the mountain. His momentum carried him safely over some jagged rocks. With a plop, he landed in a pool of something dark and wet.

Thinking he was in the creature's stomach, Aidan felt the sting of the acid beginning to eat away at his flesh. He splashed furiously and then stopped when it dawned on him that he wasn't in acid. He opened his eyes and stood up in the chest-deep water.

"Right, Aidan. It was a mountain monster!" Robby would have said. Aidan shook his head and laughed quietly at himself. The scrapes and cuts still stung, but at least he wasn't being digested.

Aidan heard a noise high behind him and stopped laughing. He spun around and looked up at the backside of the mountain. The tunnel exit was forty feet up and the noise, a high-pitched squeal now, emanated from it. The sound grew louder.

Something long shot out of the tunnel, followed by something round and dark. In a split second Aidan recognized the first item: his scroll! He backed up like a center fielder awaiting a fly ball. Then he identified the second item: It was one of the creatures he had seen on the ledge the night before!

He didn't want that thing to land on him. But he didn't want the scroll to land in the water either. Something happened at that moment. Aidan didn't think; he just acted.

He took two slow steps backward and reached up with his left hand while simultaneously feeling for the edge of the pool with his right. He caught the scroll and vaulted up onto dry ground just as the dark ball hit the water.

Aidan was stunned for a moment. Never in his life had he pulled off a move like that. *That was . . . that was almost athletic!* Aidan thought, feeling a little proud.

A few moments later, a small wet face poked up out of the water. It had large, pale yellow eyes that blinked continuously and a shiny black nose much like that of a bear cub. It looked at Aidan, emitted a gurgling growl, and began to emerge from the pool.

Ordinarily, Aidan would have been off and running, but the creature crawling out of the water was more peculiar than it was threatening. It had dark wiry hairs running back from its widow's-peaked scalp and similar fir covering its four sodden limbs. Long, fingerlike silver talons protruded in groups of three from each paw.

On the animal's back were rows and rows of sharp gray quills like a porcupine's or a hedgehog's, but the quills were webbed together by leathery folds of dark skin. The folds extended and retracted so that the rows of quills combed each other. It seemed to be cleaning—or drying—itself. After several such combings, the thing shook like a wet dog, spraying droplets of water everywhere— even onto Aidan's shoes.

Then, to Aidan's complete surprise, the creature curled up like a pill bug and began to roll. Aidan watched it cruise about twenty feet before it disappeared into a large round hole in the ground. *Another tunnel*, Aidan thought. Some distant part of him wondered if he could take one of those rolly-creatures home with him. They were cute, but Aidan figured such a creature would dig up the yard and give his father fits. Aidan smiled.

Shivering from the wetness and the cold, he turned and looked back up at the mountain behind him. It was dark and towering and gave the sense that it might shift and topple at any moment, crushing anything beneath it. It was dizzying, and Aidan turned away. He had made it over . . . through, actually, and that was enough.

Aidan unrolled the scroll to look again at the map. His original goal had been to get over the mountain to find out what the flag symbol stood for. He had hoped it might be a castle—maybe even the Castle of Alleble—but there weren't any man-made structures anywhere in sight.

The sky was red and purple like fiery paints threatening to spill upward over the dark sky canvas, but the distant mountains still hid the sun's full brilliance. To the left, the mountain range stretched out like a severe fence of stone. Straight ahead were miles of wasteland, uneven ground, pocked and rent with pitfalls and shadowy holes. And to the right, the dark mountain curled and jutted, creating a series of coves.

No flag, no castle . . . no plan.

Aidan secured his scroll with the leather lace and placed it safely away from the edge of the pond. He looked down at the dark water. It might be okay to drink. Or it might not. Aidan was too thirsty to care. He cupped his hands, drank several mouthfuls, and watched the sun climb above the distant peaks.

It was dawn. And in the new light, Aidan saw a wispy tendril of smoke rising from one of the coves to his right. Smoke meant fire, and fire meant civilization! A warm, crackling fire to dry off by sounded good to Aidan, so he set off in the direction of the smoke. Moving as swiftly as his sore, achy body would allow, he leaped over several holes like the one the creature rolled into before. Eventually, he had to slow down, for the terrain began to rise as he neared a high ridge.

The smoke came from directly behind the stony ridge, so once again, Aidan climbed. Compared to the long journey up the mountain the day before, it was an easy ascent.

Just then, a trumpet rang out from the other side of the ridge. It was not the proud blast of royalty, however. It sounded more like the dying scream of a large bird. Aidan remained very still, and he gripped the stone so hard his knuckles whitened. He had a terrible feeling that he was headed in the wrong direction, but he was just a few feet from where he might see what was on the other side of the ridge.

Moving an inch at a time, Aidan climbed closer until he could peek over the edge. Looking into the cavernous valley, what he saw stole away his breath and most of his hope. A long convoy of soldiers was entering the cove from the wastelands beyond. He could see knights in black armor riding horses and pulling people on foot chained at the neck, wrists, and ankles. All moved toward a pair of tall arched doors that were cut into the mountain. Foul black smoke escaped the thin fissure between the doors and rose like a shadow of a serpent into the sky.

A soldier in the lead of the convoy blew his trumpet once more. A second trumpet answered from some unseen opening in the rock near the doors. The caravan halted. Great belches of smoke escaped as the heavy doors swung outward.

The convoy resumed its march, and the first wave of knights began to pass within the mountain. But there was some trouble with the prisoners. They screamed and violently pulled against their captors. They clutched their own chains and dug in their heels to avoid entering the place in the mountain from which the black smoke rose. The soldiers in front spurred their horses, and the soldiers behind pressed into the prisoners, forcing them forward. They were dragged—some still struggling, some limp—into the smoky darkness.

When the last of the soldiers passed into the mountain, the great stone doors slowly closed. Aidan stared, transfixed, unable to look away and yet not wanting to see.

"You there, on the rock!" A soldier in black stood on a ledge just below Aidan. "Who are you? The Prince does not take kindly to trespassers!"

Aidan struggled to his feet. He looked left and right, adrenaline surging.

"Stay right there!" the knight yelled. He began to climb up after Aidan.

Aidan turned and leaped back down the way he had come.

"Don't move, you!" Aidan heard the soldier shouting as he ran. He also heard the distinctive metallic ring of a sword being drawn. Aidan panicked.

He bounded down the ridge, groaning with each awkward landing. He knew the knight in black must be right behind him, and he knew there really was nowhere to go.

A million hopeless options of escape flickered in his mind, but he knew the knight would get him first. Suddenly, Aidan heard a swooshing sound.

Aidan stopped running.

"There now, that's better! Stay where you are!"

Aidan turned and saw the knight leap down from a cleft of rock.

He wore a black masked helmet, so Aidan couldn't see his face. But Aidan feared the soldier would either kill him on the spot or drag him like the others into the dark place in the mountain.

The knight was only a few feet away when a shadow passed over them both. There was another *Swoosh! Swoosh!* and the knight looked up into the sky. He raised his shield as if to ward off a blow.

Just as Aidan looked into the sky and drew in a breath to scream, a burst of wind slammed him and the soldier to the ground. The wind brought with it an overwhelming warm and beastly smell, with a tinge of smoke or ash. *A dragon!* Aidan's imagination raced as he struggled between utter disbelief and paralyzing fear. Debris rotated in the violent winds. Aidan tried to cover his eyes, but the force of the turbulence was too powerful. He shrieked, turned on his stomach, and frantically clawed at the dirt trying to get away.

The creature's enormous dark wings eclipsed the sun as the beast hovered ominously above. A thunderous roar rang out and echoed violently off the mountains, and Aidan could just make out the soldier running madly away.

The beast roared again and looked directly at Aidan. Covering his face with his hands, Aidan curled into a ball. The dragon's talons closed around Aidan's waist like gigantic pliers. Aidan pried at them with all his might, but it was hopeless. Another deafening roar blasted from the creature's lungs, and being so near to the colossal beast, Aidan couldn't bear the sound. He lost consciousness as the dragon gently lifted him from the ground and took to the air.

When Aidan awoke, it was dark. He lay on his back, his arm curled around his old down pillow and the covers pulled snugly up to his chin.

As the blurring effects of sleep wore off, his memory returned in a rush. *It had me. I should be dead. The dra—dragon? Oh, man. What a crazy dream!*

A dream—that's all it had been. A door to another world, a unicorn, little creatures with glowing eyes, and a dragon!! Aidan sighed with relief. It was a good thing he had been dreaming. There would have been no escape from the dragon's viselike clutches. And even if he had broken free of the dragon, one of those dark knights would've no doubt dragged him off to that terrible place in the mountain.

Aidan shuddered, took a deep breath, and sank deeper into his bed. Relieved as he was, some distant part of Aidan was disappointed. The dream had been the adventure he'd always wanted.

And, come to think of it, I was pretty brave to climb that mountain—even if it was just a dream. Aidan smiled lazily.

Feeling very safe, he hugged his pillow tightly and closed his eyes. Aidan relaxed and was at peace in the darkness. . . . Then Aidan's smile faded. *Something isn't quite right.*

PECULIAR COMPANY

The bed was comfortable, plush, and wide, with layers of blankets, but there was no light coming from the side of his room where the window was supposed to be. There was a strange scent in the air too. Aidan thought he had smelled it before, but he could not remember when. And Aidan's favorite down pillow didn't feel soft and fluffy like it was supposed to.

Aidan's heart skipped a beat. Chills and gooseflesh raced all over his body, for Aidan suddenly didn't know what his arm was curled around.

Aidan let his fingers slide over this thing that lay under his arm and across his shoulder. It certainly wasn't fuzzy or furry. It felt leathery and ragged, like it was covered with shingles . . . *or maybe, maybe . . . they were scales? SCALES?!!*

"Ya-yaahhh!!!" The scream exploded from Aidan's lips like a great bubble popping. He sat up from the covers to stare wide-eyed into the darkness.

Aidan felt something heavy slithering off the bed.

A blue flash lit the room, and Aidan could see the creature sitting like a great big cat in the middle of the stone floor. *It had not been a dream after all!* Aidan squirmed frantically backward, bashing his head into the enormous solid-wood headboard.

"Do not fear," a musical female voice said. "You are safe here."

Aidan could only stare at the monstrous, unearthly creature that had slid from the bed and now seemed to be speaking to him.

The beast raised its head slowly. Blue, fiery slanted eyes squinted at Aidan and blinked.

Aidan blinked back and then blinked again. But each time he opened his eyes it was still there: *a real dragon!*

The creature squatted on its thickly muscled hind legs and smaller ropey forelegs. Broad wings were folded like huge leather coats behind its body, and its neck and tail were as long as and as thick as anacondas. It had gray flesh on its underside and was armored with silvery scales that here and there reflected the flickering blue light. The dragon's head was long like a horse's and tapered to a very narrow snout, dappled with patches of those silver scales on its enormous high cheekbones.

Its lengthy jaws opened, baring dozens of needlelike teeth—and it swung its head forward toward Aidan. Aidan cringed.

But instead of the piercing pain of sharp teeth, he felt a huge, slimy, sticky tongue slap wetly across his face. The creature's tongue almost knocked Aidan out of the bed.

"I told you . . . you are safe here," the voice said again. "The dragon's name is Gabby. She likes you."

Aidan wiped some goo off of his face and stared at the beast. It ducked its head shyly, bared its teeth again, and began emitting a deep, rumbling purr.

"Welcome to the Castle of Alleble," began the melodic voice again. "You are a guest of the King, so you have nothing to fear."

It occurred to Aidan that the voice was not coming from the dragon.

Aidan turned to the voice and nearly jumped out of his skin a second time. There at the foot of the enormous bed was a being—a girl. Aidan thought she was about his age, but he wasn't certain.

Her long gossamer dress of lavender was studded with brilliant multicolored jewels, and they sparkled, reflecting the flickering blue light of the candle in her left hand. But her skin, her skin was ghostly white, seemingly glowing in the shadowy room. Her eyes, like perfect blue gems, were ablaze and held Aidan still in spite of his fear.

"You are very fortunate to be here. Many who wander off the path become lost. We sent Gabby to go and find you. I'm sorry she gave you such a fright."

Aidan could not speak, but his teeth ground audibly. The spectral girl guessed Aidan's fear and spoke again. "You have never seen a being like me before. Do not fear. You could not be safer."

"Are you . . . are you a ghost?" Aidan asked.

"Ghost?" she replied, considering the word. "No, I am not a spirit, shade, or apparition. I am a living Glimpse. I am very much like you, as a matter of fact."

"But you're glowing, and I can see through you, uh—well, sort of," he said. As Aidan stared at her, he realized that she wasn't actually transparent. But when she moved, she shimmered like a bright reflection rippling in a lake at night.

"No, your eyes just aren't used to seeing Glimpse-kind." She seemed to float around the bed closer to Aidan. "I have flesh and bone—here, touch my arm."

Aidan's eyes bulged, and he backed again into the headboard. She reached for Aidan's arm, but he jerked away.

She had said he was safe, but Aidan was not yet convinced. Undaunted, she gently placed her hand on Aidan's shoulder.

"Trust your heart, for I am a friend," she assured him. Aidan had expected her hand to feel cold and dead, but instead, her touch brought warmth and a wonderful tingle. Aidan looked up at her and was enchanted once again by her eyes. His fear left.

She smiled and said, "My name is Gwenne."

"Uh, my ame is Naidan . . . er, I mean . . . my name is Aidan." He felt very awkward. Mouth dry, cheeks reddening, muscles taut. She was kind of spooky, but she was also the most beautiful being he had ever seen. Of course, there had been a few girls at school who had caused Aidan to do a double take in the halls, but nothing like Gwenne. She was beyond physically attractive.

Her movements were precise and athletic but graceful—like the act of walking was for her a dance. And every time she spoke it was like listening to a song, hypnotizing and dreamy.

"Well-met, Aidan," she said and made a brief curtsy. "I am very honored to be the first of my kind to welcome you."

"You are a Glimpse?" Aidan asked curiously. "When I read the Scrolls, I thought it was about people."

"The Scrolls you read *are* about people. You are in a region called Alleble, and Glimpses are the people of this land. This castle is the center of The Realm."

"How did I get here?"

"You were called here."

"I was?"

"Yes, silly, by the King. Gabby and I were allowed to get your attention from time to time, but it was the King of Alleble who called you here. Do you not remember a voice drawing you?"

"Yes, I remember . . ." Aidan's voice trailed off. Had she said the King of Alleble? How could that be possible?

"Wait, wait, wait," Aidan said. He leaned forward and stared. "You said the King called me?"

"Yes."

"What King do you mean?" If she answered King Paragal, Aidan was ready to bolt out of the chamber—dragon or no dragon!

"There is only one King of Alleble. It is King Eliam, of course."

THE TWELFTH KNIGHT

ow, I'm totally confused. But Paragal . . . he killed King Eliam, didn't he?"

She sighed. "Did you not read The Scrolls of Alleble?"

Aidan felt like he was being lectured by an impatient teacher. "Well, yeah, of course I read the Scrolls. But I thought King Eliam died . . ."

"He did, Aidan. But it was merely the body that was slain by The Betrayer. King Eliam is far more than flesh. He is everlasting."

"But what about—"

"In time," she interrupted. "The King bade me to bring you to the guards' quarters to be fed and strengthened."

With that, Gwenne whisked him into a long curving hallway. Aidan was mesmerized by the castle. The walls and floor seemed to be hewn out of solid gray marble and then polished to a reflective shine. There were intricately woven tapestries hung high on every wall. Some were of sprawling castles with massive walls and grand towers. Others showed valiant Glimpse knights charging into battle upon proud unicorns. Many of the tapestries had a particular detail in common: a pair of mountains with the sun rising between them. It seemed familiar to Aidan, but he didn't know why.

A series of trumpet blasts echoed throughout the castle. Aidan held his ears and looked up the hallway to see what was happening.

A tall Glimpse stood at the end of the hall near an arched pair of gray stone doors. The Glimpse was dressed in bright silver armor, and his skin also seemed to glow. He looked frightening and beautiful at the same time.

"Oh, dear," Gwenne mumbled. "Quickly, cover your eyes and turn this way!"

"What is it? What?" Aidan resisted, but Gwenne brought him to the ground and pressed his head down.

"One of the King's messengers has returned, and they are opening the King's chambers. You must not look."

"But why?" Aidan demanded.

Just as Gwenne covered Aidan's eyes with her hands, a thunderous rumble sounded. The King's enormous doors began to open. The entire hallway filled with searing light. The fierce brilliance streamed in through Gwenne's fingers.

Aidan fell facedown, burying his head in his hands. Gwenne bent down to his side as the King's chamber doors closed and the light withdrew.

"I warned you," she said sympathetically. "Are you all right?"

"My eyes!" he complained, rubbing both vigorously with his knuckles. He blinked tears and opened his eyes. The only image he could see, eyes opened or eyes closed, was the vague outline of Gwenne's fingers.

"The glory of the King . . . it is perilously pure," she said.

"You aren't kidding. It was like looking into the sun for a few hours!!"

"Well said," Gwenne replied laughing. "But do not let your heart be troubled, for your eyes have not been damaged. In fact, you may find that your sight becomes somewhat more keen. The King's light burns, but it heals as well."

Indeed, Aidan's vision began to be restored.

Gwenne led Aidan into a great hall that contained a vast table made of rich dark wood. At the far end of the room was a large arched window. Aidan was surprised to see sunlight streaming in, for it had been dark in the chamber where he awoke.

Gwenne seated Aidan near that window, and he turned to take in the view. He looked down into a vast network of parapets, arches, cottages, and courtyards. Each building was ornate with twisting trim and sloping gables. But beneath the beautiful decor, there was great strength.

Each dwelling, gatehouse, and tower was girt with dense stone and wrought iron. It seemed to Aidan that Alleble was a kingdom that desired to be at peace but was ever ready should the fight come.

There were many Glimpses traveling along the cobblestone streets and passages along, around, and between buildings. Some Glimpses wore armor and marched with serious purpose. Others were in tunics and more casual garments.

Glimpse children scurried about as well. Aidan spied one group of children playing a game of some sort with a leather ball. They kicked up a storm of straw as they each tried to get to the ball first. Finally, one young girl ran faster than the others and got to the ball with some distance between her and her peers.

With an oft-practiced motion, she kicked the ball straight up in the air, caught it with her hands, and then turned defiantly to the other children who had by that time closed in on her. They immediately shrieked with a mixture of delight and terror and turned to run. The girl flung the ball at one boy who tumbled to the ground laughing. He got up, picked up the ball, and passed it back to the girl. Then together, they chased the rest of the children, beaning them whenever possible.

Like soccer mixed with dodgeball, Aidan thought. The children disappeared around a corner with joyous screams echoing behind them. A flicker of movement distracted Aidan, and he looked into a gated courtyard.

There, many knights engaged in training exercises. Some battled hand to hand. Others dueled with lances. But the swordsmen commanded Aidan's attention. They thrust forward swiftly, parried, and counterattacked. Their swords glimmered in the sun and rang like bells with each strike. They attacked with power and ferocity as if they were really trying to kill each other, but their movements were expertly measured to avoid drawing blood. Aidan watched in awe and felt an uncanny desire to join them, to strap on some armor and wield a sword.

"They are impressive, are they not?" Gwenne said, joining Aidan at the window.

"Unreal. I'd hate to go against one of them," Aidan replied.

"They are the Elder Guard and the Knights of Alleble."

"The twelve greatest warriors in the kingdom?" Aidan asked.

"Yes," Gwenne replied. She smiled proudly at Aidan. "They serve and protect Alleble. Truly they are fierce in battle, but they save the sword as a last resort."

"What do you mean?"

"You will learn, Aidan. You will learn. Look there," she said, pointing across the inner wall. "Behold, the Seven Fountains of Alleble. Have you ever seen anything more beautiful?"

From their window, the main thoroughfare of Alleble was to the left. It ran from the castle all the way to the kingdom's outer walls. Evenly spaced and running up the center of the thoroughfare were seven tremendous fountains. Great plumes of water and mist shot high in the air, caught the sun's rays like millions of tiny prisms, and arched down into massive pools of stone. They were incredible, Aidan had to admit, but he couldn't honestly say it was the most beautiful thing he had ever seen since arriving in Alleble.

"On the last day of every month, all of the Glimpses of Alleble go to the Fountains to celebrate . . . and remember."

"Gwenne, why are only six of the fountains working?" Aidan asked, pointing to the fountain nearest their castle. It was empty and dry.

Gwenne bowed her head and looked away from the window. "Do you not know?"

"No, I just—" He snapped his mouth closed as it hit him like a thunderbolt. That fountain was *the fountain*—the fountain where the Elder Guard and their families were held captive by the treasonous knights who served Paragal the Sentinel.

But Aidan was confused. Paragal had promised to release them if King Eliam allowed himself to be sacrificed in their place.

Aidan turned to ask, but a very tall, armor-clad Glimpse entered the room.

This knight carried a gigantic, gleaming silver tray full of covered dishes and placed it gently before Aidan.

"Good day, m'lady," he said, greeting Gwenne and bowing low.

"Good day, Sir Knight," she courteously replied. "How goes the training?"

The Alleb Knight looked suspiciously at Aidan for a moment.

"You may speak freely, Sir Galorin. He is here by the King's own invitation."

"Prithee, forgive my mistrust, m'lad," he said, bowing to Aidan. "For these are such days as require careful speech."

"Uh . . . no problem," Aidan muttered, a little surprised that an adult would bow to him. Alleble seemed pretty cool, so far.

Aidan looked at the tray and then questioningly up at Gwenne. She nodded, so at once he began lifting the lids of each dish. The first platter contained a pile of the succulent purple fruit he had eaten on the mountain ledge. He eagerly grabbed one and took a bite that would put a shark to shame.

His mouth full of sweet goodness, Aidan continued exploring the platter with his free hand. Under the next lid was a roasted leg of something—Aidan didn't want to know what—but it was huge, bigger by itself than a whole Thanksgiving turkey. The giant leg-thing was garnished with purple flowers and literally surrounded by a bed of light blue flakes of various sizes.

Aidan thought about covering it back up, but Gwenne was watching him. Finicky eater that he was, he couldn't turn up his nose with Gwenne there. Using a small knife and a two-tined fork, Aidan carved a piece of meat off the gigantic drumstick and plopped it into his mouth. He chewed slowly at first, trying to determine the flavor. He found it salty and savory, very much to his liking and somewhat familiar.

"Mmmm . . . ," he said. "Tastes like chicken!"

In another dish, he found what appeared to be blue and white diamonds. When he touched the gleaming jewels, however, they were not rigid and hard like the stones they resembled. Instead, they were soft and pliable like taffy.

Aidan had no idea what they would taste like, but he was too hungry to care. He picked a blue one out of the bowl and had it just inches from his mouth when Gwenne grabbed his hand.

"A solid druble in your belly would make you most unhappy," she said. Then, she dropped the jewel into a glass of clear water and placed an unusual three-spouted lid on top. Instantly, the jewel began to fizz. Bubbles of every color of the rainbow began to shoot out from all sides of it, and the glass swirled with a tornado of color.

"Now," Gwenne announced. "Put your mouth on the long spout and your fingers in the two little ones."

Aidan reluctantly did as he was told and then looked up at Gwenne as if to say, "Now what?"

"Slowly, take one finger out of one of the spouts."

Aidan knew something was going to happen. He could see and hear the liquid fizzing away furiously in the glass. But when he took one finger out of a spout, his eyes went wide in total surprise. The glass became warm in his hand, and the heated beverage shot into his mouth. But unlike a normal drink, which you swish around in your mouth before swallowing, little droplets of this stuff bounced and ricocheted around until every last taste bud was in flavor paradise! Aidan liked it so much that he took his other finger out of the other spout to increase the flow.

"No, Aidan, not ye—" Gwenne cautioned . . . too late!

The sweet drink roared into Aidan with such pressure that he had to pull the spout out of his mouth to keep his cheeks from exploding.

The liquid had nothing holding it back, so it shot like a geyser out the window behind Aidan.

Someone on the street below yelled, and Aidan could only imagine what must have occurred.

The tall Glimpse, the one Gwenne had called Galorin, howled with laughter. Gwenne looked as if she was struggling mightily to hold back. All Aidan could do was turn fifteen shades of red and watch the glass empty.

As the last of the drink shot out of the spouted glass, Aidan laughed nervously and shrugged. "Sorry," he muttered.

Gwenne nodded and smiled at Aidan, and then glared at Galorin, who quickly contained himself. Aidan felt as foolish as he'd ever felt, but he was still extremely hungry. Shrugging again, he turned back to his meal.

While Aidan noisily gobbled up the unusual meal, Sir Galorin updated Gwenne on matters concerning the Kingdom.

"I am afraid we may be preparing too late, m'lady. The Knights of Paragory are massing even as we speak. Our dragons have counted at least four different Paragor messengers leaving the Gate of Despair. The Prince, it would seem, has a great interest in the loyalties of Mithegard."

"And why should he not?" asked Gwenne bitterly. "There are only tens of thousands of undecided Glimpses there for his misguiding."

"Agreed," said Galorin, gritting his teeth.

"When will the twelve be ready for the journey to Mithegard?" asked Gwenne.

"Eleven are ready now, but we are waiting for the King to choose the Twelfth Knight."

At that, Gwenne turned slightly to Aidan, who was sloppily gobbling down a dessert that looked more or less like a hot dog made of chocolate and whipped cream.

"Sir Galorin, the King *has* chosen the Twelfth Knight," Gwenne began, gesturing toward Aidan. "It is the lad you see here before us."

Aidan stared at Gwenne, and his dessert slipped from his fingers and hit the table with a splat.

The lad whose face was covered with cream would be the Twelfth Knight.

ARMED AND
TERRIFIED

Gwenne led Aidan down a long spiral flight of stairs in one of the castle's main towers. "If we are to make an Alleb Knight out of you," she said, "we must have you dressed for the occasion."

"How am I supposed to be a knight?" he asked. His voice bounced with each footfall. "I don't even know what I'm doing here!"

"I already told you. You were called to Alleble by the King."

"But, Gwenne!" Aidan complained. "This can't be right! Maybe, maybe the King called me by mistake."

Gwenne stopped abruptly. "King Eliam does not make mistakes," she said.

Aidan sat down hard on the stairs. He buried his head in his hands. "I'm not a Glimpse. I don't really belong here, do I?"

Gwenne sat next to Aidan and put a pale hand on his shoulder. "Be of good courage, Aidan. You belong here just as I belong. The

Scrolls you received are but a small part of the history of our Kingdom. It is also *your* history now."

Aidan looked up, eyes red around the lids, blinking.

"But how did the history of Alleble end up in Colorado or even the United States, for that matter?" Aidan asked. "It's even in the bookstores!"

"The history of Alleble is indeed well known to many where you come from, though not enough. You see, long ago in an age before time, our worlds were one and the same. But not long after, there was a great disturbance, *The Schism*, we call it, and our realms divided. The history of Alleble survived because over the centuries it was passed down through generations. Many people believed and became a part of Alleble once again. New scrolls were written and sent by the King to the faithful. But as time passed in your realm, Aidan, men grew wise in their own minds. Science, reason, and . . . what do you call it? . . . Psychology? These things beguiled the hearts of generations of people. Fewer and fewer chose to believe. The Betrayer is yet powerful and does all that he can to blind and deceive, so that no one will believe. Perhaps that is why so many have *The Story* of Alleble but deem it as nothing more than . . . a fairy tale."

Fairy tale hung in the air ominously. Aidan stared at the steps. He remembered his father using those exact words to describe the scrolls.

"I am truly thankful to the King," Gwenne continued, "that you accepted and trusted the promises within The Scrolls of Alleble. It was a step of faith to enter The Door Within, believing a story that most in your world would deem foolishness."

"When I believed," Aidan said, "I didn't know that . . . that I'd end up so involved."

"Aidan, that is how it goes with us all. King Eliam often chooses the brokenhearted, the lonely, and the cast aside. He will make something great of you. I know he will."

Gwenne said that with such unshakeable confidence that Aidan felt his burden lifted. "I still have questions," he said.

"Questions are permissible—encouraged, actually—for in time, all questions will have answers. But come, let us go to the armory, for you need battle gear."

"Battle gear?" Aidan exclaimed. "What are we going to do, start a war?"

"A war has already begun, Aidan, and the King has called you to be an important part of a battle that must be won."

"What can I do?" Aidan pleaded. "I can't fight. I even had a middle schooler beat me up once!"

"When Captain Valithor is finished with you, I should think you would have little trouble with a whole legion of middle schoolers!" She laughed. "Besides, the battle we shall fight will be better fought with truth and not swords."

"I don't even know who we're fighting—or what for!" Aidan complained, beginning to feel that he was in this up to his ears, whether he liked it or not. Gwenne stood and motioned for Aidan to do likewise.

Her golden brow furrowed. She seemed hesitant to tell Aidan something or was searching for the right words. "You read the Scroll of *The Great Betrayal*?"

Aidan nodded. "But my Scroll ended after King Eliam died."

"There is much to tell from that point, but my heart is too weak to speak of what happened next. And I am not the one who can best recount the events that followed. But what you should know is that Paragal was exiled, he and all who followed him, banished to the westernmost regions of The Realm. And, as the King declared, Paragal's name was changed to Paragor, which means 'pure light, stained forever dark.'

"The land where Paragor dwells now is a ruinous place. He pretends it is his own kingdom and calls it Paragory. He even built his own jagged black stronghold in mockery of the castle in which we now stand. He has raised an immense army that grows malignantly in the dungeons and catacombs beneath his dark lair. It is a realm of blood, Aidan, and Paragor's strength grows daily. Bloody conquest after bloody conquest. But in spite of all this, Paragor festers upon his black throne. Ever he yearns to be King, but even his own followers will not call him by that title. A power greater than his will not permit it. So, instead, they call him Prince."

Aidan swallowed. He remembered the poor souls being dragged through the dark gates. And he had been so close to joining them.

Gwenne began descending the stairs again. Aidan followed.

"So are we supposed to attack Paragor?"

"Not exactly, though our forces clash regularly. Our battle is of a different sort. You see, from the time of his exile, the Prince and his Paragor Knights have sought to gain the allegiance of all the other kingdoms of this world. Many Glimpses have accepted his cunning offers of wealth and power, turning away from the only true King. There is even now a kingdom the Prince eyes to be a new jewel in his crown of slavery. It is a land called Mithegard. Once your training is complete, we will travel to Mithegard to reach their Glimpses for the King."

"I still don't see what good I'll do." Aidan sighed audibly.

"Aidan, I have already told you, the King does not make mistakes. It may be that there is value within you that he can see—even when you cannot. So it is with all whom he has called."

Aidan smiled. The idea of someone believing in him made him feel a few inches taller, though still there were many doubts.

"Back home, I have this friend, Robby. Now, he's the kinda guy you want for this kind of thing. He lives for adventure. I . . . I don't think he's afraid of anything."

Gwenne frowned at Aidan. "I do not doubt that your friend is considered brave in your world, Aidan. But there are things here in Alleble that might give him a start."

Aidan smirked. He knew Robby better. He imagined what Robby might say. "Me afraid? Ri-ight!"

"Besides," Gwenne continued, "it is easy to be fearless when one has not yet learned what he has to lose."

As they traveled through the castle, from stairway to corridor, from corridor to keep, Aidan pondered the meaning of all that Gwenne had told him. It was mysterious and frightening. What had Gwenne meant by learning what he had to lose? And being in a war? What good would a short, cowardly teenager be in the midst of a huge war?

But there was also a sense of excitement. Gwenne had said that he was to become the Twelfth Knight. A real knight, with a real sword, on a very real adventure. His thoughts were interrupted as they passed through the massive stone fortress Gwenne had called the main keep and entered a great domed hall: They were in the Armory of Alleble.

The room was alive with light, for beams from the glass dome above found many polished objects on which to sparkle. Racks and crates of helmets, breastplates, and shields gleamed all around. Some of the shields were emblazoned with vivid designs. Aidan remembered from social studies class that medieval knights often decorated their shields with objects and colors symbolizing their kingdom or family. A lion on a shield might indicate the courage of the knight. Or a galloping horse might mean speed. Aidan spied shields illustrated with dragons, trees, unicorns—one even had a butterfly on it. What a butterfly symbolized, Aidan could not guess. He just hoped that wasn't the shield they gave to rookie knights! He imagined the laughter that might be directed at a knight charging into battle bearing upon his shield the fierce butterfly!

There appeared to be enough pieces of armor stockpiled in the huge room to equip several armies. Of course, there were weapons as well. Swords, daggers, axes, maces, hammers, bows, and some other spear-axe-looking things Gwenne called halberds. Many weapons stood in barrels or lay across vast tables and counters in the room. Others required more prominence.

On one wall, in a large glass case inlaid with lush red velvet, hung seven mighty broadswords. Aidan's eyes widened with delight, bouncing from one blade to another. Each sword fanned the passion in Aidan's heart.

Then, it was as if the lights in the room dimmed and a spotlight illuminated one sword in particular. Aidan stared, drinking in the weapon's every detail. Its silver blade was over three feet long, double-edged, and honed to razor-sharpness. It glinted iridescent blue when Aidan turned his head just slightly.

Cords, dark and ribbed, wound like a pair of black snakes down the two-fisted grip and disappeared into the silver pommel at the bottom. At the top of the grip was a crossguard of the same silver as the pommel. On the middle of this crossguard was an intricate engraving of a rising sun blazing out from behind the silhouette of two mountains—the very same design Aidan had seen on the tapestries in the castle halls. But engraved with such skill in silver, it took on special brilliance. It was a work of art within a work of art, and Aidan longed for such a mighty weapon of his own.

"Indeed, that lad 'as an eye for a blade!" proclaimed a stout Glimpse who appeared from an anteroom at the front of the armory. He waddled out toward Aidan, lifted an arm in a sweeping gesture, and bowed low. "Kindle, master of all things sharp or dangerous, at your service," he announced.

Aidan bowed in return. "Uh, Aidan. Aidan Thomas," he replied. Aidan didn't think of himself as a master of anything, so he left it at his name.

Kindle, who seemed to have one eyebrow permanently arched higher than the other, smiled wryly and scratched his stubbly beard. He was just a little taller than Aidan but built like an anvil. And though he was certainly quite heavy, it was his broad cannonball shoulders and massive bare arms that gave him the squared appearance. The chain-mail shirt he wore draped over his chest and ample stomach made him look as if he had no legs at all.

"That is an incredible sword!" Aidan exclaimed, nearly drooling. Gwenne joined them in front of the broadsword display.

"That blade, m'lad, is a broadsword fashioned by none other than Naysmithe himself!" said Kindle.

"Nay who?" asked Aidan, perplexed.

Gwenne smiled as if remembering a glad time from long ago.

Kindle cocked an eyebrow and explained. "Naysmithe is the chief metalworker of Alleble. If it can be fashioned from iron, silver, or gold, then Naysmithe can make it. Truly, I say to you, it was Naysmithe who forged *Charrend,* the sword of our King. It is known as the blade that cleaves darkness."

"Do all swords have names?" asked Aidan.

"Nay, lad, not all swords—only those made by gifted craftsmen and proven in battle. The blade you've set your eyes upon is called *Fury*—so named by a knight who wielded it against Paragory in the Cold River Battles long ago. Naysmithe finished repairing the blade only recently."

"Come, Aidan," interrupted Gwenne. "We need to get your armor and dagger."

"Dagger?" Aidan blurted out, looking sadly back to the sword Fury. "But, can't I use . . . that one?"

Gwenne smiled apologetically and looked to Kindle.

"Sorry, lad," he began. "That blade does already 'ave an owner, and methinks it will be in use shortly. Besides, a blade that size would no doubt weigh you down exceedingly. When you're ready, you'll get a weapon that'll be just right for you. For now, a dagger. Perhaps, a short sword."

Aidan's shoulders drooped. He really wanted Fury. But, of course, it belonged to someone else. Still . . . the sword seemed to call to him, every feature of the blade imprinted in his heart. No dagger would replace it, and a short sword sounded small like Aidan felt among the Knights of Alleble.

The armory keeper looked thoughtful for a moment, rubbing his chin as if considering some highly questionable course of action. Then, he shook his head, deciding "No" was the answer to the unspoken dilemma. With a brief embarrassed smile, he scuttled off behind a tall counter. He emerged a moment later carrying a bundle wrapped in flannel cloth.

"Your armor, lad. Wear it well, and may it turn the arrows of any Paragor rat who dares to fire upon a servant of the King!"

Feeling a little queasy with the thought of creatures firing arrows in his direction, Aidan walked into the changing room to put on his armor.

Kindle waited a long time before he decided he'd best enter Aidan's changing room. Kindle took one look at Aidan and chuckled deeply. Aidan was struggling mightily, attempting to dress himself in chain mail and iron plates.

"That piece of iron you've got on yer head," he said, "it's made to fit yer elbow, Aidan!"

Aidan blushed and swiftly took the piece (called a *couter*, he learned) off his head. "Don't feel low, m'lad," Kindle said with a wink. "Most of this requires another set of 'ands to put on—usually the duty of a squire. So today, allow Kindle to be your humble squire."

With yet another chuckle, the armory keeper went at once to work arming the embarrassed knight-to-be. It was not a complete suit of armor, Aidan was told, just a training suit for light fencing. Off came Aidan's favorite pair of Nikes and his well-worn blue jeans to be replaced with a pair of dark brown pants. They were thick and durable but were somewhat elastic and clung to Aidan's skin. Next, Aidan tugged on a pair of knee-high leather boots and laced them up. Off went Aidan's half-shredded T-shirt. Kindle then draped a thick overshirt called an *arming doublet*. This was topped off with a long-sleeved shirt of chain mail. The tiny linked iron rings could perhaps turn an arrow or cause a light sword blow to do a little less damage—not a very comforting thought to Aidan! Then, on top of the doublet, the keeper slung and buckled a gleaming breastplate and shoulder harness that reminded Aidan of Robby's football pads—only these were metal!

On each forearm Aidan wore a cylindrical piece of armor called a *vambrace,* and of course, on his elbows, he wore the *couters.* On his hands, Aidan wore protective metal gloves called *gauntlets.* Finishing his outfit was a thick leather belt with a *buckler* for a sword—or at least a dagger!

Aidan looked at himself in a long mirror. He had no helmet and no shield, but still he couldn't get over how knightly he appeared. Sure, the weight of it all made him feel like he could barely move, but at least he looked good.

Gwenne also approved of Aidan in his new armor. She beamed proudly as he slowly spun around before her. "You shall make a fine Knight of Alleble," she said, and Aidan glowed. He was once again dazzled by her sparkling blue eyes and pure white skin.

"Aidan," Gwenne spoke. Aidan snapped out of the trance. "Let us take our leave of Kindle's fine armory, for Captain Valithor is waiting."

"Captain Valithor?" Kindle exclaimed. His eyes were wide, and he brushed a few dark, oily locks of hair out of his eyes. "Oh, lad, I do not envy you your next few months."

"Days," corrected Gwenne. "Captain Valithor has agreed to accelerate his training regimen so that we might leave for Mithegard within the week."

"A week? Sorry for your sake, lad," Kindle replied. He shook his head and stared at Gwenne with a look that said, "Become a knight in a week under Valithor? It'll likely kill this one!"

Aidan swallowed. Being a knight didn't sound so cool anymore.

Aidan and Gwenne walked in silence to the enormous training yard adjacent the castle's main keep. Aidan's stomach turned over and over as they walked. Aidan felt he was in over his head. And though the sky was cloudless and the sun rained golden rays down on Alleble, Aidan felt he was shrouded by an enormous shadow. A shadow cast by Captain Valithor.

Basic Training

Gwenne and Aidan navigated a labyrinth of high wooden fences called *palisades*. Gwenne had explained that these rows of tall, extremely pointed stakes were temporary fortifications until stonework could be constructed.

Aidan made a mental note never to try to climb the palisades. *Ouch!* he thought.

Once inside the vast training compound, Gwenne introduced Aidan to an oak of a knight named Kaliam, who was leaning on the pommel of a long broadsword as he avidly watched the combat in the courtyard. His warrior's armor matched that of the other knights Aidan had seen, but Kaliam's massive shoulders and rippling arms had no armor except for a pair of black leather *vambraces* that struggled to contain his forearms.

"So, you are the Twelfth Knight we have heard so much about?"

said the Glimpse Kaliam. "A little short and dull for a Knight of Alleble, eh, Gwenne?"

"He is scarcely less tall than I," argued Gwenne, "and I seem to recall besting you in our most recent duel—O tall one of tall pride!"

Kaliam let out a great, deep bark of laughter. His long ebony hair bounced as he roared, "Well-met, m'lady! A lesson I shall not soon forget. Forgive my rudeness."

"I will forgive you, certainly, Sir Knight . . . and I will gladly reteach the lesson since you seem in need of tutoring."

"Nay! That will not be necessary, swordmaiden. My pride has been duly reminded of its proper place."

Aidan gawked at Gwenne. It wasn't that he thought of boys as more skilled than girls. After all, a lot of the girls in his school could trounce him in most any sport they played. But to defeat a towering galoot like Kaliam? Aidan gawked some more.

As she left, swordless and shrouded beautifully in the gossamer lavender dress, Gwenne looked vulnerable and soft. Apparently, she was not.

Kaliam turned to Aidan. "Come, lad, some of our party are there by the fire. Let us join them."

Aidan did as he was told and sheepishly followed Kaliam over to the fire. There was a thick meaty carcass roasting over the flames. A very large Glimpse stood beside it. His back was turned to Aidan, and he gestured vigorously in conversation. But it was not possible to see with whom he was speaking, for he was very wide, draped in rough black fur that made him look part bear. And by his side was an immense hammer.

Kaliam cleared his throat. "Forgive my intrusion, Sir Mallik. A word?"

"Prithee, mention it not." The beastly Glimpse turned to Kaliam.

Like a frightened pup hiding at his master's heel, Aidan cringed behind Kaliam.

Mallik was red-bearded. His chiseled face was besieged by a corona of wild coppery hair. His eyes, black as coal, smoldered beneath thick, wiry brows. And, Aidan noticed, they glinted blue at certain angles like Gwenne's eyes.

Mallik wore a permanent sneer, and his long, braided mustache bounced as he spoke.

"It is a pointless argument—the same one I have endured with Nock and Bolt here for some time now."

Aidan could now see two other Glimpses seated on a great log beyond Mallik. They were smaller than most of the other Glimpses, though still greater in size than Aidan. Each had long, straight sandy brown hair drawn back tightly. Each wore a circlet of silver like a thin crown above his uncannily arched brows and restless blue eyes. And though they appeared youthful, their stature was proud and manly. Seated side by side, turned just slightly, the two Glimpses looked like mirror images. They were, in fact, twins.

"These two, these impetuous upstarts," Mallik went on. "Though they gang up on me with their wagging tongues, they are simply in the wrong if they claim that a bow—nay, two bows, even—are better in a scrap than my hammer."

"With our bows," the twins protested in stereo, "you need not scrap in the first place. The enemy falls dead ere you draw close enough to be struck."

"Mallik, Nock, Bolt . . . a wise Glimpse would not come between two such formidable arguments," said Kaliam. He raised one hand like a referee. "But weapons may play but a token role on this errand. Diplomacy, my good Glimpses."

"Diplomacy!" Mallik snorted and stroked the haft of his hammer.

"Those Paragor rats know nothing of diplomacy. Flowering words hiding daggers—that is their craft. Pity him who falls beneath *my* diplomacy!"

"Have pity on me, Mallik," said Kaliam. He smiled and bowed. "And have pity on our Twelfth Knight, for he has patiently endured such bravado, first from me and now from you, hammer-meister!"

"Twelfth Knight?" Mallik objected. "He is but a lad!"

Aidan cringed. He felt once again that there must be some mistake. Perhaps now everyone would realize this and send him home.

"My first thoughts were such," said Kaliam. "But the King has called him here for such a time as this. Dare any of us question the King's judgment?"

No one spoke. The fire crackled. A knot of burning pine popped.

"And think on this: Were any of us anything before the King called us?"

The twins nodded to each other. "Well spoken!" they said, and in unison they stood and bowed before Aidan.

"I am Nock," said one.

"I am Bolt," said the other.

"We are from the deep forest city of Yewland," they said together. "Welcome to Alleble—and to our company."

Not to be outdone, Mallik turned to Aidan and inclined just slightly. It was the best bow he could manage, for Mallik did not bend.

"Mallik I am called," he said. His mustache twitched. "I come from Ludgeon, the chief city of the Blue Mountain Provinces far north of here. So, you too were called by the King of Alleble? I will gladly serve with you, Sir . . ."

"I'm not really Sir anything, but my name is Aidan."

"Aidan, ah?" Mallik stroked his mustache. "I like it. It is a strong name. A sturdy name. My people are sturdy folk—workers of wood, stone, and iron. This hammer was made by my grandsire and thundered in the hand of my father before me."

Mallik swept up the heavy weapon and held it on his shoulder like a major-league slugger posing for a baseball card. The haft of the hammer, thick like a bedpost, was carved from black wood and etched in silver with images of battle. Long, inlaid bars of iron ran the length of the haft and were welded into the weapon's massive head. It reminded Aidan of the hammer he'd seen his mom use to pulverize raw meat—only the head on Mallik's weapon seemed the size of a Volkswagen.

"Few in Alleble can lift it—much less wield it. When my hammer falls, mountains tremble and foes wilt. What skill do you bring to our company of twelve?"

Aidan thought for a moment. He was quite good at most video games, and his father had said he had a wicked backhand in tennis. But remarkable as those things were, they seemed useless in this context. "Uh, I don't have a special skill," he finally answered.

Mallik snorted. Nock and Bolt stared at Aidan and betrayed no emotion at all.

"Come, Aidan," Kaliam said. "Let us leave Mallik and the twins to debate hammer and bow. We have much to discuss ourselves."

Kaliam and Aidan bowed. Nock and Bolt bowed in return. Mallik nodded.

Kaliam led Aidan to a stone bench away from the fire.

"Please forgive Mallik," he said amiably. "He is brash at times. And we do not get many of your kind here . . . though more have been invited of late."

"That's okay," Aidan said. "Compared to you guys, I am pretty much a mouse."

Kaliam laughed. "Compared to Mallik, *everyone* is a mouse. But even a mouse may frighten a mighty elephant!"

Aidan grinned.

Kaliam winked. Aidan stared at the warrior's eyes. At first, Aidan thought that Kaliam's eyes were blue, but Aidan saw now that it was not so. His eyes were definitely green. But when Kaliam turned his head just so, his eyes glinted blue. It reminded Aidan of how a cat's eyes seem to glow at night when struck with a flashlight beam. Gwenne, Mallik, Kaliam . . . Aidan wondered if all Glimpses' eyes were like that.

"How much do you know of our mission?" Kaliam asked.

"A little. Though I don't think I understand much," Aidan admitted.

"It is a worthy task," Kaliam said. "One from which we may not all return."

"Now see, that's what I don't get," Aidan complained. "I see hundreds of knights around here. Why take only twelve?"

"There are untold thousands counted among King Eliam's army, here in Alleble and in other lands who are allied to us. But for this quest, our strength comes not from number, but from the message we bring," said Kaliam. He proudly slammed a *vambrace* against his chest. "The Glimpses of Mithegard will not trust in us because of the size of our army or the ferocity of our swords. Only Paragory seeks allegiance in that way."

Aidan shrugged and pulled at the chain mail at his neck. It was heavy and dug into his skin. "I still don't see how I fit into this mission."

"Aidan, I cannot say what part you will play in all of this, but I deem that you are here to learn—to learn so that you may face an even greater battle that awaits you when you return to your realm."

Aidan rolled his eyes and shook his head. *More riddles. Can't anyone around here give me a straight answer?*

"Well, what about this Captain Valithor? What's he like?"

"Captain Valithor," Kaliam began. "Well, he is—"

"ON YOUR FEET!! You beslobbering, beef-witted barnacles!!"

A Glimpse taller than Kaliam and broader than Mallik stormed into the compound. Like ants scattering from a disturbed anthill, scores of Glimpse knights escaped the courtyard by every conceivable exit. The remaining eight Glimpses, including Mallik and the twins—leapt to their feet, formed into rows of painfully straight lines, and stood in rigid, silent attention. Kaliam yanked Aidan up beside him and whispered, "That . . . is Captain Valithor."

The goliath Glimpse wrenched his head abruptly in their direction and then thundered toward them. His great chest heaved, breaths escaping in grunts. He stood directly in front of Kaliam.

"Kaliam!" he bellowed. "Thou errant, earth-vexing mumbler! Tell me that you had not the nerve to speak before being summoned!" The Captain, who towered at least a foot greater than Kaliam, stared directly down into Kaliam's eyes. Kaliam swallowed hard twice before answering his commander.

"S-s-sir," mumbled Kaliam. "I wish that I could tell you it was not me you heard, but . . . it was."

The Captain's bushy white mustache curled on one side in a half smile. "Puny, lily-livered weasle that you are—at least you had the courage to speak the truth!"

He turned to face the other wide-eyed Glimpses. "Let that be a lesson to the lot of you! No matter the consequences, the truth is always first!"

Captain Valithor visited his wrath on each Glimpse in turn. None withstood his penetrating glare or his resonating voice. Even Mallik dropped his gaze when faced by his commander.

In awe and fear, Aidan stared at the Captain. He was clad in brushed-silver armor and had a vast shield slung on his back. Snow-white hair fell in waves from his head, mustache, beard—even his eyebrows! His forehead was lined with deep furrows, and between his bristling brows and piercing eyes, his nose jutted out like the beak of a hawk. He stood erect when still and leaned forward, stalking, when he advanced. He carried no weapon, but had an ornate sheath at his side. It waited for a blade to match the magnitude of its owner.

Intimidated as he was by the Captain, Aidan thought that he caught a hint of something vaguely familiar about him.

He looked like a Viking from the pictures in Aidan's social-studies textbook, but it wasn't that. There was something in his intense, pale blue eyes that reminded Aidan of someone, but the identity shied away. The Captain's eyes glinted brighter blue when he turned, just like the others. Maybe that was it. Aidan wasn't sure. Before he had time to figure it out, the Captain turned toward him.

"And thou," the Captain bent low, close to Aidan's face, "thou weedy wagtail! It is the King's request that I make a knight of you in very short order! And so help me, I will . . . even if it KILLS US BOTH!"

Aidan felt dizzy, and he thought he must look very much like a pale Glimpse now that all of the blood had drained from his face. Fortunately, Captain Valithor turned away from him and went back to roaring at each of the other eight knights. He seemed particularly angry when he came to the Glimpse at the end of the second row.

"Tell me, Acsriot!" Valithor roared. "How is it that your armor gleams like the sun and yet your blade is stained?!"

Acsriot had no answer. He stood very still but cringed as if expecting a blow.

"Thou weepy sack of wraith-clottle! Ten thousand times I have told you: Keep your blade sharp—and clean! The sword is a reflection of the one who carries it, and no Knight of Alleble will keep a weapon so besmirched."

Captain Valithor glared at Acsriot, and Acsriot stared back. There seemed some unspoken communication between the two, a silent struggle of wills, but inevitably, Acsriot could not endure. He looked away.

"Come, Acsriot!" said the Captain in a triumphant tone. "Let us go to the armory and fetch some scrubbing tools. And after you clean up your blade . . . I'm sure Kindle will be happy to supply you with a few hundred more to scour."

After he was sure that the Captain had left the courtyard, Aidan asked, "Is he always like that?"

"Nay, lad. We are fortunate he was in a good mood today!" said Kaliam, shaking his head. "Let not his manner fool you, Aidan, for Captain Valithor appears harsh, but he has the biggest heart in the kingdom—except for the King, of course. Captain Valithor is the Sentinel of this realm and one of the most valiant warriors Alleble has ever known. The King must deem this a mission of critical importance to allow his personal guard to go."

Aidan pondered Kaliam's words. *Just what kind of mission is this? And how could I, a teenager, be of any use among these great champions? Surely I'll mess things up or, worse yet, be killed, leaving my parents to never know what has become of me.*

A great voice shook Aidan from his thoughts.

"Rapscallions! Thou ragtag lot of widge-lumps! What madness has relieved all of you of your minds? You should be training, yet you stand on the very terrain on which I left you?!"

Captain Valithor raged into the compound and stood in front of Aidan, Kaliam, and the seven Glimpse knights who remained.

"The knight who moves?" Valithor called out to them.

"His valor he proves!" the Glimpses thundered back.

"And the knight who stands still?"

"Is a target to kill!"

Valithor made his knights repeat the precept a dozen times and then paired them off to train. He sent Kaliam to help Acsriot clean fouled weapons in the armory. Kaliam walked away shaking his head, downcast at losing the opportunity to train, but the Captain called after him, "Kaliam! Never alone!"

Kaliam turned and smiled grimly. "Never alone!"

It was the first time Aidan had heard one of the knights say that phrase. It rang with importance, but Aidan didn't have time to ask about it.

Captain Valithor stood very still, silently watching Kaliam leave the courtyard. He was so large and grand . . . he looked like a monument of an ancient hero somehow brought to life. Aidan knew nothing of Captain Valithor's history or his deeds at arms, but it was clear that the Knights of Alleble feared him, revered him, and loved him. Though activity teemed around him—knights grunting, swords clanging, and Mallik's hammer swooshing through the air—Aidan could not take his eyes off the rugged sentinel. Aidan felt strangely heartened. If anyone could teach him to be a knight, surely Captain Valithor could.

The Captain turned and stormed over to Aidan. "Now, wayward

minnow, it is time for you to learn knightcraft. Catch!" In a flash of motion, Captain Valithor drew something from his belt and flung it at Aidan.

Aidan's hand shot out, and to his surprise, he had caught the missile thrown his way. It was a wooden dagger, and Aidan had caught it by the handle.

The Captain cocked an eyebrow. His mustache quivered, and he burst into laughter.

"That was good, Aidan. Very good. You have much to learn, but your reflexes are sudden and strong. Now, let us see how you handle that dagger."

Aidan looked down at the wooden dagger and glowered.

Captain Valithor guessed Aidan's thoughts. "You want steel, eh, Aidan?" He laughed. "Fear not, for you shall have it—and soon. But for now, it would not do to have you hack off one of your own arms. So wood it is. Bring the weapon and follow me."

Aidan frowned at the small wooden thing in his hands. He felt like throwing it into the fire. The Captain himself had said that the sword is a reflection of its owner. Aidan knew what a little wooden toy made him look like. True, next to the Knights of Alleble, he was just a little guy. But at the same time, he despised being treated like a kid.

This indignant spark kindled into a roaring blaze of desire—the desire to prove to Captain Valithor, to prove to Gwenne, to prove to everyone that he could be a knight. *Whatever it takes to be a knight and earn a real sword, I will do it.*

"Tarry not, thou tardy-gaited flea!" Captain Valithor's broad strides had already taken him far ahead, so Aidan jogged to catch up.

The Captain led Aidan to one corner of the courtyard, where there stood an odd-looking contraption. "This," said the Captain, "is the Training Urchin."

The urchin was a segmented post about man-high. Each section could rotate independently of the others and had several thick rods sticking out from it like arms. A different weapon or shield hung at the end of each rod. The Captain stood behind the urchin and grasped the two handlebar grips of the middle segment.

Captain Valithor nodded. "Now then, imagine this post is your enemy. Take your sword—I mean dagger—and strike your opponent."

Frustrated like never before, Aidan gathered all his strength and swung his wooden dagger wildly at the urchin. Captain Valithor steered the urchin so that the wooden sword from one rod knocked away Aidan's attack while simultaneously slamming Aidan to the ground with the post's wooden shield.

"That's the spirit!" choked the Captain, laughing merrily.

Aidan, reddening by the second, slowly stood up and brushed the dirt from his clothes and armor. It was going to be a long, long week.

SON OF FURY

Did you see that?" asked Matthias, one of the oldest Knights of the Elder Guard. He leaned on a post and stared at two knights sparring in the center combat ring of the training compound.

"Aye, I saw it," answered Tal, another member of the Elder Guard. He shook his head and smacked Matthias on the back. "I saw it, but I don't believe it."

"A true-as-life *moulinet*? He's been at this three days, and he threw a moulinet. It took me three *years* to learn that."

"Three days," echoed Tal. He whistled. "What kind of swordsman learns a combination like that in three days?"

Tal's question fell unanswered but, with the rest of the crowd, he watched in rapt silence as the two knights in the ring dueled. Kaliam was one of the combatants. And he wielded a broadsword so naturally it seemed an extension of his arms. Again and again he slashed forward, attempting to throw his smaller foe off balance.

But his opponent, the Twelfth Knight, dodged each attack and deftly countered with a creative battery of blows that drew gasps from those gathered there.

Captain Valithor coached from behind a short fence on the other side of the ring. "Don't just stand there, you vexing slow-coach lump!" he yelled at Aidan. "Do as I showed you. Guard, now quick snap! Get that basket in tighter."

Abruptly, Aidan held up his small round shield. "Stop!" he said. "My back is sore, my legs feel like rubber, and every time you hit me, my whole arm aches. Kaliam, you've worn me out. Man, it's a good thing you weren't going at full speed, or you'd have killed me."

Kaliam glanced sideways at Captain Valithor. "Rrright . . . well, of course, Aidan. I uh . . . just wanted to be sporting, you know." Kaliam bowed and walked over to Captain Valithor. They whispered briefly through the palisade as Aidan removed his breastplate and began wriggling free from his shirt of mail. Free of the armor's weight, he sighed, leaned back against a post, and smiled.

"You do not assume you are finished for today, do you?" asked Captain Valithor, tromping around the palisade toward Aidan. "Thou hasty-witted pigeon-egg, it is just time now for your wrestling lesson!"

Aidan's shoulders sagged. He exhaled audibly and trudged away with Captain Valithor.

The next three days toiled by just as the first three had. Aidan was up every morning before the sun's first rays painted the kingdom's tallest turrets pink. After a hearty but brief breakfast, he went to the castle's inner courtyard for stretching and a course of acrobatics.

Then off to the armory, where Kindle instructed Aidan in the art of "putting the stone." *A torture,* Aidan thought. *Heaving large rocks until your shoulder felt ready to explode!* Next came the Sylvan

Fields behind the rows of cottages lining the main avenue of Alleble. There Aidan learned to throw a long, fluted spear called a *javelin*. After lunch, again brief, Aidan went to the training compound to practice dueling with a seven-foot wooden pole called a *quarterstaff*.

Captain Valithor took over from there, tutoring Aidan in fencing and the other sword arts. After the sword, Aidan wrestled until sundown. Aidan had always hated wrestling in gym class. It seemed like the P.E. teacher always paired him with some big slobbering goon intent on smearing an underclassman across the gymnasium floor. Wrestling in gym meant pins, bruises, and severe mat burns.

The sort of wrestling taught in Alleble was far worse. There were no mats or pads, and there were no rules. You simply grappled until your opponent was unconscious or could no longer continue.

Aidan, by his own admission, was a horrible wrestler. He did learn quite a bit about holds and pressure points, places on the body where a well-placed finger or elbow could cause an opponent excruciating pain, but that knowledge came at a high cost.

His instructor, a short, thick fireplug of a Glimpse named Zander, tossed Aidan around like a pizza. Zander seemed to think that by slamming Aidan into the ground often enough, he might somehow learn how to grapple better. It didn't work.

And by Aidan's calculations, he had inadvertently eaten over a cup of woodchips and several quarts of sand and dirt! It was a bittersweet relief when the sun went down at the end of the day. That was the cue to end his training, but it also signaled that it was time for Aidan to begin his chores.

He had to wash his own clothes, polish his armor, and scrub his sword. At least he had a real sword now, though it was dull, heavily notched, and not much bigger than the wooden dagger with which he began.

But the worst duty of all was what Kaliam called "refreshing the dragon pens." This foul practice consisted of filling the dragons' troughs with the *second* most awful-smelling slop Aidan had ever had the displeasure of inhaling through his nostrils. Then, while the winged beasts ate, Aidan had to shovel and scrape the dragon pens clean of the *first* most awful-smelling slop he'd ever whiffed. Aidan wished many times that dragons could be more like cats and bury their business.

After lining each dragon pen with straw, Aidan could return to his chambers in the castle to bathe and sup. He spent each evening with Gwenne, studying The Scrolls of Alleble and learning the lore of a very ancient and wonderful realm.

With the exception of spending time with Gwenne, it was a grueling week. Aidan reflected on it all as he lay in bed, the very bed in which he awoke six days earlier. Every night, he went to sleep thinking he would awake and find it had all been a dream. Every morning, he awoke to rediscover that it was real.

Aidan turned on his side and rumpled his pillow. The curtains were now parted and shutters thrown open, so Aidan stared out of the chamber window at the bright full moon. Its pale light gilded the parapets, turrets, and rooftops of Alleble at rest. Here and there Aidan saw a cottage light blink out, and he imagined a Glimpse mother and father kissing their child good-night upon the brow. He thought of his own parents then. But he did not wish for them to be there to comfort *him*, to kiss him on the brow and say everything would be okay. No, he wished with all his heart that he could be home to comfort *them*. They would be terrified, frantic with visions of kidnappings and violent abductions. He wished he could be with them, just for a moment, to tell them their son was okay. He rubbed the new calluses on his hands and drifted to sleep.

"Congratulations, Sir Aidan!" announced Kaliam the next evening to the group assembled in the Great Banquet Hall of the Castle of Alleble. Gwenne, Kindle, Captain Valithor, and a large gathering of Glimpses raised their goblets to Aidan. Nock and Bolt were there as well, flanking Mallik at the table. Aidan saw that Mallik had a goblet the size of a fishbowl. He took a quick swig and winked.

Aidan was not used to all the attention and wished for the moment that he could crawl under the enormous oval dining table in front of him.

"Again I say . . . congratulations! You have survived the training that is required to be considered a Knight of Alleble!" Kaliam's words were met with a chorus of cheers and many solid slaps on the back, paining Aidan greatly as he had accumulated quite a collection of bumps and bruises over the last couple of days.

Aidan turned to Gwenne to say something, but the words vanished when he saw a tall, prominent-looking Glimpse enter the back of the banquet hall. The Glimpse wore a dark blue cape and carried a small burlap-wrapped bundle. A hush fell over the gathering. Yet the Glimpse said nothing, but he bowed low, handing the bundle to Captain Valithor.

A few of the younger Glimpses whispered excitedly and pointed at the mysterious caped Glimpse. He seemed to be someone of importance, though he bowed to Captain Valithor—an act that again reminded Aidan of his commander's rank and stature.

The stranger left just as Captain Valithor bellowed, "Just one moment, thou artless assembly of fly-bitten flapdragons! It would seem that you have declared this minnow a knight too soon!"

At that, Aidan's heart fell. All the work, the beatings, the cuts and bruises—had it all been for nothing? He looked to Gwenne who, oddly enough, wore that wry, crooked smile of hers. Aidan scanned the hall from Glimpse to Glimpse. Some whispered. Others smiled and stared at Aidan, waiting. Waiting for what? Mallik was laughing uproariously in spite of the twins' efforts to shush him. Aidan wondered if he was the only one terrified about what the Captain would say next?!

The Captain waited for what seemed like several eternities before finally speaking. "I am astonished! Even you, the weedy, idle-headed giglets I have taught so well, noticed not that Aidan is missing something. Something of great importance to a knight!"

There were smiles around the room as Glimpses laughed and pointed at Aidan. What was so funny here? Aidan felt as if he must have dressed in some comically incorrect way. The Captain cleared his throat gruffly, instantly silencing the crowd.

"For as any knight with half a brain knows, a worthy servant of Alleble must have a sword—a real sword!"

The room erupted in cheers of "Here! Here! Give the knight a blade!" The Captain picked up the bundle from the table and then, untying the black twine that bound the package, walked over to Aidan who stood flabbergasted.

The Captain dropped the cord near Aidan and handed him the now loosely wrapped bundle. "Here, lad, open it, for herein lies a token, a sign of your knighthood."

Aidan took the bundle and, for a moment, simply stared down at it. The shape was right, and he recognized the weight—it must, of course, be a sword. He peeled back the last layer of cloth and gasped, his breath stolen. There, shining out from the cloth like the sun rising behind the mountains, the very emblem on its haft, was the sword known as Fury!

Yet, it was not Fury. Aidan grasped the handle and held up the gleaming short sword, for that is what it was, a short sword, about a foot shorter than Fury but in every other way identical to the incredible blade Aidan had coveted at the armory.

"But how?" Aidan blurted out, dumbfounded. "I thought—"

"You thought correctly!" interrupted Captain Valithor. "Indeed, there is only one blade called Fury. And it already has an owner!"

The Captain threw back his dark green cloak and unleashed a blade from its scabbard. He held the gleaming sword aloft, and to Aidan's continuing bewilderment, it was the real Fury!

Just as quickly, the Captain sheathed his sword. He turned back to Aidan and stared directly into his eyes.

"Now, good lad, hand me your blade and kneel before me."

Aidan, remembering the correct way to deliver a sword, took both hands and carefully grasped the blade near the point and again just above the hilt. He gave the blade to the Captain grip-first and then fell quickly to his knees. The Captain took Aidan's sword and placed the blade upon Aidan's right shoulder. Then, he began to speak.

"You have been called by the King to serve the Kingdom of Alleble in truth and honor. You responded in faith and have chosen the narrow path."

As the Captain spoke, Gwenne and the rest of the gathering silently surrounded Aidan and the Captain.

"Lad," the Captain continued, "you have shown great skill at arms, and though truly your training has only just begun, you have been found worthy of the title Knight of Alleble! It is my duty and honor as Captain of the Guard to require of you the good confession. Do you, Aidan, confess allegiance and absolute loyalty to the one true King, the provider of all that is just and good? Even were the hordes of darkness to assail you in hopeless demand of your life—even then do you swear devotion forever to the King?"

The Captain lowered his voice so that only Aidan could hear.

"Aidan, think hard on this, lad. From your reply there is no turning back. If you speak nay, you shall be returned safely and speedily to your realm, and this—all this—can become for you the fairy tale most in your world believe it is. Only reply aye if your heart, your very soul, cries out to do so."

Aidan felt as if time had stopped. Everyone in the room except the Captain and himself had vanished, and he was alone with his decision. At home, his decisions seemed so meaningless . . . without consequence. What should he wear to school? What should he pack in his lunch? What should he spend his allowance on? This decision, however, weighed in his heart as if everything in the world depended on it. There was a sense of phenomenal joy in Aidan's heart that did indeed cry out for Aidan to accept.

But there too, lurking from a shadowy corner of his mind, a dark voice whispered, "Mis-s-s-stake."

It chilled Aidan, and he felt a dangerous presence willing him not to confess. It hovered above him like a ghostly hand.

This is serious. This isn't the kind of promise where I can cross my fingers behind my back. To make the confession could lead to war . . . could lead to death—my death! Going home would be safe. Aidan blinked.

Aidan looked up through a haze of fears, but the eyes of his Captain, like beacons for a lost ship, penetrated deep into Aidan's heart. In Alleble, there was meaning and purpose. Things happened for a reason. To leave, to turn his back on it all, would be to abandon everything he ever wanted. It would mean throwing away his dreams forever.

Staying would not be safe—that was clear. But, Aidan decided, it was the right path. And so, with courage swelling within, he cried out, "Aye!"

The crowd of Glimpses erupted in cheers, whoops, and hurrahs! The Captain's snowy mustache curled on one side in a proud smile, and he nodded.

Finally, when the roar diminished, Captain Valithor gently tapped each of Aidan's shoulders with Aidan's new sword and announced, "Then, by the heartfelt confession of your lips, I now dub thee Sir Aidan, Knight of Alleble and Servant of the one true King!"

The next thing Aidan knew, he was at the bottom of a massive pile of joyous Glimpses. He felt squashed, but he didn't care. And though he couldn't see anything through the jumble of arms and legs, Aidan heard thunderous deep hurrahs and huzzahs above all the other din, and he knew it had to be Mallik. *I have friends here,* Aidan thought.

After the banquet, Aidan and Gwenne walked to the unicorn stables beyond the castle courtyard. They leaned on the fence and watched the majestic beasts play in the moonlight. Aidan sighed, still finding it hard to believe that the legendary craftsman Naysmithe had forged a short sword just for him.

Aidan turned to his friend. "Gwenne, in the old language, how would you say Son of Fury?"

Gwenne scratched her head for a moment and then pronounced, "Son of Fury would be *Sil Furyn*—a proud name for a blade, *Sir* Aidan." She put strong emphasis on Aidan's new title. He blushed and looked down at the hilt of his sword. He was a Knight of Alleble now—a knight! *Wouldn't Robby be surprised!*

"I think *Sil Furyn* shall be your name," Aidan said drawing the weapon.

The moonlight glinted off its keen edge. Aidan held the Son of Fury high, turned, and with an oft-practiced jolt, threw a perfect moulinet at an imaginary foe. Gwenne applauded. Aidan bowed and sheathed his sword. He had never felt so valued and important. It was all too good.

As they walked back to the castle, Aidan glanced at the Fountains of Alleble, for even at night they coursed and arched fifty feet in the air. They were beautiful and hypnotic. But Aidan's eyes lingered on the one empty fountain, and he shivered. Turning quickly, he followed Gwenne into the gatehouse.

TRAITOR'S LEGACY

Aidan couldn't sleep. And the fact that he couldn't sleep made him angry. After all he'd been through—the early mornings, the grueling workouts and training, the intense emotions of the ceremony—he ought to have passed out and slept for a week. But somehow, he was still restless. He tried thinking of pleasant memories. He tried deep breathing.

He even tried counting sheep! But that just sent Aidan's mind spinning with silly thoughts like: *Are there any sheep in Alleble? If not, what do they count to sleep? Counting dragons doesn't sound very relaxing!*

Aidan couldn't stand it. He threw off the downy covers and stepped to one of the chamber's arched windows. The moon was much lower in the night sky, already well into its routine descent. The rooftops, turrets, and parapets glistened silver. The fountains sparkled as if their waters were enchanted with stardust.

Aidan stared again at the fountain nearest the castle, the empty fountain. It lay partially in shadows far below. Aidan blinked, thinking he saw something move near the fountain's base. He squinted to be sure his eyes and the shadows weren't deceiving him, but then he was sure. There was someone down there.

Aidan threw on a dark tunic, a rugged pair of breeches, and slipped on his old Nikes—glad someone had brought them to his room. Even without socks, they felt like paradise compared to the hard boots he had worn all week.

He was certain no one would care if he was out at night, but he felt sneaky anyway as he tiptoed from his chamber to the spiral staircase. The guards who were always posted at the castle's inner gatehouse nodded when Aidan passed. He was, after all, a knight himself and as such, free to roam most areas of Alleble at will.

The flickering orange of torches faded as Aidan wandered beyond the castle and onto Alleble's main thoroughfare. Slipping silently from shadow to shadow, Aidan approached the Seventh Fountain, the dry fountain. There a tall Glimpse warrior stood, leaning over the circular granite wall and staring forward. His back was to Aidan, and he did not turn around when Aidan drew near.

The Glimpse cleared his throat. "Ah, Sir Aidan," he said. "What brings a young knight out when the moon falls low and day nears the threshold?"

"Captain?" Aidan guessed. Surely it was Captain Valithor, for no other Glimpse in all of Alleble stood as tall and as broad. And yet, the voice was different. Not as gruff and commanding as usual.

"Sorry to disturb you, Captain. I, I couldn't sleep. I shouldn't be here, should I? I'll just head back to my chambers."

"Nay, lad. Join me," said the Captain.

Aidan did. He clambered up and sat on the granite wall close to where Captain Valithor stood. They both stared out over the sleeping kingdom.

Alleble was very still and quiet. The only sounds came from the other six fountains that resonated like a constant tide. Staring at the fountains and listening to their steady, hypnotic song was relaxing. Aidan almost felt he could sleep now. But then he peered into the empty fountain before him. And he remembered.

He remembered why one fountain, one of the renowned Seven Fountains of Alleble that flowed in ceaseless splendor for untold centuries, was now dry forevermore. With great sadness, Aidan stared at the vast, empty pool bed and imagined it when it was last filled. He had read in the scroll that the Elder Guard, their wives, and their children, were surprised by traitors in the still hours before dawn, dragged at swordpoint, and cast into the fountain—cast aside like refuse in a pond.

They must have been so cold, Aidan thought. He could almost see them standing in the pool of black fuel oil. He thought he knew what had happened to them that night, but he did not want to imagine it. Aidan cringed.

He wanted to look away. He wanted to run away. But the fountain-bed had a gravity that gripped Aidan so that he could not turn from it. He swayed, and for a moment he felt he would fall in— fall into the deep, dark liquid where he would surely drown or burn. A strong hand gripped Aidan's shoulder.

"You know of this fountain, then?" said the Captain quietly. Aidan blinked a moment as if waking from a dream. He numbly watched Captain Valithor pull on a pair of long silver gauntlets. He had never seen the Captain without them. Before the gloves completely hid the Captain's hands, Aidan thought he saw wounded flesh as if they had been gashed or cut. No, Aidan realized, not cut. Scarred. Burned.

Aidan stared wide-eyed with recognition. Captain Valithor nodded slightly. His white brows furrowed, and he turned to lean again on the edge of the fountain.

"I was your age at the time," he began. "My mother and father were asleep in the loft of our cottage. But, like this night, I could not sleep. My father, you see, was to take me into the mountains the next morn to search for dragon roosts. I aspired to be an artist then, and wanted to sketch them in the wild. Alas, it was not to be.

"The traitors were stealthy, but still I heard them. I had just enough time to slide out of my window onto the ledge. I wanted to cry out, to warn my parents, but fear stole my voice. I failed them, Aidan.

"From my hiding place on the ledge, I saw dark shadows—ten at least—advance toward the stair to the loft. They fell upon my father, and though he was just startled from deep sleep, he fought like a lion. He slew two of them before they struck at a weakness he could not defend—my mother. They held a dagger to her throat, the cowards." Captain Valithor gripped the edge of the wall as if he would crush it.

"My father for the first time—and the last—surrendered his sword. They took my parents away with the other Elder Guards and their families to the courtyard.

"They nearly caught me then, for I knocked a stone loose from the ledge as I clambered to the ground. They sent two knights after me, but I knew the alleys and backways. I lost them easily enough."

"You were the one?" Aidan asked. "You were the boy who escaped?"

"Yes, Aidan, I escaped. But I needed to get to the courtyard to see what they would do with my parents. I tried several streets but found them all guarded. Finally, I climbed the bell tower near the sixth fountain. And there I saw them—my mother and father, the others, the children. They were drenched in dark liquid, and I knew it was oil, for the air smelled acrid. They were surrounded by two legions of traitorous knights—all cloaked in black but streaked angry orange from the torches they carried.

"Then I saw, high on a balcony of the castle, two knights. One of them had a sword drawn. The other lay down on a bed of stone. I was young and did not fully understand what was happening.

"The sword flashed in the moonlight and fell. When my father and the other knights in the fountain screamed in rage, I knew that something terrible had happened. I felt it. Still I watched, trans-fixed, waves of dread washing over me. The knight standing on the balcony raised his sword and gave a great shout of triumph.

"It was Paragor, Aidan, though then he was called Paragal. He was filled with unquenchable lust for blood and death. I watched in horror as Paragor took a torch from the wall and flung it in a high arc away from the castle. It fell like an evil star from the sky into the fountain. At the same time, the traitorous archers loosed a hundred fiery arrows into the pool. There was a great shock wave as the fuel vapor ignited and fire roared up from the fountain, engulfing my parents and the others in its hungry flames."

"No!" Aidan almost shouted. He leaped down from the foun-tain. "No, that . . . that can't be what happened. Paragor said he'd release the other knights if the King allowed himself to die."

"Paragor is a liar, Aidan. He plotted always to murder the entire Elder Guard, for he knew that they would not rest until they avenged the King's death. I watched from that tower, watched Paragor commit a deed too foul for words. I was stricken and nearly fell from my perch, but somehow I found strength in my anger. I grabbed the chain to the great bell and set it to ringing so loud the mountains trembled.

"Noble Glimpses, aroused by the alarm, issued forth like a flood from all corners of Alleble. Some were armed, but many wielded only pitchforks, spades, or nothing at all. Still, they seemed to know something of the great evil that had just befallen Alleble, and they fought valiantly. In the chaos of battle, I ran across the courtyard to the fountain. The heat was staggering, my hair began to melt, and I felt my skin sizzle and crack. The fountain was an inferno, and I knew no one could have survived. . . . Whether it was some last evil trick in the fire, I do not know, but I thought I saw shapes of men thrashing about trying to find a way out. I looked away, but then forced myself to look back into the fountain. And for just a moment I saw the silhouette of a man, and I knew it must be my father.

"I reached then, into the fire, for I had to undo this deed and release my sire from the flames. The heat bit down hard and set to work devouring the flesh on my arms. Just as I thought I'd reach him, my father's image vanished, and I fell away from the fountain having saved no one. I lay in agony on the very stones upon which you now stand, Aidan. The last thing I remember, above the roar of the raging flames, above the screams of battling Glimpses, and above the ringing of swords, was hearing laughter—Paragor's laughter."

Aidan felt like he'd been hit hard in the stomach—he was so angry and heartbroken by the Captain's account. Aidan didn't want it to be true. He wished that the story of Alleble was just like the other fantasies he'd read where there were heroes, victories, and happy endings.

It wasn't fair. Things like that should never be allowed to happen. Tears escaped the corners of his eyes and traced angry streaks down his face.

"Weep, Aidan. Weep," Captain Valithor said. "But do not despair. Paragor's victory was not final. What he intended for evil has become the foundation for much that is good."

"How can you say that?" Aidan cried. "How could good come from—" Aidan choked. "I mean, he killed them! He killed the King! What good could ever come from that?"

Captain Valithor's eyes softened. He took Aidan by the shoulders and stooped to look him in the eyes.

"Aidan, if you only knew how many times I asked that very question. But I was blinded to the answer by the closeness of the pain. It was only by the passing of time that I was able to finally see the answer. You see, from the flames of Paragor's treachery, Alleble was reborn stronger than ever, and the destinies of many in The Realm changed in such a way that they have brought about incalculable good."

"I don't understand," Aidan whispered.

"There are many, even among the wise, who do not understand. But try, Aidan. Try to see. If Paragor had not committed his foul deeds, I may never have become a knight like my father. I would never have raised a new army for Alleble. Battles that were won . . . would have been lost. And many of the scattered kingdoms of Alleble would never have been reached for the glory of the King."

Captain Valithor released Aidan's shoulders. Aidan wiped away the last of his tears and said, "But, Captain, so many had to suffer."

"You are right, Aidan, and that must never be forgotten. But though many were lost and many left behind to grieve, ten times more were rescued from futures more terrible . . . and final."

Aidan shook his head. There was still so much he could not grasp.

"Take heart, Aidan," said Captain Valithor, throwing back his cloak and gesturing toward the mountains. The sky was beginning to glow pink. "For Paragor is in exile, and the King is restored!"

Aidan smiled grimly. The Captain's words were heartening. But also mysterious—like a riddle whose answer was maddeningly just out of reach.

"Captain, what happened? How was Paragor defeated? How did the King come back?"

"How King Eliam returned to us, I cannot say. I can only say that the King is here. And he always will be. But as for Paragor, that tale I know very well. And it is time you know also."

Captain Valithor drew aside his cloak and removed something from his belt. Aidan knew the shape. It was a scroll.

The Captain opened the scroll and placed it before Aidan. "I will not tell you this tale," the Captain said. "You must see it for yourself. Reach here, Aidan. Brush your fingers across the words. They are powerful. And they will live in your mind's eye."

Aidan let his hand hover over the page of parchment. And slowly, he lowered his fingers to touch the words. A sea of black flooded Aidan's vision. A long sword blade sliced through the darkness. Then, there was fire, and Aidan lost all sense of where he was.

Paragal passed the throne one more time. He would not sit there. *Not yet.* For one task remained.

He stopped at the foot of the stairs that led to the King's sacred courtyard, now his own sacred courtyard. A cold draft whispered and pulled at the torches in the passage. And something strange took hold of Paragal there. Looking up at that long stair, seeing the old stone, chipped and flaking, the statues of long-forgotten warriors at each landing—Paragal wondered how history would remember his deeds on this night. And he felt—what was it? *Not fear. History will see me in whatever way I see fit.* Anxiety, that was all, apprehension about fulfilling his destiny at last. That had to be the reason for the disquiet he felt.

Paragal strode very quickly up the stairs, passed through the white flames, and into The Library of Light. To the ninth level he climbed, past tables piled high with scrolls he'd read many times before. Finally, Paragal approached the chest of stone that lay below the window on the eastern side of the chamber.

The chest was gray like granite but as smooth as velvet. It was plain except for the latch and the large keyhole. No key, but Paragal was not concerned. He drew Cer Muryn, its blade stained dark, and delivered a great two-handed slash. The top of the chest fell away, for *murynstil* could carve stone like balsa wood. Within the chest was an enormously thick scroll, rolled tight in a bundle and secured by a cord. And to Paragal's ruthless satisfaction, there too was a quill pen and a bottle of dark ink. Paragal sheathed his sword, removed the contents of the chest, and sat at a long table near the window.

The cord was untied and removed, but the scroll lay unopened on the table before Paragal. He hesitated to open it, for it represented the ultimate success of his plot and the fulfillment of his ambition. King Eliam was gone. His beloved Elder Guard vanquished without a fight. And the people? *They are sheep*, Paragal thought. *They will fall in line or they will die like the others.*

All that was left to do was to open the legendary first scroll.

If the stories were true, it would contain the entire history of Alleble. And, more importantly, the future of Alleble as well. Paragal knew that with such knowledge, his wisdom would never be questioned, his decisions could never go awry, and his reign would not end until age took back the throne.

As if in a trance, Paragal stared out the tower window. The snowcapped peaks of *Pennath Ador*, the mountains of glory, were outlined in deep pink. Soon the sun would rise between the twin summits and witness the dawn of a new age. Paragal waited no longer. With great eagerness, he stretched flat the scrolls and began to read.

Only a few passages in, Paragal stopped in alarm. He already knew what he was reading. Paragal turned through several pages, but it was unmistakable. He was reading the story of his own life.

It could not be! The first scroll of Alleble could not possibly be all about one Glimpse. Paragal's mind raced. The legends claimed that the first scroll would reveal the past and the future of every Glimpse who had ever lived. How could it—? And then, he understood. Paragal went back to the first page.

He brought into his mind the image of Rucifel, the lieutenant of his rebellious horde, and suddenly, the text on the scroll changed. It was no longer Paragal's life story. It was Rucifel's. Paragal grinned wide. He had often wondered how a scroll—no matter how long or thick—could contain infinite lore.

Now he knew. Paragal began to think of other Glimpses. And with every name that entered Paragal's mind, the scrolls changed, revealing every moment of every life that he cared to perceive.

Paragal turned the scrolls back to his own story and began searching through the pages. He merely skimmed, for he was not interested in reliving his past. He wanted to discover his future. Paragal raced through his squiring, his training, his knighthood. He saw his recruitment by the Elder Guard and his selection to be sentinel.

Finally, he came to the account of his rebellion—the bloody events that had occurred that very night. He knew he was getting close. One more page.

But the next page was empty. Paragal's story had run right up to the present moment, with Paragal in the ninth-level tower of The

Library of Light reading the first scroll of Alleble. But there it ended. Paragal began to despair. What could this mean? Had he no future? Or was it that the first scroll was in fact only a record of what had been?

As if he were watching through a window, a vision began to unfold in his mind. He saw himself there at the table near the east window with the first scroll stretched out before him. But it was not the present moment, for he saw himself pick up the quill pen that he had taken from the stone chest. He watched himself plunge the pen into the jar of black ink. He saw himself begin to write on the empty parchment. There the vision ended.

Paragal smiled again. He had always assumed that when King Eliam wrote on the scrolls he was simply recording a narrative of what had already happened, like a bard inscribing the events of an adventure for posterity. But it was not so. The King was writing the future!

And now, Paragal thought, *that power has passed on to me.*

Paragal picked up the quill pen and firmly stabbed its point into the ink bottle.

He moved the pen to the parchment and began to write.

But the moment the wet point of the pen touched the page, Paragal froze. The disquiet he had felt before the stairs again took hold of him. A thought clawed into his mind. *If King Eliam saw the future, then he must have known that I would betray him.*

Paragal looked down at the parchment. Dark ink pooled where the pen's tip rested. *Why, then, would he allow me to take his life?*

Paragal shook his head. It did not matter why, for King Eliam was dead. The power was Paragal's now. He cleared his mind and sought to see his future.

Visions erupted in his mind, and Paragal wrote what he saw. *I will be wise.*

I will be feared.

I will be powerful.

Paragal wrote these three lines and smiled for the last time.

Something took control of his hand. Paragal cried out, for he could not stop his own hand from writing. The visions that followed pierced him through:

I will never know all.

I will never be loved.

I will never be King.

Crimson light poured through the eastern window as the fierce sun rose between the peaks of *Pennath Ador*. Its rays splashed upon the scroll and seared the ink into the page. When the light of that dawn reached Paragal, it kindled into red fire and began to race up his arms as if he were doused in oil. The hungry flames writhed about Paragal, afflicting him with agonizing pain, but did not consume him. He flailed at the fire, but it could not be quenched. Then Paragal felt himself being lifted.

The crimson flames carried Paragal's contorting body up, and he passed through the stone of the tower into the blazing dawn sky. Paragal saw through the flames that there were other forms captured in the fire and floating high above the courtyard of Alleble. And Paragal knew that every one of his evil conspirators was captured in the same manner as he. And the last line that Paragal had written on the scroll seared his mind.

I will never be King.

As if catapulted by a gigantic hand, Paragal and all of his horde were flung with tremendous force—an evil red scar tracing high in the sky far from the Castle of Alleble. Finally, they crashed together at the foot of a dark mountain range. The roots of the mountains smoldered like a fire left to burn itself out.

But the impact did not kill even one of the Glimpses who had been cast out. Not one of them perished from the flames or the fall. And Paragal, though he was not consumed by the fire, was changed by it. His sword could no longer be called Cer Muryn, for its blade was charred black. Paragal's eyes, glassy with shock, flickered red. And upon Paragal's chest, seared into his pale flesh like a brand, was a jagged scar: the outline of an inverted crown.

Beneath it were symbols from the oldest language in Alleble, in the same runelike manner as those engraved upon The Stones of White Fire. Paragal looked with disgust at the scar but grimly accepted his new name: Paragor.

"Come back, Aidan," the Captain said gently. Aidan awoke from the vision and blinked. He could still imagine Paragor and the other fallen Glimpses smoldering at the foot of the dark mountains. It made him shiver.

"From that time forward, King Eliam regained his rightful place on the throne. He is different now, of course, and the holy purity of his countenance takes some getting used to. But he is our King, and we love him more than ever for rescuing us from the fate that Paragor had in mind. The Prince, as Paragor calls himself, and his servants, Aidan, are our eternal enemies. And though he has not waged full-fledged war against Alleble, he is massing his forces. And he is ever at work bribing, coercing, and tricking—doing anything he can to draw the loyalty of the free Glimpses of The Realm away from Alleble. And tomorrow, tomorrow we begin a quest to Mithegard to see if we can ruin the Prince's plans and bring more of the children of Alleble back into the fold."

"Captain, I've seen Paragor."

"What?" The Sentinel looked up, his eyes narrowed, posture tensed. "Where?"

"It was in a dream I had before I entered The Realm."

Tension melted from Captain Valithor. He sighed with relief. "That is natural, Aidan. When you read The Scrolls—it is bound to influence your dreams."

"But it was a dream I had before I found the scrolls."

Captain Valithor's eyes widened.

Aidan continued. "I had the same horrible dream over and over again. I was in the ruins of a kingdom. I was captured, and Paragor told me to deny my King. I refused, and . . . and he killed me."

Captain Valithor staggered backward and steadied himself on the wall of the fountain. "Aidan, I . . ."

"What is it?" Aidan was alarmed.

The Captain swallowed. Then he mastered himself. "Aidan, no matter what, tell no one else of this dream."

"But, why?"

"No one! Do you understand? I must seek the King's wisdom, for my own is found wanting in this. Remember, no one!"

Aidan's gut churned, and the hair stood up on the nape of his neck. "I won't tell anyone, Captain," he whispered. "I promise."

"Good, Sir Aidan," he replied. And just like that, Captain Valithor seemed back to his own commanding self. He winked at Aidan. "You've been trained for this mission, very well trained, in fact. Now what you need is some rest."

"But I don't see what my part is in all this."

Captain Valithor nodded. "Nor do I," he said. "It is rare that King Eliam brings someone from your world to Alleble before his time. But things are changing. And I truly believe that things are drawing to a close. It is clear that the Prince and the forces of Paragory are making a last push to increase their influence in The Realm. It may be that Mithegard is a pivotal piece of the puzzle. And you, Aidan, may be another—even, perhaps, a bigger piece. Now, you have learned much. I suspect more than you are ready to know. Go back now to your chamber, for you will need your rest. I will not have you awakened at first call. No, in fact, I will set Gabby outside your door with orders to roast anyone who attempts to wake you before midday."

FATEFUL PLANS

"Oh, this ought to be good," Gwenne said the next afternoon. She grinned and motioned for Aidan to stop as they approached the archery range. "Look there, Matthias and Tal are at it again!"

Aidan saw two Glimpse knights standing a step apart. Each held a long bow and had a full quiver of arrows slung behind him. The first knight was portly and older, with strands of silver lacing his long, dark hair. He hung his bow over his shoulder and reached for a bag on his belt.

"Twenty gold coins, Tal," he said to the other. "First shaft to the bull's-eye and closest to the center! If the swiftest arrow is not the most accurate, we draw again. What say you?"

"Agreed," said the other knight. He was willowy and slender. Indeed, he seemed carved from the same wood as his bow. And like a good bow, he seemed supple, as if he had great power hidden within. Aidan noticed too that this knight's skin, though pale, was more cream-colored than the ivory of the other Glimpses he'd seen, and his hair was bundled in great locks. This knight also drew a pouch of coins from his belt.

"But twenty gold coins is far too paltry a sum to be won by the greatest archer in Alleble. Let's make it an even fifty, eh, Matthias?"

"I like your style, Tal," said the taller Glimpse. "And I shall like your money even more! Fifty it is, then. But we need, uh—yes, Gwenne! Gwenne, come over here, if you would, and govern this contest."

"Don't you two ever give up?" Gwenne said. She and Aidan approached the two archers.

"Nay, m'lady," answered Tal. He bowed courteously. "Not until it is decided who is the most skilled archer in all the kingdom!"

"Take your ground, then," said Gwenne. She raised her right arm. Both archers turned to face the distant target. *It must be at least a mile away,* Aidan thought. He imagined himself shooting arrows at it—missing it, of course—and probably skewering some poor farm animal nearby.

"Ready!" Gwenne shouted.

Each archer gripped his bow in one hand and let the free hand dangle at his side. Whispers teemed among the small crowd of knights that had gathered behind them.

"Steady!"

The archers glared at the target. Muscles tightened. Fingers twitched.

Gwenne looked from archer to archer, Matthias to Tal, Tal back to Matthias.

"Pull!!" she yelled.

The motion was fluid, practiced, expert. Hands swept over shoulders. Arrows fit to strings, lingered only a heartbeat. They fired with the speed of striking cobras. Bowstrings sang out, and the missiles sprang through the air.

A split second later two dark streaks whooshed through their arrows' paths, shattering them in midair. With a sharp *thok!* two black arrows stabbed into a palisade on the right, embedded up to their fletchings in the wooden planks.

Jaws dropped and the crowd was as still as old stone. Matthias and Tal looked at the shards of their broken arrows and then up at the black shafts that had destroyed them. Gwenne and Aidan stood there blinking.

Nock and Bolt, bows in hand, raced down a hill from the left and bowed before Matthias and Tal.

"If you intended to find the greatest archers in all of Alleble," began Nock, grinning.

"Then you should at least have had the courtesy to invite them to the contest," Bolt finished.

Gwenne burst into laughter.

"Thou hasty-witted flapdragons!!" roared Captain Valithor as he stormed into the training yard and up to Matthias and Tal. "It would seem that you each owe fifty gold coins to the winners!"

"Not so, Captain," said Matthias. He blushed and was clearly intimidated by their great leader, but still he argued. "They did not hit the bull's-eye!"

"No," the Captain replied. "Not one bull's-eye but two—traveling through the air at great speed. And Nock and Bolt fired from much farther away!" Captain Valithor erupted into deep, bellowing fits of laughter. The crowd joined in the mirth. Dejectedly, Matthias and Tal handed a bag of coins to each of the winners.

The twins accepted their prize and turned to Aidan. "Greetings, Twelfth Knight!" they said, again bowing low.

"How did you do that?" Aidan blurted out.

"Yewland skill!" said Nock. "We were trained to shoot before we could walk. It is the way of our kin."

"And, of course, superior equipment never hurts," said Bolt. "Our bows and the shafts of our arrows are made from the roots of the great trees in the Blackwood. Our bows launch with much greater force and speed."

"And our arrows fly straighter and pierce the air with no resistance," Nock said.

"That was the most incredible thing I've ever seen," said Aidan.

"It is no more amazing than what I've heard of your skill with a blade," said Bolt humbly. "I didn't really want to show off. It was Nock's idea."

"Ahh, they had it coming," said Nock, dismissing the offense. "Those two drive me crazy with their petty competitions. They should be content with their skill—"

"Just as we should be content with ours, brother," replied Bolt, and the discussion was over.

A few moments later, Captain Valithor and the other Glimpse knights gathered around a great round table in the center of the training yard. It was warm and still, and the late-afternoon sun dissolved into the hazy sky. A mantle of dark clouds bubbled at the horizon.

"I think it might rain," Aidan said as he and Gwenne joined the others at the round table.

"No, not today at least, Sir Aidan," she said. She scanned the distant sky and frowned. "But there is something brewing in the West. I can feel it. The worst storms always come out of the West." A light, cold breeze swirled amidst them, and the nearby trees rustled.

There, at the table, was the first time Aidan had seen the full team together.

He knew most of them. Kaliam, whom they called Pathfinder, was hunched over the map, engaged in conversation with Captain Valithor. As always, Nock and Bolt were seated side by side. Their light brown hair was tied back tightly, but a few renegade strands drifted loose and floated like phantoms on the cold breeze. Mallik stood rigidly behind the twins, his hands crossed over the haft of his hammer. He looked like he was standing guard. Matthias and Tal were next. Sir Acsriot wore a dark, weather-beaten gray cloak and sat to the right of Captain Valithor. Next to Sir Acsriot were two Glimpses Aidan had not met.

"Gwenne, who is he?" Aidan asked quietly. He pointed to the first, who stood very still, leaning on a long wooden staff. This Glimpse wore new plate armor, polished and gleaming. He seemed very well groomed, almost princely, compared to Acsriot.

"That is Eleazar. He is our team's spokesman," explained Gwenne. "He is wise in Alleble's lore and as skilled with words as he is with that staff. He will be the first to meet with Mithegard's sovereign, King Ravelle."

Aidan turned his attention to the knight who stood next to Eleazar. This Glimpse wore a long, dark tunic over leather breeches but no armor. The sleeves of his surcoat widened at the end, and his hands disappeared into them when his arms were crossed.

"Okay, well, who is that? He doesn't have any armor . . . or a weapon."

Gwenne turned to Aidan and whispered, "He is Farix, and he *is* a weapon."

"Huh? What do you mean?"

"Be glad Farix is on our side, Aidan. Were he to battle our entire team at the same time, he would disarm and slay each of us, except Captain Valithor, before we could so much as put a scratch on him."

"You're kidding, right?" Aidan asked.

Gwenne's hard stare spoke volumes. She wasn't kidding.

Just then, Farix looked up at Aidan and smiled. Aidan swallowed and immediately began studying his boots.

"Yes, Aidan, our group of twelve is formidable indeed—easily a match for a Legion of Paragor's so-called knights. We must be reminded that success in Mithegard hinges not on the accuracy of our archers or the prowess of our swordsmen. Still, we will not naively go unprepared—or unarmed."

"Gwenne, you told me there are supposed to be twelve of us going to Mithegard," Aidan began cautiously. "But including myself, I count eleven . . . and I don't remember meeting the other knight."

Gwenne glared at Aidan. "Oh . . . you've met the other knight," she began, a sly smile curling on her lips. "She is standing in front of you."

As she spoke, she opened the cloak she was wearing and revealed that she too wore armor and carried a sword. She pulled the sword skillfully from her scabbard and spun it around her wrist, carving the air in front of her.

"Sir Aidan, I would like to introduce you to *Thil Galel*, the Daughter of Light. Shall I prove to you my worthiness to accompany you on this quest, or did you not forget that I bested Kaliam in a duel?"

Aidan wished he could crawl under a rock and disappear. He knew that Gwenne was strong and athletic, that she had great swordcraft. Defeating a beast like Kaliam in battle was no easy task, Aidan knew! He looked at Gwenne—long blond hair tied back with a silver circlet, piercing blue eyes, the auburn, velvety cloak draping over her armor. It was still hard to imagine someone who appeared so delicate and beautiful—in a moment turning into a tough-as-iron warrior.

"I'm sorry, Gwenne. Sometimes I just don't think," he said. "You definitely seem worthy to me. Forgive me for shooting off my mouth."

"Oh, don't be silly," Gwenne said, sheathing her blade. "Of course you are forgiven, but I must admit it was fun to watch you jump when I drew my sword. I can only imagine how you might jump when you meet a knight from Paragory. They are far more ugly than I am."

"No, I've seen them. Or at least I think I have. Right before Gabby swooped down on me, a knight in black armor was chasing me in the foothills of that mountain with the two jagged peaks."

"The Prince's Crown," said Gwenne, thinking aloud.

"There were actually a bunch of knights. It was horrible, Gwenne. They were taking these people like slaves into a huge cavern in the mountain. There was smoke from in—"

"That is the Gate of Despair, Aidan," said Captain Valithor quietly. He and the rest of the twelve were staring at Aidan. "Those wretched souls who pass that terrible gate will endure misery and sorrows that reach beyond the end of their lives. Such is the fate of those who swear allegiance to Paragor The Betrayer. And it is for that reason we travel to Mithegard—into harm's way. We may by necessity be forced to travel near the gate ourselves, for Paragory lies between us and Mithegard."

"With all due respect, sir, we dare not travel the Prince's Crown," argued Tal. "Paragor is sure to have every available spy watching for us, not to mention his legion of foul beasts living in every crevice of that wretched mountain."

"The Prince's Crown?" Aidan blurted out, surprising himself. "That's the mountain range I came over."

All of the Glimpses stared at Aidan.

"You passed over the Prince's Crown?" blurted out Mallik, wonder in his eyes.

"Actually, I passed through it. I found a tunnel that cut right through," he said, leaving out the fact that little creatures with glowing eyes led him to the tunnel. "But I don't think we can climb back up the passage. It is very narrow and slippery."

Captain Valithor looked at Aidan thoughtfully and then said, "Kaliam, what do you say to this? You know those mountains better than any of us. Do we travel the Prince's Crown?"

Kaliam hesitated, stared at the map, and then seemingly made up his mind.

"Sir, I do not advise an attempt at the Prince's Crown. The dangers are too many, and I do not believe that we can expect Aidan's good fortune."

"Well then, Kaliam, Pathfinder, how do you suggest we travel to Mithegard?"

Kaliam began, "Let us head north and take the land bridge through the Mirror Lakes."

"No, not that way!" interrupted Acsriot, rising and throwing back his travel-worn cloak. "I am little more than an herb-meister on this journey, my skill with salves and potions being far greater than my skill with maps, but I need to have some say in this matter."

"Continue, Acsriot," said Captain Valithor. There had been some friction between Acsriot and Captain Valithor, Aidan remembered from that day when Acsriot arrived to train with a stained blade. But, Captain Valithor, harsh as he was, did not hold grudges. And he seemed eager for Acsriot to prove himself.

"Well, sir, north is certainly the safest route, but it is also the longest route. The Mirror Lakes are often swollen this time of year, and it would be disastrous if our path was flooded, forcing us to find a new and longer way."

Kaliam nodded. He hadn't thought of that.

"And," Acsriot continued, "as Kaliam rightly said, there is no guaranteed passage over the Prince's Crown." He cast an accusative eye at Aidan. "No, I suggest a middle ground—safer than the black mountains with their daunting gates, and much faster than the lakes. We should travel southwest around the mountains by the Grimwalk."

"The Grimwalk!" scoffed Tal. "That is no middle ground. That's the enemy's backyard! Acsriot, why that way?"

Acsriot smiled slightly and replied, "No way is without peril. But think on this: Paragor turns his attention north to Mithegard. They are the closest settlement of Glimpses that he has not yet consumed. He will only be concerned with his 'backyard' if Alleble's armies march upon it. What will the Prince, so full of grand schemes and designs, care about twelve pilgrims wandering in that barren land?"

Acsriot paused and looked at each knight at the table. "It is a brazen move, I admit," he said. "But the Grimwalk is the fastest route. Not to mention it may present us with a rare opportunity to see something of the enemy's plans."

"See or be seen, I wonder?" murmured Captain Valithor. "Yet if your route provides such speed as to keep one free Glimpse from passing forever into the Gate of Despair, it is worth whatever harm may come to us. Acsriot, we will take your counsel and travel the Grimwalk."

"But, Captain!" objected Kaliam. "The Grimwalk is utterly exposed. We will have no shielding, no cover. And what of the weather? Should the *stilling* begin, where will we go? And . . . what if a Tem—"

"We will not be deterred by foul weather," said the Captain pensively. "Make certain that Kindle provides each of the twelve with his best cold gear. And Kaliam, you are a remarkable path finder. You have a responsibility for finding the safe way. I understand your feelings about the Grimwalk. I think, however, that this time, speed—not safety—is of greatest importance."

Aidan was thoroughly puzzled, but the rest of the group nodded solemnly, as if they always understood the Captain's decisions.

They were to leave early the next morning, two hours before sunrise, so Gwenne suggested that Aidan try to rest all he could. As they were walking together up one of the castle's main stairways, Aidan found himself full of questions again.

"Gwenne, what's so bad about the Grimwalk?"

"I've never traveled that way myself, for normally the King forbids us," she began. "But I know that it was once green and lush—filled with every blossom, shrub, and tree. Fruit and all kinds of produce once grew there naturally, and the rest of The Realm could produce no equal. But Paragor and his fallen minions laid waste to it. And it is said that through some dark arts, he cursed the land so that it would ever be empty and barren. What little still grows is poison, and the only creatures that remain there are wretched, evil things."

"The little creatures I saw in the mountains near the tunnels seemed harmless enough," Aidan thought out loud.

"Moonrascals, no doubt," she replied.

"Moonrascals?"

"They are little burrowing creatures with keen eyes and sharp claws. They live in the mountains and rocky canyons, but they only come out at night."

"So that's what they were!" said Aidan. "They led me to the tunnel through the mountain."

Gwenne nodded. "One of the many tunnels in the network they have created in the rocky places of The Realm. Their claws allow them to tunnel through soil, clay, even solid rock! Yes, they can be very helpful, but they are often mischievous as well. They have been known to amuse themselves by leading travelers in circles."

Aidan laughed.

"But not all creatures here are so good-natured. There are things in the dark kingdom of Paragory and hidden in caverns under mountains, things dreadful and dangerous: trolls, wraithlings, illgrets, and such. There are stories of ancient monsters told in whispers during the harvest season. But let us not speak of this any longer. You will find it difficult to shut your eyes with such things on your mind."

They reached the top of the last staircase, traversed the hall, and stopped just outside of Aidan's chamber. "Just one more thing, Gwenne."

"Yes?"

"Kaliam mentioned something about *stealing* on the Grimwalk?"

"*Stilling*," Gwenne corrected him. "And, Aidan, that's the last thing I should speak of before sleep. I'd rather tell you a dozen tales of wraithlings. No, you can ask Kaliam tomor—"

"Oh, come on, Gwenne," Aidan persisted. He was beginning to think he could handle most any fear.

"Very well, Aidan." She frowned and hesitated to make sure Aidan knew that she did not approve. Then, she explained. "*Stilling* is said to be one of the worst dangers of the Grimwalk. It happens before a storm strikes. Everything becomes motionless and quiet. There is not even a breath of wind. Some say a strange scent fills the air—metallic, like recently mined copper."

Copper? Aidan thought. *Like pennies?*

"Beasts sense it, I'm told," Gwenne continued. "The *stilling* affects them before it would a Glimpse. Something begins to happen to any living creature that is not active or moving. They feel a sudden lethargy and become sleepy. But what is actually occurring is that they are freezing to death from the inside out. *Stilling* will find any exposed flesh, seep into the body, and rapidly chill one's blood. In moments, a Glimpse will fall silent, sleep, and die. That is *stilling*."

Later that evening, Aidan blew out the candle and tried to sleep, wishing he hadn't urged Gwenne to tell him about the Grimwalk.

Aidan tossed and turned endlessly, mumbling and grumbling about everything that was on his mind. Gabby, the dragon who slept each night on the floor in Aidan's room, became annoyed with Aidan's fitful movements and decided to seek slumber somewhere else!

Aidan was about to give up on sleep when he heard a voice. Not plain spoken as if someone else was in the room. It was more a deep echo of something spoken long ago. It was that peaceful, dreamy voice Aidan had heard as he passed through The Door Within. This time he could understand the words. "Be anxious for nothing," the voice urged. And immediately Aidan became drowsy and began to drift off.

Into the Wild

Before sunup the next morning, Aidan, Gwenne, and the other Alleb Knights packed and saddled up for their journey. Each knight had a unicorn to ride. And there were seven more to help spread out their load of supplies. The pack-laden steeds meandered slowly, grazing on the dew-drenched grass on the southern side of the castle. With all living beings sound asleep, it was as quiet as The Realm could get—at least it was until Captain Valithor rode out of the castle to lead them.

"Look alive, thou lumpish, beetle-headed canker-blossoms!" he bellowed, the thrill of adventure filling his already powerful voice. "We must ride hard to reach the Cold River by nightfall. There we'll camp, for no one travels the Grimwalk at night! Then, we make haste for Mithegard to do great service for the King!"

One by one, they spurred their unicorns forward past the seven fountains, up the stone thoroughfare, out the main Gates, and into the predawn twilight.

They rode at full gallop. Even without much training on riding unicorns, Aidan kept up. But Aidan knew that was only because Captain Valithor had given Aidan the calmest, most surefooted unicorn in all of Alleble's stables. Still, it felt pretty good, thundering across the countryside, Sil Furyn at his side.

The warmth and peace of the King of Alleble coursed through each of them as they put leagues far behind. They kept on until just after the sun had risen. They stopped then, but only for a brief respite and a light meal.

As the sun began to climb, they were off again. The unicorns seemed tireless and raced at great speed for long spans of time. Even the stocky beast that bore Mallik had little trouble bearing his prodigious weight on pace with the other steeds.

Other than the heavy armor bouncing up and down while he rode, Aidan was having a splendid time. Of course, he knew danger lay ahead, but so far it had been like an incredible field trip with more breathtaking sights than he could count. Occasionally, friendly dragons of many colors circled above them, and huge oxenlike beasts called blackhorne herded in the tall grasses.

They traversed bridges of ancient stonework and heard the friendly brooks trickling beneath. Here and there they passed through bands of forest, some with the massive towering trees and others with thickets of thin willowy trees and carpets of fern. It was an altogether wondrous land, though unfortunately for Aidan, most of it went by in a blur.

They rode for hours, and Aidan's mind focused on very little. But as the sun began to set, their pace slowed considerably, allowing Aidan and Gwenne to talk.

"We shall be breaking for camp soon," Gwenne advised. "I see a branch of the Cold River up ahead."

"I'm ready to camp too," Aidan groaned. "But why camp at the Cold River? It doesn't sound all that comfortable."

"It is not comfortable at all," she explained. "But it is the last decent place for making a camp. And there is at least some tree cover. To go past that point would mean camping on the Grimwalk at night."

"Oh," said Aidan. "No thanks."

Gwenne grinned. "Just remember, you were the one who wanted to know so much about the dangers on the Grimwalk."

"I know," Aidan grumbled.

Finally, they reached the edge of the river. The sun slid down in the distance, an angry red mass between the distant peaks of the Prince's Crown. Captain Valithor held up a hand and commanded, "Halt, thou reeking, fly-bitten bootlickers! Unburden your unicorns and pitch camp!"

By the time they had their tents set up and sleeping blankets unfurled, the sun was gone, leaving nothing more than a faint glow on the western horizon. After sharing a small but tasty meal, the Twelve Knights of Alleble gathered around a pleasant fire. The Captain spoke quietly with Kaliam, Matthias, and Tal. Gwenne seemed to be recounting some humorous story with Mallik and the twins. In fact, everyone seemed to have someone to talk to . . . except Aidan.

He watched them, the eleven Glimpses, their cloaks swept back and armor gleaming with firelight. *They all look so heroic,* Aidan thought. *What am I doing here? I'm not even a Glimpse!*

Aidan turned from the fire and wandered over to sit on a fallen tree. Even though he had been dubbed a knight and encouraged by everyone, he could not shake the feeling that he did not belong. And even though he had been trained well and had worked harder at swordcraft than anything he had ever done, he still was terrified by the idea of fighting someone to the death.

"Hail, Twelfth Knight!" came the deep, gravelly voice of Mallik. He strode up, hefting his great hammer, and stood before Aidan. "I could not help noticing that you left our little fireside gathering."

"I, um, was getting a little too hot," Aidan lied. "Being so close to the fire with all this stuff on, y'know."

Mallik's eyes narrowed under his coppery brows.

"I grow weary of the twins—all their talk of shaft and bow! Care you for company, or . . . do you wish to be alone?"

"No, I don't want—I mean, I'd like your company. Would you like to sit down?"

"I don't sit," Mallik replied with a wink.

Aidan laughed. "Seems to me you sat fine in the saddle! Better than I did."

"Riding a unicorn is different," replied the Glimpse. "I need not bend very much in the saddle. It is getting on and off that truly tries my patience."

They shared a laugh, but it became silent and awkward for a few moments afterward. Mallik twisted one of the braids of his mustache. Aidan fingered the hilt of his sword. The stars began to poke out in the darkening sky.

"You must be feeling somewhat homesick," said Mallik. "Being so far from your home will stretch you like nothing else can."

"Yeah, I guess," Aidan replied. "I do miss my mom and dad. And I miss my friend Robby. But I feel like I'm the only one who doesn't belong."

Mallik nodded. The light of the fire flickered in his eyes. "Lad, I think I know a bit of what that feels like. Swearing allegiance to

King Eliam didn't exactly make me the most popular Glimpse in the Blue Mountain Provinces."

"What do you mean?" said Aidan, leaning forward.

"Well, nowadays, most of my people are followers of King Eliam, and we fly the banner of Alleble. But many years ago, forty years as you would reckon it, the Blue Mountain Provinces were governed by its own Glimpses. We had our own king too, King Brower—a decent Glimpse really, but stubborn and proud like the rest of us. We didn't want Paragory or Alleble to rule over us—though we traded goods with both kingdoms. So when I came back from Alleble with eyes glinting blue, nobody wanted to have anything to do with me."

"Blue eyes?" Aidan said. "What does that have to do with anything?"

"Why, the eyes gave it away!" Mallik replied. "It was a sign that I had chosen. What are you, blind, Sir Aidan? Or have you not noticed that no matter what the base color of anyone's eyes, they all glint blue if you've chosen to side with King Eliam?"

Aidan almost fell off the log, the knowledge hit him so hard. "So that's why everyone in our team, everyone in Alleble . . . yes, now I understand."

"Blue is a color of purity," Mallik explained. "And ever since the Prince; nay, he is no prince! Ever since that traitor Paragor was thrown down, the eyes of every Glimpse tell the tale of whom they serve. But when we get to Mithegard, you will see their eyes shine out green, for that is the color for the undecided—for those who are their own masters. And if we meet the enemy, Aidan, the foul Glimpses who follow Paragor, their eyes will glint red—red for the innocent blood they spilled in the rebellion."

An image of blood-red eyes flashed into Aidan's mind, and he pulled his cloak tighter around him.

"I wonder that you had not already learned this," Mallik said.

"But it is good that you know. So you can understand how my people reacted to a 'blue eye' in a sea of green. They shunned me, made me feel like an outsider in my own land. I, uh . . . hope we haven't treated you so poorly?"

"No, not at all," Aidan replied. "The Captain's been a little harsh, but he treats everyone that way. Even so, I know he cares. Everyone seems to care. Oh, I don't know what my problem is."

"Problem, eh?" Mallik grinned. "I have found that there are very few problems in life that cannot be solved with a great big hammer!"

This time Aidan did fall off the log. He lay on the ground and laughed so hard it hurt! With a hand from Mallik, he finally got up.

"Thanks, Mallik," Aidan said, "for everything."

"We're together in this, lad," he said. "Remember that."

Weariness from the journey caught up with them all, and each retired to his or her tent for the night. Aidan was about to snuff the candle in his lantern, but the urge hit him to use the bathroom. Of course, they had no portable toilets in the wilderness of Alleble, so Aidan wandered off to find a private place. He walked away from the tents and toward the edge of the Cold River. It was just a narrow branch of the river—barely a running leap to the other side, if one was interested. Aidan had no interest in leaping across, for, somehow, the other side of the river seemed spookier. There were tall, leafless trees with gnarled branches swimming in a sea of waist-high dead grass that brushed this way and that in the chilling breeze. No, Aidan would wait until he had the other eleven Knights of Alleble with him before he crossed to that side of the Cold River!

It did look cold too. Aidan looked down from the edge into the inky black water that was far too still for a river. Aidan imagined what dark things could inhabit such water—long, segmented gray worms, slimy black fish with bulging eyes, sleek lizards, or snakes! *Blech!* Aidan shivered and stepped back from the edge.

It was not easy undoing his breeches, but he managed. He stood there, taking care of business, when he saw a flicker of light on the other side of the river. He looked up and squinted, but it was too far away to identify. Only seconds later, another light flashed on— bright yellow, a little closer. Then, two or three more lights. Suddenly, lots of them, maybe twenty or so—in the tall grass, near the trees, some only thirty yards away! Aidan's mind whirled in a frantic attempt to think. There were more now, perhaps a hundred, but what could—*Oh no! TORCHES!*

Aidan stood paralyzed. Torches could mean only one thing: The wicked Knights of Paragory had somehow found them!

Aidan thought about the others—he had to warn them! If more than a hundred Paragor Knights attacked their little band of twelve with no warning, they would all be slaughtered! That thought urged Aidan to move. He yanked up his breeches, secured them as best he could, and raced back for camp. He began screaming urgently, "The Paragor Knights! They've found us! Wake up! They're here! Captain Valithor, the Paragor Knights are here!"

Aidan expected to feel an arrow stab into his back as he ran closer to camp, but somehow he was able to keep running and screaming. In a matter of seconds, Captain Valithor and the others burst forth from the camp. Nock and Bolt, arrows fit to their bowstrings, were up in the crooks of a tree. Mallik, his hammer at the ready, bounded to Aidan's side.

"Where, Sir Aidan? Where are they?" bellowed Captain Valithor, scanning for the enemy.

"Across the river . . . there, you can see their torches!" Aidan shouted back.

The knights ran fiercely to the river's edge and looked across, but then, something peculiar happened. The intensity of battle vanished from their faces, and to Aidan's complete surprise, they all started laughing.

"What . . . what's going on?" Aidan asked, feeling frustrated.

That seemed to make things worse, for several of the knights were holding their sides from the pain of laughter. Kaliam and Acsriot actually fell to the ground and heaved in hysterical fits!

"Hey!" Aidan screamed. "Why are you all laughing? Huh? Aren't you worried about the Paragor Knights?"

Finally, after the roar simmered down to small bursts of snickers and giggles, Captain Valithor came over and put a hand on Aidan's shoulder.

"Come, Sir Aidan," he said tenderly, while obviously trying not to break into fresh laughter. "Come, let us go look at your Knights of Paragor!"

With that, the powerful Captain took Aidan by the hand and led him over to the river's edge. Then, to Aidan's horror, the Captain took Aidan under one arm like a sack of potatoes and jumped across the river to the other bank. He carried Aidan over to the closest light and put him down. When Aidan looked closely at the light, he saw that it wasn't a torch after all. It was a web nestled between the stalks of grass. And in the web was a spider with a glowing rear end that lit up all the web around it.

"They're called lantern spiders, Sir Aidan," explained the Captain to Aidan's complete embarrassment. "Their abdomens light up to attract moths and other insects into their webs."

The other knights stood watching from the other bank and

burst into a new round of laughs. Gwenne did her best to shush them, but a moment later, something else happened and even Gwenne could not restrain herself.

As Captain Valithor again picked up Aidan and leaped across the Cold River, Aidan's breeches, which he had not yet secured properly, slid right off his legs and fell into the murky water.

Aidan landed on the other bank wearing nothing but a night-shirt and long underwear.

Kaliam used his broadsword to fish Aidan's sodden breeches from the water. He handed them to Aidan, grinned, and walked back to his tent. Aidan had never felt so mortified in his entire life. First, he had scared everyone half to death because of some stupid glowing spiders! Then he had pretty much flashed all of his com-panions! At least no one teased him about it as they walked back to camp—except, of course, Gwenne, who couldn't resist.

"Well, Sir Aidan," she said, biting her tongue to keep from laughing, "I guess those spiders just scared the pants off of you, eh?"

Aidan just gritted his teeth and ignored her. *Some courageous knight I am!* he thought, flopping down on his fur-lined bedroll. *What good could I possibly be on this adventure? Maybe I could be the Royal Jester, and when the knights become sad, I could do something stupid to make everyone laugh!*

Thoughts like those picked at Aidan until he fell into a light sleep. A few hours later, in the darkest, quietest part of the night, a small sound awoke Aidan.

Nothing alarming, just a sound that broke the silence of the sleeping world in the wee hours. Instead of going out, Aidan lifted up one corner of his tent to see what had made the sound. He was thinking that perhaps a moonrascal was crawling around out there looking for leftovers from their dinner.

It wasn't a moonrascal at all. It was Acsriot, and he appeared to be leaving the camp. Curious, Aidan crept out of his tent to see where Acsriot was going. Aidan was just in time to see Acsriot leap over the Cold River and disappear into the dead grass and the darkness beyond.

Humph, Aidan thought, scratching his head and going back into his tent. *I guess Glimpses need to go sometimes too!*

Aidan went quickly back to sleep, laughing quietly to himself as he imagined Acsriot being frightened by a bunch of lantern spiders.

THE GRIMWALK

The Twelve Knights of Alleble had been traveling for hours. At daybreak, they had donned their cold gear and set out across a ford over the river on their way to the Grimwalk.

Aidan noticed the temperature decreasing as they rode closer to places ruined by the Prince. He was glad for the fur-lined breeches and surcoat.

The ground became pitted and hard. Old gray waste grass stuck out here and there like whiskers. Most trees were broken as if by wind or lightning.

Ominous gray clouds had rolled in as well, devouring every last trace of blue sky. The twelve rode slowly due to the uneven ground. The ever-present dreariness cast a pall over them, and no one spoke for quite some time.

Abruptly, Captain Valithor held up a hand and halted their journey. He gestured for the knights to circle their unicorns closely around him before he spoke.

"Alleb Knights, on the other side of the next ridge is the deso-
late land called Grimwalk," he began.

"It can't get any more dreary than this, can it?" asked Aidan, not
intending to interrupt but accidentally thinking aloud.

The Captain sent a harsh look to Aidan but softened it immediately. "The half-dead lands from the Cold River to this point are
indeed injured and bereft of anything green. But at least here we can
still be warmed by thoughts of green blossoming things, strong root,
and smooth bough. But gird yourselves, knights, for the Grimwalk
will rob you of the hope of ever seeing a green thing again. It is poisoned with despair, which is the enemy's most powerful weapon."

Aidan swallowed.

"This is the most dangerous part of our journey," Valithor continued. "For we will be out in the open in a treacherous land. The
Prince should be looking for us in other places, but we must be
wary. His spies are everywhere."

"Captain, have you taken note of the weather?" asked Kaliam
anxiously.

"I have. Indeed . . . it does not fill me with hope, though I still feel
Acsriot was right in suggesting we go this way. Come now, let us travel
on. We need to keep a steady pace to cross the Grimwalk by nightfall."

Aidan wasn't sure what to expect when he first saw the
Grimwalk, but as they crossed the last rocky ridge and looked down
into the vast valley below, Aidan felt as if every ounce of hope was
sucked from his heart. He looked upon the sad land and wept.

It was miles and miles of dead land. Other than a few patches of
leftover snow, the land was entirely black as if poisoned and rotten.

Here and there were icy pools of dark liquid that gave no reflection, and as their unicorns marched slowly forward, the ground
crunched like the snapping of brittle bones left there to rot.

It was as if the loss of all things green and beautiful had created a horrible vacuum, and any who trod upon that barren land would be doomed to grow slowly cold, wither, and die. Aidan kept his unicorn moving.

Across the Grimwalk, far off in the distance, stood the menacing twin mountains called the Prince's Crown. Aidan had seen them from another side, from another vantage point where there were living things and some hope. But there was no hope on the Grimwalk.

To the right of the two jagged peaks were smaller mountains, and eventually ridges and foothills. Tendrils of dark smoke issued up from behind these ridges, and Aidan knew that the Gates of Despair were there. He felt as if an icy claw were around his heart.

"Do not look, Aidan," Gwenne said. "It will only drag your spirit down."

Aidan tried to turn away, but he felt compelled to look. Echoes of a voice came from shadows of memory. *Come to the darkness. You can hide there. Come.*

Aidan stared at the height of the Prince's Crown and then down at the mountains' knees shrouded in a gray, unhappy mist. For the first time, he became aware that there was something there. It was far away, but he saw that there was an immense fortress. It seemed not built from the ground up, but rather hewn, gouged from the black rock of the mountains. There were dark towers, cruel-looking keeps, and sharp parapets. Here and there, like the empty sockets of a skull, were irregular windows and gates. And surrounding it all were massive, impenetrable-looking walls.

Aidan was drowning in despair when Gwenne reached out and touched him. Her hand was warm. He looked upon her. Her smile was warmer. And there was a trace of hope reborn in him.

"Remember," she said. "Never alone."

"Never alone," Aidan repeated. And he found that it brought peace to his troubled heart. They spurred their unicorns lightly and began their crossing of the Grimwalk.

As the party of twelve continued, the temperature fell lower still. They were all bundled as tightly as they could make themselves, but the frigid wind found every open spot and bit at any exposed skin. In a day, they had gone from a comfortable spring in Alleble into the dead of winter, and the low, puffy clouds threatened to make it more wintry.

Aidan looked ahead at Captain Valithor who was talking quietly with Eleazar. "You have any idea what they're talking about?" Aidan asked Gwenne, who was riding beside him.

"They often speak of deep things," she said. "But my guess is they are becoming more concerned about the weather."

"Why? Is it going to storm?"

"Yes," she replied, pointing skyward. "Look at the clouds. Do you see how dark they are? And notice the slight purplish color. I am certain that a snowstorm's coming."

"Snow?"

Gwenne pointed to the dark castle at the foot of the Prince's Crown. "The Prince has many dark powers, Sir Aidan, and his heart is cold and violent. Some of the most terrible storms occur in this land, and it snows here often."

Just then, one of the pack unicorns began to tug at its reins.

"Easy, easy!" yelled Eleazar. Farix rode up to help try to calm the steed.

"Something has her spooked," Farix said.

"Is it any wonder, in such a place?" asked Eleazar.

They were able to restrain the unicorn, but only to a point. She still seemed uneasy. In fact, all of the steeds became restless, as if they might buck at any moment. Aidan had no idea what he would do if his unicorn started to buck.

No words were spoken as their party of twelve rode on.

It was utterly silent. The chill breeze had stopped completely. Even the clop of hooves seemed muffled. And it seemed to Aidan that their pace had slowed down considerably. He rubbed his eyes.

How long have we been riding? he wondered. It felt like an eternity, and Aidan was exhausted. He shrugged his shoulders. He wanted to rest. Maybe they would all take a break soon. He felt so sleepy. And there was a strange smell.

A hand grabbed Aidan's arm. "Aidan!" a voice said.

"Aidan, wake up!" It was Gwenne. "Aidan, wake up! You've got to move! Captain Valithor, come quickly! Aidan, please move!"

"Look alert, thou fog-pated slowcoach! Get your arms moving, RIGHT NOW!!" Aidan felt a roar of heat surge through him, and there were Captain Valithor and Gwenne. Their eyes were wide, and then they broke into relieved smiles.

"The *stilling*, Aidan. It is happening," Gwenne cried. "It almost took you!"

"Hear me, Knights of Alleble!" Captain Valithor's voice rang out. "We must push forward as fast as we can! Watch the ground for ruts, but get the unicorns moving! The *stilling* has come—"

Several of the unicorns reared. Mallik fought to stay in the saddle. Eleazar shouted, "Farix, get her up! Get her up now!"

Farix wheeled his steed around to the pack unicorn that had been so restless earlier. It was beginning to slowly kneel several yards back.

Farix grabbed her reins. "Get up, Girl! Stand!" he called to her. But it was too late.

Aidan watched in horror as the unicorn went to her knees. She swayed drowsily and lay down. The unicorn became unnaturally still. Her eyes were wide, lids rimmed with blue. But she was no longer breathing.

Aidan realized that he, too, had almost died. He spurred his unicorn and hugged himself to keep warm. Immediately, the wind kicked up, and snowflakes began swirling down from the angry sky. In a matter of minutes the ground was dusted in white.

"Faster, Aidan!" Gwenne called, and she was riding beside him.

"I'm trying, Gwenne!" Aidan spurred his steed again, and it responded with a burst of speed. Rigid icy flakes cut into Aidan's eyes and stung so fiercely he had to turn his head to the side as he rode. Through waves of howling white, Aidan discovered that there were some living things on the Grimwalk after all. A pair of moonrascals peeked over the edge of an opening in the ground. While the first moonrascals Aidan had seen were as black as the rock of the Prince's Crown, these were downy white and blended in with the snow that poured all around them. In a moment, they disappeared, apparently into their tunnels beneath the surface.

"Gwenne," Aidan called out. "I just saw a couple of moonrascals!"

"What?" she called back. "I can barely hear you!"

"Never mind!" he yelled, his voice quick-frozen and stolen away by the wind.

Captain Valithor was just a gray shadow in the swirling white landscape ahead. At last, he halted the group and motioned for the others to circle around him. The Captain's bushy, snow-flecked eyebrows furrowed in deep concern as he began to speak.

"We dare not stop for long, my good Knights of Alleble!" he yelled hoarsely over the wind. "The *stilling*, I fear, is just the first assault of a fierce storm that could wreak havoc on our mission, and I—"

Kaliam interrupted. "You don't think that a Tem—"

The Captain raised his hand to silence Kaliam. "Do not say it! But we must be ready if it comes! We must decide now!" roared the Captain. "Either press on or turn back, for there is no shelter on the Grimwalk!"

No one spoke. Aidan looked into the eyes of every Glimpse in the circle—though Acsriot had drawn his hood down to shield his face from the wind.

There was steely determination in their eyes, and Aidan knew they would not turn back.

"Then valiant knights," bellowed the Captain, "we ri—"

A brilliant, blinding flash of purple lit up the Grimwalk, followed by a deafening clap of thunder.

The blast startled the unicorns, and most of them reared back on their hind legs. Aidan wasn't a very skilled rider, and he fell right off and landed hard on the frozen ground. It was difficult for him to stand back up, for his armor was heavy and he was disoriented from the fall. Many of the other knights were struggling to settle their unicorns, and Aidan hoped he would not be trampled. Mad with fear, they stamped and thudded closer. Captain Valithor, who alone had managed to quiet his steed, rode in front of the terrified beasts. He seemed to have some way with the unicorns, and they became calm again. For the moment, Aidan was safe. He yelled out to thank his commander, but Captain Valithor had already ridden a few paces ahead.

There the Captain seemed to be staring through the strengthening storm in the direction of the mountains. Lightning flashed again, bathing the Captain in eerie purple light. The thunder followed, crashing and echoing terribly off the mountains.

Aidan finally made it to his feet. The wind wailed, but there was another sound. It was a peculiar deep humming sort of noise— growing louder each moment.

The sound became louder still, and Aidan thought it was like the roar of an enormous freight train barreling their way. The Captain turned abruptly and rode back to the other knights.

"It's a Tempest!" he bellowed. "Fly back! Fly back to the Cold River! Ride reckless and do not stop! A Tempest is upon us!"

Aidan's thoughts raced. *A Tempest!!* He looked around for someone to help him.

Before anyone could act, however, the roar of a dragon pierced the commotion of the storm. Acsriot rode quickly away from the others, stopped, and turned toward them. Aidan was shocked. Acsriot was laughing.

"Enjoy the weather, you fools!" he shrieked, and a white dragon materialized from the clouds and swooped down. The winged beast fought the wind to hover above Acsriot before finally grasping his outstretched arms and lifting him from his saddle. Aidan watched in horror as the blue flicker in Acsriot's eyes burned away and kindled to bright red, and the dragon whisked him away into the sky.

Captain Valithor drew Fury from its sheath and slashed the air as he roared. "Mark my words, Acsriot!" he yelled. "You will fall by my sword for this treachery!"

Aidan realized then that Acsriot had betrayed them all along. Betrayed them before they even left Alleble when he suggested they travel the Grimwalk. Betrayed them when he left camp late the night before, no doubt to meet a spy of the enemy. Betrayed them so that the dark Prince could conjure some perilous storm to waylay their team where there was no shelter.

Aidan turned and looked through the blowing snow at the horizon. It was dark, but there was something there, something enormous. Lightning flashed, and Aidan saw a menacing shadow growing in the distance.

Again, Captain Valithor's voice rang out. "Ride for your lives! The Tempest is upon us! Ride!"

Lightning struck again—jagged, violent streaks in the sky. In the fierce but momentary flash of light, Aidan saw the unmistakable form of a tornado—only it wasn't like the ones he'd seen on TV. This one reached down from the sky but then went sideways like an immense steamroller of wind and snow. With each streak of lightning, Aidan watched as the Tempest churned closer, devouring both the sky and the ground as it came.

The deep, continuous roar of the Tempest shook the ground and rattled Aidan's armor. The swirling winds pelted him on all sides with snow, ice, and frozen debris. The unicorns bucked and galloped in terrified circles, and the knights fought for control. The wind blew so fiercely that no one could hear anything but the storm. The only Glimpse Aidan could see was Gwenne. Her unicorn was going berserk with fear. Aidan knew he had to help, so he ran toward Gwenne, dodging the poor unicorn's frantic kicks. He reached up for Gwenne's belt and pulled her off the unicorn. She fell heavily on top of him.

As they struggled to their feet, another flash of lightning showed them that the Tempest was closing in, ripping up the Grimwalk and everything else in its path. They were doomed. They were in the middle of a vast wasteland with no shelter. But then Aidan had it! The moonrascals! Without a word, Aidan grabbed Gwenne by the arm and dragged her in the direction he thought the moonrascals had been. He was right! There were two small openings in the ground where the moonrascals had burrowed. One looked like it might be barely large enough for a person to fit through. They had no choice. The Tempest was there. Hoping it would protect them from the deadly storm, they each dropped down into the tunnel.

SHORTCUT

In the tunnel, Aidan and Gwenne could hear the howling winds of the Tempest churning up the Grimwalk above the opening.

They found themselves sliding on their rear ends and picking up speed. Gwenne was ahead of Aidan, and she was the first to exit the tunnel. She landed with a clumsy crash and looked up just as Aidan slammed into her.

They stood up awkwardly and looked around. They found they were in an underground chamber of some kind, lit dimly by several glowing streaks gouged into the ceiling. The chamber was circular and had other openings to tunnels all around.

Aidan was the first to notice they were not alone.

"Look!" he pointed. "Look, Gwenne, moonrascals!"

Gwenne did look, and huddled in several of the tunnel openings were little groups of white moonrascals. They stared at Aidan and Gwenne with their peculiar glowing eyes as if trying to decide if their uninvited guests were friends or foes. Then, one by one, the moonrascals scurried away up or down the various tunnels.

Aidan and Gwenne stood for a moment in awkward silence. The reality of what had just happened came crashing down on them. Aidan was the first to speak.

"Gwenne, the other knights, is there any chance? I mean . . . are they?"

"If anyone was caught in the Tempest, yes . . . they are gone," Gwenne confirmed grimly.

Memories flashed through Aidan's mind. During the time he'd spent with the knights, many had become his friends. Aidan felt as if his insides were being crushed.

"But if there is anyone besides the King of Alleble who could somehow lead the knights to safety, it would be the noble Captain Valithor."

Aidan nodded. *Valithor, Mallik, the twins—all gone in an instant. How could this happen?* Aidan searched his heart for answers. There were none.

"What now?" Aidan asked. "Do we try to climb back up that tunnel?"

"I don't think that will work," Gwenne replied. "Those tunnels are slippery, and even if we could somehow climb, the Tempest has probably filled in the top of the tunnel with snow and debris."

"What about these other tunnels? Are they blocked too? Are we trapped underground then?" Aidan asked, pointing frantically at the openings all around the chamber.

"Aidan, I know it's hard," Gwenne said. "But with King Eliam's help, we will find a way. Most of the tunnels come out somewhere on the Grimwalk. It may be that they are not all blocked."

"So, what if we do get back out on the Grimwalk? What'll we

do then?" Aidan asked pathetically. "Eleazar was supposed to meet with the King of Mithegard, but he's gone. Captain Valithor too. I mean, it's just the two of us. Are we just supposed to go back out there and plod our way to Mithegard without any help?"

"Thanks to that double-crossing, foul Glimpse Acsriot, the Grimwalk will probably be crawling with Paragor Knights," Gwenne raged. "I know we are sworn to complete our mission, but I don't see how—"

"Shhhh . . . I hear something," Aidan whispered. There came a scratching sound from one of the tunnels. Aidan looked from opening to opening, and then he saw it! There was a glowing arrow on the inside of one of the tunnels.

Aidan had been on the verge of despair, but now there was something he could grab hold of, a thin strand of hope. "Look, Gwenne!" Aidan exclaimed excitedly. "The moonrascals are trying to help us! I bet that tunnel will lead us somewhere safe. Maybe even to Alleble!"

"Alleble is leagues away," Gwenne argued. "And so close to Paragory, how do you know that those snowy moonrascals are not under a spell of the Prince? That tunnel could lead us right to the enemy's front door!"

"Yeah, but what choice do we have?" Aidan said. "We can't just stay here!"

Reluctantly, Gwenne agreed. She paused for a moment, looked thoughtful, and then said, "You have made quite a knight, after all, you know. With the Tempest bearing down on us, you could have made other decisions, and the disaster would be complete. When you pulled me off my unicorn and threw me into the tunnel, you . . . you saved my life."

"C'mon," Aidan said. "You're acting like I did something brave. I was scared out of my wits when the Tempest came tearing through!"

"That is the very essence of bravery," she said. "We all become frightened in the face of danger, but it is those few, like you, who act in spite of their fear—who are the heroes."

Me? A hero? Aidan thought. *If Mom and Dad . . . if Robby could see me now.*

While Aidan was imagining sharing his adventures with Robby, Gwenne came close to him and kissed him on the cheek. All the thoughts in Aidan's mind quickly turned to mush! He felt dizzy and short of breath, and the place on his cheek Gwenne had kissed felt warm and tingly.

"Sir Aidan," Gwenne called, snapping Aidan out of the trance. "Shall we travel this tunnel?"

"Verily, we shall," Aidan replied, trying to sound herolike.

The tunnels had been created by moonrascals for moonrascals—not humans. It was always night in those narrow passages, and the air was thin and foul-smelling. Aidan led the way, but he didn't feel much like a leader. His heart raced the whole time, and he felt like he could barely breathe as he inched along the passage. It seemed like forever passed between each glowing arrow, but they always appeared.

Every once in a while the tunnel would split, and a glowing arrow would direct them left or right. The moonrascals were obviously leading them somewhere.

The tunnel had been level for several hours, but it gradually began to rise.

"We're going up," Aidan whispered back to Gwenne. "Maybe we'll come out soon."

"I hope so," Gwenne replied. "My knees are aching rather fiercely!"

But they did not come out soon.

The tunnel curled, swerved, and banked. Occasionally, it would level out for a time, but it always began to rise again. Though their straining muscles suggested that they had been crawling for an eternity, Aidan and Gwenne had lost any real sense of time.

"How many arrows have there been?" Gwenne asked.

"I stopped counting," Aidan admitted. "I think there were thirty-three when I stopped, but that was hours ago."

More time passed, and Aidan simply fell over on his side.

"How can it keep going up like this?" Aidan asked, weariness in his voice.

"I do not understand it either," Gwenne agreed. She fell to the side of the tunnel. "By my reckoning we should have come out by now. Though where we might come out, I have no idea. There have been so many turns, I have completely lost any sense of direction."

After another couple of hours of climbing, Aidan felt a warm breath of wind sail through his hair. It was startling in the dark.

"Did you feel that?" he asked.

"Yes, we could be nearing the surface!" she replied excitedly.

They increased the speed of their climb, hoping to find an exit soon, but what they found was a large hole in the floor of the tunnel. It had glowing arrows all around it.

"Uh-oh," Aidan muttered.

"What?" Gwenne asked, straining to see.

"There's a hole with arrows around it. I think it's a slide!"

"A slide? You mean . . . like the one in the hole when the Tempest was coming?" she asked.

"Yes, exactly. I think this is another one. And unless you want to crawl all the way back the way we came, it looks like this is the only way. The tunnel ends here."

"There is no way we are going back," Gwenne argued.

"I know, but I feel like we're so high up . . ." Aidan was unsure. The warm breeze wafted up through the hole. *What if the slide leads to some fiery dungeon in the pits of Paragory?* he thought.

"Look, Sir Aidan," Gwenne said as if reading his mind, "we need to go. We will die anyway if we stay in these dreaded tunnels any longer." With that, Gwenne gave Aidan a surprisingly strong push, and he tumbled into the hole. Gwenne quickly eased herself over the edge, and just like that, they were gone.

SPEED! It was the only word Aidan could think about as he screamed headfirst down the tunnel slide. He had always enjoyed the power dive of a roller coaster, but this was ridiculous! It was almost straight down, and his hair whipped in his eyes as he struggled to see what was ahead. Aidan felt his cheeks stretching backward as he picked up even more velocity.

He tried to bring his hands up over his head in case he hit something, but the wind pressure kept his arms pinned to his sides. *Besides,* he thought, *if I hit anything going this fast, it won't matter one bit if I have my hands over my head.*

Gwenne didn't know it, but she was sliding only about twenty yards behind Aidan. She couldn't hear Aidan screaming because the wind whistled in her ears as she sped down the slide.

They continued to plummet for several minutes, accelerating as they went, but suddenly, the slide began to bottom out. It curved at the bottom and then went back up.

Aidan's stomach did flip-flops as he hit the bottom of the slide and jetted up the other side. He opened his eyes a crack and saw he was nearing a light—it was an opening. *Yes!* he thought. *A way out!*

But he was going too fast. What good would it do to escape the tunnel, only to slam into a rockface or a tree trunk at a hundred miles an hour? But there was nothing he could do.

With a yelp, Aidan launched from the tunnel like he had been shot out of a cannon. When he opened his eyes, he found himself sailing through the air far above the ground. He looked down and saw that his momentum was carrying him through the air over some rocky foothills and then over some trees. But slowly the speed from his launch started to wear off, and he began to arc downward.

That's it! Aidan thought. *I'm dead. I'm going to smash into a tree or splatter all over the ground somewhere!*

He screamed as he looked ahead and saw the ground rising up to greet him. He closed his eyes and tried to curl into a ball just before impact.

Gwenne shot out of the tunnel feetfirst, so the only thing she could see as she flew was the sky. But she could feel herself starting to fall, and she, too, thought the end was near.

They hit the ground in different spots, fortunately, but rather than being smashed to bits on hard ground, they bounced and rolled on something purple and very springy. Aidan rolled a couple of times and flopped onto his back.

Relieved to be alive, Aidan stood up, wiped something sticky off of his face, and turned to look for Gwenne. She stood up about fifteen feet away. And she was laughing hysterically.

"What?!" Aidan yelled.

"You . . . you have . . ." She was laughing too hard to speak clearly. "You have moss hanging out of your nose!"

Turning bright red, Aidan swiped at his nose. Sure enough, there was plenty of purple moss up there! It was everywhere else too. The force of impact had jammed tons of the stuff into his hair, behind his ears, and all over his armor. Aidan shook his head, laughed, and let himself fall backward into the moss. It was good to be alive!

After cleaning themselves off, they climbed down from the huge mound of purple moss.

"The moonrascals' tunnel must have taken us under the Prince's Crown!" Gwenne announced, looking back at their exit from the tunnel. "Those tunnels are an incredible shortcut! Sir Aidan, do you know where we are?"

"Near Alleble, I hope?" Aidan answered.

"Nay, Sir Aidan. Apparently, the King of Alleble has decided that we must continue our quest without the other knights. Look over there, not five miles from here . . . Mithegard!"

Aidan looked in the direction Gwenne had pointed. Indeed, across the fields, dotted with mounds of that purple moss, was a beautiful city with seven towers. It was Mithegard—their destination!

MITHEGARD

Their quest had begun with Twelve Knights, but in a matter of days, decimated by a Tempest and treason, their number had dwindled to two. And the storm on the Grimwalk had taken more than just their companions. They had no unicorns, no spare clothing, no fresh water, and very little food. After eating the last of the dried meat from their pouches, Aidan and Gwenne rested for a short time before making their way between huge humps of moss across the plains to Mithegard. Now it was up to the two of them to complete the mission for King Eliam and the Kingdom of Alleble.

"So the Glimpses of Mithegard haven't decided whether to join Paragory or Alleble?" Aidan asked, still picking pieces of purple moss out of his hair. "And we're supposed to help them understand that Alleble is the right way to go?"

"Yes, Aidan," Gwenne replied. "Mithegard is an ancient kingdom, and they have great pride in their own sovereignty. For ages, they have turned aside all offers of allegiance from Paragory, as well as those from Alleble. It is said, however, that their new ruler, King Ravelle, is more open to agreements."

"But if the Prince is so totally evil, why would anyone follow him?" Aidan asked.

Gwenne smiled sadly. "Lies, Sir Aidan . . . lies. You see, the Prince promises wealth, power, fame—anything a Glimpse might desire! He gives them all of these things to try to trick them out of what they truly need . . . the peace and love that can be found only in the Kingdom of Alleble. Many Glimpses are fooled by the Prince and willingly become his servants. He is wicked but cunning beyond compare."

"So what chance will the two of us have compared to the might of the Prince and his armies?"

Looking him straight in his eyes, she replied, "Very little chance, Aidan. Even were our party of twelve still intact, we would accomplish nothing by force of arms. Mithegard is a powerful realm. Their mounted cavalry is fierce, and their foot soldiers are valiant. It is for this reason alone that Paragor has not before now attempted to overthrow Mithegard by force. But his dark armies have grown. Even the famed Seven Towers of Mithegard may not withstand Paragor's new strength. And so, we come bearing only truth, our greatest weapon. We bring King Eliam's offer in peace—and should they refuse, we will depart in peace."

Aidan pondered Gwenne's words as they approached the great outer walls of the city. Mithegard was not as vast or as tall as Alleble, but its grandeur was in the craft of its design.

"Mallik told me once that his people constructed these walls," Gwenne explained. "They are not made with stones and mortar in the traditional way. Instead, his people carved whole slivers of granite

from the Blue Mountains and cut them into solid blocks as tall as a
man and as wide as a young dragon, tail to snout. Do you see the blue
color in the stone of the walls?"

"Yes; it's in the castle too!" Aidan replied, looking up beyond
the walls to the magnificent blue castle with seven towers.

"Mallik's people carried each block sixty leagues," Gwenne continued. "Then, they were shaped and assembled such that they fit
together perfectly, so perfectly that not even a hair can be passed
through their joints."

Aidan had trouble carrying a couple of gallons of milk from the
van to the house. He could not imagine what a massive block of
solid granite would weigh. He thought of how strong and crafty the
Glimpses of the Blue Mountains must be. And . . . he thought of
Mallik.

Mithegard's front gate, an enormous triple *portcullis,* was raised,
and a pair of tall, well-armed Glimpse knights stood at attention on
each side of the entrance. Each of the Mithegard Knights wore a
pale blue tunic over his shining armor. They stared at Aidan and
Gwenne as they approached. Aidan stared back, for there was something different about these Glimpses, but he wasn't sure what.

"A little far away from home, are we?" one of the Mithegard
Knights asked scornfully. "We seldom have such young visitors from
Alleble!"

The other Mithegard Knights laughed. "Yes, do the elders in
your land allow their youths to venture out so far from home?"

Aidan bit his tongue. *Okay, I'm pretty much a little squirt,* he
thought. *But insulting Gwenne? This has to stop!*

Hand on the hilt of Sil Furyn, Aidan stepped toward the first knight, but Gwenne gently but firmly held out an arm to hold Aidan back.

"We have business in the city," said Gwenne. "We were told that Glimpses here are friendly, so we should have no fear to travel here."

"Oh, but we are friendly," said the first knight. He made a show of stooping so he could look eye to eye with Aidan. "And you are welcome to enter. Join the many guests who have arrived of late. And, there's a toy shop near the fifth tower for your, hmmm, business."

All four of the knights shared a great laugh at this. Aidan wanted to draw his sword and cut off the Glimpse's nose. *Toys, indeed!*

Aidan and Gwenne entered the walled city and marveled at the formidable defenses. Beyond the first wall and the triple portcullis stood another immense wall, this one much higher and pitted with narrow windows, through which volleys of arrows could be fired. Bands of archers could just barely be seen along the length of the inner wall.

As they passed through the gatehouse of the inner wall, they saw enormous barracks for Mithegard's soldiers. Aidan had no doubt that knights armed to the teeth would issue forth like hornets if the city was attacked.

Once beyond the defenses, they found Mithegard strangely empty. There were a few Glimpses here and there: a blacksmith sitting by his hot kiln and hammering out shoes for a unicorn, a woman hanging wedges of various cheeses in a storefront window, and, of course, Glimpse children scurrying about. But it wasn't the expected bustle of thousands of Glimpses, out traveling and doing business on the city's many shop-filled avenues.

"So, where is everyone?" Aidan asked. "The guards said there are a lot of visitors."

"I do not know, Sir Aidan," Gwenne replied. "Seeing this grand city so lifeless gives me an uneasy feeling."

"Maybe we should go to the castle. There has to be someone there," Aidan suggested.

"Yes," Gwenne agreed. "Perhaps we can find answers there."

They navigated the city's many streets until, finally, they arrived at the castle's front gate. It was open, but there were four more Mithegard Knights standing guard.

Aidan and Gwenne made it clear that they were planning to cross the drawbridge and enter the castle. But the knights moved in front of the gate to block them.

"Where do you think you are going, young Allebs?" one of the knights asked.

Not again! Aidan thought.

"We are here to see the King of Mithegard," Gwenne answered, trying to sound important. She apparently was also fed up with being called a child. "We are on an errand for His Majesty, the noble King Eliam of Alleble."

"Oh, really?" sneered the knight, and the others smirked. "Well, I'm afraid King Ravelle is a little busy now holding court. So . . . why don't you take your little blue-eyed self back to Alleble?!"

The four knights laughed and then stared at Gwenne and Aidan, apparently expecting them to leave. Then, finally, Aidan discovered what was different about them.

All the Glimpses of Alleble had eyes that glinted blue, but these four Mithegard Glimpses, and the others outside the city, had eyes that flashed bright green!

Mallik was right . . . the eyes do tell the tale.

"Good Knights of Mithegard," Gwenne spoke again. She stood to her full height and cast a disdainful look upon the guards. "I shudder to think of what Captain Valithor would do to those who insulted citizens of Alleble . . ."

The guards stopped laughing as if the air had been vacuumed right out of their lungs.

"C-Captain Valithor!" one of the guards stuttered. "He's coming here?!"

Gwenne grinned. "As a matter of fact, we were traveling with him, but a great storm separated us. We hope he will be along any day now."

The guards looked terrified. Apparently, Captain Valithor was well known—and feared outside Alleble as well! Apologizing continuously, the guards stepped aside and allowed Aidan and Gwenne to enter the castle.

Once past the gate, they entered a great hallway decorated with ornate banners and tapestries. They had barely gone ten steps when Aidan stopped.

"Why did you say that Captain Valithor would be coming?" Aidan asked solemnly. "He's probably dead."

Gwenne nodded. "I didn't say he *was* coming. I said we *hoped* he was coming—and we do! Right?"

Aidan agreed. Captain Valithor was as tough as they came, and Aidan certainly hoped he had somehow made it through the Tempest.

"Sir Aidan, I hear voices up ahead," Gwenne said, starting to walk on. "I am anxious to see with whom the King of Mithegard is holding court."

"But, Gwenne," Aidan persisted, grabbing Gwenne's arm. "Did you see? Their eyes sparkled with green!"

Gwenne seemed stunned momentarily. Her cheeks grew pink in

embarrassment. "I cannot believe I have not explained this to you before now. The eyes—"

"No, that's okay. Mallik told me about it. Blue for those who serve Alleble. Green for the undecided. Red for the followers of Paragor."

"That's exactly right."

"But what about Acsriot?" Aidan asked. "His eyes changed from blue to red."

"I do not know how Acsriot was able to do it," Gwenne replied. "Acsriot was a master of all the herbs and elements in The Realm. Or perhaps Paragor has taught his minions some foul new art."

"But what about my eyes, Gwenne?" Aidan began, alarm in his voice. "My eyes are blue, but they don't glint any color at all. What does that mean?"

"It means, Sir Aidan . . . ," she began thoughtfully. "You are not a Glimpse. Your eyes do not change unless—"

Gwenne never finished the sentence, for several trumpet blasts shattered the quiet and echoed throughout the enormous arched hall. Gwenne immediately ran down the hallway. And Aidan, dumbfounded as usual, tried to keep up.

Eventually, they found themselves at the doorway to the Throne Room of Mithegard. But they couldn't get in or even see in because of the mass of Glimpses who had gathered there. Gwenne spotted a door off to the side of the throne room. "This way, Sir Aidan," she said, gesturing. "Most castles have passages to allow servants special access to their royalty."

She was right! The passage led them right to the head of the room, only ten yards back diagonally from the King's throne! Because they were slightly behind the throne, they couldn't see the King, but they could see almost everyone in the crowd.

And because they were peeking out between two curtains, no one noticed them there. Aidan turned to Gwenne to speak, but she looked stricken. If it were possible, her skin looked even whiter than usual! Then, Aidan looked out into the assembly and saw immediately what had affected Gwenne. He, too, fell silent.

There in the center of the throne room was a large band of Glimpse knights. They were dressed in black armor streaked violently with scarlet, and each knight had the same terrible stabbing red eyes. They were armed, and their shields bore a strange red symbol that looked like an inverted crown. They were the Knights of Paragor.

One of them, a particularly menacing Glimpse who wore all black armor with a dark red hooded robe, stood in front of the rest. His face looked stretched and aged, and his eyes seemed somewhat sunken beneath his wildly bushy gray brows. On his forehead he wore a gold circlet. A confident smile played across his lips as if he were the King of Mithegard and ruled all before him.

"That is Lord Rucifel, the enemy's second in command," Gwenne explained. "Paragor does not usually send him forth as an ambassador. I wonder what that could mean."

Aidan shuddered. There seemed to be something dark and venomous that emanated from the warriors of Paragory. But Lord Rucifel was far worse than the rest. His sunken eyes and stretched face made Aidan think of things that were dead and decaying.

"Worthy King Ravelle, it is my honor to appear before you," Lord Rucifel began, his voice high and musical, dripping with flattery as he spoke to the unseen ruler of Mithegard. "Under your mighty hand, Mithegard with its famed seven towers has become a thriving kingdom."

Cheers erupted, mostly from the other Paragor Knights. Their commander was a crafty speaker, and they hung on every word.

"We come in peace from Paragory, yet another prosperous land—your nearest neighbor to the south. And we seek to form an agreement. An agreement, noble King, that would make both of our lands more wealthy and powerful than our wildest, most fantastic dreams."

The ambassador paused to let each Glimpse of Mithegard imagine matchless armies and vaults full of gold. They would fantasize themselves into a greedy trance—just as he had planned.

"The mighty Prince of Paragory," the ambassador continued, "has asked me to present you with a gift if I may. It was forged by the Prince's personal blacksmith in the fires deep beneath the Prince's Crown. Please accept this gift as a pledge of friendship from the land of Paragory."

The ambassador unwrapped a long bundle, revealing an unbelievably marvelous sword. Its grip was polished silver with six red gems set in the hilt. Its blade, however, was what caused many jaws to drop and eyes to stare. The blade was black and reflective as if it had been dipped in a dark ink that never dried. It looked beautiful and priceless. Even Aidan, though he already had a magnificent blade, found himself desiring the dark sword.

Rucifel bowed in an exaggerated fashion and held out the sword with both hands. Aidan and Gwenne watched as the King of Mithegard stood up from his throne and walked down the four steps to where Lord Rucifel knelt.

King Ravelle was a tall, dark-haired Glimpse, and he wore a splendid blue robe that shimmered as he walked. Aidan watched the King take the sword from Lord Rucifel. Aidan still could not see the King's face, but he could easily hear him when he spoke.

"On behalf of Mithegard," the King announced, "we welcome you into our land. And though there is much to discuss before we will be bound by any agreement, we gladly accept your token of friendship!"

There was deafening applause. The Glimpses of Mithegard seemed only too happy to welcome evil into their kingdom. Gwenne shook her head sadly. Paragor's ambassadors had reached Mithegard first. They had come with a full brigade of knights in full armor. And they brought a special gift and promises of much more.

Gwenne and Aidan had no ambassador. They had no sparkling gifts. Their mission had just become immeasurably more difficult.

But Aidan wasn't thinking about the mission. All he could think about was the voice of King Ravelle. His voice was so familiar—but that wasn't possible, was it? Aidan had never been to The Realm before. Aidan had never met a Glimpse before. And he certainly had not met the King of Mithegard before! Still, his voice sounded so similar to someone else's.

But whose?

The answer was there, flitting around in Aidan's mind, but he just couldn't grasp it. Aidan stared at the back of the King who was talking privately to Lord Rucifel.

"C'mon, come on . . . turn around," Aidan muttered to himself. "I know you. I know I know you—just turn around so I can see your face."

As if in answer to Aidan's silent command, the King of Mithegard turned to hand the dark sword to a nearby servant.

For the first time, Aidan saw King Ravelle's face. Aidan choked and staggered backward from the curtain. There was a sharp ringing in his ears. Blackness swirled in from the fringes of his vision.

REVELATIONS

Gwenne caught Aidan as he crumpled to the ground, or the noise might have attracted the attention of one of the Mithegard Knights. For several long minutes, Aidan lay unconscious, breathing heavily until, at last, he began to wake up. *Where am I?* he thought. *What happened?* But as he gazed up into Gwenne's blue eyes, memories began to fill in the blanks.

"Sir Aidan, are you all right?" she asked. "I almost didn't catch you!"

"Gwenne," he whispered urgently. "The King of Mithegard . . ."

Aidan stood up clumsily and went to the curtain to look again. He had to be sure. He parted the curtains ever so slightly and looked at King Ravelle, who was talking quietly with a group of knights but still facing in Aidan's direction. The dark, bushy eyebrows, the large dignified nose, the squared jaw—there could be no doubt!

"Gwenne, the King of Mithegard . . . is my father!"

"What?" she gasped. "Your father?"

"It's him," Aidan insisted. "I mean . . . he's got the white skin and flickering eyes like a Glimpse, but it's definitely him. Gwenne, how can that be?"

Gwenne pulled Aidan away from the curtains, and they both sat down with their backs against a stone wall. Gwenne hesitated, drew in a deep breath. "Sir Aidan, you must believe me when I tell you that I had no idea you would meet your father's Glimpse here in Mithegard. It is rare for King Eliam to allow one of your kind to see a Glimpse of a family member or a close friend."

Aidan struggled to understand. "A Glimpse of my family?"

Gwenne frowned. "Oh, Captain Valithor should be the one to explain this to you! I'm no master of Alleble's lore."

"Well, the Captain's not here, Gwenne," Aidan said, feeling a breach in his trust of Gwenne. *Is she hiding something?* he wondered.

"Very well, Aidan. You certainly should know this. Your father, and every person in your world, has a Glimpse twin."

"A twin? Like an identical twin?"

"Now, see," she said growing frustrated, "I don't know everything, but if by identical you mean exactly the same, like Nock and Bolt, then no . . . not identical. Time works differently in The Realm as compared to your world. And while King Ravelle is like your father in most ways, he may be a different age entirely."

Aidan stared blankly at her.

"I know it is difficult to grasp," Gwenne continued. "There are many in The Realm who do not understand, and many more who simply deny it is true. Remember I told you that long ago, before time was reckoned, our worlds were one. One world, Aidan. But something happened, and only the wisest of The Realm know exactly what, but it was something of extraordinary evil. The fabric of the universe was torn apart, and instead of one world, there was The Realm and there was Earth. That was The Schism. Each world still mirrors the other. Each Glimpse has a human twin. Each human has a Glimpse twin."

"Wait, Gwenne," Aidan said. "So if King Ravelle's a Glimpse of my dad, he'd have a son—a Glimpse just like me!"

"That is possible, Aidan, but you must understand the time difference, for it is just as possible that King Ravelle has not even had a child yet. Your Glimpse may not yet be born. I certainly haven't seen him."

"But if King Ravelle did have a son, he could be here in Mithegard. We might even run into him!"

"Shhhhh," warned Gwenne. "A guard might hear. As far as meeting your Glimpse here, I do not believe that is possible," she whispered. "Again, I do not fully understand this, but it has something to do with The Schism. A person may travel here, and a Glimpse may travel to your world—but what I have been told is that can only happen once, and only for a short time. And that the Glimpse and the person can never be in the same realm together."

"So that means there could be a Glimpse of me running around messing things up for me in Colorado?" Aidan asked.

"I do not know, Aidan. But if your Glimpse is in your realm, he would do nothing evil unless you do something evil here. For whatever a person does in your world affects what his Glimpse does in our world. You see, Sir Aidan, when our worlds divided, there remained a connection, like an invisible tether linking the lives and events of The Realm and Earth."

How many mysteries can there be in this world? Aidan wondered. He remained quiet and Gwenne went on.

"Something else you should know," Gwenne said. "When someone in your world chooses to believe in the story from The Scrolls, then a Glimpse here becomes a citizen of Alleble."

". . . and gets eyes that glint blue?"

"Yes, that's right!" she said.

"Gwenne, what happens if someone doesn't believe in the story of Alleble?"

"That person's Glimpse would go his own way for a time but would eventually become enslaved by the Prince. Perhaps, Sir Aidan, you are here for that very reason. Your part in saving Mithegard might lead your father to believe in the story of Alleble before it is too late."

"Too late?"

"Yes, people have only their lifetime to choose whom to follow: They can believe in the story of Alleble and follow the King, or they can follow the dark path of indecision and disbelief."

Aidan's fear for his father was mounting, so he asked, "What about when someone dies?"

"When a person dies, his Glimpse also dies. If that person believed in the story of Alleble before death, he would become one with his Glimpse and go to be with King Eliam in the Sacred Realm Beyond the Sun. But if someone dies who disbelieves or is undecided, he and his Glimpse become locked eternally in the torturous dungeons beneath the Prince's Crown."

Aidan remembered the captives, chained and terrified, being dragged into the Gates of Despair. Aidan felt numb and angry. How could this be?! He and most people spent their whole lives playing, going to school, and working—without ever having the slightest clue that the story of Alleble was real and that their lives forever depended on whether or not they believed.

"Gwenne, I've got to get back to my world!" Aidan stood up, eyes wide, the panic evident in his tone of voice. "I can't let my father go on not believing!"

Gwenne stood up and put her hands on Aidan's shoulders. "No, don't you see? It is King Eliam's will that you are here! The only way you can help your father is by helping his Glimpse, the King of Mithegard, to follow the right path!"

Suddenly, there was a tremendous crash. Aidan and Gwenne spun and looked down the passageway. One of King Ravelle's servants stood there, a dropped tray of dishes and goblets at his feet. He looked just as surprised as Aidan and Gwenne felt! Before they could run away, the servant began screaming, "Guards! Guards! There are spies behind the throne! Hurry, before they escape!"

There was no chance of escape, for in an instant a swarm of Mithegard Knights had grabbed Aidan and Gwenne by the arms and dragged them out into the center of the throne room.

They were surrounded on all sides by knights and citizens of Mithegard, as well as the dark Knights of Paragor. And worse still, the King of Mithegard approached them, scrutinizing them with his eyes, eyes of dark brown but ever-flickering green.

"Ethelbred," said the King to the servant who had discovered Aidan and Gwenne. "Your desire to keep your sovereign safe is admirable. But I think there is little to fear from these—they are but youths!"

A number of the Mithegard Knights laughed heartily, but the Paragory ambassador, Lord Rucifel, strode forward. His face, which had been confident and cordial before, flashed with furious anger.

"Do not be too hasty, good King," said Lord Rucifel. "The lad is a crossover, a dark skin from the Other Land. The girl, however, is from Alleble. I believe the King of Alleble is against our treaty!"

The King of Mithegard looked at Gwenne's eyes more closely. "Ah . . . yes, you are right. She is from Alleble! So, young one, is that it? Are you here to spy on our meeting with the good Glimpses from Paragory?"

Aidan had heard his father use that tone a million times. It was the old "I'm an adult, and I know better than you" tone! Aidan didn't like it from his father or his father's Glimpse!

Apparently, Gwenne didn't care for the tone either. "We were not spying! We simply couldn't get in the front door to the throne room, so we found another way in! Besides, I am part of the company from Alleble you invited here yourself!"

A look of recognition appeared on the King's face. "Where, then, is the rest of your party?" he asked. "And Valithor was to be your leader."

"Your Majesty," replied Gwenne, remembering to be more respectful. "We do not know what has become of our companions. They were swept away by a Tempest devised by the Prince of Paragory to keep us from getting here!"

A shadow passed over King Ravelle's face, and for a moment, he looked stricken. "Is this so?" he asked in a tone that was almost pleading.

"She lies!" shrieked Lord Rucifel. "My Prince does nothing to create those storms! They occur naturally! Besides, had there been a Tempest, these two scrawny imps would certainly have perished!"

The Knights of Paragor howled with laughter. Aidan could barely stand it.

"We escaped into some moonrascal tunnels just before the storm hit!" he argued. "The storm passed over us, and we traveled through the tunnels to get here!"

"Impossible!" bellowed Lord Rucifel. "These are imaginative

stories—nothing more! Could two little wags such as these escape the terrible winds of a Tempest? My good King, send them away. We have important matters to discuss."

The King of Mithegard looked closely at Aidan and Gwenne, apparently judging them and their story. Aidan wondered if the King of Mithegard recognized him. If he had a son, Aidan reasoned, there would be a resemblance. But there was no recognition in King Ravelle's eyes. Only suspicion.

"We find the two of you hiding in my servants' passageway," the King began skeptically, "and you tell us an unbelievable tale—what do you expect me to do? Welcome you with open arms?"

Gwenne spoke up. "Our story is unbelievable, but it is true. Unlike those from Paragory, servants of Alleble speak only the truth!"

"How dare you insult my guests!" thundered the King. "Is that how everyone from Alleble behaves? Guards, escort these two mischievous *children* out of the castle. And throw them out of the Kingdom of Mithegard. Perhaps Alleble will send someone more mature next time!"

Aidan and Gwenne tried to argue, but it was no use.

The Mithegard Knights turned them around and directed them toward the throne room doors. The Paragor Knights sneered at Aidan and Gwenne as they left. One young Paragor Knight left the crowd. He ran up to Aidan and teased him.

"You! Dark Skin!" he ridiculed. "What are you doing with this beggar from Alleble?"

Aidan's blood was boiling. He wanted nothing more than to belt the rude Paragor Knight in the jaw, but he knew they had already made a terrible impression on the King of Mithegard. He couldn't risk giving him any other excuse to distrust the Kingdom of Alleble.

The other Knights of Paragor urged the young mouthy knight on. He continued to insult and smirk right in Aidan's face.

"What's the matter, pipsqueak?" he sneered, pushing Aidan slightly. "Do you not know how to defend yourself?"

Aidan looked away, trying to ignore the brash Paragor Knight, but that just seemed to make him angrier. When Aidan wasn't looking, the Paragor Knight rammed into him from behind, sending Aidan flying forward. He crashed awkwardly to the ground, banging his chin smartly on the solid stone floor.

The Paragor Knights looked on, laughing merrily at the sport. The King of Mithegard also watched, but he wasn't smiling.

The Paragor Knight who had pushed Aidan sneered, shook his head with disdain, and announced, "How weak you are! Do not parents in your world teach you how to wield a blade? Stand and fight, you gutless coward!"

Aidan had heard enough, so he did stand up. After wiping the blood from his chin, he drew Sil Furyn from its scabbard. The sword made an echoing metallic ring as it came loose. He held it menacingly with the razor-sharp tip pointed directly at the Paragor Knight.

Immediately, tension filled the throne room. The other Paragor Knights stiffened, and their hands silently grasped for their own swords. The King of Mithegard stepped down from his throne. Gwenne, terrified, wondered what Aidan would do.

The Paragor Knight stood no more than five feet from the edge of Aidan's sword. He hadn't expected Aidan to actually do anything! The fierce look in Aidan's eye and the powerful-looking sword had him worried, but he drew his own blade. He couldn't back down in front of everyone!

"C'mon, then," the Paragor Knight challenged. "Do your worst."

Gwenne could barely watch. She knew their mission depended on truth, not bloodshed. If Aidan killed this Paragor Knight, it might appear to be brave to some, but for the King of Mithegard, who already distrusted them, it could turn him against Alleble forever.

As the Paragor Knight continued to provoke Aidan, Aidan stepped forward and did something remarkable: With both hands, he grasped the Son of Fury and laid it at the feet of the young taunting knight.

"I offer you my sword," he announced, "as a sign of peace. For the Kingdom of Alleble is a kingdom of peace!"

The Paragor Knight looked shocked! "Keep your blade, Dark Skin!" he groaned, turning his back on Aidan. Gwenne smiled.

The King of Mithegard suddenly spoke. "Guards, I told you to take these two from Alleble out of the castle! Do this, but give them shelter in a cottage just inside the main gate. In a short time it will be nightfall, and . . . I do not want them traveling at night."

That was hopeful, Aidan thought as the Mithegard Knights escorted him and Gwenne out of the castle. At least they got to stay in Mithegard! As the guards took them out to the courtyard, the sun had fallen behind the mountains, and already the sky was alive with stars. There was a chill in the air, and Aidan and Gwenne were thankful to have a place to stay—even if it was just a tiny two-room cottage with no furniture but a wooden bed in each room.

Gwenne couldn't wait to talk to Aidan in private. "That was incredible, Sir Aidan," she exclaimed. "How did you keep yourself from attacking that Paragor rat?"

"I didn't," Aidan replied simply.

"What?" Gwenne asked, dumbfounded. "But you didn't strike him—you, you surrendered your sword!"

Aidan shook his head. "Gwenne, I can't take credit for that. I wanted with all my heart to pound that no-good loudmouth! I very nearly did! But at the last second, I saw his eyes flicker red. And, I don't know, I felt sad—that's when I got the idea to surrender my sword. Boy, I'm sure glad that he didn't take my sword!"

Aidan and Gwenne laughed uncontrollably. It was the silly, bouncy laughter of ones who were utterly exhausted. Neither Aidan nor Gwenne had ever been so tired in their lives. In two days' time, they had traveled the Grimwalk, narrowly escaped death in the Tempest, crawled and slid through countless miles of tunnels, and arrived at Mithegard, only to find their mortal enemies had arrived there first!

A few minutes later a tray arrived, and Aidan and Gwenne shared their first real meal since leaving Alleble. It was only bread, salted beef, and a few pieces of fruit, but it was a banquet to them. After eating, Gwenne went to her room. Too tired to clean up, Aidan reclined in his bed. Sleep overcame them quickly, and Aidan and Gwenne slumbered peacefully deep into the night.

Some hours later, Aidan was disturbed from his sleep by some noises in the cottage. It was too dark to see anything, but his hearing was alert. He could hear the crickets and other night sounds from outside, but there was something else—it was footsteps on the stone floor inside the cottage. Gwenne was in the other room, but it wasn't her. The footfalls were heavy like a large man's. The footsteps came closer. Someone was in the room. Aidan reached for his sword when suddenly, there was a bright flash of light!

"Dad!" exclaimed Aidan, for in front of the bed stood King Ravelle, holding a brilliant candle that illuminated much of the room in an eerie blue light.

"What did you call me?" asked the King curiously.

"Uh . . . er . . . I mean, Your Majesty, what are you doing here?"

"It is my kingdom, is it not?" he replied playfully. "I have come with questions for you and your companion." He arched an eyebrow and nodded over his shoulder at Gwenne, who had entered the room. She too stared in wonder at their unexpected royal guest.

"My first question is quite simple, really," the King continued. "Since your arrival in my chamber was a bit, how shall I put it— unusual, I did not get to hear your names."

Gwenne bowed low. "I am Gwenne, daughter of Lienne and Gamaliel, and servant of the noble King Eliam of Alleble. I am at your service."

The King nodded politely at Gwenne and then turned to Aidan. Aidan felt incredibly odd. Not only was it strange to introduce himself to a Glimpse who looked just like his dad, but he didn't have any flashy titles or anything to make his name sound more important! He scoured his brain for something.

Finally, he muttered, "Your Kingship, sir . . . uh, my name is Aidan, son of Charles, and I come from the land of, er . . . Colorado, but I am also on the King of Alleble's, um . . . team."

The King stared at Aidan in awe. "Then I was right," he said. "You are from the Realm of Legend, the Mirror Realm! How did you pass into this land?"

"I was given scrolls, the story of Alleble," Aidan explained. "And I learned about your world. When I had enough faith, the King of Alleble called me here."

Gwenne added, "Sir Aidan was called by the King of Alleble to be the Twelfth Knight in our company."

"You mean the company from Alleble?" asked the King. "The one that was lost when the Tempest hit?"

"Yes," Gwenne replied. "We still don't know what has become of our friends."

"And Valithor was one . . . one of the lost?"

"He was near to us when the Tempest struck," Gwenne replied. "But in the debris of the storm I did not see if he stood or fell."

"But Captain Valithor, well, he's a champion—the bravest and the strongest of anyone I've ever known," Aidan said. "I just know he had to escape . . . somehow."

"But against a fist of ice and wind," the King said sadly. "He would need more than courage and might."

Aidan stared at the floor.

King Ravelle cleared his throat and said, "Servants of Alleble, let me come to my point of being here, for I must return soon to the castle lest anyone notice I am not in my chambers. My visit to you is a secret and could cause quite a stir if someone discovered it, but I had to come. When you told your story in my throne room, I did not trust your words, but your actions spoke clearly.

"The brash young Knight of Paragor seemed intent on provoking you to violence, even having the nerve to assault you in my presence—a presumption I will not soon forget. Rather than striking back in anger, you surrendered your sword in peace. That was a gesture of such courage and nobility as few Glimpses in my service have ever demonstrated! How were you able to do this?"

Aidan thought for a moment and then replied, "The King of Alleble gave me the power—I couldn't have done it on my own."

"That is the way of King Eliam and all who serve him," Gwenne added. "He does not tempt with gold or promise swords. He offers you and your kingdom peace and hope for the future."

The King stared hard at Aidan and Gwenne. "So that is why you have come? You are here on behalf of the King of Alleble, seeking a treaty with Mithegard?"

"Not a treaty," Gwenne replied, choosing her words carefully. "The King of Alleble asks only that you trust in him and be willing to serve the Kingdom of Alleble in its mission to bring peace to all the kingdoms of Glimpses in this land."

"Uh, King, sir," Aidan stammered, "we also came to warn you."

"Warn me?!" The King's expression became fierce. "Warn me? Does the King of Alleble threaten the good Kingdom of Mithegard?!"

Aidan gulped. In the presence of a being so like his earthly father, he felt sure he'd just earned a lecture or worse. "No, no, no . . . what I meant was . . . we came to warn you about Paragory."

To Aidan's great relief, Gwenne spoke up. "Good King, the Prince of Paragory offers you riches and power, but it will not last. The Prince is evil, and he will not share his power with anyone! He will pretend to be your friend, but faster than poison, he'll turn on you and seek to make slaves of every last Glimpse in Mithegard!"

"Slaves?!" barked the King. "That is a very serious charge, young lady. How can you be so sure of this?"

"You may be sure of the Prince's corruption," said Gwenne, a tear welling up in her eye. "For the Prince and his bloodthirsty Paragor Knights have done this before. Long ago, when I was only five, the Paragor Knights invaded my home, the tiny province just south of Alleble called Acacia. They spoke of peace and friendship, but the moment our guard was down, they attacked. Those cruel Paragor Knights captured many Acacian Glimpses and slaughtered the rest. They . . . they murdered my parents . . ."

Aidan stared in disbelief. Gwenne had never told him! The King of Mithegard stared as well. He seemed shocked, sad, and angry— all at once.

"I am deeply moved by what you have told me," the King whispered. "And I am afraid I have not judged rightly in this matter, perhaps to all our peril. Earlier this evening, Lord Rucifel advised me to sign a treaty promising that Mithegard would join with Paragory as allies. I refused because I wanted more time to consider the matter. Lord Rucifel seemed a bit offended, and he demanded I agree to the alliance. Again, I refused. Finally, he asked if I would grant permission for him and his men to return to Paragory. He claimed that he would bring back additional treasures from the Prince—treasures that might help persuade us to join with them. I was blinded by glittering images, so I allowed Rucifel and his men to depart."

"Good riddance," Aidan said. "Maybe they'll look to some other kingdom."

"No, you do not understand," Gwenne said, her eyes wide with fear. "The Prince will not shrug and accept Mithegard's rejection, not any longer. Either way King Ravelle chose to go, Paragor would have had his armies camped nearby—to invade or attack."

"Rucifel and his men," King Ravelle spoke, turning his head slowly toward Gwenne. . . . "they have been inside the walls of my city. They know my defenses. They know where we are vulnerable. And my armies, my armies are not prepared. . . ." An uncomfortable silence fell over them.

Unexpectedly, harsh orange light flashed in the cottage's windows. A deafening explosion shook the ground beneath their feet. From afar came distant rumbling and the haunting blare of trumpets being blown.

"We are under attack," said the King. He rocketed from the cottage. "Mithegardians, awake! The armies of Paragory are coming!"

THE CURTAIN OF RED

Led by King Ravelle, Aidan and Gwenne fled from their cottage into the streets of Mithegard. Nothing could prepare Aidan for the chaos he would see there.

Burning projectiles launched from Paragory's catapults gouged arcs in the predawn sky. They crashed into the kingdom with thunderous fury. One slammed into a cottage, collapsing and igniting it. Another bounced upon the stone of the courtyard fifty yards from where Aidan ran. It left a burning path and careened into the side of a one-lane bridge that spanned Mithegard's natural spring. The bridge splintered and plummeted into the water.

Burning debris from the explosions flew in every direction, causing hungry fires to spring up all over the kingdom. It seemed the enemy's fire weapons could burn the very stone from which the kingdom was built.

More horrible to Aidan than the explosions and fire were the screams. Animal-sounding wails that rose from every part of the city.

It seemed that all of Mithegard filled the streets. Families stumbled toward the castle, ducking with the impact of each strike. Soldiers in their royal blue livery raced to support the guards upon the kingdom's outer walls, screaming as they ran.

Aidan and Gwenne scrambled to keep up with the King as he sprinted through the crowds and over piles of burning wreckage.

Then, above even the screams and explosions, there came a sinister rumbling from behind. It sounded as if a great storm was about to hammer the Kingdom of Mithegard.

"Gwenne!" Aidan yelled. "What's that sound?"

"Horses!" Gwenne screamed. She looked over her shoulder and stumbled. "Paragor must be bringing his full army to bear on the city!"

"They'll have to stop at the walls, right? The walls will hold, won't they?" Aidan asked. Gwenne did not answer.

The thunder abruptly stopped, and a chorus of trumpets rang out. For a split second everyone stood very still. A sense of danger hung heavy in the air. No one dared move. Aidan felt as if someone stood behind him with a knife raised to plunge into his back. But he would not turn.

"THE ARCHERS!" bellowed the King, breaking the spell. "The Archers of Paragory are preparing to fire! Everyone seek shelter from the skies!"

Aidan looked back toward the city walls and up into the sky. The walls seemed to be intact, though some were burning in places. Gwenne tugged at Aidan's shoulder, but he would not look away from the sky. There wasn't anything alarming there but smoke. *What was the King talking about? There were no arch—* Then, he saw it!

Rising above the city walls, devouring the dawn sky, came an evil red curtain—undulating and billowing high above the kingdom walls. The arrows flung from the longbows of a horde of unseen Paragor archers looked like thousands of teeth. They seemed to pause at their pinnacle, and Aidan, mesmerized, stood and stared.

If it weren't for Gwenne grabbing his arm and pulling him into a nearby farmhouse, Aidan's adventures and his life would have ended there. For, in moments, it literally rained arrows. Thuds, smacks, ricochets, and horrible stabbing sounds filled the air as the barrage of arrows pelted the city.

Though they were inside and protected by the structure's sturdy roof, Aidan and Gwenne covered their heads with their hands and ducked down. A few seconds and several thousand arrows later, it became dreadfully silent. Reluctantly, Aidan looked out of their shelter's window. Anything that wasn't made of solid stone had become riddled with dozens of the cruel-looking, red-shafted arrows. But there was no sign of King Ravelle.

"The King! Where is he?" Aidan cried out. He was frantic, remembering that the death of a Glimpse had dire consequences on Earth. "I don't see him."

"I don't know," Gwenne answered. "He was just in front of us. . . ."

His eyes wide and fearful, Aidan turned to Gwenne.

"He must have made it to the castle," Gwenne called back. "He knows his way around Mithegard better than anyone else!"

Aidan nodded. He wanted Gwenne to be right. He smiled grimly and looked at a post at the front of the farmhouse. There were five crimson shafts embedded in the wood up to their fletchings.

"That could've been me, Gwenne," Aidan whispered. "I guess that makes us even. If you hadn't grabbed me . . ."

"It is well that you were not pierced by even a single arrow, Sir

Aidan," agreed Gwenne. "For the Paragor Knights dip their arrow-heads in *mortiwraith* venom."

"Mortiwraith?" Aidan asked.

"Perhaps the deadliest creature in all The Realm," Gwenne explained. "A large cave-dwelling creature, like a serpent but with many sets of taloned limbs. Row after row of poisonous fangs, it has, and each is filled with a dreadful poison. Even a tiny bit of its venom will kill even the strongest Glimpse warrior."

"I hope I never run into a mortiwraith!" exclaimed Aidan, shuddering at the thought.

The Paragor Knights once again began catapulting flaming projectiles into the city. One vaporized a bell tower very near to the farmhouse in which Aidan and Gwenne had been hiding.

"That was close!" Aidan choked. The air was warm and smoky—difficult to breathe. "What are those things? Did you see what it did to the tower?"

"I am not sure, Aidan. Long we have had oil for our lamps and torches, but nothing that explodes like that! We'd better get to the castle!" They left the shelter of the building and ran, crunching the arrows that littered the cobblestone streets.

As they entered the main avenue to the castle, Aidan and Gwenne were greeted with a sight that would haunt their dreams forever. They had wondered why it had become so quiet after the arrows . . . why the screams had stopped—now they knew.

Lying dead in the wide road, pierced with innumerable arrows, were hundreds and hundreds of Glimpses. Aidan choked back tears and looked upon the lifeless bodies of men, women, and children who were struck down just a short run from safety. Their faces were locked in terror, eyes bulging, mouths agape, and their beautiful ivory skin was streaked violently with blood.

Even those who had taken just a single arrow in the arm or leg had perished and looked as though they had suffered in death. Mortiwraith venom was horribly efficient.

Then Aidan looked up at Gwenne, who shook and wept openly. He wanted to cry too, to rage and shriek against the reality of the horror all around them, but he could not. For somehow he knew that Gwenne saw more on those streets than just the dead of Mithegard. He knew that she also saw the ghosts from her past—memories of her parents dying, murdered in cold blood by the merciless armies of Paragory.

Without saying a word, Aidan wrapped his arms around her and held her. Gwenne put her head on Aidan's shoulder and convulsed into wrenching cries as they continued toward the castle.

To see Gwenne—the swordmaiden whose eyes had silenced Aidan's fears and whose words had made him feel like a hero—to see her in such agony kindled an inferno in Aidan's heart. *Someday*, he thought bitterly. *Someday, I will pay Paragory back for the pain it has caused.*

Mithegard Knights appeared on the high walls of the castle. One called out to Aidan and Gwenne: "Friends! You must get inside the castle! Our small force is overrun, and the outer wall is nearly breached. Get inside! Hurry, before the armies of Paragory are here!"

Aidan called back to them, "Is the King alive?!"

"Yes! The King of Mithegard is rallying his captains in the main keep. He is as safe as may be, but you are not safe! You must hurry!"

Because of the dead there was no way to hurry. So, carefully, Aidan and Gwenne tiptoed around the bodies and made slow progress toward the castle. It was just a hundred feet, but it felt more like a hundred-mile journey through a hideous nightmare. They didn't want to look down because of the dreadful scene at their feet, but they had to look down to avoid stepping on a leg, an arm, or fingers of the poor victims.

They were halfway to the castle of Mithegard when the ground began to shake. Aidan and Gwenne looked back down the avenue to the gatehouse and Mithegard's outer walls. There was a deafening grinding noise and a tremendous explosion. For a moment, they couldn't see because the smoke was so thick. When the cloud of debris settled, Aidan and Gwenne realized that a huge section of the wall had been knocked down. And through the gaping hole, like a sea of black and red, poured the armies of Paragory.

Aidan and Gwenne looked on in horror as the armies stopped and formed into horizontal lines that were several dozen Glimpses deep. *What are they doing?* Aidan wondered.

"They are going to fire another volley!" Gwenne cried. "Run!"

A lone trumpet sounded, and another wave of red arrows sped upward into the sky. Aidan and Gwenne turned to sprint for the castle, but they stopped short. The castle's massive drawbridge had been raised. A sheer fall into a deep, inescapable moat lay in front of them. The ruthless forces of Paragory clamored behind them, and a blizzard of poison arrows was about to crash down on them from above. They were trapped.

THE SIEGE

Expecting at any moment to feel the bite of an arrow through plate armor, mail, and skin, Aidan frantically sought anyplace that might provide shelter for them from the sky. At last he spied a long overhang in front of the stables on the right side of the road.

"C'mon, Gwenne!" he yelled, but she did not answer. Aidan spun around; Gwenne was gone. Then he saw her. She was about twenty feet away, kneeling, and holding something in her arms. A limp form in a small tattered dress. A child.

Gwenne's liquid eyes were wide with questions, her face contorted in anguish, and her lips trembled. Aidan felt he had been pierced through the heart.

But Aidan knew to wait was to die. "Gwenne!" he screamed in a voice so strong he surprised himself. "You've got to get out of the road! The arrows!"

He looked to Gwenne who was moving too slowly, still carrying the child. He looked back at the stable. There'd be no way he could reach Gwenne and get them both back to safety. Then he saw on the other side of the road, behind Gwenne, a cottage with its door ajar.

"Snap out of it, Gwenne!" Aidan yelled. "Never alone!"

Gwenne looked up as if awakening from a trance.

"Get to the cottage, now!" Aidan said pointing. Gwenne hugged the child and ran just as the first arrows struck the road. Aidan sprinted toward the stable. He lunged beneath the overhang, rolled into a post, and lay still.

A hail of poison arrows fell. There were clatters, clangs, and snapping sounds. And then there was silence.

The moment the crimson barrage ended, Aidan heard the heavy cadence of many soldiers marching. He stood, raced to the front of the stable, and froze. He saw the armies of Paragory surge into the main avenue. In terror, Aidan searched the road for his friend. Had she made it to the cottage?! There were so many bodies, but he could not tell if hers was one of them.

The soldiers marched closer. They would kill him if he entered the road, but Aidan had to find Gwenne. And in that moment, he decided she was worth his life. He drew his sword and stepped out into the road.

"Aidan!" Gwenne's voice rang out above the rumble of the advancing knights. "Get back in there!"

"Gwenne!" he yelled. He saw her. She was in the cottage. "Are you all right?!"

"Yes!" she called back. "I've found a trapdoor, leading to a cellar of some kind. I think I can hide there! You must stay where you are! It is too late to get across!"

Aidan looked and saw the grim-faced Knights of Paragor less than a hundred yards from their location.

Gwenne disappeared from sight just as scores of Paragor Knights charged up the avenue between Gwenne's cottage and Aidan's stable. The knights trampled the dead as they came and looked hungry to add to the destruction. Aidan crouched down but watched to see what the knights would do.

A mighty shout came from the castle, and at least fifty Mithegard archers appeared from behind the *battlements* high atop the stronghold. They drew back their long bows and loosed their arrows into the heart of the Paragor offensive. There were shrieks and short-lived curses, as the first two rows of knights toppled over in heaps upon the road. From what Aidan could tell, every arrow had found its mark.

But for every Paragor Knight who went down, there were five to replace him. They fired back at the Mithegard archers. Some fell several hundred feet from the battlements and disappeared beneath the dark water in the moat below. There was a frantic exchange of fire, and Aidan watched in sick fascination as warriors from both sides dropped and moved no more. Aidan stayed low for fear that he might be seen. But the warriors of both sides were far too intent on the battle to notice Aidan in the stable.

So Aidan looked on. The forces of Mithegard in their mighty castle held their own against the siege. The foundation of the stronghold was solid. The walls were high, with dozens of *lancet* windows and parapets from which archers could send volleys of arrows and then quickly disappear to avoid being hit by return fire. The Knights of Paragor, on the other hand, had only their shields and horses to hide behind. And they fell a dozen at a time, many adding to the heaps of carnage on the road, and some sliding slowly into the moat. Then, as if raked in by a giant invisible arm, the Paragor forces pulled back.

Where are they going? Aidan wondered. *Are they giving up?*

But the archers from the castle kept firing. In fact, they seemed frantic, firing shaft after shaft recklessly, without aim or pause. Cautiously, Aidan stepped out of the stable and craned his neck around a post to see where the army of Paragory had gone.

Aidan's heart lodged in his throat.

They were not fleeing.

Spanning the road and drawn by huge, armor-clad steers, heavy catapults rolled slowly forward. Behind each was a massive tarped wagon and scores of soldiers. The convoy halted. The Knights of Paragory, seemingly unconcerned by the hail of arrows from the castle, went to work, winching down the throwing arms of the catapults and removing the tarps from the wagons. They took great black barrels from the wagons and loaded one upon each catapult. In unison, the fuses of every barrel were lit. A horn blared and all at once, the catapults fired. Aidan dove back into his hiding spot, but still watched.

The first volley soared high over the battlements and disappeared. For several ominous moments there was silence.

Then, as if a bolt of lightning had struck, detonating its earsplitting thunder, explosions rocked the castle and shook the ground. Aidan collapsed and covered his head. Great plumes of black smoke rose from behind the parapets and issued forth from the lancets. The castle of Mithegard was burning!

No one moved atop the walls.

Abruptly, another volley from the catapults careened toward the castle. This wave hit the walls directly and exploded on impact. Volley after volley of Paragory's powerful black projectiles were hurled at the walls of Mithegard's stronghold.

Dust fell and the stable groaned as if it might collapse. Tears blurred his vision. Still, he managed to look out from the stable into the swirling mass of smoke.

Flames crawled up the stone on creeping vines, but the castle walls were not breached.

Then, as Aidan watched helplessly, the Paragor Knights approached the moat and stood there as if willing the iron portcullises to be raised and the drawbridge to be lowered. From the midst of them strode forth a tall warrior. He wore a scowling black helmet and armor so jagged and fierce that it seemed he could kill without a weapon. But this foe had a sword in each hand.

It is him! It is the twin-bladed warrior who stood with Paragor in the dream. Aidan clutched his chest. *Is this where it happened? Will I be captured, brought before the Prince, and executed in cold blood?*

Aidan felt a powerful urge to run out into the field of battle to surrender, to explain that this was all some sort of mistake, and to beg for mercy. And perhaps the old Aidan might have done just that. But this Aidan had made a promise. *Even were the hordes of darkness to assail you in hopeless demand of your life—even then do you swear devotion forever to the King?*

"Aye!" Aidan had answered.

Aidan looked down at the Son of Fury. The sword burned in his hand. If it came to it, Aidan would die, but it would not be a coward's death. Aidan went back to see what the dark knight would do.

Trumpets rang out. When the echoes faded, the Glimpse raised both swords and declared aloud, "By order of the Prince, Lord of Paragory and Master of all Glimpse-kind, you are commanded to open the castle of Mithegard and surrender!" It was the voice of Lord Rucifel. Aidan was stunned.

Another voice answered, coming from high in the middle tower of Mithegard Castle. And a lone figure appeared atop the walls and fearlessly stood upon the battlement. It was King Ravelle. "Rucifel, at last I see you as you truly are," the King of Mithegard thundered. "Liar! Murderer of the innocent! We will not surrender to the likes of you or the mongrel you serve!"

Lord Rucifel placed his helmet on the ground and sneered up at the King. "Powerless fool!" he exclaimed, slashing the air with both blades. "The mercy of Paragory should not be so rudely cast aside. If you had but accepted the Prince's offer of friendship, you would not be reduced to this—"

"Friendship!" barked the King. "You stretch out one hand in friendship while in the other you hold a dagger! Nay, there is no friendship or love in slavery! I know now where Mithegard's true friends dwell. In the east by the Seven Glorious Fountains!"

Aidan's heart leaped when he heard this. Was the King allying himself with Alleble? Did that mean his own father would come to be—

"Seven!" Rucifel laughed cruelly. "Did you say 'seven' fountains? Know you not that only six of those fountains still flow? The other is cold and barren. It stands as a monument of what follows when my Prince is defied! Your last chance, King Ravelle. Yield to me! Surrender—if not for your own sake, at least consider the lives of your loyal subjects . . . what few remain."

Like the crack of a whip, King Ravelle flung something dark straight at Rucifel. It turned end over end. Rucifel tripped over his helmet as he dove out of the way. His scowling helmet rolled over the edge and plopped into the moat.

Embedded deep in the ground was the black sword Rucifel had delivered to King Ravelle as a token of Paragory's goodwill.

"There's your filthy sword back!" The King's voice exploded. "Mithegard will not surrender! We would rather die first!"

"And die you shall," replied Lord Rucifel, standing awkwardly and nodding to a group of extremely tall, muscular warriors who had come to the front of the massive army.

The brawny Glimpses turned and walked back into the crowd of knights. Moments later the ranks parted and the warriors returned, leading several of those great horned beasts with their wagons and their deadly payload. Six wagons, each still tarped and very full. They led the steers to within several feet of the moat and turned them so that the back of the wagons reached just over the edge.

The musclebound warriors of Paragory opened the backs of the wagons. Barrel after black barrel tumbled out and fell into the moat. *How many are there in each wagon?* Aidan wondered. But he could not tell, although he suspected more than a dozen.

Finally, when all of the wagons were empty, Rucifel himself came forward carrying a single barrel on his shoulder. With some effort, he removed the peg from the barrel and repulsive brownish fluid began to gush out into the moat. He traversed the edge until the liquid was spent. Then, he ordered his knights to withdraw. The entire army of Paragory marched back a hundred yards from the castle.

Aidan watched in fearful suspense, wondering if Gwenne was still safe, wishing she were with him. Surely she would know what to do! But there was nothing that either of them could do.

A single Paragor archer stepped forward from the crowd. He raised his bow, and Aidan saw that he had a flaming arrow fitted to its string. Aidan wasn't sure what happened next. He saw a vision of the fountain in Alleble, and in it, waist-deep in oil, were the Elder Guards, their wives, and their children. And standing high above on a balcony was Paragor with a torch. With a chilling laugh, Paragor cast the torch high in the air. The moment the torch hit the fountain, the vision was gone, and the archer let fly his flaming arrow.

Aidan stared in horror, for if the archer's aim was true, Aidan knew that the arrow would sail down into the moat. And he knew that when those dozens and dozens of black barrels exploded, it would level the castle and obliterate everything near it—including the stables. Aidan threw himself to the ground.

THE BATTLE BEFORE
THE SEVEN TOWERS

Aidan waited for the roaring fiery explosion, for the searing wave of heat that would follow and the burning debris that would fall. But there was no explosion, and Aidan thought for a moment that the archer had missed.

Then, Aidan heard something that made his heart soar: "Hold, thou weedy, weather-bitten canker-blossoms!! Mithegard Castle shall not fall if I can help it!"

Aidan looked up, and beyond all hope it was true! There in the sky, the morning sun shining gold upon his armor, was Captain Valithor!

"Now, Swiftwing!" he cried out to his dragon steed, and the agile creature craned its neck down, opened its jaws, and snatched the flaming arrow out of the air moments before it would have hit the fuel in the moat!

The Paragor Knights had been watching all this, but before they could light and fire another flaming arrow, the other eight Knights of Alleble soared down from the sky and drove their dragons into the front lines of the enemy. Soldiers were thrown cartwheeling into the air. Others fell like dominoes.

Then, Kaliam, Matthias, Tal, Eleazar, Farix, Nock, Bolt, Mallik, and, of course, Captain Valithor leaped off their dragons, readied their weapons, and surged into the enemy's foundering ranks.

So terrified at the onslaught of the unexpected assault, the companies of Paragory fled. In fact, the small force from Alleble clove a path right through the enemy. But Rucifel blew his war horn, and it seemed the Knights of Paragor quickly remembered their numbers were a hundred times those of their attackers.

Those fleeing turned, raising sword, axe, and bow. And the path that had been cut through the middle of the enemy army began to close like jaws of a steel trap. Aidan feared for his friends, ferocious in battle as they were, for they were about to be sealed off by their enemy like a small island at high tide.

Then, the drawbridge of Mithegard opened.

The army of Mithegard flew out, more than a hundred knights on horseback disgorged as if shot from a cannon. They were led by none other than the King of Mithegard himself!

"Go, Dad!" Aidan yelled.

"Now, Rucifel, the tables are turned!" roared the King, the lust of battle thick in his voice. "Let's see now if you can wield a sword!"

King Ravelle spurred his horse toward Rucifel. The Paragor Commander stood defiantly near a catapult and let his gray cape fall to the ground. He drew not one but two long swords, and it seemed to Aidan that he laughed as the King approached.

The King rode at Rucifel until the last moment, and then he dove from his saddle and crashed, sword and shield, into the twin blades of his foe. But Aidan did not see what followed between King Ravelle and Rucifel, for Mithegard's mounted soldiers clashed in that moment with the enemy legion, cutting off Aidan's view.

"Alleb Knights, keep moving!" roared Captain Valithor, and Aidan turned and saw the great Captain of Alleble. He was surrounded by Paragor Knights, but Fury cut through his foes like a scythe through summer wheat. Free for a moment, he motioned to Nock and Bolt.

As if bounced from a trampoline, the twin archers sprang up out of the mass of fighting Glimpses.

Aidan watched in disbelief as Nock and Bolt ran across the heads and shoulders of the enemy knights as if hopping stone to stone in a shallow riverbed. Nock landed on the roof of a cottage, Bolt upon the highest beam of a catapult. There they opened fire.

With incredible speed, their pale hands snatched dark shafts from their quivers, set them to the strings, pulled, and fired. Their Blackwood Arrows flew razor-straight at the speed of thought.

So fast was their flight, so powerful the force behind them, the shafts went right through the bodies of two Paragor warriors and stuck in the chests of two more behind them. Four enemies fell in wide-eyed silence.

Then, there was an explosion. Or at least Aidan thought it was an explosion. In the midst of a sea of combatants, five Paragor soldiers were hurled into the air. But there was no smoke, fire, or thunderous boom.

Again Paragor Knights were catapulted. And again it happened. They were launched in bunches as if an invisible giant were brushing them aside. Then, Aidan saw the cause of these strange sights, and he grinned. It was Mallik and his great hammer!

With powerful two-fisted strokes, Mallik swept the hammer into his foes. That fearsome weapon was immensely heavy, but Mallik wielded it as though it were a staff of balsa wood. Swords splintered into shards and shields crumpled when the hammer crashed into them. None withstood Mallik's heavy strokes.

Aidan saw no sign of the other knights from Alleble. He hoped they were all still alive, but even with King Ravelle's knights, the forces of Paragory outnumbered them greatly.

Gwenne! Aidan remembered. In the hypnotizing spectacle of the battle, he had forgotten that Gwenne was hiding in the cottage across the road. Aidan knew she could take care of herself, but he could not let her face the enemy alone.

Aidan slashed the air with the Son of Fury. It felt light in his hand. He paused a moment, took a deep breath, and left the safety of his hiding place.

Hoping to make his way to the cottage on the other side of the road, Aidan stumbled through the battle. All the knights seemed too busy fighting one another to notice Aidan.

Then, Aidan heard a great ringing clash to his left. There was a guttural, desperate scream, a nauseating crunch, and a strange sucking kind of gasp. And something wet sprayed across Aidan's face.

Aidan stumbled to one knee, stood slowly, and wiped at the red spray. He looked down at the chain mail of his gauntlet and saw angry smears of deep red. He turned his head as if in a trance and saw a fallen Mithegard soldier. The Glimpse lay on his back. His ivory skin was filthy with grime and painted with his own fresh blood. Transfixed on the motionless stare of the dead Glimpse's eyes, Aidan did not notice the Paragor Knight standing there with a bloody war axe.

Eyes gleamed red from the sockets in his skull-like helmet. His huge body heaved, and with both hands he raised the heavy axe. He took one step over the fallen Glimpse. One step toward Aidan. And he brought the axe crashing down.

The next thing Aidan knew, he was shoved forcefully to the ground. He found himself looking up at Farix, who had caught the falling axe blade in his bare hands. In a flash of motion, Farix twisted the axe and flipped the enemy onto his back. He brought his elbow down hard upon the Paragor Knight, and the knight lay still.

Breaking the axe over his knee, Farix yelled, "Keep your wits about you, Sir Aidan. As our Captain says, 'Stay in motion, if you want to stay alive.'" And with that, he raced away into the storm of steel and flesh.

Aidan blinked. *Gwenne was right . . . Farix is a weapon.*

He shook his head and stood. He had been spared from death for the moment, and he did not intend to be caught unaware again. Ducking blows and sidestepping struggles that suddenly blocked his path, Aidan finally made it to the stone cottage where he had last seen Gwenne.

The heavy wooden door to the building had been torn from its hinges. Aidan raced inside, looking for the trapdoor. There was nothing but a fireplace and an overturned table and chairs in the first room he checked. Then, in the center of the floor of the next room, he found it. But the trapdoor was wide open, hacked off its hinge and thrown aside. Aidan looked down into the basement room. The stairs down were spattered with fresh blood.

"Gwenne!" he screamed, knowing with heart-crushing certainty that his friend would not answer.

KNIGHTFALL

Aidan ran frantically down the stairs beneath the trapdoor, but the cellar was empty. There were, however, signs of a great struggle. An overturned table, broken glass, and a toppled bookcase—but what riveted Aidan was an awful spray of blood on the wall.

Aidan flew back up the stairs. He searched and re-searched every room in the house. They were all empty.

The cold, still eyes of the dead Glimpse in the road invaded Aidan's mind.

"No!" he roared, swinging the Son of Fury recklessly at a vertical wooden beam. The beam split and the top portion fell. Dust rained down on Aidan, and the roof protested loudly. "No, you can't be dead, Gwenne! You can't be."

Aidan trembled in the cottage doorway, and all the doubts and fears rushed in and began to make themselves at home. And for a moment, it was as if they had never left. Aidan heard voices in his head.

His father's: *"Believing in something doesn't make it real!"*

Grampin's: *"If what you believe in turns out to be a lie, then you could end up humiliated . . . or worse."*

Valithor's: *"Try to understand, Aidan. What Paragal intended for evil has become the foundation for much that is good."*

Nothing, Aidan thought. *There was no result, no future that could justify Gwenne's death. How could King Eliam allow Gwenne's family to be murdered by Paragor's armies? How could he let her survive as an orphan and give her hope, only to let her be killed anyway—It wasn't just unfair—it was . . . evil!*

Rage boiled up within Aidan. Rage at his parents for making him move. Rage at Grampin for making him believe. Rage at Gwenne for making him think he was something he was not. And rage at King Eliam or whoever caused all of this to happen. Hot tears burned trails on his dusty cheeks, and he trembled and heaved as if he would be sick.

He could not save Gwenne, and he could not make it all go away. But there was something he could do.

His eyes smoldering, he wiped away the wet streaks and burst forth from the cottage . . . with the Son of Fury in his hand.

One of the Paragor Knights spotted Aidan immediately. With a lustful screech, the beastly Glimpse charged and raised his sword high, his intent to chop Aidan in half. But he made a fatal mistake, for he did not expect skill from one as young and short as Aidan.

The Twelfth Knight knew that his enemy would throw himself off balance with such a mighty high-to-low chop. Aidan simply side-stepped, and in one motion he snapped the Son of Fury and thrust it into the Glimpse's side. Aidan winced as his sword went quickly in and then back out.

Within minutes, seven enemy knights had fallen by Aidan's hand. Then, out of the corner of his eye, Aidan saw a familiar face. He still wore the long, weather-beaten cloak, and it fluttered in the wind as he barked orders to other knights. But the knights who followed his commands did not wear the silver armor of Alleble or the blue and gold of Mithegard.

"Acsriot!" Aidan said aloud. His adrenaline surged, and Aidan rushed forward toward the traitor. Several blades slashed Aidan's way as he ran, but he brushed them aside as if swatting flies.

He came upon Acsriot like an unexpected storm, raining down blows, snaps, and thrusts. But Acsriot was not without skill. He parried each attack away, then took a quick step backward.

"You!" Acsriot rasped. "You survived as well?"

"Yes, I survived!" Aidan yelled, throwing a quick snap at Acsriot. The Son of Fury traced a circular arc from outside in. Acsriot blocked it, but Aidan's sword slid off his block and put a notch in the black vambrace guarding Acsriot's forearm.

"Whelp!" Acsriot spat. "Think you that one week's training is enough?"

"I may not be as skilled with the sword, nor as strong as you, but my heart is pure, devoted to King Eliam the Everlasting, and I am not alone!" Aidan said.

Like lightning, Aidan struck with his best move, the moulinet—throwing Acsriot a half step off balance. In the split second that Acsriot needed to right himself, Aidan lunged forward with all his strength and drove the Son of Fury straight through Acsriot's breastplate.

But when Aidan looked up, he saw that Acsriot was not dead. He was not even wounded, for Aidan's sword had not pierced his enemy. Acsriot had, with the speed of a lightning strike, knocked the thrust wide so that it sawed across the armor rather than through.

Acsriot laughed. "You see, I saw your move in your eyes before you made it. If a moulinet is all you can manage, then you are without hope!"

Acsriot's blade seemed to come at Aidan from every angle. Aidan stumbled, blocking recklessly and unable to regain the balance to attack. Acsriot was driving him backward, and there was nothing Aidan could do but retreat. His arm ached from the blows, and he dropped his guard just slightly. Acsriot saw and stabbed forward. He missed Aidan's eye by a fraction of an inch but opened a gash on his right cheekbone. Aidan felt the warm blood trickle down his face.

Acsriot came on again. His sword flashed and stabbed, forcing Aidan up a hill near one of the catapults. The Twelfth Knight had run out of room. With a swift hacking motion, Acsriot knocked the Son of Fury from Aidan's hands. The blade flew end over end and landed with a dull clang on the road, far from Aidan's grasp.

Aidan awaited the final thrust. Acsriot, the traitor, would win— plunging his sword through Aidan's chest. And it would all be over.

But Acsriot did not kill Aidan. Instead, he picked up an iron-tipped spear from a fallen knight and drove it through Aidan's shoulder armor into the heavy wood of the catapult's base.

"I could have run you through," snarled Acsriot. "But I have learned from my master to savor the kill. And so I will not allow you to die without watching you suffer first. Have you heard of morti-wraith venom?"

Aidan's eyes went wide, and he struggled to free himself. But he was pinned.

"I see that you have," Acsriot said, and he laughed. Stepping backward down the hill, he turned slightly and motioned with his sword to three Paragor archers perched on a distant roof, with drawn bows aimed directly at Aidan. "Wriggle all you want, little Dark Skin. Your end, your painful end, is near."

Aidan watched as the archers let their arrows fly. The crimson-shafted, poison-tipped arrows were racing through the air when two dark blurs streaked horizontally through their path. Two of the red shafts were snapped, splintered in the air by the swifter arrows from Nock's and Bolt's longbows.

But the third red arrow flew on.

With a great shout, Captain Valithor appeared from nowhere and leaped between Aidan and the final arrow. It pierced the Captain's armor and was buried halfway into his chest. He crashed to the ground at the base of the hill where Aidan was caught.

"Noooo!" Aidan shrieked. He wrenched all his weight against the armor, desperately trying to go to the Captain's side, but he could not. He could only stare down at his fallen commander.

Captain Valithor struggled to reach for Fury. But Acsriot snatched up the famed blade and carelessly flung it behind him. He back-handed the Captain across the chin. The Captain, already weakened by the venom, fell on his back.

Acsriot, his cloak swirling, stood at Captain Valithor's feet and smiled triumphantly at his prey. "I thought I'd killed you before, old one," he said, sneering and gesturing to the sky with his sword. "And as much as I would like to see the mortiwraith's venom twist you and run its course, there would be no glory in that for me. I want to be the one remembered for slaying the famed Captain Valithor of Alleble."

Acsriot clutched his sword with both hands and raised it overhead. Captain Valithor looked up, his eyes darting left for the briefest of seconds before they locked with the flickering red eyes of his attacker. The Captain raised his trembling hand and opened his lips to speak. Acsriot delayed his strike.

"What is it, Captain?" Acsriot said with feigned pity. "Do you wish to beg for mercy?"

Captain Valithor, a glint in his eyes, spoke, "I told you, Acsriot, that for your treachery, you will die by my sword!"

Acsriot grinned smugly and tensed to deliver the killing stroke. But his smile vanished.

"This is Fury!" said a voice from behind. And the point of a long sword burst through Acsriot's chest. He had forgotten the Twelfth Knight.

Acsriot writhed like a beetle on a pin as his sword fell harmlessly to the ground. With all his might, Aidan shoved Acsriot's body off of Fury and down the hill.

With his shoulder armor torn off and hanging by a link of chain mail, Aidan knelt by Captain Valithor. Kaliam appeared, saw the crimson shaft, and grimaced.

Before anyone could speak, however, a blinding flash of light bathed the road from moat to outer wall in angry red light. And a sound like a hundred cannon blasts seemingly shook the whole world.

A shock wave of scalding hot air surged out into the road, incinerating those near the castle and slamming Aidan and Kaliam to the cobblestone.

Aidan sat up, spit grime from his mouth, and crawled back to Captain Valithor. The Captain looked withered and frail, and his breathing was too fast. Aidan carefully removed the Captain's helmet. Then the Captain rested his head on Aidan's lap.

Aidan looked toward the castle. The main gate was blasted, and it seemed the main wall and the battlements were bulging inward as if it would collapse upon itself. And everything, everything burned: the towers, the parapets, the keep. It all burned. Fire reached up from the moat like a molten beast, clawing, escaping from cracks in the earth.

From the moat for fifty yards nothing moved upon the road. Blackened, twisted Glimpse forms lay heaped and tangled, smoldering. Closer to Aidan, soldiers, mortally wounded, some in the dark livery of Paragory, a few others in blue and gold, lay groaning, gasping for air.

There was still the rumor of battle behind Aidan—the ring of swords, the cries of victory and defeat—but it seemed so far away.

Aidan blinked back tears. He was alive, but it didn't matter. He had lost Gwenne, the Castle of Mithegard was in flames, and Captain Valithor lay dying in his arms.

AIDAN'S CHOICE

Paragory had won. The outer walls of Mithegard had been thrown down; every cottage and home had been raided and destroyed; the once proud Glimpses of Mithegard were scattered, killed or captured; and Mithegard Castle was in ruins.

The army of Mithegard, aided by the Knights from Alleble, had fought valiantly, defeating more than half of Paragory's invading force. But in the end, Paragory had too many soldiers and too much firepower for the tiny resistance to handle.

Led by Lord Rucifel, the enemy's remaining forces gathered and stored all salvageable weapons and war machines. They also herded together hundreds of captured Mithegardian peasants and soldiers, put them in chains, and began their long journey around the mountains of the Black Crescent back to Paragory.

Aidan, Kaliam, and their mortally wounded Captain were left in the middle of the carnage-filled battlefield. How they had been missed by the scavenging Paragor Knights, Aidan did not know. He was so focused on caring for Captain Valithor that he had no thought of other concerns, including his own survival.

A single red arrow remained deep within Captain Valithor's chest, close to his shoulder. Such a wound would not ordinarily be life-threatening, for the arrowhead did not pierce the Captain's heart or any vital artery. But the mortiwraith venom was perilous and swift. That amount of toxin would have killed Aidan in a few agonizing seconds. But so great were the strength and courage of Captain Valithor that even with the venom coursing in his blood, he remained alive for some time—though reduced to a weak shadow of his former self.

"Can't we take the arrow out?" Aidan asked, blinking away tears.

"Nay, lad," responded the Captain softly. "That would do more harm than good."

"Is there nothing we can do? No remedy or medicine?" Kaliam pleaded.

"The poison has already found my heart," the Captain replied. "But weep not, Aidan! Soon, I will go and join the King, my wife, my mother and father and, at last, be among those in the Sacred Realm Beyond the Sun."

"It's all my fault! I should have gotten free sooner! I tried, but the armor wouldn't come free." Aidan groaned. He looked at the glistening blood on his trembling hands. It was not his own blood, but he felt it should have been. "Captain, you shouldn't have saved me! Alleble needs you . . . more than me."

For a moment, the Captain returned to his fiery, cantankerous self. He stared Aidan straight in the eye.

"Sir Aidan, thou tottering, beetle-brained lummox! How dare you measure yourself against another! No one who follows the King of Alleble is greater or lesser than the other. We are all equal in the King's eyes!"

"But, I'm just a kid, and you, you're a mighty knight, the Captain of Alleble's armies!" Aidan argued. "You've won countless battles for the King!"

"I have lost more battles than I have won, as the King measures victory," sighed the Captain, putting his hand on Aidan's shoulder. "And any glory in battle belongs to King Eliam, for it was his might in me that led to every victorious deed. His unyielding strength . . . is within you now as well."

With a groan the Captain closed his eyes, and it seemed a great effort for him to speak again. "Now, Aidan, Kaliam, listen to me closely . . . I have but little time to remain. You must not despair, for our mission did not fail, and it is . . . not . . . over . . . yet!"

"But, Captain . . . ," Kaliam objected. "Mithegard is in ruins—"

"Yes, young Kaliam," the Captain interrupted. "Mithegard the city is destroyed, and yet . . . many of the Mithegardian Glimpses are now allied with the true King, and that is a victory worthy of a new scroll in the great Story of Alleble! Before that chapter is written, however, there is much work to be done. Kaliam, there must be survivors still hiding in Mithegard. Many of the cottages have underground shelters—if memory serves—so stay here and do not rest until every last Glimpse is found. I do not know how many of the twelve survived. I thought Mallik, Farix, and the twins were yet alive. Find whom you can. Then, lead those who are willing to the safety of Alleble."

"Aye, Sir!" replied Kaliam, standing up. The Captain had given him a new mission to accomplish and with it, a new hope.

"And you, Sir Aidan . . . ," said the Captain, his voice weak and congested. "You must rescue Gwenne and—"

"Gwenne?!" Aidan interrupted, unexpected hope pulsing in his heart. "She's alive?"

"Yes, lad, . . . she was captured by Rucifel . . . hundreds of Mithegard's citizens and soldiers were taken captive as well. Even now they are traveling at speed to the Gates of Despair."

"Was King Ravelle captured as well?"

"If I know my s—" The Captain's body shuddered, and he coughed. "I . . . I cannot imagine Ravelle allowing himself to be captured alive, and yet, I did not see him here among the dead . . . I cannot say," his voice trailed off. His eyes fixed on a point beyond Aidan for a moment, but then he blinked and spoke again.

"In any case, you must hurry! You must catch them when they make their first camp, for once they cross the border into Paragory, all hope for their rescue will be lost!"

"But Captain," Kaliam spoke, "our dragon steeds, they are all slain."

"How can I catch up to them?" Aidan protested, feeling more like a pudgy, slowpoke teenager than a battle-tested Alleb Knight. "They have a huge head start, and I don't have a dragon—or even a unicorn to ride!"

Captain Valithor had closed his eyes and clenched his teeth, struggling against the pain to think.

". . . And even if I could find a moonrascal's tunnel heading in the right direction, there's no guarantee it would come out where I need to go."

But when Aidan mentioned tunnels, the Captain's eyes snapped open. "There is a way," he announced. "Kaliam!"

"Sir?" answered Pathfinder, kneeling again next to the Captain.

"You know the way to Falon's Stair?"

"Yes . . . but—"

"Show Sir Aidan the way. If my guess is correct, the Army of Paragory will make camp upon the plains of the Black Crescent. If Sir Aidan travels Falon's Stair and through the underground labyrinth, it will bring him up behind the enemy's camp!"

"But, Captain," Kaliam objected, "that's suicide! No one who enters Falon's domain ever comes out again!"

"Who is Falon?" Aidan asked.

Captain Valithor, his voice thin and distant, replied, "Falon is a creature, the greatest of all mortiwraiths. She lives in a stone maze beneath the mountain—"

"You mean I need to go where a mortiwraith lives?!" Aidan blurted out. He knew as much as he needed to know about mortiwraiths. He was watching just a touch of its venom slowly draining the Captain of life.

"Falon lives in this maze, but she does not slay those of pure heart for sport. And . . . she owes me a favor. Many years ago, I came across a rank of Paragor Knights who had captured one of Falon's wraithlings. They were beating the young creature with clubs, trying to kill it so they could harvest its poison. I rescued it and returned it to Falon. She vowed to repay me someday. Today is that day! It is the only hope of getting to Gwenne and the others from Mithegard in time."

"Let me go instead!" argued Kaliam. "Or at least let us wait until one of our own can go with him."

"No, Kaliam. Do you see Mallik, Tal . . . anyone?" The Captain gasped, blood trickling from one corner of his mouth. "We have no time to wait. You know what our enemy will do to the prisoners from Mithegard . . . to Gwenne once the Gates of Despair close behind them. And I feel in my heart that this task is meant for Aidan . . . or no one at all. Will you go, Sir Aidan? Will you travel Falon's Stair?"

An incredible array of thoughts kaleidoscoped in Aidan's mind. He remembered Gwenne's description of a mortiwraith: a long, snakelike creature with many sets of clawed feet, and huge jaws filled with flesh-ripping teeth. And Falon was the largest, craftiest mortiwraith to ever live! Aidan could not imagine facing such a creature, but even if he did somehow survive the mortiwraith, what would he do once he came up from underground? It would be Aidan against Lord Rucifel and hundreds—maybe even a thousand—Paragor Knights!

He thought as well about how he had come to such a point—so many pieces had to fall into place to bring him to this exact moment. And none of it was a result of chance.

Aidan thought of Gwenne too. Gwenne had become his best friend. Now she was held captive, destined to be tortured and killed.

"I'll go," Aidan declared softly.

Captain Valithor nodded. "Sir Aidan, loyal servant of Alleble, you have truly become a knight on this journey. You will need to become even more as you face the perils that lie ahead of you . . ."

The Captain closed his eyes again and whispered, "When you face Falon, remind her of my name, and . . ." He placed Aidan's hand on the hilt of the sword called Fury. "Show her this sword. She will be reminded of a favor I once did for her when my beard was more brown than gray. Tell her it is your sword now . . . and the favor must then be repaid to you."

Aidan looked down at the sword. No blood could mar its shining blue blade, for it gleamed just as brightly as it did the first time Aidan saw it hanging in Alleble's armory. But he didn't want the sword. Not this way. He wanted Captain Valithor's wound to heal.

"Sir Aidan," Captain Valithor spoke again, barely audible, "though you will face many trials by yourself . . . you are never alone."

Tears flowed freely down Aidan's cheeks. Valithor, the noble

Captain of the Elder Guard, was gone from his body—gone to live forever with King Eliam in the Sacred Realm Beyond the Sun.

Though Aidan knew that precious seconds were ticking away, he needed a final moment with the fallen hero. Captain Valithor had been tough on Aidan, very tough. But he had trained Aidan well and made a fearful teenager into a confident Knight of Alleble. Then, in a sacrifice Aidan thought he would never understand, the Captain had stepped in front of a deadly shaft meant for Aidan.

Aidan found his own sword, the Son of Fury, and placed it on the Captain's chest. Aidan gently crossed the Captain's arms over the short sword.

Then, with both hands, Aidan picked up the mighty blade called Fury and placed it in his own sheath. It was heavy, and the tip of the blade would drag on the ground at times, but he would wear it with honor. Aidan hoped he could accomplish something to justify the gift.

Kaliam gestured to Aidan that it was time to go, but Aidan let his eyes linger on the Captain just a little longer. The fierce expression always worn by the Captain, even the pain from the fatal wound, had faded in death.

He now looked peaceful and relaxed—more like he was sleeping.

In fact, Aidan was reminded of his grandfather when he used to fall sound asleep in his wheelchair. In some ways, Captain Valithor looked much like Grampin. Very much like him indeed . . . Then Aidan realized, from the moment the Captain thundered into Alleble's courtyard to address the knights, his piercing blue eyes flashing, Aidan had always felt there was something familiar about him. And now he knew. Captain Valithor was the Glimpse of his grandfather.

Aidan felt a heavy weight upon his heart, for he realized what the Captain's death meant. "Good-bye, Grampin," Aidan said quietly as he and Kaliam walked away.

FALON'S STAIR

Those lonely peaks rise steadily into the Black Crescent range and then, eventually, to the Prince's Crown," Kaliam said as he led Aidan south of Mithegard and pointed to a dark, curling mountain range.

Aidan knew the path he would need to take already. "Gwenne and I came that way."

"So then, did you see the gate hewn into the mountain? That is the entrance to Falon's Stair."

"No, um, the way we came, we kind of shot past it, I think."

Kaliam stooped to the ground. "It is clear that the Army of Paragory traveled west to go around the mountains. Captain Valithor is right; they will camp inside the Crescent. But you will not follow, Sir Aidan. You shall continue north and find the entrance to Falon's Stair. You will need to run, if there is to be any hope. The Black Crescent is a full two leagues from here."

"Have you ever been there, in Falon's Labyrinth?" Aidan asked, swallowing hard.

"What, me? In the mortiwraith's lair? Nay, Sir Aidan. I have traversed many paths in my time, but that is one trail I have avoided. And if I had not heard it from the Captain's own lips, I should never let you pass that way either!"

Aidan shook his head in agreement. Favor or not, Aidan didn't want anything to do with a mortiwraith.

"This, then, is farewell," said Kaliam, holding out his hand to Aidan. "I need to return with haste to Mithegard."

"Before you go, Kaliam . . . may I ask you something?"

"Of course."

"Back on the Grimwalk, when the Tempest came, how did you and the other knights escape? I mean, Gwenne and I jumped into a moonrascal hole!"

"Dragons," replied Kaliam. "Just like that traitor Acsriot, only it was the King of Alleble who sent the dragons for us! The storm forced us to fly east of the Cold River. Finally, when the winds and snow had stopped, we flew back to the Grimwalk. We too wondered what had become of you—we searched for you through the night, in fact!"

Aidan shook his head.

"I hope we shall meet again," said Kaliam. "You are a valiant lad, Sir Aidan, and a true servant of Alleble. Remember . . . never alone!"

"Never alone!" Aidan replied, though in truth he had never felt more alone in his life.

Kaliam sped off, backtracking to Mithegard, and Aidan turned and looked across the fields with their humps of purple moss. Two leagues, Kaliam had said. Aidan didn't know how long a league was, but he knew it was long enough.

King Eliam, Aidan called out in his mind. *If ever I have needed your strength and your help, it is now.*

Aidan took off. He ran at full sprint, but after only a hundred yards or so, his heart crashed against his rib cage, and he found himself gasping for air. *This isn't working,* he thought, and he stopped.

Reluctantly, Aidan stripped off his armor. Off went what was left of the shoulder harness, off went the breastplate, the vambraces— even the couters! When Aidan was finished, all he had left was his tunic and his breeches. He removed Fury, still in its sheath, and carried it by hand.

Then, Aidan took flight—or at least it felt like flying. Removing all that heavy metal made a huge difference, and Aidan ran light on his feet.

Aidan rocketed across the fields, driven by thoughts of Gwenne in danger. How he would rescue Gwenne if he somehow emerged from beneath the mountains, he had no idea, but he resigned himself that, if need be, he would die trying.

As he ran, he thought too of his friend Robby back in Maryland.

Aidan remembered a conversation he and Robby had shared the night before Aidan left for Colorado. It was a troubling conversation, full of anger and fear. Robby had asked Aidan hard questions. They were questions that Aidan could not answer . . . then.

"When I was ten, my parents started fightin'," Robby had said, *staring at the floor and wringing his hands continuously. "Dad'd complain about the house or the money. Then, Momma'd be upset that he was never around. I mean, they'd just holler at each other, callin' each other things and slammin' doors. I got so scared sometimes, I hid in my closet until they stopped. After a while . . . it got even worse. Then, one night my*

*Dad didn't come home—haven't seen him since. Don't even
know if he's still alive. It doesn't make any sense, Aidan. Is this
how life's supposed to be?"*

"What do you mean?" Aidan had asked.

"I mean, first I lose my dad. Now I'm losin' my best friend.
It's like life is some cruel joke. Doesn't seem like things ever
work out for anybody, especially me."

"It's not that bad," Aidan replied hollowly. He was
instantly reminded of his father attempting to explain how
great moving would be.

"It's not?!" Robby objected bitterly. "Then, tell me . . . why
do awful things like this happen? Why'd my dad take off? Why
do you have to move? Why do all those horrible things on the
evening news have to happen?"

That night, Aidan had nothing to say. But now Aidan had all the
answers Robby needed to hear. *But who will tell him,* Aidan wondered . . . *if I don't survive?*

Spurred by the fear that no one would tell Robby—or Aidan's
own mom and dad for that matter—the truth about Alleble, about
the reality of The Realm, Aidan reached deep within himself and
found a gear he did not know he had. He traversed the final mile of
the journey at top speed. The dark mountains of the Black Crescent
loomed in front of him.

At the base of the mountain, some fifty yards away, a small but obvi-
ous cavelike entrance gouged the smooth face of rock. Aidan threw
away his sheath, took Fury in both hands, and approached.

The entrance had no door, fence, or gate of any kind. It was simply a rectangular opening cut right into the side of the mountain. On a large stone next to the entrance was carved an odd and unnerving poem. Aidan read it to himself and shivered.

> Ye have come to Falon's Stair,
> But enter not ye unaware,
> For better men than thee have fled.
> They that entered soon were dead.
> The darkness spins your mind with fright,
> As you descend into her night.
> Beyond the steps the labyrinth waits,
> With dangers untold and treasures great.
> Know ye this as ye travel the maze:
> Lest ye fall under Falon's gaze,
> There is one path alone to the light of day.
> And death will come if ye lose your way.

With considerable dread, Aidan looked into the opening. The diminishing late-afternoon sun provided just enough light for him to see that Falon's Stair actually was a spiral staircase. It curled down and in before disappearing into darkness.

This was no spooky legend or an imaginary boogeyman. To step down would be to enter a living nightmare. Either Aidan faced almost-certain death under these dark mountains or he turned back, allowing the wretched Knights of Paragor to take Gwenne and the others into a nightmarish land of torment and pain. Aidan took a deep breath. He simply could not allow his friend and other innocent Glimpses to die while he did nothing.

"Never alone," he said aloud, and he stepped out of the waning sunlight into the darkness of Falon's Stair.

Aidan held Fury out in front and began to descend. It was some comfort to have such a mighty blade as Fury with him. Even so, he took each step cautiously, stopping from time to time to listen for anything that might be traveling up the steps to meet him. Soon, the last glimmer of faint light was gone, and Aidan found himself in the deepest darkness he had yet encountered.

Of course, the moonrascal tunnels were dark too, but they seemed almost cheerful compared to the smothering black that surrounded Aidan now.

Holding the sword up as best he could with one hand, Aidan used the other hand to feel his way along the cold stone wall of the stair. *What was that?* He stopped. Aidan was certain he'd heard something down the stairs move just slightly. Aidan's heart hammered away, and he used every last ounce of hearing ability, straining to pick up the sound again.

He waited and waited, but he did not hear anything. *My mind is playing tricks on me.*

Venturing farther, he began wondering if the gigantic slithering beast could be silently hunting him. Or maybe it was simply waiting with its tremendous jaws open at the bottom of the stairs, waiting for Aidan to blindly fall right in!

Aidan didn't want to be so afraid, but his body betrayed him. Aside from his breathing and racing heart, Aidan's mouth felt full of sawdust, his throat full of gravel, and every muscle in his body was as tense as a bowstring.

To make matters worse, the temperature began to fall. Aidan was cold, for a tunic and a pair of leather breeches did nothing to turn away the eerie chill of the underground. Aidan guessed that he must be half a mile or more beneath the surface, and still the stairs went down.

The sound again! This time closer! It was too much for Aidan; he simply reacted. Grasping the mighty Fury with both hands, he swung the sword frantically in front of him. It clashed and clanged off the stone walls, sending sparks flying and a near-deafening metallic ring echoing up and down the stairs.

Aidan cringed, holding the sword pitifully out in front of him. *She knows I'm here now,* Aidan's mind raced. *Would Falon come? Was this the end of the adventure?* Aidan soon had an answer.

"Welcome," came a raspy, purring voice. The word was stretched as long as a fully exhaled breath. Icy wind swirled up the stairs. "It's been soooo long since I've had a visitor . . . and a young one too, if my sense of smell is still keen . . ."

Aidan heard a whistling as the great beast inhaled deeply. "Mmmm . . . yes," the voice continued, exhaling. "It is a young visitor, young but not Glimpse-kind. A nice surprise for Falon. What brings a savory young lad into a dark, dangerous place, hmmm? Is it treasures you seek? They are here . . . the finest gold, the most precious silver, and simply exquisite jewels . . . all for the taking, hmmm?"

Aidan was frozen. He tried several times to open his mouth to speak, but the words would not come.

"Pity . . . ," came the voice again. "Not much to say . . . hmmm? Then perhaps riches are not what you seek. Then, could it be . . . you've come down my stair to slay little old Falon, is that it? Well, delectable one, is that what you aim to do?"

The beast laughed a sinister, mocking laugh that eerily echoed up the stairway.

Feeling that he'd better say something lest Falon get the wrong idea, Aidan forced himself to reply. "No, I . . . I don't wish to harm you," he stuttered. "Nor do I want to be harmed by you. I j-just want to get through because someone is counting on me."

"Well then," Falon replied, "why didn't you say so, hmmm? You're just a noble lad seeking passage, that's all . . . Come, then, your path leads through my little labyrinth. Come on, hmmm?

"Don't be afraid, for though I am very hungry, yes . . . famished, I promise not to harm you. No, I won't even take so much as a nibble . . . as long as you find the right path through my maze. But you must make it all the way through, your first try! The moment you make even a single wrong turn . . . I'll come visit you, my delicious stranger. Is it a deal, then, hmmm?"

"But, wait!" Aidan stammered. "There's a fav—"

"Good then," Falon decided. "You come on down to my little maze, hmmm? And I'll just sneak off to my secret hiding place. Remember, not even one wrong turn . . ."

Aidan heard a great slither of motion from not too far below and then, silence. "Wait!" he cried again. "Captain Valithor said you owe him a favor!"

There was no answer, only silence . . . waiting, hungry silence.

How could an enormous man-eating creature be trusted? Aidan decided that he didn't really have much of a choice, so he grasped Fury with both hands and continued down the stairs.

Eventually, it began to get lighter—not the glad, golden light of the outdoors, but rather a ghostly blue glow. Aidan could at least see the steps in front of him, and for the moment, that was some comfort.

Aidan followed the stairs around a bend. He lowered his sword and gaped. For his first sight of Falon's Labyrinth literally stole his breath. The labyrinth lay in an underground cavern lit from above by glittering, gem-covered stalactites of deep purple and blue. The cavern floor was a garden of dark green rocks and coral-like stalagmites. And in the center of it all, more captivating than all the jeweled stones, was the labyrinth itself. Vast, intricate, and clever, the network of passages, turns, and dead ends ambled all over the cavern floor.

Its walls were twenty feet high and dotted with an array of jewels that sparkled and winked in the strange underground light. Aidan had expected a dark, dreary place, one fraught with jagged edges, cold pools of water, and pale, sightless creatures. And he wondered that such a sinister, evil creature would live in a place so marvelous and beautiful. If Aidan's life hadn't been in danger, he would have liked to just sit and look at the wondrous maze. As it was, however, he knew he had to figure out a way through.

Aidan was above the labyrinth, looking down at its entrance. *How am I supposed to do this?* he wondered. The walls were far too high to climb, the twists and turns were too complex, and Aidan had never been very good at solving puzzles or mazes. But as Aidan stared, he remembered a conversation he had shared with Gwenne one night while studying lore in the castle's lower library.

"I don't think I'll be much help on this mission," he had said.

"Fear not, Aidan," Gwenne replied. "You have the best teachers in all of Alleble to help you complete your training."

"No, that's not what I mean." He shifted nervously in the tall chair. "See, I'm just not good at doing things on my own—even when I know what to do! I get afraid, all stressed-out, and I mess up."

Gwenne smiled and had that mischievous look in her eyes. "You seem to think that you must rely only upon yourself. Have you forgotten King Eliam?"

"I can't even go see him. And the scrolls don't deal with every situation."

"True. But, Aidan, there is something you must understand. When you opened The Door Within, it was not just so that you could pass through it, as you might go into a shop or a cottage. No, it was so that the King could become a part of you. King Eliam lives within you now, and you will never be alone."

NEVER ALONE. Aidan felt peace, in spite of the task before him. He knew that King Eliam was with him and that, somehow, he would guide him through.

Aidan stared intently at the labyrinth, and suddenly, the sparkles in certain areas of the maze began to glitter more brightly. A pattern began to materialize: right, pass two; left, pass one; left, pass one; right, pass two; left, pass one; left, pass one . . . He couldn't see it all the way through to the end, but he hoped he could figure it out once he got in.

"Not fair, appetizing one!" Falon's voice echoed throughout the cavern. "You must begin now, or I will come for you!"

Aidan had no idea which direction Falon's voice had come from. It seemed to bounce all over as if she were somehow everywhere all at once. Aidan didn't want her to get angry, so he ran down the steep hill and into the entrance to the labyrinth.

"Right, pass two; left, pass one; left, pass one; right, pass two; left, pass one; left, pass one," Aidan said to himself as he made his first turn to the right. It was a much different point of view inside the maze. Everything looked the same. The walls were all solid-looking marble with unusual patterns running through them, and each turn he skipped looked like it could have been the right way.

But Aidan didn't second-guess. He stuck to the pattern: right, pass two; left, pass one; left, pass one; right, pass two; left, pass one; left, pass one . . .

As he made his second left, however, something went wrong. He skipped one turn, but there was supposed to be a right turn right after the one he skipped! He looked ahead, far down the passage. There were several left turns, but the next right turn was a lot farther away than it should have been. Aidan sat down on the ground for a moment and placed his sword across his lap. He had to be careful—one wrong turn, and he was history.

"Well," he told himself, "the pattern has been right so far . . . otherwise Falon would have eaten me already." Eventually, Aidan decided that it was the King of Alleble who had given him the pattern, so he needed to follow it. Right, pass two; left, pass one; left, pass one; right, pass two; left, pass one; left, pass one . . .

He jogged up the hallway and took the right turn. *No mortiwraith—that was definitely a good sign!* He continued with the pattern, even though, two or three times, the distances between the turns seemed much different from what he remembered. One time, Aidan stopped to count turns. He thought he heard a noise behind him, so he spun around to look. His jaw dropped because the end he had just passed through was now closed—sealed off! The maze had changed behind him.

I must be seeing things, Aidan thought. He shook his head comically and then continued on, following the pattern. There was still no sign of the mortiwraith. Finally, he came to a place where the pattern seemed to stop. Ahead of him was one left turn and a long, long straight passage.

This must be where the pattern ends, he thought, walking cautiously up to the left turn to see if he could find out where it led.

Holding his breath anxiously, he peered around the corner. He exhaled that stale breath in awe, for down that hall was a vault full of TREASURE!!

Not in all the museums he'd ever visited had Aidan seen such wealth.

Sparkles of red rubies, green emeralds, and blue sapphires blinked and winked at Aidan from enormous dark-wood chests. There were great piles of gold and silver coins. And barrels full of sharp iron battleaxes, huge powerful-looking bows, and quivers full of arrows. Wrought-iron helmets, chain-mail gauntlets, jewel-studded war horns, broad silver shields—every imaginable precious thing seemed to be there.

Aidan turned and looked up the long, straight passage. There weren't any riches in that direction that he could see, but if the pattern repeated itself, he should continue that way to search for a right turn. Still, he looked back left . . . he couldn't decide. Every time he made up his mind to go straight, he kept thinking of things he could do with the treasure. *With all that gold and stuff, surely I could bribe the Paragor Knights into letting Gwenne go . . . I could maybe use that shield in battle. . . . Or, perhaps, one of the battleaxes would be nice. . . .*

Finally, he chose, and though there was a quiet, nagging feeling tugging at him to go straight, the temptation of treasure was too much. Aidan turned left and walked toward the fortune.

As he walked toward the first chest, he thought, *I guess this must have been the right way after all.* Then Aidan picked up a shiny gold coin from a large chest.

The ground began to tremble, and there was a thunderous, angry roar.

"Greedy fool!!" shrieked Falon, her voice again echoing from all directions.

Aidan cowered in fear, grasping his sword and looking every which way for a sign of the creature. As he looked on, the ground shook even more violently. But then Aidan noticed something: The walls of the labyrinth were changing!

The solid stone seemed to soften, and the unusual marble pattern in the walls became more regular, like interconnected squares or shingles. And right before his eyes, the huge twenty-foot walls began to lift from the cobblestone floor. They rose from the ground and began to move, twist, and bulge.

In one corner of a wall, the outline of something appeared, and something unfolded from the stone. Aidan stared and realized with dreadful certainty that it was a leg sticking out of the wall—a leg ending with a four-toed foot and razor-sharp talons.

In various other places along the other twisting walls, other legs extended. Then something locked in Aidan's brain. He was beyond the ability to think or move. He just watched as all the walls of the labyrinth uncoiled into a monstrous, snakelike body with innumerable pairs of clawed legs. From the middle of the spiraling body arose an enormous round head, with creased ears folding backward and mingling with tufts of dark purple fur. Its eyes were moon yellow split by black, fanglike reptilian pupils. She stared down at Aidan in ravenous hunger. Her jaws opened, dribbling poisonous saliva and revealing row upon row of dagger-like teeth.

"Ssssso! You made a wrong turn, hmmm?" Falon laughed menacingly as she reared back to a great height, ready to strike.

Finally, the thought crystallized in Aidan's fear-struck mind. The mortiwraith wasn't *in* the labyrinth . . . the mortiwraith *was* the labyrinth!

No Small Favor

Aidan stood still, barely able to raise his sword a foot off the ground. It was all too clear now why no one who entered Falon's Labyrinth ever returned. The maze wasn't just difficult—it was alive! Falon, the largest and craftiest mortiwraith to ever live, had learned to make the coils of her tremendous serpentine body appear as stone and form the walls of the maze. Anyone who wandered in and became lost was doomed, for Falon was everywhere.

Towering over Aidan ominously, Falon prepared to strike. The monstrous beast's haunting yellow eyes flashed, and she lunged forward. Aidan feebly held up the sword called Fury. In those bleak moments before death, Aidan's mind raced. He wondered if he would die quickly, injected with Falon's lethal poison, or would he feel her dagger-filled jaws close around him, piercing his flesh in a hundred places at once? Aidan closed his eyes.

"I have a question for you, young one," said Falon, her steamy, reeking breath washing over Aidan. Opening his eyes, and glad to still be alive, Aidan saw that Falon's enormous head was just a few feet in front of him. He backed up reflexively and found a mighty clawed hand behind him.

"The sword you carry . . . ," she continued. "Tell me, where did you get it, hmmm? The truth, boy, for Falon knows if you lie. . . ."

Aidan came to his senses, and he remembered the favor the Captain had told him about. It was his only chance.

"This sword was given to me by Captain Valithor, the Captain of the Knights of Alleble and Sentinel of the King," Aidan announced.

Falon's eyes flashed, and her huge lips curled into a snarl. "I know the name Valithor! But he would not give up his blade to such as you!"

"Captain Valithor was killed," Aidan's voice cracked. "Shot with a poisoned arrow, deadly poison from one of your kind. He, he took the wound that was meant for me. Before he died, he gave me his sword and—"

"Lies!" Falon bellowed, slamming a clawed foot to the ground with a thunderous echo.

Aidan knew it was now or never—Falon was losing her temper!

"The Captain told me that you owe him a favor," Aidan pleaded. He slowly lowered Fury to the ground in front of the creature's great head.

"Captain Valithor said that a long time ago, he saved one of your wraithlings from some Paragor Knights who were trying to steal all of its poison. Captain Valithor said if I showed you his sword," Aidan swallowed hard, "that you would give that favor to me!"

Falon's demeanor changed instantly. The muscles, which tensed and rippled all over her snakelike body, relaxed. The fierce glow in her eyes paled, and her open mouth, drooling with hunger, closed with a wet snap. She crossed her two front legs and rested her chin on them.

"He and I alone know that story," she said softly. "Had it not been for good Sir Valithor, those greedy Paragor rats would have drained my baby's blood till there was nothing left of her. You see, our poison is not in our glands or stored in the hollows of our fangs. The poison is our blood. The servants of Paragor have nearly wiped my race from this land—and for what? So they could use our poison for their own dark purposes. One day, I will forget my fear of the sun and moon, and I will go to Paragory. In that day, I will satisfy my growing hunger for vengeance from Paragor and his brood.

"It saddens me that you speak the truth, for then the Captain has passed from this world. I owe him not only the life of my child but the preservation of my race. So I will honor him by granting you the favor. What is it you wish?"

"I just want to get through to the other side of the Black Crescent," Aidan replied. "The Paragor Knights have taken some friends of mine, and that is where they will camp—I think."

"Yesss . . . they camp there often." Falon nodded, her enormous, shrublike black eyebrows wrinkling and her lips curling in an exasperated sneer. "I've watched them, many times from my caves, longing for them to camp close enough for me to get at them. Oh, . . . what sweet revenge that would be!"

"Why don't you just go out after them?" Aidan asked.

"Nay, young one . . . ," Falon replied, shaking her head. "We mortiwraiths are cave dwellers. Longer than a few moments under the sun or the moon, and something happens to our blood. The poison within, the very life-bringing essence of it changes. And it becomes toxic to our own bodies. I would fall dead before I could exact a just price for what they have done to my kind. But," Falon said, inhaling deeply, "if ever they venture too close on a moonless night, I will come for them. And were they to dare to enter my caves, and travel into my maze, that would be a little different . . . hmmm? Then, they would know the wrath of Falon!"

It was quiet for a moment and Aidan had an idea. It was something, perhaps, but not all the pieces were there yet.

"Confirm something for me, young one . . . ," Falon said. "Was it the Paragor Knights who killed good Sir Valithor?"

Aidan nodded and stared at the ground. "Yes . . . they were trying to kill me, and Captain Valithor stepped in front of the arrow. He saved my life."

"It was a noble sacrifice," Falon replied.

"I wish it had been me," said Aidan, thinking of the Captain and his grandfather back home.

"Nonsense!" shouted Falon, slamming a clawed fist to the ground. "Wishing yourself dead isn't going to help the living! You said you have friends who were captured by the Knights of Paragory?"

"Yes, but—"

"And," Falon interrupted, "you said you need to get to the other side of these caverns so that you can save your friends, right?"

"Yes, but—"

"Then, young one, I suggest we leave soon, for the sun has set. When it rises again, the Paragor Knights will march toward their black kingdom."

"I guess you're right," Aidan replied. "Though I still have no idea what I'm going to do once I get there. What good is one person against an army?"

"You are a servant of Alleble, aren't you?" Falon asked, staring intently at Aidan.

"Yes, I am," Aidan answered, the meaning of Falon's question becoming clear. Fresh hope surged in his heart. "I am a servant of Alleble, and I am never alone!"

"That's the spirit, young one!"

"Aidan, my name is Aidan."

"Then, young Aidan, I shall hold Fury, and you climb onto my back," Falon said, smiling and extending an arm like a ramp for Aidan. "It is a long journey to the Black Crescent . . . a journey full of winding caverns and hidden pitfalls. It will be faster and far safer for you to ride."

Aidan carefully clambered up. He examined the creature a little differently now that he wasn't afraid of being eaten. The morti-wraith was scaled in layers like a dragon, but each scale was different and beautiful in its own way. Some were deep purple or blue like the luminous stalactites from the cavern's roof. Others were the dark green of the cavern floor. But all had embedded stones and precious gems. Aidan supposed the color and the gems had rubbed off as Falon traveled through the tunnels beneath the mountains.

As he climbed to her neck and sat down, he thought that Falon was a beautiful creature—though nevertheless fearsome in a pinch.

"Hold on to my hair, young Aidan," warned Falon. "I know every twist and turn of these caverns, so I tend to navigate them rather swiftly!"

Aidan gripped a couple of the thick cords of the creature's dark purple hair. He felt like he always did before a ride blasted off at the amusement park.

In moments, Falon began trotting along, increasing speed as she went. Aidan looked back and watched almost in a trance as Falon's numerous legs rose and fell rhythmically like pistons all along her lengthy body. *How many legs does she have?* he wondered.

The eerie blue light continued wherever Falon turned, and Aidan saw the openings to innumerable tunnels and caverns. And he knew there was no way he'd have ever made it through without Falon.

Her speed increased more and more, until she began to make turns, banking hard left and right. Struggling for a better grip, Aidan held on to Falon's ropelike locks for dear life as the air whipped by him. The muscles in Aidan's forearms burned with pain, and he screamed when his entire body went airborne as Falon dove low into underground valleys. When Falon leveled out each time, Aidan slammed into the back of her neck.

Unlike any roller coaster Aidan had ever ridden, Falon's ride seemed to last forever. Up, down, hard left, jerk right—all the while zooming at breakneck speed. He tried to look backward and side-ways, but everything was now a blur of various shades of purple, blue, black, and green.

If this ride didn't end soon, Aidan thought, he would surely fall off and be lost forever in these puzzling caverns.

Eventually, the air whistled a little less in Aidan's ears, and he sensed that Falon was slowing down. When she finally came to an abrupt stop, Aidan slid off her neck, down one of her front legs, and plowed facefirst into the mossy tunnel floor. He sat up and clutched at his forearms—they burned as if thrust into a furnace.

"Well, young Aidan," Falon said, breathing in heavy huffs and handing him Fury, "not bad for an old mortiwraith, hmmm?"

Aidan had to laugh in spite of the pain. "Yes, that was quite fast." He chuckled. "You just about bounced me off three or four times!"

"Well, young Aidan, I am glad you survived, for I guess you have much to do," said Falon, pointing with one clawed hand to the wide paths ahead. "Come this way, for these passages you see before you open into the caves of the Black Crescent."

Aidan followed Falon up the middle path. He had to walk to the side of her never-ending body as she half slithered, half crawled up the path.

"Falon, how many sets of legs do you have, anyway?" he asked.

"Many . . . ," she replied with an amused snort. "Mortiwraiths grow a new pair of limbs every five years, and as you can see . . . I've been around for quite some time."

The path wound onward and upward a short distance until, finally, the blue light of the caverns began to fade and was replaced by the subtle gray of night. The path ended, and an incredibly vast opening was before them. It was an opening to the plains of the Black Crescent. Aidan looked out, and he could see where the mountains got their name. The moonlit black peaks curled left and right before tapering off toward the horizon.

Inside the Crescent was an enormous plain dotted with hills and craggly trees. Aidan's attention was drawn to the center of the plain, for there was an immense dark mass, dotted with the light of torches and campfires. It was the army of Paragory—they were still there!

Great! Aidan thought. *Now all I have to do is sneak past a thousand heavily armed soldiers, release Gwenne and the other prisoners from Mithegard, and get back out without anyone noticing.*

"I'll be back in a second," Aidan whispered to Falon, and he ventured out of the cave. He needed to get closer to the enemy camp if there was any hope of finding out where they were keeping their prisoners. Gwenne's life depended on his coming up with a plan of rescue, and the odds of his success were stacked heavily against him.

There were patches of tall dead grass everywhere, and Aidan

crouched down as he passed through it to avoid being seen. As he did, a few tiny glimmers of light sprang to life in the grass. *LANTERN SPIDERS!* Aidan realized immediately. He had jostled them awake as he walked through the tall grass. They seemed to be all over the place, for every step Aidan took, the spiders' lights blinked on.

Aidan smiled, remembering early in the journey to Mithegard how terrified he had been, thinking that the lantern spiders were torch-bearing soldiers preparing an ambush.

Man, I need to catch some of these to take home, Aidan thought. *If I ever get out of here!*

He wandered through the tall grass as close as he dared to the Paragor Knights' camp. Aidan suspected they would have numerous sentries, watching for the slightest hint of an intruder. Sure enough, there were soldiers moving around in the camp. They were marching back and forth near the many tents. Aidan guessed that Gwenne and the other prisoners must be somewhere in the center tents—much more difficult for them to escape, or be rescued, for that matter.

There's no way I'm going in and out of there, unless, Aidan thought, *unless I could somehow get some of the Paragor Knights' armor . . . Maybe Falon would have some in her treasures! Still . . . they wouldn't just let me walk out of there with Gwenne and the others.*

Aidan knew there had to be a way. The King of Alleble wouldn't have brought him this far only to have him fail. So, Aidan looked from one end of the camp to the other. Then, he looked into the mountains and all over the plains. Could he start an avalanche? *Nope, no good.* The rocks would barely reach the camp. Maybe a fire . . . the tall dead grass would burn easily enough, but perhaps only enough to let the enemy know his position. *Okay, so that's not going to work, but then what?*

There just didn't seem to be much to work with: rocks, grass, a small stream that wound behind the enemy's camp. Aidan's eyes wandered along that tiny stream.

Strangely, it disappeared into a large dark clump of something. Trees maybe? Aidan stared at the huge mass, and he couldn't tell if his eyes were playing tricks on him or not, but it seemed like it was moving . . . how strange. Aidan shrugged and hurried back to the caves to talk to Falon.

He sprinted through the tall grass and hurtled up the hill into the caves. Falon lay there, her eyes gleaming somehow even in nearly complete darkness. "See anything useful, hmmm, young Aidan?"

"There are guards all over the place," Aidan replied shaking his head. "I might be able to sneak in, but I don't know . . . there are so many!"

"I wish I could help," Falon growled. "But even though the moon is veiled in clouds at this hour, it would be enough to finish me."

"What is that big gray clump beyond the camp?" Aidan asked, pointing toward the horizon.

"That, young Aidan, is a massive herd of blackhorne," Falon replied. "They graze upon the tall grasses. Mmmmm, what a feast that would be."

"Blackhorne, huh?" Aidan replied absently, his thoughts wandering. But suddenly, he felt a peculiar prickle on his neck. In a quick, reflexive movement, he swiped at his neck repeatedly.

"Looks like you picked up a stowaway while you were out playing in the grass," Falon laughed.

Aidan looked down at the floor of the cave, and there, skittering around, blinking frantically, was a rather large lantern spider.

"Yuck!" Aidan exclaimed. "That thing was on me?!"

In that moment, Aidan became very still. Something clicked in his mind. It was like turning the last number of a combination lock. A memory flittered through his mind, and the pieces of the plan came together all at once.

"Falon!" Aidan nearly shouted. "I think I know how I'm going to rescue my friends! And I think you can help!"

"Tell me, young Aidan," Falon replied, her enormous ears perking up like a bat's wings.

After Aidan explained his plan, a wide, mischievous smile spread across Falon's face. "Mmmm . . . sounds like a delicious plan," she said.

"Can you bring me those items from your treasures?" Aidan asked.

"Oh, yesss indeed!" Falon replied, turning back toward the tunnels. "I will make all speed, for the night will not wait for those who tarry."

THE PHANTOM ARMY

Falon returned in moments—apparently, she had been moving rather cautiously earlier, but with Aidan off her back, she was able to hurtle quickly through the tunnels and caverns beneath the mountains.

"Here is everything you asked for," Falon said, opening a hefty canvas satchel she had flung around her neck. "One Horn of War, quite loud, for I remember the fellow who carried it blowing it like mad when he saw me! Guaranteed to get the attention you want. One clay pot with a lid, large enough, hmmm? One longbow—it is from the Blackwood, the best there is—and a quiver full of arrows. And, of course, the armor and helmet of a Paragor Knight. It may not fit you just right, but it was the only one I could find that wasn't fouled or much too big. Oh, and this, I thought you might want a sheath for the sword of Valithor. It is heavy, hmmm?"

Aidan was amazed. "This is great, Falon, really. I can't thank you enough!" he said excitedly.

"Well, young Aidan," Falon replied playfully, "it is for Sir Valithor that I do this. But if your plan works out the way you described, you will have paid me back many times over, hmmm? Go now, save your friends! I will be waiting. . . ."

"Good-bye, Falon!" Aidan called after her. "I hope we meet again some day!"

"Perhaps." Falon's voice echoed, then faded.

Never alone, Aidan thought as he struggled to strap on the Paragor armor. He felt creepy putting on the black-and-crimson armor of the enemy, and the helmet was plainly too big, but it had to be done for the plan to work. The quiver of arrows slid easily over his shoulders, and the War Horn hung around his neck, but he had to carry the longbow in one hand and the clay pot in the other.

Aidan hopped cautiously out of the cave and down the little hill into the tall grass. Immediately, lantern spiders began to blink all around him. Aidan needed both hands for the clay pot, so he put down his longbow. As fast as he could, he meticulously began plucking the black-and-green arachnids from their webs in the grass and putting them in the clay pot. Aidan had never asked if the things were poisonous, but he didn't want to find out the hard way.

I wonder if anyone who dies from lantern spider bites would glow in the dark? With such thoughts, he continued brushing through the tall grass, grabbing every lantern spider that gave itself away by lighting up. Fortunately, the lantern spiders were numerous, and in a short time he had the great clay pot stuffed with hundreds of unhappy glowing critters.

With stage one completed, Aidan put the lid on the clay pot, picked up his longbow, and ran as fast as he could for the herd. The enemy's camp was between Aidan and the blackhorne, so he took a long, curving route to get to the animals. As he ran, the War Horn smacked against his armor on the front, and the quiver of arrows smacked him on the back, and worse still, his helmet kept sliding over one side of his face. Even so, Aidan hurried on.

Aidan could smell the large beasts long before he reached them. It was a mixture of thick animal sweat and tons of freshly deposited manure, and it was not pleasant. He wished he had a third hand to pinch his nose shut.

Blackhorne were similar to cows, Aidan noticed, but much, much bigger. Their coats were jet black and extremely shaggy, and all of them had a set of thick horns that protruded from the sides of their skulls and ran backward to a sharp point.

As Aidan got closer, he was surprised at the size of the herd: There were thousands of blackhorne. And even though they were peacefully munching on the dead grass, they looked dangerous. And Aidan was counting on that!

Aidan ran to where the blackhorne were closest to the camp of the Paragor Knights. There he again put down his longbow and opened the spider-filled clay pot. Swiftly, he took out the spiders, one at a time, and placed them atop the heads of the blackhorne. Most of the big, smelly animals didn't notice the spiders, though a few snorted and flopped their ears around a little. Aidan repeated the process over and over and over again, until the clay pot was empty and well over a hundred blackhorne had little glowing hitchhikers.

Then, he discarded the clay pot, retrieved his longbow, and circled around behind the herd. There seemed to be enough of the tall dead grass. There would have to be, for there was no time to cut and gather piles of grass—no, this would have to do.

Now begins the most dangerous part of the plan, Aidan thought as he reached down and picked up some mud. He smeared the dark, muddy soil on his face and all over the armor. Then, he drew Fury.

Aidan put the blade to his forearm and gritted his teeth. In one swift motion, he ran the sword across his arm, opening a large gash from which blood began to pour. He let the warm red fluid run down his arm and drip on his clothing, then his armor—he even spattered some on his helmet. The wound on his arm would leave an ugly scar, but it would be a scar Aidan would wear proudly . . . if he survived.

His costume complete, Aidan began the long run back toward the Paragor camp.

"Great King of Alleble," he said aloud. "Be with me, please, and guide me!"

With only a hundred yards between him and a thousand Paragor Knights, Aidan stopped and took in the deepest breath of nighttime air he could manage. He put the War Horn to his lips and let loose a tremendous blast on the horn. Its sound was a blend of a freight train and a thunderclap, and it echoed off the mountains of the Black Crescent. Again and again, Aidan blew the horn, shattering the quiet of the night.

Then, as Aidan sprinted again toward his enemies, he saw frenzied movement in the camp. He slowed down as he neared the first tent and began to hobble-run, dragging his left leg as if it were broken. Suddenly, a deep voice rang out from the shadows. "Halt! Declare yourself or be shot dead!"

"It's me, Dreadlock!" Aidan replied, giving the most evil-sounding name he could think of. "Don't shoot! Don't shoot! I was bringing a message from our master when I was attacked by some scouts from Alleble."

"What's this you say?!" exclaimed a huge ironclad Paragor warrior. Many other Paragor Knights were drawing swords and running up to join him.

"I barely escaped with my life," Aidan explained, trying to deepen his voice. "The armies of Alleble are on the way—thousands and thousands of knights. As I ran, I could see their torches behind me and hear the thunder of their steeds."

"I see nothing!" complained a short, stocky slant-eyed Paragor Knight. "Where are they?"

"Just over that ridge!" Aidan swallowed hard—they didn't seem to believe him, so he summoned his courage and lashed out at the Paragor Knights. "Listen, you fools! We can stand around here arguing until they swoop down on us and cut us to shreds! Or we can man the catapults and make ready for battle!"

There was a great murmuring among the knights until, finally, the tall one spoke again. "I don't see any—wait! There is something there. I see lights, lights in the shadows! We must make haste! Prepare the catapults!" He bellowed, pointing his long sword at the other knights. "Knights of Paragory, draw your blades, dip your arrowheads, for tonight we get to slay the armies of Alleble!"

The moment the order was given, the whole camp erupted in a flurry of activity. Well-armed knights ran every which way—some carrying supplies, others relaying orders, and still others manning their posts at the catapults. All of the knights near Aidan ran off as well—except one: the short, stocky Glimpse.

"You say you came from Paragor himself, bearing a message, eh?" he said, eying Aidan suspiciously. "Well then, what was the message?"

Aidan hadn't thought that far, but before he could answer, another Paragor Glimpse appeared and ordered the short one away. For the moment, Aidan was left alone and pretty much ignored. Aidan whistled a sigh of relief.

Then, dodging other knights as he went, Aidan started searching. There were boxes and crates everywhere, but so far he didn't see any barrels. After a brief moment of despair, he realized that the barrels would have to be near the catapults. Aidan ran from catapult to catapult, searching for the barrels he needed.

Finally, Aidan found one. Without hesitation, he drew his sword and poked a hole in the barrel. A thick greenish-brown fluid began to ooze out. Aidan took off his quiver of arrows and began dipping their razor-sharp tips into the oily liquid. He even let about four inches of the stuff pour into the quiver before he put the arrows back into it. Aidan wanted the arrows to soak in as much of the flammable liquid as possible.

The fuel-laden quiver slung over his shoulder again, Aidan ran for the edge of the camp. Hoping no one had seen him, Aidan ducked behind a tent. He took out one of the arrows and fitted it to the string of the longbow. Then, he held the point of the arrow in the flames of a nearby torch. The arrowhead ignited instantly, and Aidan took aim.

He pointed the fiery arrow in the direction of the herds of black-horne. He hoped that the blackwood longbow could fire as far as the twins had claimed. The arrows had to reach the dead grass behind the herd, or the whole plan would fail. Aidan pulled the bowstring back till he thought it might break, and then he released the arrow. It soared high into the night sky and disappeared. Aidan loosed another flaming arrow . . . then another. He fired until he had but one arrow left. He let the arrowhead catch fire from the torch, and he prepared to let it loose, but suddenly, a voice rang out from behind.

"Hold, Dreadlock! What are you doing?"

Aidan spun around, the burning arrow still fitted to the bow-string. To his horror, it was the short, slant-eyed Paragor Knight who had stopped Aidan before.

All Aidan could do was stare—there was no answer he could

give to explain why he was shooting flaming arrows into the sky. Then, with the worst timing in history, Aidan's too-big helmet slid down over half his face and then fell off entirely.

"Wait a sodden minute," said the brute. "You're not a Paragor Knight. Why, you're not even a Glimpse at all!"

The furious Paragor Knight drew his sword and charged at Aidan. There was only one thing Aidan could do. He quickly pulled back the bowstring and shot the flaming arrow right at the warrior's chest. The knight stopped abruptly and looked at Aidan with strange, questioning eyes. At first Aidan thought he had missed, but then, the Paragor Knight fell forward, flat on his face. On his back was a cruel wound still burning from the fuel that had rubbed off the arrow as it passed through the knight's body. The burning arrow was stuck firmly in a beam of a nearby catapult.

Aidan stifled the urge to throw up as he stepped over the body and ran out from behind the tent. Now he had to find Gwenne and the others. If he could find them, and if the flaming arrows hit their target, then maybe they would all get out of this. *If the arrows didn't make it, well* . . . Aidan thought, *they might as well all die together.*

Aidan threw the longbow to the ground and drew his sword. Paragor Knights were still rushing about preparing for battle. Aidan tried his best to look like he too was a Paragor Knight doing something to get ready for the attack. He ran from tent to tent, peeking in only briefly, hoping to find Gwenne.

But almost every tent was empty—no sign of Gwenne or the Mithegard Glimpses who had also been captured. Then, he saw it— about fifty yards away, in the center of the camp, were three large tents, and there were still dozens of guards posted around them. That had to be it! Before he could take another step, however,

Aidan heard something strange. There was a distant rumbling.

"They're coming!!" a Paragor Knight yelled.

"The Knights of Alleble are upon us!" another knight screamed, pointing at the horizon.

Aidan turned and looked, and there, with the horizon ablaze with orange, was a massive torch-bearing army. Only Aidan knew that they weren't knights at all. The arrows had reached the dead grass behind the herd. Now the mass of huge animals, many of them bearing lantern spiders, was stampeding in blind terror of the fire behind them. In moments they would crash into the camp. The plan was working!

Aidan immediately put the War Horn to his lips again and blew several short but deafening bursts. "The Knights of Alleble are too many!" Aidan yelled at the top of his lungs. "Hasten to the caves or we will be overrun!"

Someone nearby joined in. "Yes, run to the caves beneath the mountain! We can defend them better there than we can on this open ground!"

Thunderous sounds filled the air as thousands of blackhorne hooves pounded the earth.

Aidan continued yelling as he ran toward the guarded tent. "We cannot hope to win! The Knights of Alleble will kill us all! Run away! Hide yourselves in the caves! Find holes that you can defend. It's our only hope!"

The guards around the big tents already had their swords drawn when Aidan arrived. Once again, his helmet had slid down over his face. Aidan quickly adjusted it and began shouting at the guards, "What are you doing? Haven't you heard? The full army of Alleble is attacking! They're everywhere—ten thousand more than our force. And they bring upon us a wave of fire!"

The leader of the guard objected, "But what about the prisoners?"

"Let the prisoners burn!" Aidan commanded. "Are they worth your lives? Look!"

The guards turned just in time to see the first wave of blackhorne crashing into their camp! Only in their minds, it was a battalion of fierce Alleb warriors coming for them. Screams of agony arose from the camp's front lines as many Paragor Knights were trampled and crushed.

Seeing this, the guards bolted away from the tent, heading directly for the caves!

Aidan looked up as well, and he realized with horror that his plan had a major flaw: He, Gwenne, and the other prisoners were right in the path of the stampeding blackhorne!

Knowing he could be trampled at any moment, Aidan ran to the tent and ducked inside. There, bound and gagged, were Gwenne and five Mithegard Knights.

The King of Mithegard was not one of them. Aidan wasn't sure if he should cry for joy or sorrow, but he knew there was no time for either. He took his sword and cut the bindings off Gwenne and the others.

"Sir Aidan!" Gwenne shouted, spitting out her gag. "Praise the King! I thought you were dead!"

"Not dead yet!" Aidan barked. "But if we don't get out of here, we all may be killed. There's a huge stampede of blackhorne heading right for us! We need to get to the caves beneath the mountains!"

"Blackhorne?" Gwenne said, staring at Aidan.

"Where are the other Glimpses from Mithegard?" Aidan asked.

"There are nearly seventy spread throughout the big tents."

"So few?"

"Many were killed on our journey," Gwenne said through gritted teeth. "They were dragged and trampled to death."

"We'll save all we can," Aidan said. "We've got to go, now!"

The seven of them ran out of the tent into a chaos even worse than the slaughter at Mithegard. Enormous blackhorne were running wildly everywhere, stomping and crushing. Many Paragor Knights had already been killed, but those who were still alive were fleeing toward the mountains.

It was no trouble finding swords for Gwenne and the five Mithegardian Glimpses. Weapons littered the ground. Together they went from tent to tent, slashing the bindings and releasing the prisoners. At last, they could find no more.

"All the Paragor Knights are heading to the caves," Gwenne said anxiously. "We can't go there!"

"Yes we can!" Aidan replied. "It's a long story, but we don't have any choice. There are over a thousand blackhorne heading our way, and behind them is a raging fire—look!"

Gwenne looked at the horizon and saw the orange glow. She also saw the dark tide of terror-stricken beasts still crashing into the camp. Without another word, Aidan, Gwenne, and the others sprinted toward the caves. The blackhorne bounded by them on both sides, several times knocking one or more of them to the ground. They continued on, following the hundreds of Paragor Knights fleeing frantically toward the caves.

At last they bounded up the slight hill and over the lip of the cave entrance. Aidan swiftly led Gwenne and the others to a corner of one of the caves where he thought they could safely wait. They waited and watched as hundreds more Paragor Knights poured in through the many cave openings. The Paragor Knights were so frightened that they didn't even notice Aidan, Gwenne, and the other Mithegard Knights. They ran for cover, to save their own necks.

Row after row of Paragor Knights entered the caves and disappeared in Falon's endless tunnels. Their screams echoed everywhere
as they ran, but for some of the Paragor Knights, their screams
stopped abruptly . . . for Falon had come upon them in the dark.

THE COST
OF FREEDOM

In all my long years, I have never had such a splendid feast," said Falon, curling back part of her serpentine body so she could scratch her back on a row of stalagmites. "And now, young Aidan, I will take you and your friends back to my stair. I can carry many on my lengthy frame, and it is the least I can do since you have fed me for the next ten years!"

It was hours after sunup, and the once-menacing army of Paragory was no longer a threat to anyone—except, perhaps, to Falon, who, after such a large meal, might expect a hefty case of indigestion!

Falon laughed a deep, throaty laugh as Aidan, Gwenne, and the other Glimpses scrambled up her legs to find a spot for the ride. Aidan looked back at the survivors, and was content to be alive and reunited with Gwenne.

Falon again traveled through the tunnels and caverns beneath the Black Crescent, slower than before, because this time she had a very full stomach and more than seventy passengers holding on for dear life. The trip allowed Aidan time to let his mind wander over all he had learned. Gwenne explained how she had been captured when a squad of Paragor Knights found the trapdoor leading to the cellar in which she had been hiding. Fighting fiercely, she had wounded several enemies, but in the end, Gwenne had been taken captive. Lord Rucifel had planned to use her as a hostage to bargain with the King of Alleble.

The other Mithegard Knights had been captured during the huge battle at Mithegard or caught trying to flee the city. Had Aidan not rescued them, they were destined to become slaves beyond the Gates of Despair.

Everyone stared in amazement as Aidan recounted his ordeal and how he had tricked the enemy army.

"That was a brilliant idea, Sir Aidan," said Gwenne. "They thought Alleble had emptied, that the bulk of our army was attacking. Lantern spiders, indeed! Absolutely brilliant."

"It was so brilliant that it nearly got us all killed," Aidan replied. "Those blackhorne could have trampled us just as easily as the enemy. I don't know what influence King Eliam has on beasts in the wild, but I bet he had something to do with our not getting run over."

"That may well be, Sir Aidan," she said, her eyes glassy. "But still it was the bravest thing I've ever seen."

It had been an incredible victory, but for Aidan it was still a hollow victory, for no one had seen or heard from King Ravelle of

Mithegard, the Glimpse of Aidan's father. And of the twelve who originally set out from Alleble, Aidan only knew for sure that he, Gwenne, and Kaliam still lived. Aidan did not yet have the heart to tell Gwenne this or of what befell Captain Valithor as the castle of Mithegard was burning.

Falon finally dropped the knights off at the bottom of the long stairway back to the surface just a few miles outside of Mithegard. Not a single ray from the sun reached all the way down the stairs, so Falon gave Aidan and his friends a few torches to light their way. Aidan turned and looked at the gigantic mortiwraith. When roused, her appearance was terrifying, but at peace she was a beautiful, radiant creature.

"Falon, thank you for everything," Aidan said. "If it wasn't for you . . ."

"'Twas a benefit to us all, young Aidan," she replied, shaking her head. "Finally, I have repaid good Sir Valithor for the kindness he showed me long ago. And in the repaying, I have gained a friend, I think."

"Several friends!" Gwenne replied, correcting Falon. "We all are grateful for what you have done. We will make sure that everyone in Alleble knows that you are a hero—not the evil creature written about in the legends."

"Now, let's not be too hasty, hmmm?" Falon laughed sinisterly. "I have grown fond of that reputation—it keeps away unwanted visitors, you see."

"I'd like to come back and visit you some time," Aidan blurted out.

"Is that allowed, Sir Aidan?" Falon asked. "Well, no matter. You, Sir Aidan, are forever welcome here." Falon turned to leave, but quickly looked back at the young knight. "Now, on your way. Farewell, young Aidan. Farewell all!!"

And with that Falon was gone—back to the dark caverns and tunnels beneath the mountains. Aidan turned and led the way up the steep, winding stairway.

Somehow, the climb was so much easier than the descent, for Aidan had nothing left to fear. In a flash they reached the top, where the late-afternoon sun all but blinded them.

"It is glorious to be out in the sun again," one of the Mithegard Knights declared.

"It is glorious to be free!" another agreed.

Aidan turned, looked at the Mithegard Knights, and couldn't help but smile. They were filled with tremendous joy—the joy of freedom that can only be felt by those who realize what it's like to have that freedom taken from them. It was at that moment, staring into their eyes, that Aidan realized something amazing.

"Your eyes glint blue!" he yelled at the Mithegard Knights.

"These knights," Gwenne announced, gesturing, "have decided to follow the King of Alleble."

"We should have made this decision long ago," said one of the knights, his long blond hair dancing in the light breeze. "We were entranced by the shiny gold trinkets from Paragory's poison vaults. . . . Our greed has cost us much."

Aidan recalled the slaughter at Mithegard. It just didn't make sense how so many could be so blinded by their desires for riches and power. But then Aidan remembered how, deep in Falon's maze, he himself had foolishly gone after the golden treasures, ignoring the right path.

"Yes," Aidan nodded gravely. "We are all very fortunate to have survived our poor decisions."

"Well said," agreed one of the Mithegard Knights. Aidan fought the urge to laugh. It had been well said, but where in the world had this surprising wisdom come from?

Before this adventure, Aidan had struggled just to get a C on a math test, but now . . . now things were different. Aidan could know more, see more, and do more than he ever could have alone. *And I will never be alone again,* Aidan thought.

They walked for another hour, their pace quickening as they drew nearer to the burned-out walls of Mithegard. When they approached the smashed gates, Glimpses in bright silver armor poured out to greet them, but they were not from the ruined city. They were Knights of Alleble, and leading the way were four familiar faces.

Kaliam, Farix, Nock, and Mallik charged into Gwenne and Aidan. They held one another for long, silent moments as only soldiers who have battled side by side can embrace. In the looks that were exchanged there was grief, exhaustion, understanding, and relief. Great joy there was also, but tragedy tempered every smile.

"Sir Aidan, I feared you would perish in that dreadful creature's lair!" Kaliam declared, grasping Aidan by the shoulders. "And, Gwenne, it was almost beyond hope to have you both back safe!"

"Almost," Gwenne agreed, hugging Kaliam in turn. "But, with the mighty King of Alleble behind us, nothing is beyond hope! It was an extraordinary adventure!"

"I knew you'd make a first-rate knight the moment I saw you!" declared Mallik with a gleam in his eyes. Nock cast a disparaging look at his hammer-wielding friend.

"Your arm, Aidan!" exclaimed Kaliam. "That nasty wound needs attention."

"I'll be all right." In a weird kind of way, he was hoping it would leave a scar.

"How did you do it?" asked Farix. "How did you pass Falon's Stair? And how did you liberate Gwenne and the Mithegardians?"

"I'll be glad to tell you," Aidan said, looking among the other knights who had come out to greet them. "But where . . . where are the others?"

Mallik's jaw trembled, but he mastered it and threw his shoulders back. Tears burst forth from Nock's eyes. Kaliam seemed the only one who could speak. "Tal is in the city, for he could not bear to leave the wounded. But . . . the rest of our company, the rest fell in the battle."

"No," Aidan said, choking. He looked questioningly into Nock's eyes. "Bolt?"

"My brother was slain," Nock said slowly. "We emptied our quivers on the dark knights, but still they came. We fought with sword and dagger, but they rushed us with spearmen. Bolt was slain from behind, and I would have died with him if it weren't for the valiant onslaught of Sir Mallik. He brought his hammer on those villains and drove their bones into the earth! Never again will I argue my bow against his hammer."

"I only wish—" said Mallik. "I only wish I could have gotten to you sooner. But my hammer cannot reach like your bows."

Kaliam said, "Matthias and Eleazar were defending the castle gates when . . . when an explosion took them."

Gwenne stared wide-eyed like a lost child. Her question was barely audible. "You did not speak of Captain Valithor?"

Aidan, half-choked with tears, told Gwenne of the Captain's brave sacrifice. She fell into Aidan's arms, and they wept.

Finally, Kaliam said, "There will be time for mourning, but there is much left to be done—not the least of which is to get you a warm bath, a warm plate, and a warm bed lest your spirit fail utterly. Come, the city is not wholly destroyed, and with the supply sent from Alleble, the board is not as bare as you may suspect."

As Kaliam and the other Alleb Knights ushered them inside, Aidan began to realize just how dirty, hungry, and weary he had become. His armor, still the black-and-crimson Paragor armor he had borrowed from Falon, was caked with dirt and dried blood. The fabric of his breeches and other garments was filthy with sweat and grime from the horrific battles and difficult travels. He longed for a warm bath and a fresh set of clothes. Never before had he so much wanted to be clean.

For days, Aidan had been forced to survive on very little food. So when Kaliam mentioned being fed, Aidan's stomach churned with hunger.

But perhaps even overpowering his other felt needs was the desire to rest. He wanted sleep in the worst way. But a young attendant from King Ravelle's court insisted on tending Aidan's arm.

"This dressing will need to be changed twice a day," the attendant said. "Or else the wound could turn green and you could lose that arm. Do you understand?"

Aidan nodded yes.

"There, that should do it," said the attendant. "Now, I think your friends will lead you to your quarters and a soft bed."

A bed sounded like paradise.

Kaliam led Aidan and Gwenne inside a cottage near the kingdom's outer walls and showed each of them to a room. Aidan fell into his room's small bed.

As he lay there, tears flooded his tired eyes. In such a short time, he had witnessed unspeakable horrors. So many innocent souls slain and cast aside. He thought of Eleazar, Matthias, Bolt, and Captain Valithor—friends for far too short a time.

Aidan awoke to the sound of Kaliam banging on his door. "Arise, Sir Sluggabed, arise!" Kaliam bellowed. "Or do you plan to sleep another day away?"

Another day? Aidan thought with a start. He ran to the door and let Kaliam in.

"How long have I been in here?" Aidan asked.

"Almost a day and a half," Kaliam replied with a smile. "Now, up with you. I've drawn you a warm bath and filled a table with food. Make haste, for we must leave for Alleble in time for the great ceremony."

"What ceremony?" Aidan asked, still rubbing sleep from his eyes.

"What ceremony?" Kaliam echoed. "Why, tomorrow is the last day of *Minuet*, what you call July. Ere dawn, we will go to the fountains to celebrate many things and to remember."

With that, Kaliam was gone. A bath had been drawn for him, so Aidan bathed. And in the washing away of those stains, it seemed a great burden was lifted from Aidan's heart. He was rid of the filth, rid of the evidence of the evils he had lived. But not all reminders had been washed away. Wounds, there were still. Some would be treated and vanish. Others could not be healed by salve or bandage, and scars would remain.

Aidan's spirits lifted more as he dressed in the silver of Alleble. And he was amazed at the armor that was left out for him to wear. For upon his new breastplate, engraved with careful artistry, was the symbol of the sun rising between the two mountains. He was equipped also with a new belt for his sword. And as he slid Fury into its sheath, he discovered that it did not feel as heavy as it had. In fact, the blade did not drag the ground any longer. It was as if the armor was custom-made just for him.

Moments later a small feast was delivered, and Aidan ate. He ate a lot.

With a contented, overstuffed grin on his face, Aidan sat at a table in the cottage until Gwenne came in.

"Good evening, Sir Aidan," she said. "I'm glad you've eaten, for it is time to go. Kaliam has saddled several dragons for our return trip to Alleble."

Aidan nodded and stood. And it seemed that Gwenne was awestruck. She stared at Aidan and went pink in the face.

"What's the matter?" Aidan asked, feeling like he'd put his armor on wrong again. He checked his couters, just to be sure.

"Nothing, Sir Aidan," she replied. "It is just that you look different in your new armor." And she would say no more.

They left the cottage, and as they walked through the courtyard, Aidan looked around with amazement. The last time he had seen Mithegard's courtyard, it was soaked with blood and littered with the bodies of knights from three armies. But now, it was totally cleared. The Knights of Alleble, led by Tal, had been busy reforming it from a place of horrors to a place that could be rebuilt.

There was much evidence still of the tremendous battle: stone was cracked and shattered, buildings were reduced to rubble, and anything wooden was charred or rent. And worst of all, the once-proud Castle of Mithegard lay in ruins, its seven towers laid low.

Kaliam, Nock, Farix, and Mallik greeted Aidan and Gwenne when they entered the stables and pens behind the remains of the castle.

"Ah, Sir Aidan and Lady Gwenne, good evening to you both," said Kaliam, bowing low. Mallik, Nock, and Farix simply stared at Aidan.

Mallik seemed especially affected, and he turned and whispered something in Nock's ear.

Kaliam spoke again. "We have a long journey ahead of us this evening. Let's mount up, shall we? Gwenne, your own dragon, Gabby, is here for you to ride. And Sir Aidan, if you will, join me on Blazewing. I would like to hear of your adventures since we parted the day of the battle."

"No fair!" said Mallik, his coppery brows in a knot. "Sir Aidan was to ride with me! Indeed, I am in need of something to distract me from the smell of the beast I must ride!"

The dark green dragon near Mallik flexed its wings and growled.

"You see?" exclaimed Mallik.

"I will ride with you," said Nock with a wry grin. "I have tales to tell you of my brother Bolt that may distract you from your fear of flying."

"What! Fear of flying?" Mallik objected. And he mumbled something inaudible.

"What say you, Sir Aidan?" asked Kaliam.

"Gladly, Kaliam," Aidan replied. "But first, have you heard any news of the King of Mithegard? Did he make it to Alleble? Or was he . . . was he killed in the battle?"

Gwenne and Kaliam exchanged odd glances before Kaliam answered hesitantly. "The King of Mithegard was not found among the dead, Sir Aidan. But many have passed between here and Alleble since the siege."

It wasn't totally disheartening news, but it didn't guarantee anything about Aidan's father.

So Aidan tried to put his anxiety aside for the trip. After all, he had never ridden awake on a dragon before! He had been unconscious when Gabby had brought him to Alleble, so this time he planned on enjoying the ride.

THE KNIGHT
OF THE DAWN

The creatures began to extend and flap their awesome batlike wings. Dirt and dry grass swirled beneath them, and one by one the dragons went airborne. Watching the ground fall away so quickly stole Aidan's breath, but he kept his eyes open as the recognizable trees, hills, and mountains shrank into a patchwork quilt—colored crimson by the setting sun. And as the light faded, stars began to blink to life in the vast night sky. Aidan stared at the stars and wondered how anything could be so beautiful.

Kaliam interrupted Aidan's thoughts to ask him how he had rescued Gwenne, so Aidan told him the entire tale, beginning with the terrifying walk down Falon's Stair and the secret of the labyrinth.

"You mean there is no maze?" Kaliam had asked. "It was the creature itself?!"

"An amazing creature," Aidan had replied.

Kaliam listened in awe to Aidan's adventures. His tale lasted for several hours, and when it was over, Kaliam had simply replied, "Well done, servant of the King . . . well done."

Kaliam began to tell of his own adventures, but the rhythmic beat of the dragon's wings pulled Aidan into a deep, peaceful sleep. And Aidan slept through the rest of the trip.

After the landing, the knights dismounted. Kaliam carried Aidan to his chamber and laid him, armor and all, on his bed.

There came a soft knock at Aidan's door. It was Gwenne. Her armor was gone and she again wore the beautiful jewel-studded lavender dress she had worn the first time Aidan had seen her.

"I let you sleep as much as I could," she said. "But come now, for we do not want the sun to rise without us."

It was all rather mysterious, and as he trotted down the stairs, Aidan wondered what to expect from the celebration. Gwenne would not tell him anything. She simply smiled and said, "Come and see."

Finally, they left the stairs, turned the corner, and walked out of the gatehouse into the blue-gray before dawn. And Aidan stood as one turned to stone. He gazed out into the main thoroughfare of Alleble, but it was not the Seven Fountains that made him still. For such a crowd was gathered there as Aidan had never seen. It seemed that every Glimpse in Alleble must be there, shoulder to shoulder, side by side, all around the fountains and upon every foot of available space along the entire expanse of the road. And all were absolutely silent—even the tiniest of children seemed to know the reverence of the moment and made no sound.

There, before Aidan and Gwenne, standing on a podium constructed in the heart of the dry seventh fountain, was a tall Glimpse. But his back was turned so that he could face the gathering.

He seemed to know that someone was behind him, and he turned his head and smiled.

Aidan was stricken with gladness, for it was King Ravelle of Mithegard. He had survived after all. He gestured for Aidan and Gwenne to come closer, and the crowd parted and let them through. When they stood near, King Ravelle began to speak.

"Good people of Alleble, Glimpses young and old," he said, his voice like thunder announcing rain after a drought. "This is a solemn occasion, and I do not feel fit to speak to you who know what I have only just learned. But if for no other reason than gratitude, I will speak."

Aidan stared at his father's Glimpse, straining to see the color of his eyes.

"Today we mourn," said the King. "We mourn the loss of a champion. And I say 'we,' for were it not for his valor, I and the rest of my people would have perished. For the noble Captain Valithor died—in much the same way as he always lived, I am told—in sacrifice!"

Aidan's eyes grew wet. Gwenne reached down and their hands met.

"And it was his sacrifice and the sacrifice of many from your beloved land that has brought me and my kingdom to this point."

If the vast crowd had been silent before, it became more silent still, and they waited on King Ravelle's words.

"We Mithegardians were a proud nation. Our Seven Towers stood tall, and we were pleased to be alone. I am sorrowful to confess that it was I who drew us away from Alleble. For though many of you do not know this, I was born in Alleble. My father was a great servant of King Eliam."

King Ravelle's father? Aidan's mind raced. He had never really thought about it before. But he reasoned that if everyone on Earth had a Glimpse, and Grampin's Glimpse was Captain Valithor, then . . .

The King drew in a deep breath and continued. "But when my mother died, I was filled with grief . . . and with wrath. But I blamed King Eliam most of all, for it was he who sent my mother on her final journey. I forsook Alleble, and in my youthful rebellion I fled to Mithegard. I fled from my father because he did not blame King Eliam, and he would not abandon his trust in your King. In all that time while I squired and trained to be a knight for Mithegard, while I campaigned and became King, while I ruled selfishly over my people—all that time I shut my father out. And now, I have lost him, but not before he taught me the single most important lesson of all."

Aidan squeezed Gwenne's hand.

"You see, my father, Captain Valithor, told me . . . ," began King Ravelle, and his thunderous voice faltered. A collective gasp like a wave surged through the crowd. Tears ran freely down the faces of every Glimpse, and Aidan as well. King Ravelle mastered himself and continued. "He told me about King Eliam—about the sacrifice he made on the balcony behind where I now stand. And in my bitterness, I did not believe him. But I have seen the truth of his words in the lives of all who serve the Kingdom of Alleble. I saw it when your people came to me and showed me real offers of peace. I saw it when your knights, with no care for their own lives, defended my city. I saw it when my father laid down his life for a friend! So, I come here to mourn with you, for I have lost as you have lost. But also I come to confess. So hear me, Glimpses of Alleble! Hear me, as I confess with my lips that I will return to Mithegard. The Seven Towers shall be rebuilt, and forevermore they will be allied with the

Seven Fountains! For as for me and my kingdom, we shall serve King Eliam the Everlasting!"

A roaring cheer rose up from the crowd, and it seemed that they all spoke with one great voice, with one accord that it was good and right.

King Ravelle descended the podium while the cheers continued, and he sprang lightly over the fountain wall and ran to Aidan.

"I spoke of you just now," he said. "When you offered your sword to the enemy—do you remember?"

Aidan could say nothing. He simply nodded and stared into the eyes of his father's Glimpse. His eyes glinted blue and he embraced Aidan.

"You know," said King Ravelle, drawing back and holding Aidan by the shoulders, "I have a son, but my wife grew tired of my self-seeking ways, and she left Mithegard and took him away while he was very young. I hope wherever he is that he has grown into a lad like you."

Aidan cried tears of joy and he smiled, thinking, *Oh, I have a hunch he's a lot like me.*

The King turned as Kaliam strode forward.

"King Ravelle?" Aidan said, and he glanced at Gwenne. He wasn't sure if he should ask. Gwenne, for once, had not guessed his thoughts. She just stared back at him quizzically.

"Uh, one moment, Kaliam," said the King. "Yes, Aidan?"

"Your son . . ."

"Yes." King Ravelle looked at him strangely.

"Well, I was wondering, what is his name?"

Gwenne shot Aidan a glance that was half curious and half worried. She apparently didn't know if Aidan was allowed to ask such a thing either.

"Aelic," said the King. "His name is Aelic. It means, *One who overcomes fear.*"

Suddenly, trumpets rang out, and the crowd once again was as silent as stars seen from a hilltop in the wild. Kaliam stood at the podium in the seventh fountain. He waited, for what? Aidan could not tell. But Aidan saw Kaliam in a new light as he stood there, tall, broad-shouldered, wearing the silver armor of Alleble and mantled with a dark blue cloak. Princely, he looked now, commanding. Until then he had always seemed so, well . . . regular. It was the only word Aidan could think of, for Kaliam had always been the most friendly, joking with everyone and sharing advice with Aidan. Before, he had always dutifully followed in Captain Valithor's shadow. Aidan wondered what had changed about him.

Finally, Kaliam spoke. His voice did not carry the thunder of King Ravelle's voice, but it was clear and precise. And those who heard him understood and felt as if Kaliam were speaking directly to each of them personally.

"Captain Valithor shall be remembered," he said, "in the lore of Alleble and in all of our hearts forever. King Eliam has decreed that our great Captain shall be laid to rest in Mithegard, not Alleble, so that he may be near his son."

Kaliam smiled warmly down at King Ravelle.

"But this morning," Kaliam continued, "this morning is not solely about grief! For though many of their kin have fallen, Mithegard is now allied with Alleble, and not even death can break that union! We must welcome the Glimpses of Mithegard, and we must come alongside our new brothers as they rebuild what was wrongly destroyed."

Kaliam went silent and looked into the crowd from face to face. He raised his fist and spoke again. "No, this morning is not solely for grief! For though we stand where of old the Great Betrayal was consummated, this is also the hallowed ground of Alleble's greatest victory! For it was here that King Eliam rose with the dawn and cast out the enemy! And today, as the sun rises between the peaks of Pennath Ador, we have the privilege to add a name to the King's Hall."

Entranced by Kaliam's words, Aidan was shocked when two knights escorted him to the podium. He stood there shaking, for he was now visible to every Glimpse in Alleble. But there was something else, some immense gravity to what was about to happen.

Kaliam smiled down at Aidan. "Do you see, fine Glimpse-kind?" Kaliam said, turning Aidan to face the crowds. "Do you see the armor worn by this young lad? Perhaps you cannot yet. But you will. For though Aidan will not remain among us for much longer, he will remain a hero of Alleble forever. For his bravery in the face of a terrible enemy, for his valor on the field of battle, and for his faith when there seemed no hope at all—this day, Aidan is named Knight of the Dawn!"

The crowd roared with cheers, but it was abruptly muted. And a great golden light blazed behind Aidan.

Turn around, Aidan, a voice said.

Aidan turned and looked into the light. And this time, it did not burn. All images faded in the brilliance, but Aidan saw clearly, up on the huge castle balcony, a lone figure. He was dressed in white armor, and a great white robe waved around him. And the light shone forth from him. Aidan knew him, for it was his voice that drew Aidan beyond The Door Within. It was King Eliam the Everlasting!

Aidan could not see his face, but he felt that he was looking into the eyes of hope. And indeed, as he stared at King Eliam, Aidan was filled with a peace like he had never known. It was as if every good and precious experience in his life had somehow been captured and was channeled through the King's eyes. The proud, desperate love of his parents looking down on their newborn son, the feel of cool water on a hot day, Robby's grin as they waded in the creek, the comfort of blankets against the cold whispering wind outside, the feel of Gwenne's hand in his, the sun rising over the Atlantic Ocean . . .

Then King Eliam raised one hand high, and a clear beam of the purest white light streamed forth and fell upon Aidan's breastplate. The image engraved there, the sun rising between two mountains, blazed with that same white light, like molten iron fresh from the fire.

And then the light dimmed, and Aidan could hear the crowds once again. He turned to them, and they saw his armor then. And behold, the light of dawn poured into the thoroughfare. For the sun had finally risen between the majestic peaks of Pennath Ador.

And Aidan wept, for the fountains of Alleble were all aglow with the splendid rays of the rising sun. And King Eliam spoke once again, *My good and faithful servant, well done.*

EARLY DEPARTURE

Two days had passed since the celebration by the fountains—two days of the most powerful happiness Aidan had ever experienced. Some of the time Aidan spent with friends, old and new.

He went to Alleble's armory to visit Kindle and to thank him.

"It was you, wasn't it?" Aidan had asked, a finger pointing with amused accusation.

"What, me?" Kindle replied. He held his hands up, feigning innocence.

"I saw the way you looked at me when I first saw Fury in your case! You went to Naysmithe, didn't you? You asked him to forge Son of Fury."

"Aye." Kindle relented. He stared at Aidan's breastplate. "And though I doubted it then, I see now that my course was charted by the King. For that blade served you well, m'lad."

"It did, Kindle," Aidan replied. "And now it rests with Captain

Valithor in Mithegard. But I thank you for all that you've done. And, Kindle, guess what?"

"What's that, Aidan, me boy?"

"I finally know which piece of armor goes on my head!" They both laughed long and hard, and for several hours they spoke of many other glad things.

Later Aidan went to the training yards, from place to place visiting his teachers—telling them how what they taught him was well put to use during his adventure.

He spent time too with the knights of the Elder Guard, especially Mallik and Nock. They spoke of the Timbers of Yewland and the Blackwood and of fields where untamed unicorn roamed free. They spoke of the Blue Mountains, of tall stone keeps and the doughty folk who made them, and of the quiet moors beyond.

But most of the time was spent with Gwenne, walking in Alleble's gardens, wading in the streams at the foot of Pennath Ador, and reading the lore of Alleble's Knights of the Dawn—of which Aidan now was one.

But there was a longing within him that he could not quite identify. His heart was content, but it felt as if there was something yet unfinished. So it was not surprising to Aidan when Gwenne appeared one late afternoon at the entrance of his chamber.

"It is time," she said with a tear cascading down her pure white cheek. She stooped and picked up a package and brought it into the room.

"You'll find your clothes, the clothes you wore when you came

. . . all washed and mended," Gwenne said, handing Aidan the package. "Summon me when you've changed."

Aidan went into the room and reluctantly took off his armor. The sunlight sparkled off each piece as he laid them on the bed. He liked being a knight. He didn't want to go back to being just plain Aidan. But as he put on his old jeans and his T-shirt, he realized that no matter what he wore, he was and always would be a servant of Alleble.

Aidan walked over and opened the door for Gwenne to come in. She smiled, and Aidan's stomach churned. She led him over to the arched window where they looked out upon the sun-bathed land of Alleble. There was the courtyard where he had trained to become a knight. It looked strange and empty this time of day, and Aidan's imagination conjured ghostly images of Glimpses dueling and sparring as they no doubt would at dawn.

Aidan's eyes wandered out of the courtyard to the Seven Fountains and beyond The Realm's main gate. Somewhere in the darkness was the trail that had led Aidan and Gwenne to the Grimwalk. Farther still was the dark mountain range called the Prince's Crown where the enemy dwelt, smoldering over his losses but ever plotting new conquests. Somewhere beyond the enemy's land lay the curling ranges of the Black Crescent where, in the caverns beneath, Falon waited. And then Mithegard was there too. Mithegard, rebuilding with stone, mortar, and hope.

Gwenne's hand found Aidan's. And they stood and watched as clouds drifted slowly across the quiet sky.

Gwenne let go and sat down. Tears streamed down her face. "I don't want you to go," she whispered.

Aidan sat next to her. He didn't want to leave either, but he knew he had to. His family was waiting. His life was waiting.

"Gwenne," he said, "I need to go back. My mom and dad, my friend Robby, they've got to know—my whole world has got to know the truth. But I'll come back."

"You do not understand." Gwenne choked out the words.

"What do you mean?"

"You were called here by the King," she said. "And King Eliam rarely brings people from your home here. I know of none he's allowed to return until . . . until you die and go to be with all who have passed into the Sacred Realm Beyond the Sun."

The news hit Aidan like a thunderclap, but the storm passed quickly. And somehow, Aidan did not feel alarmed. He knew that King Eliam had allowed he and Gwenne to become friends for a reason, and now Aidan knew that the King was allowing them to part for a reason.

"Can you visit me?" he asked.

"If the King wills it, I could visit you. But it is unlikely."

He did not say anything to Gwenne. He reached over and lifted her chin with his hand. Then he wiped away her tears. And for a long moment, they just stared at each other. Gwenne smiled again.

"I brought you something," Gwenne said as she stood and walked out of the chamber. "Since the Tempest took the one you brought with you into The Realm . . ."

She brought Aidan a thick bundle of scrolls, tied round with silver and blue embroidery. She handed it to Aidan.

"I'll keep these safe," Aidan said, and it was his turn to stifle tears.

"Our story is in there, you know," she explained.

Aidan nodded.

"You need to open to the end," she whispered. "When you touch the final word of the final page, you will begin your journey home."

Aidan stood, untied the lace, and opened the scroll to the last page. But he did not touch the last word. Not yet.

"Gwenne, I was wondering," Aidan said. "You said you never met my Glimpse."

"That is true. I never met him. In fact, it was not until King Ravelle said he had a son that I knew if your Glimpse had even been yet born. Remember that time works differently in our world."

"Okay," Aidan replied, squinting, deep in thought. "But that means I do have a Glimpse out there somewhere. And he looks just like me, right?"

Gwenne smiled. "Yes and no," she said. "Yes, your Glimpse would look just like you—though he might be older or younger. But no, your Glimpse is not out there, for a Glimpse and his twin can never meet. He has gone to your world for a time and will return to The Realm when you return to Earth."

Aidan frowned. *If Mom and Dad saw Aelic!?*

But then Aidan had an even stranger thought. "So then, my Glimpse will be here again, after I leave?" he asked.

"Yes, that's true—"

"And all the Glimpses here," Aidan interrupted, an idea budding, "have a person just like them in my world—even you, right?"

"Yes, but why do you—"

Before she could finish the question, Aidan kissed her on the cheek. He stared at her with a sly grin and said, "I'll see you soon!"

Gwenne looked perplexed. "But, Sir Aidan—"

Aidan held up a hand and winked at Gwenne. Then, he placed his hand upon the final word of the final page of the scroll and left Alleble, never to return until his life's end.

PASSAGE

Aidan had once again passed beyond The Door Within, and as before, his senses were changing, transforming. He felt that peculiar movement from within, and walked again the gray road. There were voices and visions. There appeared an image of a dark army marching forth from a black castle. They carried torches that blazed violently in the wind. The torchlight became the candlelight of a large chandelier in a grand room of some kind. There in the room was a great assembly of Glimpses. Some had red eyes and some green. Before the image flickered away, it seemed to focus on a young Glimpse who was somehow familiar to Aidan. The young male Glimpse's pale skin hid his exact identity, but he had to be someone. . . . The vision faded, and a new one replaced it. There was a young girl on a lonely tower that reached high above the clouds. But soon this image dissolved into yet another, and another after that. Aidan could not follow them, they came so fast, but suddenly, they stopped, and everything went black.

The visions and voices had disappeared. Aidan felt his senses returning to normal, and his thoughts began to organize. It was then that he realized he knew the young Glimpse he had envisioned in the elegant room. That young Glimpse was a Glimpse of Robby . . . and his eyes had been . . . red!

EYES THAT SEE

idan did not know if he had been asleep or unconscious, but he became aware that he was back in his bedroom in Colorado Springs. It must have been after sundown because it was almost totally dark. But after crawling blindly through moonrascal tunnels and feeling his way down through the blackness of Falon's Stair, the dark in his room was nothing. He shook the disorientation from his head and stood.

But there was no illusion this time. He knew where he had been, and he knew it had not been a dream. Aidan had the new scroll from Alleble in his hands, and he had a large fresh scar on his right forearm.

Aidan gripped the scroll and strode out of his room. There was light from the stairs, so someone had to be up.

But Aidan froze at the top of the stairs.

How long have I been gone? Nearly two weeks?! he wondered.

Gwenne had said that time was different, but how much different? And had Aelic been here?

Aidan knew his parents, and he knew they would have been frantic. *They probably started a nationwide manhunt for me after I was missing for a couple of days!*

He laughed nervously as he imagined his picture showing up on milk cartons all over the country. Aidan knew his parents and everyone else would no doubt demand to know where he had been and why he had been gone. This presented an unusual problem. Aidan would tell everyone the truth, but who would believe it?

King Ravelle now followed the King of Alleble, Aidan reasoned. So then, his father would come to believe someday. *But what about Mom? And Grampin, Grampin would—*

A tide of sadness rushed into Aidan's heart as he remembered that Grampin was linked to Captain Valithor. And the Captain had died in the battle at Mithegard. *How soon would everything take place?* Aidan did not know.

Standing there wondering in the dark was doing Aidan no good, so he trotted down the stairs and looked around. There weren't any policemen or FBI agents hustling around planning a rescue. In fact, there were no noises coming from anywhere in the house. Aidan walked into the kitchen and saw the digital clock on the microwave. It was ten o'clock—so perhaps they were all asleep.

Then, Aidan walked into the dining room, and there he found his mom. She was asleep at the table with her head resting on her arms.

"Mom," Aidan whispered gently. No answer. "Mom? It's me . . ."

Slowly, his mother's head rose from her arms.

She brushed aside her long dark bangs, and Aidan saw her eyes. Puffy, swollen from crying, but opening wide with recognition.

"Aidan!" she cried, standing up abruptly and knocking her chair backward. She ran to her son and threw her arms around him. Her body shook, and Aidan could feel her warm tears on his neck. Then, suddenly, she released her embrace and held Aidan at arm's length.

"Aidan, where have you been?!" she demanded, hands on her hips and her eyebrows pinching. "And what happened to your arm?"

"It's a long story, Mom. I—"

"Do you have any idea what you've put us through?!"

"Mom, I'm sorry. Let me explain—"

"Explain?!" she echoed. "Son, you were supposed to be home over four hours ago! How can you be four hours late and not even call?!"

If Aidan had been in a plane, the orange oxygen masks would have dropped out of the little overhead compartments. There was definitely a loss of cabin pressure in his head!! *Four hours?! But I've been gone for weeks . . . did time pass that much differently in Alleble?*

"Four hours, son," his mom continued, interrupting Aidan's puzzled thoughts. "You should have at least called." Her tone then softened. "Aidan, we can talk about your punishment later, but we need to talk about something else."

Aidan knew what was coming.

His mother took a deep breath. "Aidan, I don't know how to tell you this, so I'll just say it. Your grandfather had a heart attack this afternoon. Dad found him when he got home from work . . ." Her voice began to crack. "He, he's in intensive care now. Your father is with him at the hospital."

"It's okay, Mom," Aidan said, gently putting his hand on her shoulder.

"No, Aidan it's not okay," she corrected. She wiped her eyes, smearing the mascara. "The doctors say it's very serious."

"I understand, Mom. But really, Grampin will be okay, " Aidan persisted, and taking a deep breath himself, he charged ahead. "Grampin believes in Alleble. If he dies, he'll be with the King . . . in the Sacred Realm Beyond the Sun."

Mom shook her head and put her hand up. "Oh, Aidan, not that story again. I know that story might make you feel better, and I suppose that's okay, but this is real life."

"Mom, I've been there . . . to Alleble. It's ALL real, every bit of it, and Grampin believes, so he'll be just fine no matter what. You'll see."

Aidan's mom tried to smile, but her cheeks showed tension and her lower lip trembled. She started to speak but hugged Aidan instead. She hugged him so tight he thought a rib would crack. Again, he felt the tears on his neck. Aidan hugged back and lightly scratched his mother's back, wishing she could understand and believe. Then it wouldn't hurt so much.

"Can we go up to the hospital to see Grampin?" Aidan asked as they parted.

"We'll go see him in the morning, son," she said quietly. "I think you need to get some sleep."

Mrs. Thomas walked Aidan into his room and tucked him in. She kissed Aidan on his forehead like she used to do when he was little and then clicked off the overhead light.

"Good night, sweetheart," she said tenderly, sliding easily off the bed and walking to the door. She stood there, half illumined by the golden hall light. Longer than usual she stayed, just staring at Aidan warmly. She turned to leave, but paused one moment more.

"Y'know, Aidan," she began, an eyebrow raised, one corner of her mouth showing just a hint of a smile. "You seem different to me. I don't know what it is exactly. Something about the way you reacted when I told you about Grampin—I don't know. It's probably nothing. I'm just so glad you're home safe. Good night."

"Night, Mom," Aidan replied. *Mom is right*, Aidan thought. *I am different.*

Something awakened Aidan in the still hours before dawn. He had a fleeting thought that maybe, like before, he would find himself in Alleble with Gwenne standing near his bedside. Perhaps the King had called him back for some other adventure.

No, Aidan wasn't in the castle—just his own room in Colorado. His arm wasn't around the neck of a friendly dragon—just his down pillow. And it was not Gwenne who awakened him—it was his father.

It was dark, but Aidan knew it was him, silhouetted against the window. He was sitting on the edge of the bed, and he seemed to be rocking back and forth slightly.

"Dad, what is it?"

He nodded ever so slightly. "Aidan, I-I'm so grateful that you're okay. I wouldn't be able to bear it if . . . if you and my father . . ." His voice trailed off for a moment, but then he gathered his strength and spoke more assuredly.

"Grampin was in a coma, for almost the whole time after the heart attack, but once, when no one else was around, he just woke up and started talking to me. He told me a whole bunch of crazy stuff about the Kingdom of Alleble, just like you said the other night. He said all I had to do was believe it was true and choose to follow the King of Alleble, and it would all become real to me.

"He even got a little mad at me when I told him I didn't buy into any of that pie-in-the-sky fantasy garbage. He said, 'Boy, ye better open up yer eyes to see, fer it gets too late!' I think we both fell asleep after that, Aidan. But I tell you, I had the most amazing dream. I don't remember too much of it, but Grampin was in it. He was dressed in bright silver armor, and he looked younger, happier, and more alive than I have ever seen him. In fact, he was riding on a flying dragon, doing loop-the-loops in the sky above a breathtaking castle."

Aidan's dad paused for a while, swallowed hard, and then continued. "When I woke up, Grampin was already gone. He . . . he died, Aidan."

Dad wiped his tears with an abrupt swipe of his forearms. Aidan just waited patiently and listened.

"Y'know, on the drive home from the hospital, I got to thinking about what Grampin had told me. In some ways, I wanted to write it off as the nutty fantasies of a senile old man. But I just couldn't, Aidan. I mean, when he was speaking to me, he seemed as clear-minded as can be. He completely believed everything he said to me, and there was such a powerful look of hope in his eyes that I had to listen.

"He must have known that he was close to death . . . he had to know. But there wasn't the slightest hint of fear in his eyes. I think my crazy old man was actually looking forward to it! Then, it hit me so hard, I had to pull the car over to the side of the road. I made a decision there, son, and I wanted you to be the first to hear it."

Aidan was so thrilled he thought he was going to pop!

Aidan stared anxiously at him. Aidan could tell his father was staring back. Finally, he announced: "Aidan, I believe it. I believe it all!"

The happiest of tears bounced down Aidan's cheek. "I know," he replied joyfully.

"What!?" Dad blurted out.

"It's a long story, Dad," Aidan said, smiling. "It's a long story."

Epilogue

The weeks that followed were a whirlwind of ups and downs. Aidan and his dad read and reread the Scrolls of Alleble—the whole time his mom thinking they had gone collectively off their rockers!

Aidan occupied most of the last days of the summer preparing for the upcoming school year. And every spare moment he had, he spent trying to contact Robby. For some reason, no one ever answered at his home, and Robby didn't return a single email Aidan sent.

Being home, and knowing he could not return to Alleble, left Aidan with empty pangs of sadness now and then. But even within that sadness there sprang hope. For though he was away from Alleble, Alleble lived within his heart. He would never be alone, and he knew he had much work to do in his lifetime on Earth.

And though Aidan knew he could not see Gwenne for many, many years in The Realm, he had a plan. . . .

THE ADVENTURE CONTINUES IN THE
SECOND VOLUME OF THE DOOR WITHIN TRILOGY:

THE RISE OF THE WYRM LORD

Adventures are
funny things,
and they always begin
with the unexpected.
But the best adventures of all
are the ones
that never end.

THE LOST CHAPTERS

[EDITOR'S NOTE: Have you ever gone a trip and forgotten your battery charger for your cell phone, game, or some other electronic gadget? Suddenly, you have to start making choices based on how long the gadget will last on one battery charge. In a way, authors and editors are in the same situation. Publishers provide authors with guidelines that include a specific number of pages and an estimated word count. Part of the job of an editor is to be sure that an author's work fits within those guidelines. As a result, often the editor and author must make tough choices on what to cut from the storyline. They base their choices on what the reader might be most interested in reading about, things that will help move the story forward, things necessary to the story, and ways to rework sections to be more concise so they can keep the essence of the chapter but in a shorter form. In *The Door Within*, Wayne chose to rework the opening chapters to be more concise so that the reader would enter The Realm earlier, and he'd be able to keep in more of the events that happen in The Realm. He also agreed to age Aidan and his friends, so they could have more adventures in The Realm. In doing so, we agreed to cut or rework some of the opening chapters. As you'll read in his notes following each cut chapter, it was a difficult choice for him to make. But it would have been equally difficult to choose other sections to cut.]

The Unexpected

It'll be better than you think, son," Aidan's dad said. He placed his hand on his teenager's shoulder and gave a firm, reassuring squeeze. That same hand had once stopped tears during thunderstorms and after knee-scrapes. It had brought comfort and security, but now, Aidan shrugged it off as if it were a wasp.

Mr. Thomas grimaced. Silence hung like a dark cloud between father and son. Aidan felt like he'd been smacked in the head with a bat. The unexpected news had hit him hard.

Aidan's mom stood nearby, hands on hips, head with a slight tilt. She frowned at her husband as if to say, *I told you so.* He looked toward his son, who sat stiffly at the dining room table.

Mr. Thomas knelt to be at eye level with his son, and spoke softly. "It's a really big house—plenty of room for everyone," he said. He raised his eyebrows comically high, and with an encouraging smile playing on his lips he added, "I know it's a bit of a surprise, Aidan, but look on the bright side. Your room'll be twice as big as you're used to."

Bright side? Aidan could see only a dreary blur like hard rain on a window, washing away a sunny day. But Aidan could not will the move away any more than he could dismiss a storm. He just didn't want it to be. It couldn't be, could it? Any minute his parents would laugh and say, "Gotcha!" It was all just a cruel joke, right?

Aidan's face smoldered and his eyes swelled. He wanted to be far away, to escape, but he just sat there feeling like a punching bag as his dad continued.

"Just think of how great it'll be to have Grampin around all the time. I know how you love his crazy stories."

Aidan trembled with anger.

"And, maybe in July we'll go rock climbing . . . and in the winter. . . . Son, it's Colorado, there'll be more snow than you've ever seen."

Each time his father spoke, Aidan felt as if the walls were closing in a little more. "The backyard is huge, and the side yard has a serious hill.

Please, stop it! Aidan thought.

"It's a big neighborhood. You'll make tons of new fr—"

Aidan sprang up. His chair teetered and nearly fell before settling with a sharp wooden *Thok!* next to the table. Aidan rushed from the kitchen, stomped up the stairs in an angry fog, slammed the door to his room behind him, and flopped facedown on the bed.

Aidan faced his bedside table and the twelve tiny figures precisely arranged around his castle-fortress lamp. The pewter knights, dragons, and unicorns were, as always, still and quiet—ready to listen.

"It's not fair," Aidan said to them. "How can they just decide to move without even asking what I wanted to do?"

Of course, none of the small medieval beings replied. That's why Aidan talked to them. They didn't offer advice. They didn't lecture. They simply listened.

"I mean, so what if Grampin's getting too old?" Aidan continued. "Somebody else should take care of him. Why us, huh? My life was finally starting to look up . . ."

Aidan glowered at the fantasy figures. He'd been collecting them for several years, buying a few each time he visited the Maryland Renaissance Festival. At least they had each other to keep company. "I finally get one friend—a good friend—and now, they're gonna drag me to Colorado? That's halfway across the country from Maryland!"

The "one" friend Aidan was thinking of was Robby Pierson. Robby and his family had moved from Florida to a house up the street in September, and everything had changed for Aidan. Until that time, Aidan had been known to the kids in the neighborhood and at school as the overweight weirdo who sat around all day drawing castles and space ships. Then Robby showed up. He was tall and muscular and had long blond hair and an earring. And given his good looks and ability to play every sport better than everyone else, he was instantly crowned "so cool" by all the seventh and eighth graders.

For reasons Aidan still didn't understand, Robby had decided to become his best friend. They hung out between classes, after school, and sometimes had PlayStation sleepovers on the weekends.

As if *coolness* were a magical golden powder that could rub off, Aidan found that he had become a little cool himself just by standing in Robby's shadow. It was, after all, a large shadow, and Aidan liked it there. He didn't have to worry about being picked on, and better still, he never had to think about what to do in certain situations—Robby always knew what to do. And, while Aidan still drew pictures of castles and spaceships and was still chunky and peculiar, he had a reliable friend, a new reputation, and something to look forward to every day—that is, until now.

"I HATE my life!" Aidan shouted, he hoped loud enough for his parents downstairs to hear him.

Aidan let out a furious, animal sort of grunt and buried his head in the pillow. In that moment, tears came. Hot, stinging tears. He was bitter, exhausted, and unhappy. And while he was often sad, Aidan almost never cried. Once, when he was eight, he had fallen out of a crab apple tree in his front yard and broken his arm in two places. He had yelled a lot and kicked the tree vengefully a few times, but not a single tear had fallen from his eyes. It was different now.

There was something about feeling trapped—trapped in what seemed to Aidan the most unjust situation to ever occur. There was no escape. Aidan's vision blurred and his eyes began to burn. He dragged the corner of his pillow across his face and stared miserably at the medieval creatures on the table. Each one was forever frozen in action: two blue and black armored knights on horseback preparing to joust, several others with swords raised high for a duel they would never fight, a trio of sparkling unicorns rearing or in mid-gallop, and one particular silver dragon that seemed to be staring back at Aidan.

Aidan longed to join them, to leave the relentless pain of reality and disappear into another world. *Maybe that world*, Aidan thought, *would make more sense.*

Turbulent thoughts of losing things whirled in Aidan's mind. Summer vacation, gone. Looks of approval from kids at school, gone. Tree forts, crab apple battles, and Brae Brook Creek, all gone. Worst of all, Robby, gone.

Aidan's eyelids began to feel heavy and liquid. The anger and sadness had drained him of energy. Sleep was a welcome escape. He started to drift off, but gooseflesh suddenly erupted on his arms. The hair on the back of his neck stood on end. Aidan felt like someone was there, in the room, watching him. But he hadn't heard the door open. Aidan sat bolt upright, but the bedroom door was still shut.

He felt it again . . . a strange presence. This time behind him—like the weight of someone staring in at him from the bedroom window. Aidan hesitated to turn. There couldn't possibly be someone outside. But still . . .

Aidan jumped. A commercial airliner screamed by high overhead. Aidan spun around, bounced off his bed, and went to the window. He stared past the front yard crab apple trees and through the power lines across the street. The tall oaks beyond swayed in the wind. Aidan stared up into the darkening sky. No sign of a plane. Just the roar of jet engines, not shrill like before but deep, throttling up against the turbulence.

Aidan plopped down on his bed. The strange sensation was gone. He shrugged. Of course, no one had been watching him. Aidan laughed quietly at himself and fell backward onto his pillow. He heard the jet again. It really did sound like a roar.

He turned his head and stared drowsily at the pewter figures on the bedside table, especially the silver dragon. Then, he faded away to sleep.

AUTHOR'S COMMENTARY:

Chapter 1 was one of the few chapters that existed almost from the beginning of the whole Door Within concept that I conceived in 1993. I loved it because it helped to build Aidan's character as kind of a follower, not yet confident enough to find his own way. You also begin to get a picture of Robby Pierson. He's the most popular guy, but not full of himself, not so caught up in his own image that he wouldn't have a friendship with a kid like Aidan.

There are many ways to build suspense and gain reader interest. I chose to use intense emotion and unusual phenomenon. The book opens with Aidan hopping mad at his parents, and I wanted the reader to wonder why Aidan's so upset. I also wanted readers to connect with the pain Aidan feels over having to move. In my sixteen years of teaching, I've seen the heartache some kids go through when they have to move. It can truly be like ripping away a part of yourself. The scene grew out of an experience I had growing up. My best friend lived in Panama City, Florida, and my family would drive there every summer to visit my grandfather. But one year, my grandfather died. I grieved for him, but also because I knew that meant I wouldn't see my best friend anymore. I delved into that memory to give Aidan's emotion the ring of reality.

The phenomena, of course, was the feeling that someone could be watching Aidan and then, the roar of the jet sounding so much like the roar of a beast. I thought that would be the first hint that this story was going to take a left turn into the fantasy genre. I hoped it would really get the pages turning.

So why did we cut the chapter? In the end, it came down to action. The scene, though touching, was a little too slow to open this kind of adventure. The trend in fiction today is to drop the reader into the middle of the action—force them to hang on for dear life and figure out the characters later. You may have noticed, I scavenged as many lines as I could from this deleted scene and used them in chapter 2, The Unexpected, of the published version. Aidan shrugging his father's hand off like a wasp was an image I had to keep. I also kept the pewter figures and the strange "I'm being watched" sensation. In the end, I like the published chapter 1 better because it allowed me to do some heavy foreshadowing for the rest of the trilogy.

A Swoosh and
a Shadow

Three weeks later, Aidan sat on the edge of his bed and finished filling yet another cardboard box.

"I can't believe I have so many clothes!" he complained. He wound one more turn of clear packaging tape to seal it up. "How in the world did I ever end up getting enough socks and underwear to fill a big box like this?!"

"Shoot, this is nuh-thin'," replied Robby in his Floridian drawl. "You should see my sister. She's got a different pair a' shoes fer every day a' the year! I mean every style, every color—even spares a' the ones she really likes. I think she's fixin' to open a store right outta her closet. Call it somethin' like Snob-Mart."

Aidan smiled in spite of himself. This wasn't supposed to be fun. But at least Robby was there to help. Aidan looked up at his best friend who was busy stuffing a box with baseball card-filled photo albums. Robby looked up and grinned the little sideways smile he always did. It seemed impossible that, in just a couple of days, he'd have to say good-bye to Robby, and perhaps never see him again. Aidan shook his head and grabbed another box.

His castle lamp was packed already, but he still had the medieval figures from the bedside table to do. One by one, he meticulously wrapped them—first with several layers of tissue paper and then with a half-dozen turns of bubble wrap.

"Dang, Aidan," Robby teased. "You got enough bubble wrap on those things? You think the movin' van's gonna go off a cliff or something?"

Aidan rolled his eyes but didn't stop with the bubble wrap.

"What are you gonna do with the aquarium?" Robby asked. He pointed to the empty five-gallon fish tank on Aidan's dresser.

"Throw it away, probably," Aidan replied. "I don't think they have crayfish in Colorado. It's yours, if you want it."

"Oh, yeah!" Robby grinned. "I'll put a snake or somethin' in it and keep it in my room. It'll drive my sister crazy!"

Aidan laughed. He enjoyed listening to Robby's war stories about his older sister, Jill. As fierce as Jill was, Robby always seemed to win the battles.

Aidan finished the bubble wrap on the dragon—an extra layer or two—and then placed it softly in the box.

He stared at the aquarium and his eyes fixed on something unseen. "That was the best time, though, wasn't it?" Robby asked.

"No doubt," said Aidan. He and Robby had shared many adventures in their short time together, but this one often came to mind.

It had been a very warm day for Maryland in late September. Summer refused to yield to fall and still held the magnifying glass in place over the East. Aidan and Robby had just met, and the afternoon beckoned.

Robby had lived next to a saltwater bayou in Florida and fancied himself a champion crabber. But he'd never caught crayfish before. So, after grabbing a couple of mason jars and paint buckets, Aidan led Robby along a seldom-trodden path through the woods to the best crayfishing spot around: Brae Brook Creek.

Robby looked down from the one-lane bridge. In the shallow areas of the creek, water trickled in happy spurts over mossy rocks. "The water looks clear," Robby said.

Aidan cautiously descended the rocky bank to the water's edge. "Let's try to keep it that way," he said. "If you step in the mud or lift up a rock too fast, the water'll cloud up. We won't be able to—"

"Got it," Robby said abruptly. He joined Aidan and put down the bucket he'd been carrying. "So these things are pretty much like little lobsters?"

"Yup, smaller than a lobster—maybe six, seven inches long. But they still pinch pretty hard!"

"Can't be that bad," Robby insisted.

Aidan frowned. "Do you want me to show you how to catch—"

"No, no, I'll figure it out," Robby replied, and in moments, he had waded in up to his shins and was bending over to lift up his first rock.

"Hey, I see one," Robby announced.

This ought to be good! Aidan thought. He scrunched his eyes and could barely watch his new friend reach barehanded into the water.

He knew what was coming.

"Yeowww—ch!" Robby bellowed, pulling his hand out of the water. On the end of his middle finger, pinching with all its tiny might, was a four-inch crayfish. Robby waved it around in the air, but still it held on.

"Let go, ya' little booger!" Robby hollered, and finally, it let go. It dropped into the water and sped away backward to safety.

Aidan stumbled backward from laughing so hard and almost fell in the water. "I told you they could pinch."

"Didn't hurt," Robby argued weakly. ". . . much. Okay, smart guy, so how do you catch 'em then?"

"Well, I don't use my fingers like you do. I think the best way is to use a mason jar. Hold the jar with one hand. You have to submerge it carefully behind the clueless crayfish. Then place the other hand a little underwater in front of the critter and wave it. The crayfish thinks the danger is in front, and shoots backward—right into the jar. Cover the jar with your free hand, and the crayfish is trapped."

With just that brief explanation, Robby had soon become every bit as good as Aidan at catching crayfish. That's the way Robby was with things. He mastered in moments what took others months of practice to learn.

They had spent the rest of that afternoon filling their buckets with little claw-pinching, tail-flicking, temperamental lobster-midgets. And Robby was right: it had been the best time.

"That takes care of this dresser," Robby said, stacking a box full of t-shirts on top of the cardboard pyramid near the door to Aidan's room. "What time is it?"

Aidan put down his box of mummified medieval creatures and checked his watch. "It's almost noon."

"I gotta go," said Robby.

"You can have lunch with us," Aidan suggested. There weren't many hours left that they could be together, and Aidan wanted to make the most of them.

"I can't. Momma said I need t'cut the grass 'fore my dentist appointment at one-thirty."

Aidan still found it odd that kids in the South, even in their late teens, still sometimes called their parents "Momma" and "Daddy."

"You have a dentist appointment?" Aidan frowned. "You're not getting braces, are you?"

"Ri-ight." Robby always said the word in two syllables. It had to be his favorite word, for he used it all the time to mean a great many things. In this case, "Ri-ight" basically meant, "Me, get braces? You can't be serious."

Robby smiled broadly, revealing two gleaming rows of perfectly straight teeth. Aidan's teeth were straight too, but not movie-star-straight like Robby's.

"Besides, I said dentist—not orthodontist. Just a check-up. I'll call ya' when I get home, okay?"

Aidan nodded, and his best friend left. He was alone again in his room, only now it didn't seem much like his room anymore. The posters had been removed and rolled up. The bookshelves were bare and the dressers were empty. Everything that had been in his room was now stuffed away into little square prisons of cardboard. There was nothing left to say, "Hey, a kid lives here!"

About the only thing that wasn't imprisoned in cardboard was the aquarium.

Aquarium, shoot! Robby! Aidan stumble-stepped down the stairs, arriving with a horrendous thud at the bottom. This earned him a stern, "Hey! Quit thumping!" from his father, who was in the basement.

"Sorry, Dad!" Aidan hollered as he bolted out of the front door and onto the porch. Already breathing heavily and beginning to sweat, Aidan plodded across the lawn and into the street.

"Rob—bee! You forgot the fish—" Aidan's mouth snapped shut. Robby was long gone. *Man, Robby can really turn on the jets when he wants to.*

Turning to leave the street, Aidan jerked to a halt. He heard a noise. He wasn't sure what it was, but it registered above the hum of distant traffic and the incessant chirping of cicadas. Aidan cocked his head sideways, listening. Nothing for a few moments, then—there it was again in the distance, a series of rapid swooshes—somewhat like the swoosh heard after a car speeds by. Then silence.

Then more swooshes, a little louder, followed by silence. Aidan looked up high in the sky and then scanned the street far ahead where the sounds seemed to be originating. No airplanes, no birds, nothing at all.

Then, the familiar sound of old Mr. Filbert driving his old light blue Dodge Dart made Aidan jump. Aidan hurriedly moved out of the street to let the car pass. It was a relief to see someone else, to not be alone on the road. Aidan waved. Mr. Filbert ignored him. Old Mr. Filbert never had liked kids.

The moment the car had passed, the swooshing sounds began anew. They were somewhat louder now. And there was something else, too. A shadow had appeared, just a ragged blur stretching across the road far ahead.

Like trying to get at an itchy spot on his back that he could never quite reach, Aidan struggled to think of something that could cast such a shadow. An airplane, maybe, but there was nothing in the sky—not even a cloud.

The shadow came slowly closer, and Aidan noticed that it seemed to be changing size or shape from time to time in rhythm to the swooshing sounds. It was wide enough to span the whole street at one moment, but then the next, it became thin.

Every swoosh, and the shadow narrowed for a moment. But immediately after, it spread wide again. And it stayed wide when there was silence. It was like a giant bird flapping its wings to stay aloft as it closed in on Aidan—only, stare as he might, Aidan saw nothing casting the shadow!

Tiny prickles of fear tiptoed up and down Aidan's spine. The sound swooshed louder still. The shadow was closing, a few feet away, and there was still nothing to be seen overhead.

Aidan covered his head and ducked, but he kept his eyes open. For a brief, paralyzing moment, Aidan felt the presence of something monstrous above him, and all sunlight was eclipsed. Seconds later, the feeling was gone, but a gust of wind followed it, causing Aidan's hair and clothes to flap in all directions.

Then it was still. No breeze. No shadow. No sound—except for Aidan's heart pounding away like bongos at a luau. A warm, sickly sweet, unfamiliar smell drifted over Aidan.

Aidan sprinted out of the street, up his front porch, into the house, and slammed the front door. This earned Aidan another stern, "Hey, stop thumping around up there!"

AUTHOR'S COMMENTARY:

"A Swoosh and a Shadow" was originally chapter 2 in the book. When I wrote it, I had three immediate goals: 1) Foreshadow events later in the story; 2) Increase the reader's awareness that something otherworldly is going on; 3) Establish Aidan and Robby's characters through their friendship. *The Door Within* was the only book of the Trilogy that I did not outline—that's probably why it took thirteen years to write. Yikes! I won't ever do it that way again. But even with the lack of an outline, I always had certain end-of-the-book events in mind. The method Aidan and Robby used to catch the crayfish in the flashback scene foreshadows how Aidan tricks the Paragor Knights with his Phantom Army. In both cases an apparent threat from behind flushes the enemy into an even more dangerous situation.

The swooshing shadow scene may seem familiar to you. I used

a variation of it in chapter 2, "The Unexpected," in the published version. But in the original, I wanted the reader to wonder what this invisible flying thing was and why it was following Aidan. The creature, by the way, is Gabby, Gwenne's dragon—sent over The Thread by King Eliam to look after Aidan.

There's a lot more character development here. You realize that Robby had moved to Maryland from Florida, and you get a little taste of his southern accent. However, it became cumbersome to spell out all the dialect, so we thinned it out a little in the published version. You see what a natural Robby is at almost everything. But you also see that Aidan is a thinker and has some leadership qualities somewhere deep inside.

There was one other reason I liked this scene. It included one of my favorite pastimes as a kid: crayfishing. My friends and I in Seabrook would grab our mason jars and buckets and head for the creek! Even today, I have a blast taking my own four children to our local creek for a little crayfishing. We've caught some monster pinchers together. My son Tommy calls these gigantic crayfish Bajos (pronounced Bah-joes).

This chapter naturally had to go because the original chapter 1 was cut. *The Door Within* begins with Aidan in Colorado, not Maryland, so this chapter wouldn't work. I really wanted to include the crayfishing scene as a flashback, but there just didn't seem to be any natural place to put it without seriously slowing down the pacing. Pacing is the speed at which events seem to be moving. It's especially important in the beginning of a book to keep the pace high so that readers will stay alert and interested. Still, I'm glad readers can now get to know Aidan and Robby—and the crayfish—a little bit better.

ROBBY'S BASEMENT

I'm serious, Mom, it was this huge shadow," Aidan mumbled, his mouth half full of Bambinos pepperoni and extra cheese pizza.

"I'm sure you saw something, Aidan," she replied. "Maybe it was an airplane?"

"Mom, airplanes don't go *swoosh, swoosh!*" Aidan said, trying to make the sound.

"I went out there and looked," offered Aidan's dad. "I didn't see—or hear anything."

"Maybe it was a helicopter?"

"Mommm!"

"Sorry," she said, holding up her hands. "But helicopters do go *swoosh, swoosh!*"

Aidan scowled.

"It was kind of a slow, steady sort of . . . oh, never mind!"

Aidan went back to working on his pizza. It seemed to Aidan

that his parents always expected him to believe them without question. But if Aidan had something to share that was the least bit doubtful, they became so skeptical. Just because they were older didn't have to mean they were automatically right all the time. Whatever it was that had flown over his head, Aidan knew he had never heard—or felt—anything like it ever before.

"Did you get the mail?" Aidan's mom asked.

"Nope," Mr. Thomas replied. "Didn't think it had come yet. I'll go check."

A moment later, Mr. Thomas returned with an envelope in his hand.

"What is it?" asked Aidan's mom.

Aidan watched his father tear open the envelope. "A letter," he replied, unfolding the paper within. "It was stuck way back in the mailbox. It's postmarked two weeks ago. How'd I miss that?"

There was a brief pause while Aidan's dad read the contents of the envelope. "This is from the moving company. Our truck, the big one, will be here sometime tomorrow, late afternoon," Aidan's father announced.

Aidan stopped chewing.

"They could've called." Mrs. Thomas crossed her arms. "It's a good thing we're almost ready. I thought they were coming later in the week!"

"Just as well," said Aidan's dad. "After the movers, all we need to do is load up the minivan and we'll be ready to roll."

Great, Aidan thought. *Just what I wanted to hear.*

"Still want to leave early, like one or two a.m. tomorrow night?" Aidan's mother asked. "Avoid a lot of traffic that way."

"Absolutely," he said. "I love driving at night anyway. It's cooler, no glare off the road . . ."

If they didn't stop soon, Aidan was going to be sick.

"Then, tonight," his mom added with a big grin. "Tonight, since it's our last full night in Maryland, we arranged for you to spend the night over at Robby's."

"Spend the night!?" Aidan nearly spray-painted his parents with shredded pizza. "Cool! That is so cool! Yes!"

"Y'all help yourself to any a' the snacks," said Mrs. Pierson, holding open a tall cabinet door. "You get messy, you clean up, hear?!"

"Okay, Momma," replied Robby.

"Sure thing, Mrs. Pierson," agreed Aidan.

"I'm goin' on up—my shows are on, so I'll see y'all in the morning."

Robby's mom turned and disappeared up the stairs. His sister was at a friend's slumber party. Aidan and Robby were alone and free for the evening. The prospects were good.

"Know what we should do?" said Aidan, eyes gleaming. "We should build a cushion castle!"

"I was just fixin' to say that." Robby grinned.

With a conspiratorial nod Aidan and Robby left the kitchen to seek different areas of Robby's house. Aidan zoomed into the living room and came waddling back with two square sofa cushions stuffed under each arm. Robby went up his stairs two at a time and came down three at a time carrying enough blankets to smother a dinosaur. They met at the door at the top of the basement steps.

Robby put down his pile of blankets and flipped the switch to the basement lights, but when the lights came on, Aidan and Robby immediately noticed that something was very wrong. The door at the bottom of the stairs was open.

"O-kaaay . . . whose turn is it?" Aidan asked.

"Yers, I think," Robby replied.

"Great."

Aidan shuddered. The door at the bottom of the stairs led to the unfinished side of Robby's basement, the work side, a dark and foreboding place that, quite frankly, scared the crud out of both of them—especially Aidan. He'd had the nerve to go in there just once, and that was during the confidence-boosting light of day. One side of the basement, the side they stayed on, was carpeted, comfortably furnished, and well lit. The work side, on the other hand, had a cold cement floor and cinderblock walls that were originally painted a dreary gray but had been stained through the years with unguessable dark liquids. There were cobwebs aplenty, as well, and more than a few skittering spiders happily making new webs each day.

In every shadowy corner of the room were piles of cruel-looking old tools and half-rotten scrap wood left by the previous owners of the house. The only light in the work side was one naked bulb that dangled from the ceiling like a hangman's noose.

Aidan remembered the work side all too well. It was a cold, lonely, and forbidding place. And no matter how many times Robby and Aidan had closed the door to the work side; it always seemed to end up open.

Aidan dreaded the notion of reaching into the mysterious work side to grab the doorknob. His powerful imagination conjured visions of dark, tentacled beasts and cold, skeletal apparitions just waiting to grab the arm of anyone who dared reach into their domain. And it was his turn to shut the door.

"Great," Aidan muttered again.

Then, suddenly, before Aidan could stop him, Robby charged down the stairs. Five steps from the bottom, he sprang into the air. And in one coordinated motion, he landed on the basement floor, reached into the work side, and pulled the door shut.

"Ta daaa!" Robby took a bow and beamed.

Aidan immediately held up an imaginary scorecard like the gymnastics judges in the Olympics. "Nine-point-five," he announced. "And, thanks."

Aidan was immensely relieved—though in some dusty corner of his mind he wished he had been the heroic one to shut the door to the work side. But, at least the door was shut.

Robby bowed low. "Now, let's get our castle built."

For the next ten minutes, few words were spoken, but Aidan and Robby were busier than ants in a gingerbread house. They scooted furniture, set up card tables, spread and draped blankets, tossed pillows and cushions—they even used a piano to support one of the walls. And that was just the outside.

Inside, they stored everything good castle residents could need: comics and flashlights, folding chairs and walkie-talkies, drawing paper and colored pencils, ranch-flavored tortilla chips, and ice-cold sodas.

Aidan and Robby smiled with creative satisfaction as they surveyed their finished work. To the unenlightened observer, their fort looked like a rectangular, quilt-covered igloo. But to Aidan and Robby, it was the impenetrable Castle Courage, the home of truth, justice, bravery . . . and the largest assortment of hand-held video games known to mankind!

They crawled in through one of the couch cushion tunnels and flipped on a half-dozen flashlights. Then, sprawled out side by side on a mat of blankets and sleeping bags, Aidan and Robby allowed themselves to escape into a pile of comic books. Aidan ventured into King Arthur's legends and imagined himself as Lancelot, the brave and clever swordsman. Robby, on the other hand, found the super-naturally gifted X-Men more to his liking. He saw himself as the swift and stealthy Nightcrawler, who could scale walls and teleport to safety when surrounded by dangers.

The basement filled with old house sounds—rattling pipes, creaky boards, dripping water—and time passed unnoticed. Comic books gave way to video games which, in turn, surrendered to sketch pads and pencils. Aidan had just drawn the outline of a dragon when he felt that Robby was staring at him.

"I wish you didn't have to move," Robby said, glancing up at Aidan and then staring at the ground. Something churned and fell heavily in Aidan's stomach.

"The thing I hate most," Robby continued, "is I'm gonna be alone again."

This was the very last thing Aidan expected Robby to say. "Are you nuts?" Aidan exclaimed. "Everybody thinks you're cool. I mean, you've got all those friends from soccer, football, and baseball. And half the girls in school are waiting in line for your phone number."

"Well, they're . . . *sorta* friends," Robby replied as if English were a second language and he couldn't find the right words. "It's like some a' them, they're like *outside* friends. They like what they see on the outside. You watch, if I couldn't play sports like I do, those *friends* would disappear faster than greased lightning. And if I wasn't what those girls call cute, ya' think they'd call me? Ri-ight! They'd walk on by with their pretty little noses stuck so high in the air—you could shoot spitballs in 'em from ten feet away!"

Yup, Aidan thought. *That's exactly how they all treated me before you showed up.*

"But not you, Aidan. You'd still be my friend even if I looked like a catfish on a bad hair day and couldn't hit the broad side of a barn with a baseball. You're an *inside* friend. Am I makin' any sense?"

Aidan nodded. In less than a year their friendship had grown. And they were real friends. Not "sorta" friends. It made the thought of moving hurt even more.

Robby made an irritated clucking sound and continued. "It just seems like every time things are goin' good, somethin' happens t'mess it all up."

"You mean when you moved from Florida?"

"No, well . . . yes, sort of. I left a few friends behind in Panama City—no one as cool as you—but I was thinkin' of my dad."

An awkward, speechless moment passed. Aidan found himself staring at a fort wall and listening to the crickets' bug symphony outside one of the basement windows.

"It was 'bout two years ago, they started fightin'," Robby explained, staring at the floor and wringing his hands continuously. "Dad'd complain about the house or the money. Then, Momma'd be upset that he was never around. I mean, they'd just holler at each other, callin' each other names and slammin' doors. I got so scared sometimes, I hid in my closet until they stopped. After a while . . . it got even worse."

Aidan cringed inside, wondering what Robby meant by "worse."

"Then, last year," Robby made that clucking sound again. "Dad didn't come home one night—haven't seen him since. Don't even know if he's still alive. It doesn't make any sense, Aidan. Is this how life's supposed to be?"

"What do you mean?"

"I mean, first I lose my dad. Now I'm losin' my best friend. It's like life is some cruel joke. Doesn't seem like things ever work out for anybody, especially me."

"It's not that bad," Aidan replied hollowly. He was instantly reminded of his father attempting to explain how great moving would be.

"It's not?!" Robby objected bitterly. "Then, tell me . . . why do awful things like this happen? Why'd my dad take off? Why do you have to move? Why do all those horrible things on the evening news have to happen?"

"I don't know, maybe—"

"I'll tell ya' why. It's because that's the way life is. Nothin' good ever lasts. It's just a waste. You get born, waste away in school, get a job ya' hate, get married, have kids, get divorced, and die!"

Aidan wished he could say something really bright, but every argument seemed empty. And scratching at the back of Aidan's mind like a dull knife's blade was the feeling that Robby might be right. Life did often seem to be just one disappointment after another.

Shaking his head slowly, Robby sighed and flopped backward onto a couch cushion. His eyes were clamped shut at first, but as anger gave way to exhaustion, the tension released, and Robby fell into a deep sleep. Aidan sat there in a stupor for several moments. This was not the way he had intended to spend his last evening with his best friend. He felt guilty, but he wasn't sure why. After all, it wasn't his fault he had to move to Colorado! His stupid grandfather—he was the one to blame. *Too old to take care of himself. Too stubborn to move into an old folks' home. So Mom and Dad to the rescue!* Aidan shook his head, trying to shake the madness of it all out of his mind.

Drained and becoming sleepier by the minute, Aidan crawled around the fort and turned off all the flashlights—except one. Then, still pondering Robby's words, Aidan stretched out on his stomach and closed his eyes.

Some time later, Aidan awoke with a start. He pushed himself up a little, blinked drowsily, and looked around. The flashlight he had left on was nearly out of battery power, but in the dimming light, Aidan saw that Robby was still asleep. And the crickets were into the second movement of their concerto, but there seemed to be nothing loud or dangerous about.

Just as Aidan decided that it was okay to go back to sleep, a sharp hiss cut through the fort's thin blanket walls. Aidan jumped. His heart and thoughts racing, he commando-crawled forward and warily peeled back the blanket. The moon was high enough in the sky to cast an eerie pale light through the two basement windows behind the fort. It was enough light to see that, a few feet from Aidan, facing away from the fort, was Buddy, Robby's cat. Buddy's back was arched severely, and he let out a deep, threatening growl. The provoked feline hissed again and bared its tiny fangs straight ahead at the open work side door.

A wave of gooseflesh surged up Aidan's arms, and every hair on his body stood at full attention. *How in the world did that door get open again?*

Buddy let out a wounded howl, and ran off as fast as his little paws could carry him. Aidan wanted to do the same, but something held him there. He could not will his limbs to move, nor turn his head to look away. He stared at the open door and the lightless depths beyond. The crickets were no longer chirping.

A noise suddenly rolled out from the swirling blackness of the work side. It was a deep and heavy growl—like the angry rumbling of thunder that makes windowpanes rattle. And like thunder, Aidan felt it in his bones.

Aidan tried vainly to see. Then, about a foot above doorknob height, something pierced the darkness. As if two dark curtains were being raised, huge eyes were revealed. They were slanted and lit from within by blue fire. The eyes blinked once, and then the work side door slammed shut.

Aidan screamed.

Robby jumped up from his sleep and bashed his head on their fort's card-table roof. "What? What is it?!" he yelled.

Clutching the flashlight in one hand, Aidan pointed at the work side door.

AUTHOR'S COMMENTARY:

"Robby's Basement" is another chapter that fell like a domino once the first chapter was cut. Again, this takes place in Maryland, and again there wasn't a logical place to sew it back in as a flashback. For one thing, the chapter is too long for a flashback. The editors felt too that Aidan and Robby's building of the fort out of cushions made them seem much younger than they are supposed to be. They asked: Would high-school freshmen still do this kind of thing? And I answered: Probably not.

All that said, I really hated to see this chapter go. One reason is that it completes the promise of the prologue. "Adventures are funny things . . ." Events of the book mirror the prologue. Things do creep out of holes: moonrascals, Falon, etc. Things do appear down a seldom trodden path: a good crayfishing spot, The Ancient Tree of Yewland, and Paragor's Army. Things do fall out of trees:

Aelic and Antoinette, the Seven Sleepers, and such. And in this deleted chapter, by opening an envelope, we learn that Aidan is going to move even sooner than he thought. I know, it was a subtle artistic touch and most likely overlooked in the published version—but I like for my stories to have layers of mystery.

There were many other reasons I was sad to see this chapter go. First, Aidan's parents escape the clichéd mean-never-understanding-parent image by arranging for Aidan to stay the night at his best friend's house. It's a peace offering of sorts and really humanizes Aidan's parents.

The whole basement journey is foreshadowing of Aidan's descent of Falon's Stair. Every person has a fear—especially when they're growing up. A closet, a tree outside the window, sirens, the wind, the space under the bed—we all remember those places and things that creeped us out back in the day. I wanted the readers to understand Aidan's fear of dark, underground places so that, later on Falon's Stair, the reader can enjoy the same terror that Aidan experiences.

I was able to steal parts of the scene where Robby reveals his bleak outlook on life and sew it into chapter 28, "Falon's Stair." There just wasn't room for the whole scene, so I don't think it impacts the reader as I would have liked. In the deleted chapter, however, you can feel the depth of pain and despair Robby experiences. I wanted for kids to have a "grown-up" conversation. I believe that kids are far more capable of asking the big questions of life than adults might think. Kids want to know why bad things happen, they want to know if someone out there has a purpose for them, they want to know if it's all random and cruel, or if someone is watching over them. Knowing that you are "never alone" is a recurring theme in the trilogy.

The eyes-in-the-work-side scene was a favorite of mine. To write it, I just conjured up my own worst-case scenario. Being in a creepy basement in the middle of the night, awakened by strange noises, seeing a door opened—a door you had closed—and then, of course, the eyes and the growl. As a young teen, that would have sent me over the deep end. The students who helped me edit this version of the book really liked this scene. I've gotten letters from some of them wondering how in the world I could cut it. Alas, like a surgeon's incisions, edits hurt—and heal. And in the end, the patient—or story—is better off.

IN THE STILL
OF THE NIGHT

Thanks a lot, Aidan," Robby said, waddling with a heavy suit-case out of Aidan's house. "After that dream you had last night, I don't think I'll ever sleep in that basement again."

Aidan came puffing along behind him. "It wasn't a dream."

"Ri-ight." This time it meant, "Oh, grow up!"

"I saw eyes in there . . . right before the door slammed," Aidan argued, feeling a bit silly.

"We looked, Aidan, remember, with Momma? There was nothin' there."

"There was something there," Aidan mumbled. "Your cat saw it, too."

"Aidan, I'm fixin' to call the hospital, get 'em to bring you one a' those jackets with the real long sleeves. . . ."

Aidan couldn't help but grin. Robby could get laughs in a ceme-tery.

"Robby, I really appreciate you helping us pack up," said Aidan's father as he took the bags from Robby and then Aidan.

"No problem, Mr. Thomas." Robby nodded coolly.

Mr. Thomas hoisted one more suitcase up into the luggage carrier on top of their minivan. It was the last suitcase.

Nearly ten o'clock that evening, Aidan and Robby sat on Aidan's front porch with the nearby streetlight scattering some yellowish rays through the big crab apple tree that had guarded Aidan's front yard for so long. It remained hot and humid—not unusual for a July night in Maryland. There was no relieving breeze, and the woods across the street were still. The last few fireflies blinked forlornly in shadowy corners of the yard.

"You have my new address, so I'll be expecting some mail," Aidan said. "We could even trade cards through the mail." They had been talking, there in the dark, for over an hour, speaking awkwardly about things that didn't really matter. But it was painfully difficult to speak from the heart, so they stuck to safe topics. And while there was much left to say, their time had run short.

"We can email, too." Robby smiled weakly. "Get one of those free accounts, so we can message each other—that is, if my sister ever gets her fat tub away from the computer!"

Aidan smiled back. Robby had been the brother he never had and the friend he always wanted—always needed, Aidan corrected himself. Somehow, Robby filled in all the holes in Aidan's life. With Robby, Aidan fit in and always had direction. What would happen without him? Aidan hurriedly put that thought into his very full closet of fears.

A phone rang somewhere in Aidan's house, and moments later, Aidan's mom turned on the porch light and opened the front door.

"Robby, that was your mom. She wants you to come home now," Mrs. Thomas said, smiling sympathetically. Then she quietly shut the front door and turned out the porch light. Aidan was thankful for the darkness. It was easier that way.

Aidan walked Robby down to the sun-bleached wooden fence that corralled the crab apple tree and marked the end of Aidan's front yard. They exchanged high-fives, and Robby backed away toward the street.

"I'll send you some comics from Colorado, if they have any different ones out there," Aidan said, wanting to say something more meaningful, but stupid, less courageous phrases kept getting in the way.

"Catch some crayfish for me—keep 'em in the aquarium to bug your sister," he said, continuing to babble. "Good luck with football this fall. Who knows? Maybe I'll even try out for a team. Thanks to you, I can sort of throw a spiral now."

"Ri-ight," Robby said with a slightest tremor in his voice. This time it meant, "I'll miss you too."

Robby turned away and slowly walked up the street. Aidan noticed that he didn't cut through any of the neighbors' yards. He was taking the long way. Aidan watched until the night hid his friend from view.

Aidan's parents awakened him in the middle of the night, and ushered him down the stairs and into the already running minivan. Doors closed. The van crept out of the driveway. Aidan watched numbly through the rear window as the only home he had ever known grew smaller and smaller until finally, it was obscured by darkness and distance. The neighborhood went away next.

Then, the little strip mall with the arcade where he'd played so many times and the family favorite, Bambino's Pizza—all dark and deserted. Soon an interstate sign appeared, and unlike many vacations where that sign had been the first marker of good times to come, it seemed now so cold and final.

Miles and time passed, and Aidan could hear his parents talking in hushed tones in the front seat. The warm, almondy smell of coffee drifted back to Aidan every time his parents opened one of their tall plastic thermoses.

Laying on a foam mat under a light blanket in the back of the van, Aidan drifted in and out of sleep. The intermittent flash of the interstate's streetlights through the car windows and the steady *thrump-ump* of the tires on the highway put him into a reflective trance. His mind wandered lazily from thought to thought without reason or order, like a leaf falling on autumn drafts.

Mostly, Aidan wondered a lot of things. He wondered if his new house in Colorado could compare to his home in Maryland. He wondered if he would ever be able to have adventures like the kind he and Robby used to have or if he'd ever even see Robby again. Lastly, he wondered if he would ever get along with his grandfather, whose fault it was that Aidan's world had been turned upside down.

The answer to all of his questions was "Yes."

AUTHOR'S COMMENTARY:

Another casualty to the Colorado opening in the published version, "In the Still of the Night" had to go. Here, Aidan and Robby demonstrate the devastation that occurs in the lives of children who have to move far away from a home they've lived in for a long time. It really is like grieving for a lost loved one. Aidan numbly watches as his home, his neighborhood, and all he's ever known fades into the night. Description can be overdone, but in this scene, I wanted to paint emotion into the natural surroundings. The last of the fireflies blinking forlornly was always a favorite image if mine. The chapter's a real downer—but I didn't want to leave it that way. So as Aidan ponders all the questions near and dear to him, I let the reader know that Aidan will have adventures, that he will see Robby again, and that he will be able to forgive Grampin. I wanted readers to know that even in the bleakest moments, there is hope.

Acknowledgments

To my bride who has never doubted, not once: I thank you for your faith and your sacrifice. To Kayla, Tommy, Bryce, and Rachel: I am rich because of your presence in my life.

To my incredible students over the years at Arundel, West, Oklahoma Road, Sykesville, Mount View, and Folly Quarter: Wherever you are now, I deeply thank you for your inspiration and encouragement. In gratitude, I leave you two things. First, a commission: You are already asking the big questions of life. Ask and seek until you find the answers. And second, a warning: Be very careful putting the pen to a page. You never know where it may lead. Pip-pip-cheerio!

How do you thank those who have made your life's dream possible? Nothing I say will ever come close to repaying the debt I owe to each of you.

To Leslie, Jeff, and Brian: Thank you for sharing the adventure that was growing up together—and the adventure has only just begun! To Diedre (Cuz): Thank you for handing me a copy of *The Hobbit*, for it was then I discovered that reading is cool. To Bill: Still the best man, thank you for daring to dream big things for everyone you touch. To my community group: Thank you for your prayers and encouragement. To my friends on the staff at Folly Quarter and elsewhere: Thank you for understanding why I've been reclusive of late, as well as for your kind efforts to generate interest in the book.

To Gregg Wooding, my agent and friend: Thanks for putting yourself on the line for the story I've been dying to tell. To Dee Ann Grand, Beverly Phillips, June Ford, and the entire editorial staff at Thomas Nelson: Thank you for taking a chance on me and for shepherding me toward a greater mastery of the craft.

To Patti Evans and the design team at Thomas Nelson: You guys rock! I have never seen such immeasurably, impossibly cool graphics!

And finally, to my parents: Thank you first for your love, unbelievable generosity, and unwavering support. And though it may seem silly to some, thank you for reading to me and before me ALL THE TIME. It mattered.

The Door Within Trilogy continues with . . .

BOOK 2

THE RISE OF THE WYRM LORD

Aidan needs to reach Robby with the message of Alleble, but how? Enter bright, headstrong Antoinette Lynn Reed, a young lady with a passion for full-contact Kendo. Then Antoinette is called to Alleble, and Aidan sees his chance. Hoping it's not too late, he solicits Antoinette's help to rescue Robby's Glimpse.

But where is Robby's Glimpse? Antoinette finds The Realm in turmoil. Some of King Eliam's closest allies inexplicably threaten to turn away from Alleble. And dark rumors surface that Paragor is seeking an ancient evil to crush Alleble.

Will Antoinette stay and join Alleble's finest knights to stop the rise of the Wyrm Lord?

BOOK 3

THE FINAL STORM

Still staggering under Paragor's relentless attacks, Alleble's remaining allies flee from the four corners of The Realm to safety within the Kingdom's walls. Once there they find chaos, the forces of Alleble grieving a fallen hero, and the Kingdom's citizens clinging to an ancient legend about Three Witnesses who can bring victory. But who are they? Where are they?

There is little time for Alleble to mourn before Paragor, the Wyrm Lord, and the deadly Seven Sleepers unite against the followers of King Eliam.

As Alleble begins to lose hope, Paragor unleashes the final storm. Will anyone survive to see the dawn?

Coming the Summer of 2007 . . .

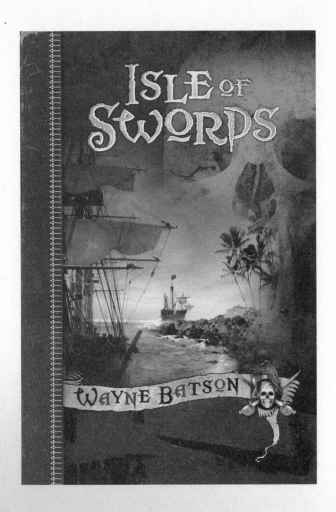

A lad with no memory comes between the
Caribbean's two most notorious pirates and the
greatest treasure the world has ever known.